R. MOODY

NULL
AND
VOID

ISBN: 978-0-646-59883-3 (paperback)

First edition, August 2024

Chapter headers and dinkus art by Jessica Rebell (@jessicarebell)

Cover art by Pollyanna (@pollyanna.d.art)

Cover typography by Christian Bentulan (@coversbychristian)

Map by Cartographybird Maps (@cartographybird)

Editing + Formatting by Shelly | The Fiction Editor (@the.fiction.editor)

Proofreading by Emma Hatton (@starlitnook)

Sensitivity read by Evren D (@nonbinaryknightreads)

Character art by Pennie Beresford (@penellope.art)

NULL & VOID

PATRONS OF THE DIVINE
BOOK ONE

R. MOODY

For anyone who has ever been told how to feel.
Embrace the rage.
It probably won't solve any of your problems, but it'll be a lot more fun.

Stay moody.

"Fear of the unknown is the root of almost all hate. It is born of ignorance and fed by those who would keep us divided."

— TINNEKKE BEBOUT

PRONUNCIATION GUIDE +
GLOSSARY

<u>CHARACTERS</u>

Amarilyss – *AM-AH-RILL-ISS*
Andt – *ANT*
Anerea – *AH-NEAR-EE-AH*
Arpi – *ARR-PEE*
Aurelius – *OR-RELL-EE-YUS*
Bitty – *BITT-EE*
Cristoph – *CRISS-TOFF*
Eryn – *EH-RINN*
Frankie – *FRAN-KEE*
Gamiyan – *GAM-EYE-AHN*
Jaena – *JAY-NAH*
Kino – *KEE-NO*
Leian – *LEH-YAN*
Liesolette – *LEEZ-OH-LET*
Lilleck – *LIL-LECK*
Lottie – *LOTT-EE*
Lylle – *LIE-ALL*
Mika – *MEE-KAH*

Otto – *OTT-O*
Pasha – *PAH-SHAH*
Petia – *PET-YAH*
Riko – *REE-KOE*
Riley – *RYE-LEE*
Sehna Ziemia – *SEH-NAH ZYEM-YAH*
Stol Brud– *STOAL BROOD*
Tovi – *TOE-VEE*
Zinniani – *ZINN-YAHN-EE*

WORLD

Sunyanile – SHOON-YAH-NEE-LIH

NATIONS

Erdu – *ERR-DOO*
Laguz – *LAH-GOOZ*
Mieva – *MYEH-VAH*
Nemoris – *NEH-MORE-ISS*
Osraed – *OZ-RAID*
Sadori – *SAH-DOOR-EE*

TOWNS

Forsto – *FORSS-TOE*
Holbec – *HOLL-BECK*
Jundamara – *JUN-DAH-MARR-AH*
Koppa – *KOPP-AH*
Lyngby – *LING-BEE*
Norli – *NORE-LEE*
Teorann – *TEE-OR-RAN*
Vavabora – *VAH-VAH-BORE-AH*
Waadi – *WAH-DEE*

OTHER

avyon – *AYE-VEE-ONN*
cacote – *CAH-COAT-AYE*
drogalyf – *DROE-GAH-LEAF*
elomak – *ELL-OH-MACK*
faegel – *FAY-GULL*
frasteria – *FRAS-TEAR-EE-YAH*
kajal – *KAH-JAHL*
kakahu – *KAH-KAH-HOO*
ofori – *OH-FORE-EE*
ritha – *REE-TAH*
Talamu – *TAL-AH-MOO*

GLOSSARY

aging-up – Patrons moving into secondary housing at age thirteen

applemint – A type of candy

avyon – Enormous creature of flight originating in Sadori

beetleberries – A wild berry that resembles the shape of a beetle, native to Erdu

bonded – Two people who have committed to an eternal union (not recognized for Patrons)

cacote – An earthy and nutty substance (like chocolate)

coming-of-age – Patrons becoming available to purchase (at the age of twenty-one)

doxy – Concubine

drogalyf – Plant that can be smoked or chewed to experience a euphoric feeling

elomak – A large tree, native to Nemoris

faegel – Berries

firecat – Small fire-breathing feline originating in Erdu

frasteria – Large flowering trees

Gift – An ability or enhanced skill

Junky – Patron of the Divine with a useless or boring Gift

kajal – A black paste often used to decorate skin

kakahu – A plant with large, fabric-like leaves

moon – A month

Mutt – Mixed nation blood

Null – Patron of the Divine with no Gift

ofori – Plant steeped and ingested to make you care less

ollie – Enormous trees with dense foliage

Patron of the Divine – A person born with violet eyes (usually with a Gift)

peacekeeper – Nulls or Junkies assigned as guards

revolution, or rev – A year

ritha – Inedible nuts that can be used as soap

secondary – Slang reference to the living arrangements of Patrons of the Divine between aging-up and coming-of-age

skin traders – Mercenaries involved in the trade of people (usually sexually motivated)

sneak – Similar to a spy, used for intelligence gathering

sneaksuit – A full-body suit made with fabric from Sadori that absorbs the light

snowolf – Large working canine originating in Mieva

spidergrass – Sturdy blades of grass, used in fibre arts

Talamu – A card game consisting of two teams of two

windcaves – Purpose built caves in Erdu used for shelter during dangerous windstorms

"-born" country suffix – The blood that runs in your veins and colors your eyes

"Of-" country prefix – Both your citizenship and last name

Please see a list of content warnings at the back of this book, or go to rmoodyauthor.com/books

THE SIX NATIONS OF
SUNYANILE

CASTLE CITY

INAROO

VAVABORA

LYNGBY

ERDU

GLENMAI

LOKNIK

FORSTO

NORLI

HALLAPORT

WAADI

JUNDAMARA

YOKIRANNA

WINDABERG

TEORANN

FERRY ROUTE

TEORANN

RUNE

NORVIK

HOLBEC

KOPPA

MAMA'S HOUSE

NEMORIS

ORFLEUR

CASTLE CITY

LARNES

AEGARN

MAARSI

FR

THUNDAL

ONDING

ELJORD

DRAKHEIM

TO THE UNCHARTED NORTH

MIAGA

FARIFF

HOTOROI

MATATOUI

SADORI

SETCA

NABAMI

OTOBU

SORI

SAPA

ALIECA'S NECK

PUKUA

HO TU

SAMSO

HAVIA

TUEL

PANGA

LAIS

SOKIKI

PALACE
ISLAND

TONGANEREE

LAGUZ
UPULU

SOARDE
PRISON

NORTHOS

OFERITI

KOLA

OSRAED

RESDOA
PRISON

MANTANGA

ESTOS

EASTOS

WAVEI

THE
COMPOUND

FALCON
TOWER

ADESOK
PRISON

DRAESO
PRISON

FONOSSI

RADOS
RISON

SOUTHOS

NEMPEST

MELTE

SANLUND

THE ORDER

AEROS

IGLIS

KOLD

CASTLE
CITY

MIEVA

WITMOOR

HYBER

THAWSON

PRELUDE

Many centuries past, Sunyanile was all one land and there were no Gifts.

A cataclysmic event referred to as the Divine Intervention split the land into six divisive nations.

And then the Gifted were born.

CHAPTER ONE

I kick over the wooden chair with a growl, not caring if I look like a child having a tantrum. This isn't like being told I can't have any more cake or candy: I'm being sold as a slave to a foreign country.

"There is nothing I can do. The council has already voted." Jaena's icy calm voice rises from behind her enormous wooden desk, so at odds with the furious heat radiating from me.

"Why was it even an option? I'm a Null!" I protest.

A frozen finger skips down my spine. Only one king in the Divine world has a proclivity for Nulls. "I will not be a doxy, Jaena." I pitch my voice dangerously low. "I will not be King Oferdu's *sex* slave."

"Oh Mika, for Divine's sake! *Nemoris* asked for the Silent Assassin," Jaena replies, sounding exasperated and finally revealing more than her calculated demeanor.

I grip the righted chair with white knuckles as I speak through gritted teeth. "The Silent Assassin *retired* Jaena." Jaena's eyes narrow dangerously. "Why *me*? Why an assassin at all?"

"You know your reputation precedes you, Mika. They want a sneak who can fight. The Princess Ofnemoris has been kidnapped." Shrugging, she adds with an edge of menace, "And it is not like I can put you on assignment anymore, can I?"

My rage takes over, and I slam the chair into the nearest wall. Jaena must have a sound barrier around us because her personal guards don't come running in. This is ridiculous. I don't *rescue*, I'm a killer. A fucking retired killer!

"I'm not going, Jae—" I don't have time to finish before my air is choked off and I'm unable to move. It seems Jaena has decided to create a Mika-shaped barrier that's just a *little* too tight.

"That is *President* Jaena, and yes, you *will* be going. You would do well to remember who saved your life more than a decade past, Mika. You have not been executed because of the protection I have afforded you." She stands slowly to her feet and looks down her nose at me, violet eyes glowing in barely contained fury. "They will be back to collect you in five days. You are dismissed."

The barrier drops, and I collapse onto the ground, quietly gasping for breath.

Jaena sits back down as she smooths non-existent escaped hairs from her tight gray-blonde bun, looking younger than her fifty-six revolutions but every bit as sharp. "Guards," she calls, with practiced disinterest.

Two of Jaena's guards file in and stand on either side of the door, their violet eyes not revealing what their Gift might be. Jaena gives me a pointed look.

I smirk. "You know two guards can't stop me."

A barrier briefly closes around my throat in warning as she looks down and starts reading as further dismissal. I stand and stalk through the door with my head held high and rage swirling in my stomach. At least her guards have the decency to look afraid of me.

I take the long way back to my rooms, needing the battering Osraed wind in my hair. I keep it short for this exact reason—long enough to tie my unruly, white-golden blonde hair back when I want to, but short enough to leave it free and be ruffled by the breeze.

I'll miss the wind. Nemoris isn't very windy, the entire country is little more than dense forest surrounded by beaches. At least it stays cold like Osraed. I'm not sure I would've survived if I'd been purchased by Sadori with their never-ending seasons of heat.

Unfortunately, the wind does nothing to calm me, and my rage continues to build. It's my earliest memory, rage. The fluttering bird in my chest became a full-grown firecat clawing to get out. As a child, I was unable to control myself when it took over, so Jaena took me under her wing, assuming my violent outbursts were a sign of my Gift manifesting.

How disappointed she was when I was finally branded Null & Void with no Gift.

I arrive at the training grounds not realizing my destination, too focused on the crunch of my feet on the loose stone path in an attempt to calm my rage. Unsurprisingly, I see Leian inside, tidying up the mess of practice weapons. The Laguzborn man—the closest thing to a friend I have—is yet to notice my arrival.

Leian keeps his black hair cropped short and face cleanly shaven. He has square features and full lips, but unlike others from the sixteen main islands that make up Laguz, Leian's skin is not the darkened bronze of his fellow Laguzborn.

Though I'm a revolution older, we grew up together, both suffering through similar cruel taunts from our peers.

Me, because I looked dirty—I am no pristine Mievaborn—and Leian because his skin was not a dark enough brown. We both went unsold at our coming-of-age and got to know each other more during the last few revs.

Leian is a Junky, Gifted with calm and patience…kind of. What that really means is his heart rate never increases above resting. He never gets overwhelmed with confusion or irrational decision-making. He can remain steady in his emotions because his heart doesn't race for any reason—not even physical exertion.

It occurs to me that Leian's Gift is the complete opposite of my rage, and I audibly snort at the irony that he's the one here tonight.

"Mika," Leian says with a startled smile, his violet Patron eyes popping up to where I stand in the doorway.

"Evening Leian. Are you packing up to go home, or…" I let the words trail off as I grab a bo staff.

He grins. "I was packing up but would never miss an opportunity to spar with the best."

Not bothering to warm up, I wait for Leian in the barn that's used as a training area. "Probably the last time we'll do this, Leian," I mention as we settle into fighting stances.

Leian stops and stands up straight with a querying look, but I charge him with no warning.

He easily blocks my blow. "Oh, tiny little Mika, would you like me to practice on my knees so we are the same height?" he jibes and then tries to jab me in the stomach.

I dodge effortlessly, amused by his usual taunts. "Does it bother you that I am the size of a child and still beat your ass?"

He laughs heartily before chasing me, our bo staffs slamming together in multiple crosses. We swap blow for blow, charge for charge, taunt for taunt, both trying to catch the other off guard.

4

It's not long before I'm panting and sweating, though Leian remains composed. I block one of his charges, but he immediately recovers and aims for my head. I narrowly miss being smashed in the ear as I duck, then use the opportunity to swing at his feet.

Leian realizes it too late, and I sweep him onto his backside with a thud. I offer him a hand up as he groans. "Small and deadly as always. Just once, I would like to win against you, Mika," he laughs and readies himself for another round.

"I could let you win if you'd like?"

He charges me without another word.

I usually win but Leian is never anything but eager and enthusiastic to keep going. We continue until I'm shaking and breathless, and I've not lost a round.

"So, can I ask why this is the last time, or should I just be grateful there was one?"

As we stretch on the giant mat in the center of the barn, I give him an emotionless rundown of what Jaena told me, cursing myself for saying anything at all.

"I'm sorry Mika. I'll miss your presence," Leian says, sounding genuine.

He's likely the only one who would, except for maybe the kids I nanny in the children's compound. The thought of breaking the news to them tomorrow completes the souring of my mood.

I help Leian finish packing up the rest of the practice weapons before saying a final goodbye. Sweaty and sticky, I debate risking the bath house. It's still too early, the private baths are usually all occupied at this time, and there'll definitely be too many people in the communal ones. Far too many for my volatile state right now.

My housing complex is a mass of double rooms with a shared bath house nearby. The kitchens where we eat are shared with another three housing complexes, and there are four separate sittings for each meal. I've already missed mine, so there will be no dinner for me, but I always keep a stash of supplies in my room.

Once I reach my rooms, I start a pot of water for a quick soup and get changed. I note I'll need to do laundry before I'm collected by whatever Nemoris escort is sent for me in a few days.

Stalking around my room in my underwear, I contemplate Leian's words while I gather up dirty clothes. He's right—I'm small. Everything about me is small actually, except for my bug-looking eyes. It works in my favor when sneaking about, making it easy to disguise myself as a child or young man. I'm proud of the lean muscle coating my body, even though my lack of more interesting curves can sometimes grate. I snatch up the last tunic on the ground from in front of my mirror.

The dim light makes my skin seem darker than it is, though I'm still very pale, as is typical for all Mievaborn. No freckles or birthkisses. And somehow, despite the many fights I've been in, not a single scar…except for the ones I've accidentally given myself. I flex a palm in the mirror, the lantern light reflecting the silvery lines on my fingers.

I am unmemorable, like a good assassin should be.

Why am I even looking at myself? Worried about what my new Ofnemoris overlords will think of me? I snort in disgust at my vanity but cannot help myself as I turn to appreciate my butt with a smirk.

I plop onto my sofa near the stove. My sitting room is basic and unadorned, with only this gray sofa, a small table with two wooden chairs, a stove, and a large cabinet full of kitchen items. My bedroom is through an archway in the back with a tiny window. Similarly sparse, the focus of both rooms are the weapons leaning against the walls.

The pot starts to boil, so I throw on a tunic before digging through the kitchen cabinet. I add mushroom powder, a wrinkly potato, an onion that's starting to sprout, and some nondescript dried meat to the pot. It's simple but delicious and filling.

With a satisfied stomach, I stretch out on my sofa again and let my mind wander about who kidnapped the Princess Ofnemoris and why. It intrigues me that Jaena didn't give me more details, but maybe she doesn't know. Monarchs from the five countries stopped requesting to purchase the Silent Assassin many revolutions past when they were consistently told she wasn't for sale. The fact that Nemoris put in a bid now, surprises me.

That they succeeded, chokes me with rage.

I haven't been an assassin for almost an entire rev. I quit when my last job required me to kill a woman who threatened the Ofmieva crown. I didn't realize the threat she posed was because the king had raped her, and she was now carrying his bastard child.

I did it though. If it wasn't me, it would've been someone else. I put a sleeping draught in her dinner and sliced across a lifeblood line in her neck as she slept. She went to sleep and never woke up. I was never allowed to ask why I couldn't simply ensure the baby died and let the mother live, considering she was almost full-term.

The whole thing was the last straw for me. Especially when I learned that the king had died of a heart attack *before* I assassinated the woman. His only other living relative is now the queen. My suspicions have always been that the king's death was not natural. But it matters naught to me now.

After that, I told Jaena I was done being her assassin for hire. I'd sneak and spy, but no longer kill for her. I'm sure Jaena thought I was bluffing, especially after everything she's done for me. But it's ten moons later and I've refused three jobs, losing her the gold I would have brought in.

Few people outside Osraed city are aware that I am—or was—the Silent Assassin. They might know the legend, but if they'd met me or heard my true name, they wouldn't be able to connect the dots. A handful in the compounds know who I am and what I used to do for the council, especially the Patrons living in Osraed who've never been sold, like Leian.

A small few took it upon themselves to learn exactly who I was several revs ago. Jaena said it was my own fault and nothing could be done, even though I wasn't the one who leaked my identity. *Apparently*, I should've stayed locked away in my rooms unless I was actively on assignment. Jaena expected me to be her monster on a leash and nothing more. Thankfully, my anonymity has mostly remained intact for the last few revs.

Other assassins weren't vilified like I was, but being a Null—*and* a woman—made me especially heinous. Petitions to the council about my position as a nanny arose not long after my identity was leaked. *"Corrupting the youth,"* they'd said. Everything was reviewed in massive hearings that took moons. Denied. Every single one was denied, and it was never petitioned again.

The Silent Assassin title started circulating about a decade past, and at that time, *no one* knew it was me. Jaena had me doing jobs long before my coming-of-age, knowing that as a Null, an announcement wouldn't be posted for the other five countries to make a bid to purchase me.

It became a game to me. How quietly could I assassinate someone? I got cocky, making sure other people were home, or doing it in public. I never once had a close call.

The only times I've ever had to physically defend myself was while traveling to and from my destinations, and mercenaries or skin traders saw me as an easy mark. Some were smart enough to wonder why a lone woman would be traveling, or what Gift I might have because of these violet eyes marking me as a Patron of the Divine.

Most of the time they were just idiots, and I was able to take out another group of scum from this difficult world.

CHAPTER TWO

Informing the children went about as well as I expected. The younger ones don't really understand yet, but I've known some of the older kids their entire lives, and their devastated faces made it all the worse.

You'd think being the Silent Assassin, I would've gotten a work assignment literally *anywhere* else, but I like it. These kids aren't afraid of me. They don't know the things I've done. Their unfiltered opinions and attitudes are usually the best part of my day, and they don't hold back which never fails to make me laugh.

We spend the day tending to our herb garden, making new ferments and pastes, and cooking meals together. I've always wanted the kids to feel like they could survive by relying on themselves. Teaching them about the plants they can forage to feed their bellies and heal what ails them. How much of it stays with them, I don't know, but their flushed cheeks and filthy smiling faces tell me they're having a good time.

I remain upbeat with them despite the truth. While it may be wrong to give them a false sense of what our world is really like, it also seems unnecessarily cruel to add more fear and uncertainty to their lives.

Most kids manifest their Gift before they age-up and move to secondary housing the season they turn thirteen. A lot of what we do here in the children's compound is about managing their Gifts. Some nannies are specifically tasked with encouraging Gifts to manifest through testing and trying to trigger something.

Obvious Gifts like an increase of abilities that already exist—strength, hearing, taste, vision—are easy and usually the first to manifest. Children whose Gifts don't manifest until they're in a unique situation and they feel the pull, are slightly more difficult. Healers tend to be like this, with most of them manifesting after they've aged-up into secondary.

Like me, some never feel the pull.

The children I nanny are all Junkies. Their Gifts are considered useless and they're unlikely to be sold—if they are announced at all—in their coming-of-age, during the season they turn twenty-one.

One five-rev-old Nemorisborn kid can change the color of all the hair on his body. Hilarious and fun for a child, but useless to the monarchies paying gold for Gifts. Though Nemoris will surely still make a bid, as they do for anyone born of the forest.

Farra, a twelve-rev-old Mievaborn girl, is about to age-up. She knows she's a Junky and will likely stay in Osraed forever as all she can do is make her fingernails grow at will. The news that I'm leaving is particularly hard on her. Being the oldest kid, she's been my right hand for moons. I know she's trying to be brave, but the devastation on her face is unmistakable.

I knew today would be hard.

Pulling Farra aside before I leave for the day, I hand her a small parcel. "I was going to give you this when you aged-up, but I won't be here for that now. Don't open it until then!" I order, playfully poking her ribs while she bats me away.

She gives me a tight hug and then sniffles her way back to her dorm. She'll open it the moment she leaves my sight. I hope she loves the book on wild, edible, and medicinal plants across the Divine world. It's full of beautiful diagrams of plant stages, their uses, and how to prepare them. I'll miss her bright and sassy personality. I do not doubt she will thrive, even as a Junky.

As I'm leaving, I run into a woman I grew up with, a Gifted wet nurse. Some Gifted stay in Osraed simply because their Gifts are of use to the council, and Petia is one such Patron. I absolutely detest her, and the familiar flutter of rage in my chest becomes rampant the moment I hear her voice.

"Mika. What a pleasant surprise to see you on this side of the compound," Petia says acerbically. A couple of other Patrons look over at us and then dash away, leaving me alone with Petia in the small receiving room off the hallway.

Around us are soft chairs, small tables, and a dresser with a pitcher of water and glasses—everything a grieving parent needs to hand over their child while the rest of the Patrons and children can walk by and look in. Not even the dignity of a closed door for privacy during the worst day of their lives.

"I'm taking some paperwork to Gamiyan," I say, regretting that I didn't plan to drop it off early tomorrow morning while fewer people are awake.

"Fascinating," Petia replies, with an insincere smile plastered on her face.

She knows I was the Silent Assassin, and I wish she was

afraid of me instead of this confident hostility. Petia thinks of me as the little girl I was, smaller than my peers, and desperate to be loved. Oh, how I've changed—that little girl is now only desperate to be alone. Maybe I can leave her the parting gift of a few broken bones.

She and I, and two other Mievaborn women of a similar age were best friends when we were young. Too little to be bullies or know the way of the Divine world we live in. As the four of us got older, my differences became more apparent, and I drifted further and further from them. Their Gifts came in early, including Petia's wet nursing, though she didn't have to start feeding the new Patrons until she was much older.

And of course, my Gift never manifested. My Patron life file was updated to Null & Void the season I turned sixteen, officially branding me a Null. Though, I'd already been teased about it long before I even aged-up into secondary.

I'm snapped out of my memories by the sound of a soft mewling coming from the bundle in Petia's arms.

"A new Patron of the Divine just arrived. Can you believe it? I haven't seen a new Mutt in revolutions!" The slur shamelessly rolled off her tongue.

I shouldn't be surprised by the way she speaks, it's not like she's alone in her views. The child looks about a moon old with a head of pale blonde hair like a Mievaborn, however, their little face is covered in Nemorisborn freckles.

I shudder to think of the life this child would have suffered through if they hadn't become a Patron. Petia is right, I haven't seen anyone risk bringing a child into this world with someone from a different country in a long time. Certainly, not many of them are in Osraed.

"Actually, can you take that to Gamiyan since you're going to see her? Thanks," says Petia, with a small flick of her eyes to a folder on a side table as she strides off cradling the new little Patron. Clearly, it wasn't a request as she doesn't wait for my response.

I grab the folder she indicated and flip through it to find it's the child's intake paperwork. A Mievaborn mother and a Nemorisborn father. A little boy, given the name of Ketia. I'm not surprised since it must've been Petia who named him, and she's conceited enough to name a stranger after herself. "Of the mountain" is listed next to his eye color, indicating he had gray eyes before they shifted to the violet eyes of a Patron of the Divine.

Gamiyan is still in her office when I arrive to hand everything over. The Sadoriborn woman's velvet-looking skin —rich brown like fresh and fertile earth—is deeply wrinkled and her once-black hair is now entirely gray. She's a highly respected Junky with the Gift of being able to dislocate and open her jaw grotesquely wide, like a snake. Obviously, her Gift is of zero use here in the children's compound, but the elderly woman was the Director of Young Patrons long before I was even born.

When the petitions came in over my position as a nanny, Gamiyan was a steadfast supporter of mine. She spoke on my behalf at the hearing, and the nice things she said about me were unexpected. I wasn't sure if she was making it all up to look after my well-being or to gain some kind of future leverage over me. I would never disrespect her to ask such a thing, she's a woman of her own mind and has never called in the favor. But I couldn't— and I still can't—understand why she believed in me so much.

We exchange pleasantries, and her eyes crinkle with kindness when I hand over my notebooks. They contain all of my notes and observations about the children I nanny. Someone will be taking over their care, and I want the transition to be as smooth as possible.

As I pass her the intake file from Petia, I wonder where it

will be kept—where *any* of the Patron's life records are kept? *Have they filed my bill of sale to Nemoris yet?*

"Thank you, Mika. I'll file this on my way home," Gamiyan says, as she looks at me with trust.

It's fortunate she knows me and my aversion to maintaining eye contact. Otherwise, she might have seen it written in my eyes when I looked away. I was going to follow her.

I RACE HOME and get changed into my sneaksuit while stuffing nuts and dried fruit into my mouth. The suit is essentially a form-fitting sock that covers my entire body and face, with a hood. It's more like a second skin with reinforced feet that act as shoes. The Sadori-made fabric is dark and swallows the light like an endless void, making it perfect to sneak about in at night. My fingertips and the top half of my face are the only skin visible. I use kajal to blacken the skin around my eyes so they're less noticeable, pull the hood down, and then I'm out the door.

It's well into the evening, and Gamiyan is still in her office. I've been blessed with a moonless night, so I get comfortable in my vantage point on a nearby roof shrouded in darkness. I find myself digging at a fingernail through the sneaksuit, frustratingly unable to chew my nails while wearing it. If I get this wrong and she leaves through the south exit, I likely won't have another chance before I leave for Nemoris.

Fortunately, I'm not wrong, as half an hour later, Gamiyan is ambling her way past me. For an elderly woman, she is spritely, her shadow bouncing under the tall street lanterns at a quick pace. I need to move from my position almost immediately to keep up.

My footsteps are silent as I creep along behind her, keeping to the shadows. She takes an unexpected sharp turn to the left toward the Registry Office. When I'm no longer an Ofosraed citizen, I'll have to come here to check in once a rev. They keep records of where everyone is supposed to be living, though I'd always assumed the Patron life records were elsewhere.

However, Gamiyan unlocks the door to Permissions and Requests, not the Registry Office. Unable to follow her into the building, I go around the side to watch her through the windows. She lights a lantern and I follow her shadow as she moves deeper inside where information like work assignments and travel permissions are stored. Like the Registry Office, these records are not guarded or protected by more than a locked door.

Between the shelves and shelves of records, I watch Gamiyan's lantern light slowly disappear until it's gone entirely. This doesn't make sense...I would still be able to see the lantern if she were between shelves.

I wait patiently, and after maybe fifteen minutes, I see the lantern light begin to flicker and dance around the room again. Gamiyan weaves her way back out of the storage area, through the offices, past the main reception area, and out the exit. She's no longer carrying the file.

I test a few windows hoping to find one unsecured so I don't have to pick the lock to the front door, and I'm in luck. I crawl through an office window on the far west side of the building, slinking into the inky darkness within.

I sit for a moment, allowing my eyes to adjust. I'm not even afforded a stream of light from the street lanterns as this office only faces another building. I don't dare light a lantern yet for fear of being spotted, and make my way through the offices the same way Gamiyan had.

So far, it's only rows upon rows, shelves upon shelves, and files upon files, of records. Crouching to the floor in the area where Gamiyan disappeared, I feel my way around the ground until my hand catches on something. A small indent almost under the shelves about the size of a small coin, and the gap in the planks is minutely wider along here. I follow the entire length, finding another small dip a few feet away.

I stick my finger into one of the shallow holes and feel some give, but nothing happens. I have the same result with the other one, so I press into both at once until I hear a clunk and a lip pops up along the gap. I lift, and the entire length of the boards swivel up, creating an even darker passage into the floor, where I'm greeted with the cold touch of concrete stairs.

Leaving the trapdoor open, I begin my descent. I've never heard of someone breaking into Patron life records before, but the effort to keep them hidden suggests it wouldn't be a good idea to be found down here.

I reach what I assume to be the bottom when I stumble after expecting more steps down. Fumbling, I finally light the lantern, the opening above barely visible and the stairs look endless. *Of course*, the door at the bottom of the steps is locked.

I retrieve my set of picks that I carry with me inside the stretchy fabric around my chest and work on opening it. Luckily for me, it's an incredibly easy lock—the type I first learned how to crack when I was being taught the ways of the sneak.

The irony of the situation is not lost on me. Jaena insisted I was taught to pick locks, and now here I am using that skill in defiance of her. The memory almost makes me chuckle— it was Gamiyan herself who taught me lockpicking. Why *she* knew the skill and why Jaena had her teach me remains a curiosity.

The lock clicks satisfactorily and I open the door with a rush of frigid air, my lantern light quickly swallowed by the sheer magnitude of the room in front of me. Rows of shelves extend at least as far as the lantern can illuminate in all directions, with a small set directly in front of me, perpendicular to the rest of the shelving in the room. Calling it a room is insufficient: it's an underground field of records.

The shelves directly in front look the newest, and I spot the one for baby Ketia. These files are sorted in alphabetical order and appear to be for the children currently in the compound.

I start flipping through a few files on the next lot of shelves. These look to be for everyone who's had their Patron file number assigned—and tattooed—but not yet come-of-age. When children age-up and move into secondary housing, Patron file numbers are tattooed onto our forearms. We're also put through a procedure that changes us forever, so it's a big season for someone who is essentially still a child.

A dusty, old set of shelves sits off to the far right within my lantern light. Looking separate from the rest, my interest is piqued. I grab a couple of files and realize quickly that these are the files of Patrons who died before they reached their coming-of-age.

Sickness, injuries, even murder. Osraed suffered a lot of disappearances before the children's compound was built a century past, and missing Patrons were often merely presumed dead after a peacekeeper investigation.

Patrons were once executed, even before their coming-of-age ceremony, if they defected—though the last death was twenty revs past. Now they're placed in an Osraed prison for life. I bet those files are down here somewhere too.

The rest of the shelves are large and looming but look to

be totally empty. I walk down the first aisle and have to go past thirty rows of shelves before I start seeing files again.

I stop, grab a file and flip it open. It's for an Erduborn man named Niko and he's an Oflaguz fish catcher. The bill of sale says he was purchased on his coming-of-age with no contest, around two revs past. Putting that file away, I pick up one from the same set of shelves but from the top. It's from the same coming-of-age season, this time a Mievaborn woman named Annikasia.

Testing a theory, I grab another file. Another name that begins with A, but their coming-of-age season was the one prior to the two other files I read. It's definitely in date order, and then alphabetical.

Leaving this row, I move deeper into the record field until I find it.

The season I came-of-age.

CHAPTER THREE

Deep in the bowels of the records room, a shiver overtakes me. I've never had a desire to know my parents or family. We're brought up knowing they don't matter, and we will never know who they are. There is no need to make the records public for fear of children born from incest, because Patrons of the Divine cannot procreate anyway; they make sure of it.

I eventually find my file. My bill of sale is not yet in here, perhaps it isn't fully finalized until I leave. I smirk when I see the words Null & Void stamped at the top where a Patron's Gift is supposed to be written.

Eye color: "of the mountain" gray, just like baby Ketia.

I freeze, and my heart immediately starts slamming into my throat. Kneeling shakily on the ground, I reread the dates multiple times. My birthdate on my paperwork is correct, but the intake date is more than a revolution after that. Even if someone wrote the wrong revolution accidentally, it'd still be far too many moons after my birth.

Children's eyes change to violet within their first day or two of life and parents have one moon to give them over as a

Patron of the Divine in Osraed. They forfeit all rights to the child—it is essentially as if they had never been born—parents can't even name them.

But I was almost a rev and a half before I was brought to Osraed…

I keep reading. My mother's name is Sehna Ziemia Ofmieva, a Mievaborn woman the age of twenty-six. The same age I am right now.

Did she hide me away?

It doesn't say anything more about my mother. If she kept me a secret for that long, she would've surely ended up in prison…I wrack my brain as to whether they still executed parents for this back then and cannot remember. Rage rises dangerously in my throat. The section for "father's name" is blank. The box for "unknown/unclaimed" has been ticked next to it.

This is worse than not knowing. I shouldn't have come here.

I pack the file back up and put it away, not wanting to look any further. Running down the aisles and back to the exit, the lantern flame flickers wildly. I'm halfway up the stairs before I remember I need to relock the door and have to go back.

I don't remember getting home or getting out of my sneaksuit. I'm sitting on the edge of my bed, replaying everything I read over and over.

Null & Void. Intake date. Unknown/Unclaimed father.

I HAVE the frosty morning to myself, so I hire a horse to visit the markets on the east coast, the ones closest to Laguz waters. I need to forget last night. I need to do something—

anything—to take my mind off what I've read. I need new underwear, so that's the goal today.

Being the last day of the moon, the markets are exceptionally busy. I enjoy the markets on the border of Laguz because of entertainment like carnival games to test your skills, though cheating is far too easy among the Gifted.

Singers, dancers, and acrobats are performing on stages. A Gifted Nemorisborn woman is shifting her body into various animals while keeping her own head, which is mildly entertaining, if not a little disturbing.

A man selling firecat kittens is arguing with peacekeepers as he doesn't have a permit. Only Erdu can issue permits, as this is where the creatures originate from, and the country is very protective of them. With their distraction, I poke my head into the pen. Long, sleek tails on short, stumpy bodies and excessively large whiskers. A light fawny color, shining gold in the sun, with their points slightly darker. Their stupidly wide heads and overly large ears with dark tufts on the end are adorable.

The kittens can't make fire, which is usually why they're sold at such a young age. I cannot get close enough to see if these kittens have already been defired, but I hope not. It's a barbaric procedure to remove the fire-producing glands, and it causes chronic pain and drooling for the rest of their lives. Despite being banned, it continues to happen. I watch them for a little while, pouncing and tumbling over each other, making small chirps.

Next, I buy a steamed bun filled with…I'm not sure what, but it's not fish, thankfully. I meander through the market stalls looking at things I definitely don't need. Eventually, I find somewhere to buy new underwear and the fabric I use to bind my chest when I travel. It's easier to ride a horse or fight when your breasts aren't jiggling about. Not that there's much to jiggle on me.

A group of acolytes are harassing passers-by, handing out fliers for their Order of the Divine. They're a religious sect that thinks Patrons are an abomination and the Divine's way to punish those who do not follow their teachings. They're all Mievaborn women, as is most of the Order of the Divine. They don't offer me a flier.

A Laguzborn woman standing beside me in line for some fresh produce threatens her kids with hiring the Silent Assassin if they don't stop misbehaving. I choke on my swallow at the unexpected mention, and she raises her eyebrow at me.

"You okay, love?" she asks, reaching for me.

Assuming she's about to clap my back in an attempt to help me stop choking, I wave her off with a smile as I compose myself. "I thought the Silent Assassin retired?" I ask, hoping I hide my small, knowing smile.

Before she can answer, a procession of snowolves passes by noisily and we both turn to stare. Almost as big as a horse but ten times as dumb, the creatures are hard workers and only wish to please their owners. Their shaggy black and white coats flap in the breeze as they carry their carts of people and property.

I had a snowolf as a pet once. She was only a puppy, and I named her Anerea. She was mine, for a whole moon. Until she…died. Maybe leaving Osraed isn't a bad thing if I can leave all the memories behind and start afresh.

The woman startles me from my dark memories, answering my previous question. "As if she *actually* retired. And even if she has, my kids don't know that." She finishes with a wink before running after one of her children who is about to bite into an apple they haven't purchased.

I watch the woman tending to her gaggle of children, and then I continue to sit and observe the people in the market. This is probably the last time that I can feasibly come to this market, as Nemoris is on the west coast. I highly doubt there would be any reason for me to be coming this way again.

It's not until the sun has started to set that I finally decide to leave the market. My hired horse has the personality of wet porridge, and I wonder if it's been abused into submission. I always treat the horses I hire with respect, but I never know if the stables are treating them well.

After dropping my wet porridge of a horse back to the stables in the outer compound, I start the cold walk home, but a strangled cry carried on the wind piques my interest and my rage. Slipping up the hood of my cloak, I stick to the darkest shadows of the trees as I follow my ears toward the cries.

It doesn't take me too long to discover the source: a pair of young women—perhaps only girls—being harassed by a group of men. Women should be safe to travel without the need for protection by another man, *from* other men. The thought alone boils my blood and fuels my rage as it takes over.

I would like to think I am in control, but there are times when my rage steps in.

I sneak as close as I can to the group. The five men have the two young women on their knees, as they plead for the men to leave them unharmed.

As if this traumatic experience hasn't harmed them enough.

It would have probably been better to observe for a moment longer before I made my presence known, but as soon as I witness the unbuckling of a belt, the choice is clear.

Leaning against a tree nearby, I clear my throat. Seven sets of eyes jump to my position, and three swords are drawn within seconds. *Interesting.* No Patrons of the Divine, all the men are Nemorisborn, and the girls are Sadoriborn.

"This doesn't look like a very fun party," I say, stifling a fake yawn.

One of the girls makes a pleading sound I pretend to ignore, not taking my eyes off the men.

"Aye, but it's a party you weren't invited to, lad. So, fuck off before you get hurt," says the man closest to me.

I chuckle as I push off the tree to standing. I wasn't even trying to pretend I was a young man this time. But, of course, why would these men think a woman would be bold enough to approach them? Sometimes, I wish I could hide my violet eyes that mark me as a Patron, as too many people back down for fear of what my Gift might be, never realizing that my Gift doesn't exist and it's just *me* beating their asses. I keep the hood of my cloak low.

"If you let the girls go now, *I* won't hurt *you*."

All five of the men laugh, and I almost do too. They never take my offer, and I hope they never do. What comes next is far too much fun.

In an instant, three throwing knives hit the first man's thigh before anyone realizes I've thrown them. He howls and falls backward, crying and looking around for someone to help him.

Pathetic.

One man clumsily swings his sword, and I duck under it to punch him in the crotch. That'll keep him down for a moment.

"You're dead!" the last man with a drawn weapon threatens.

Picking up the discarded sword from the man cradling himself between the legs, I pretend to wield it. As he approaches, I throw the sword at him instead, and then fling a knife from my wrist into the chest of one of the men holding the girls. I hit my mark.

As the sword I threw is knocked aside, I spin and kick the

side of his hands, and he drops his own sword. He reaches down to pick it up, and I knee him in the face with a satisfying crack. Blood sprays deliciously from his nose.

The man with my throwing knives lodged in him cries as he pulls one from his thigh and throws it at me. He misses, of course, and I laugh as I run at the last man standing. He immediately puts his hands up in surrender, but it's too late for me to care. They had their chance.

Once he realizes that I'm not backing down, he swings a punch. He connects with my cheek, but fortunately, I've taken worse punches. He's not very strong, but he's adept at hand-to-hand. However, it's over far too soon when I get him to the ground.

With his arm wrapped behind his back, I look up to see two of the group have disappeared. I barely even touched the guy I punched in the crotch, and he's already gone, along with the broken-nose guy. I think the one that took a knife to the chest may actually be dead.

"Say you're sorry," I demand to the man under me.

"Fuck you."

"Wrong answer." I continue to pull his arm until a loud crack sounds, and he screams. "That would be your shoulder. You should have apologized."

Standing up, I give one swift kick to his side and turn to the girls.

"Are you okay?"

No answer. Instead, they stare up at me, still on their knees.

I sigh. Not at the girls but at the man trying to hobble away with my throwing knives still embedded in his leg. "I'll be right back," I reassure them as I jog after him.

He cries and tries to hobble faster once he realizes I'm heading after him. I catch up quickly and push the pathetic man over. He begins to plead with me, but I pull out my last two knives and then knock him out with a hilt to the temple.

I turn and almost burst into laughter. Either the guy with my knife in his chest isn't dead, or these girls are just as vicious as I am. One is kicking the shit out of him, while the other goes to town on the guy whose shoulder I dislocated.

Confirming the man is not dead, I take back my knife.

"Do you girls need an escort somewhere or..."

They reply in unison. "Yes, please."

By the time I walk them back to their family's caravans and return home, it's well after midnight.

Who would have thought buying underwear would turn out to be such a fun excursion?

CHAPTER FOUR

"Your presence has been requested in the receiving hall."

I narrow my eyes at the rather tall Mievaborn man who looks to be sweating profusely after his announcement, his pale cheeks flushed a deep pink. I'm already packed and ready to go, but I keep the door cracked open only a couple of inches so he can't see in.

"They're early," comes my tart response.

The sweaty man opens his violet eyes in alarm—which, to be honest, is surprising in and of itself considering how wide open they already were—and takes a step back. Not that he's looking me in the eye, thankfully. I don't like the connection, the power in it. Having people avert their eyes first also gives me the opportunity to study them more easily.

An angry breath rushes from my nose, and I swing open the door all the way so the man can see my bags packed in a pile behind me, but he flinches. Having people afraid of me has its advantages, but today, it's irritating me. Does this moron really think I'm going to *assassinate* him for delivering a message? It's possible this man has no idea who I am, and his nervous demeanor has nothing to do with me. Still, I'm annoyed.

The man clears his throat. "Right. I'll let the council know you're on your way and have someone sent to collect your bags," he squeaks.

He can't get away fast enough and skids around the corner down the hall. I roll my eyes and slam the door as hard as I can so he hears it and hopefully shits his pants.

Still smirking at the thought, I quickly change into travel clothing and check the last of my belongings. Patrons of the Divine don't usually stay past their coming-of-age; however, as a Null, I was given a permanent residence and a work detail in addition to being Jaena's favorite assassin. I was afforded a small stipend for my work as a nanny in the children's compound, which is nowhere near as much as I used to earn as the Silent Assassin, but even so, I rarely spent it on anything other than necessities or my weapons.

I try to pack most of my dried herbs and spice pouches, my jars of ferments and pastes, and bottles of extracts and essences, assuming we will be on horses the entire journey. I may be traveling, but I'll be Divine-damned if my trail meals are going to be tasteless.

I'm bringing all of my weapons that can be worn on my person or packed into my bags. It's probably not appropriate to bring my giant bo staff, my pair of ornate—but still deadly—single-bit hatchets, or the bow and arrows that are almost larger than me. Though, the latter is more because the bow was one of the only weapons I couldn't master. This was amusing for all the weapons masters I worked with over the revs, considering Mievaborn usually have an affinity for archery. I'll give them all to Leian.

One roll of throwing knives is wrapped low around my waist under my shirt, while the other is packed into one of my bags. I have knives hidden in my boots, strapped to my ankles, and up my sleeves. It took me a long time to create straps that would safely secure knives on me while also being practical when I needed them in a hurry. I'd be taking all my straps even if I couldn't take the weapons.

I have a thin dagger sheathed around each thigh that I access through my pockets, my pants having been altered for this purpose. I leave my short sword attached to the belt and lean it against my bags, deciding against wearing it to the receiving hall to meet my new *owners*.

One of the hatchets slips over with a thud, and I pick up the familiar weight like an old friend. I don't want to leave my stunning hatchets with beautifully crafted wooden handles behind. The bits have intricate swirls and geometric lines etched into them too. They may look decorative, but they're amazing weapons to fight with. Well, they *would* be if I'd ever been able to use them outside of practice.

I admit, the woman who sold them to me had an easy job of it because I was in love the moment I saw them. They were the first weapons that I purchased myself almost a decade past. The heads are the size of my palm; each weapon is only the length of my forearm in its entirety. I've never once had to sharpen the bits, as the lady who sold them to me had promised. I wish I'd figured out a way to holster them. But I can't without hurting myself, making them too cumbersome, or not easily accessible. Wrapping them in a thin piece of leather, I put them into one of my bags. I just can't leave them behind.

I stand with my hands on my hips, surveying what has been my home for the last five revolutions. I thought I would live out my life here, or that's what Jaena had led me to believe. The two bags at my feet make up the entirety of my existence in Osraed, and someone will move into this room and erase that I was ever here. Impulsively, I grab one of my knives and carve MIKA into the door frame. I grab the weapons for Leian and walk through the door for the last time.

I'M LATE, of course. I stride in with confidence even though Jaena is giving me a glare that would have the ability to light me on fire if that was her Gift. I swallow the smirk that tugs at the corner of my lips.

The receiving hall is enormous, unnecessarily so. Nothing much happens in this part of the compound except Patron sales. Osraed is full of old architecture, and it makes me wonder what this country looked like before the world split. This beautiful hall is clearly from *before*, and what a waste it is to use it for this purpose only. Tall ceilings, large slab concrete walls, and wooden balustrades circling above, as if this was once a place filled with so many people that they would spectate from above.

The air is crisp as no fire has been lit; a clear sign that this won't take long. Standing tall with my arms behind my back, I nod a greeting at the three people who must be my escorts.

The first thing I notice is that while the two men are clearly Nemorisborn, an Erduborn woman is with them. All three are giants, although the woman looks a little short for Erduborn, who are usually at *least* six feet tall, even the women. But maybe it is because the Nemorisborn men are amusingly large.

Both the Erduborn woman and the larger of the two men are violet-eyed Patrons of the Divine. The other Nemorisborn man has regular, normal, green eyes of the forest. Eyes that keep stealing a look in my direction while he should be paying attention to the council president. He's probably noticed the blooming bruise on my cheek from last night. *Oops.*

They are all wearing the tall leather boots and layered clothing of Nemoris, covered in various leather vests, straps and holsters. I'm sure they'd be an intimidating sight to someone else.

"Commander Cristoph Ofnemoris, this is Mika. Please accept my apologies for her tardiness. We were not expecting you so soon," Jaena's pleasant voice rings out while the rest of the five council members sit quietly in their seats on either side of her. Their apprentices stand like good little statues behind them, and I spot the sweaty man and curl my lip. He knows exactly who I am if he's a council apprentice. It's odd that he was the one to deliver the message.

"Please, join us for refreshments," Jaena asks, drawing my attention back to the Council President and her practiced smile.

"While we appreciate the offer of hospitality, ma'am, my companions and I are eager to get back on the road as our journey is already a long one," Commander Cristoph says, and I try not to giggle. The tallest of the group, the giant man's voice is so deep and gravelly that it sounds like two rocks scraping against each other, as though it takes real effort to speak.

"Understandable, Commander. We will not keep you any longer. Mika's bags will be taken to your horses, but otherwise, there is nothing preventing you from departing. Commander Cristoph, Tovi, Riley, it's been a pleasure. Good luck on your journey, and Divine blessings to you all." Jaena's *friendly* presidential persona can be so lovely when she turns it on, even if her offer for them to stay was empty.

With that, Jaena stands, and then so does the rest of the council, all filing out of the room, followed by their apprentices. Leaving me with the three living mountains. Not a look back, no attempt from Jaena at all to say goodbye. I shouldn't have expected anything different.

"Well, she's not any less terrifying the second time," the slightly less giant of the two men—Riley—jokes as he folds his arms across his chest, the muscles of his forearms bare. His eyes now unabashedly take me in, and this time not just my bruised face.

He might be attractive if it didn't look like he was constantly smirking or was in on a joke that he knew you weren't. His heavy-lidded eyes, which are surveying me closely, hold an obscene amount of long, lush eyelashes the same color as his brows—a blood-red so dark they're almost black. The hair on his head is only a shade lighter, slightly longer than mine with a definite wave and worn half up in a small bun. Quite the contrast to the commander's fire-orange beard and shaved head.

I was clearly mistaken in my original assessment. All three *are* a minimum of six feet tall; the two men are definitely more than a foot taller than me and maybe a couple of feet wider too. All of them angle their heads down to look at me as I walk toward them, and an awkward silence descends.

One smirking, one grinning, and the other giving me a cold hard stare.

"So...I'm Mika," I say, introducing myself redundantly.

The commander's face—full of freckles—bursts into a grin as he claps me on the shoulder, nearly knocking me off my feet. His pounding laugh echoes through the receiving hall. "Nice to have you, Mika!"

"You're much smaller than we were expecting," Riley says, and Tovi elbows him in the ribs. "What I mean to say is, hello, I'm Riley."

Tovi rolls her eyes and heads for the door, without so much as a word of greeting.

"Nice to meet you, Riley. I can assure you that my stature has no bearing on my abilities."

He nods as he starts backing toward the exit, a smile that turns into a smirk the longer he stares. "Oh, I'm sure. Especially if that bruise is anything to go by."

The commander clears his throat and Riley spins around, jogging after Tovi before I can reply.

"Let me introduce you to your horse for the trip, Mika," the commander offers, humor tinged in his voice.

"MEET APPLEMINT," the commander says with a flourish as he attaches my bags to a beautiful gray and brown dappled mare. "Oh, and before I forget, here are your pins." He hands me five pins of varying sizes after digging into his pockets.

These pins are my ownership tags. They're forest green triangles with my Patron number in gold. I must wear one at all times lest someone think I am a defector. I remove my violet, circular Osraed pin attached to my collar and replace it with the Nemoris one.

"Thank you, Commander Cristoph."

"Woah," he says as he puts his hands up in mock surrender. "I'm going to need you to drop the formality, or this is going to be a *long* journey." He puts his hand forward to shake mine. "You can call me Beans."

I shake his outstretched hand, observing that my hand looks like a child's in his enormous paw. "Beans?" *Beans?*

"That's the one!" He turns and gives one final tug of tension to my bag straps, now attached to Applemint, before cheerily strolling off.

Applemint seizes my distraction and immediately starts nudging around my pockets.

"She's looking for her namesake," Tovi says. She pulls out a bag of applemints from her pocket, feeds the horse one, and hands me the rest.

"Thank you," I say, smiling at her.

"Don't feed her too many or she shits herself," she says over her shoulder, walking off.

Cold. Everything about her screams it, even the stiff way she ties up her long and curly brunette hair, so shiny that even on this cloudy Osraed day, it reflects the light. Her features are all harsh lines, with nothing soft about her. Clearly a very fit woman, her Nemoris leathers do not hide her muscles or the curves of her full breasts and hips.

Riley crosses into my line of view, riding his horse and leading another almost identical one by the reins alongside him. Both are Nemoris cloud horses, gray in color with exceptionally full—but short and stumpy—tails, manes that are basically just a thick fuzz, and coarse hair that grows from knee joints down to their hooves.

Just as I was beginning to think Tovi could be entirely unyielding, her face blooms into a beatific smile…at the horse Riley is leading. I mount Applemint, watching Tovi's lips move, and realize she is speaking to her horse. She looks like an entirely different person right now, stroking the face of the creature, her olive Erduborn skin almost glowing.

I look away, not wanting to be caught watching her and suffer another one of those cold stares she seems to reserve just for me.

CHAPTER FIVE

Our party travels in silence until we're through the main gates of the Osraed outer compound, heading west toward the Nemoris border bridge.

Beans slows down to bring his massive black stallion alongside Applemint. I hadn't realized how enormous the beast was (the horse, not the man) because he looked normal sized with Beans on his back. But Beans isn't *normal* sized. Ditch—the horse's ridiculous name—is easily so large that his back would be above my head if I stood next to him. Applemint nips at Ditch's neck playfully as he matches her pace.

"Did the council explain our mission to you, Mika?" Beans' deep voice rumbles.

"Princess Ofnemoris kidnapped. Dangerous. Need a sneak who can fight." I shrug, hoping he doesn't notice my surprise that we're already *on* the mission. I shouldn't have assumed they were only my escort into Nemoris.

"I guess that's it in a nutshell. But there's a lot more," he says as he frowns toward Tovi and Riley ahead of us.

"Just over four moons past, our queen received a missive from King Stol Oferdu. A Nemorisborn man had snuck into his castle, completely undetected, and attacked his doxies. Tried to blow them up with some kind of explosive."

Beans tips his head in my direction as if he's trying to figure me out. I try not to squirm under the scrutiny. Switching to a smile, he continues. "The king stated that he had managed to capture the man responsible, and he was in his dungeons awaiting trial and execution. However, he wanted restitution from Nemoris, of course." He rolls his eyes. "He demanded a Gifted healer to come and heal every single one of his doxies, and since he has many and they were in varying states of injury, it would take a few weeks. He didn't want to risk using his own healers in case they were needed elsewhere."

It dawns on me that we aren't speaking about Nemuel, the 15-rev-old youngest Princess Ofnemoris, but of Amarilyss—a Gifted healer who resumed her place as first Princess Ofnemoris when she came-of-age—though only Nemoris recognizes her as royalty.

A Patron of the Divine being named a princess caused all kinds of controversy. She will never be allowed to inherit the throne, nor can she produce any heirs. The queen technically *owns* Amarilyss and her Gifts. Speculations ran rife about Queen Neoniri getting her hands on documents to prove that she was her daughter.

"But why send the princess?"

Beans is giving me another calculated look and I hope he's not noticed my inner ruminations of Divine law.

"Firstly, Nemoris is the only country to treat Patrons as anything other than property, so technically Lyss *wouldn't* be a princess in the king's eyes, only a Gifted healer to be used. Secondly, his stipulations were only that it had to be a female healer. We're fairly confident he knew that all other Gifted healers across Nemoris are male, but—"

"Wait," I interrupt. "Why did the healer have to be a female?"

"Because he didn't want to risk a male touching his doxies," Beans says patiently, even though my questions and interruptions are surely grating on his nerves.

"Well, that doesn't clarify anything, what about the king's male doxies?" I laugh.

Beans contemplates me for a moment, before kicking Ditch forward between Tovi and Riley. I can't quite hear everything being said, but he's asking about male doxies.

Beans drops back after a few moments. "Do you know for certain he has male doxies or is it speculation?"

"Either he has male doxies, or he's lied to the Osraed council when he's purchased male Nulls. All the bills of sale for male Nulls have said they're to be a *Royal doxy* Oferdu."

You cannot purchase a Null unless you specify exactly what position they will fill in your country. Before I was assigned work as a nanny, and during the time of the petitions to oust me, I worked in the Registry.

Each country has its own set of records separate from the Patron's life records. Erdu was the country I looked after both times. I filed a copy of any bills of sale, updated any deaths, and mostly ticked off scheduled check-ins. My least favorite part of the work was whenever I had to check a request for information, confirming someone was who they said they were. When they weren't, it was a safe bet that their life was forfeit.

Beans has one hand on his hip, and the other is absentmindedly stroking his neatly trimmed, bright orange beard. "Hmm."

Tovi suddenly punches Riley in the shoulder, and then

her horse is running at full gallop. Riley recovers quickly and chases after her. I look at Beans in alarm, but he smiles in their direction and shakes his head as if it's a totally normal interaction for two people on a royal mission.

"If the princess went willingly to Erdu, how is it kidnapping?" I ask, continuing the conversation.

"Right," he says with a start, as if I woke him from a stupor. "Well. Lyss went as requested within a few days since it would take her almost a moon to get there via horse and escort. Not wanting to waste an avyon."

Avyon's are *enormous* creatures of flight. They have the skin of a reptile with plumes of thin feathers covering their heads so that only the wide mouth full of needle-sharp teeth and beady black eyes can be seen. Originating in Sadori, countries now breed their own, though only a handful are born every decade. The creatures are so large that up to five people can be seated on their backs with the aid of a contraption, allowing them flight across the world. Avyon's can cover a week's travel by horse in only a day or two.

Less than twenty mature avyons in the world means they're only used in the most special—or dire—of occasions. And a demand by a foreign country to heal your doxies doesn't equate to an emergency.

I've never seen one in person, or at least not close up. From a distance or in the sky, as they shoot by at terrifying speeds, they make an impressive sight to behold. People will stop mid-conversation when the loud beat of their wings is heard to watch them in awe.

"So, a moon to get there, plus a week or two to cure every doxy, and a moon to come home. Two-and-a-half moons at most," Beans says as he counts on his fingers. "A week after she was due to be back, the royal family hadn't heard from her and started to worry. They contacted the

King Oferdu, who said she had left as planned the moon prior, and he assumed she was already home."

"He lied?" I ask, observing the large man with his arms crossed, trusting Ditch to know where to go.

"That's the going assumption. We investigated for a couple of weeks, and aside from a few random people, no one saw her leave."

"But there *were* people who saw her leave?"

"Well, here's the thing. Everyone who said they saw her, eventually admitted that *they* didn't see her, only that they knew someone who had. But we couldn't find a single person that clapped eyes on her themselves."

"Hmmm. What about her escorts?"

Beans is nodding, stroking his beard again. "Gone. None of them were allowed to be near the doxies' wing in the castle. Oferdu guards would escort her between there and her room in the healer's wing every morning and night. Up until her supposed departure, everything was reported as smooth." His expression is somber as he looks down at Ditch's neck. "Four of the best Royal guards and two Gifted Patrons all disappeared and never made it home to their families."

"To what end? No offense to the princess, but Gifted healers aren't exactly rare."

"We can only speculate. She's particularly Gifted in that she can heal what ails the mind as well as the physical body. But we are unsure why that would be worth waging a war over."

I had forgotten about that. Amarilyss is over five revs older than me and left Osraed more than a decade past. The Gifted Princess Ofnemoris has the ability to heal the mind, but I have no idea how that works. Most healers can focus the Divine into physical wounds, encouraging them to heal rapidly. I've heard it described as being able to *see* what needs to be fixed and imagining it happening—like gluing a broken bone or knitting flesh together. But how does one know what needs to be fixed in someone else's mind?

"What happened to the accused man? Was he trialed?"

"He was executed before Nemoris could claim him for questioning. Again, we found not one witness to his crimes, more of the same bullshit. Not that we were able to question his doxies who would have actually witnessed it. Same with his trial. Though we did confirm that his execution was a spectacle and people really did witness *that* themselves."

I'm beginning to wonder what the Silent Assassin is going to be able to do when it sounds like all the investigations have been done.

Beans whistles to get Riley and Tovi's attention after a few hours of silent riding. "Let's find somewhere to make camp for the night in Osraed before we take the main road toward Nemoris."

"Why are we even going to Nemoris and not straight through to the bridge into Erdu?" I ask.

"Well, we aren't exactly going to go knocking on the king's door and ask where he's keeping the princess, are we? Stealth and discretion and all that," Riley says, with amused sarcasm.

"Not what I asked, but I appreciate the input." I roll my eyes with a smile. "Beans?"

Beans is hiding a smirk under his hand as he fingers his rather elaborate mustache. "What Riley is trying to say, is that we're going to enter Erdu from Nemoris."

"Won't that take double the time?"

"Officially, we're only in Osraed to collect you and return to Nemoris within two weeks. If we don't, the Nemoris gate peacekeepers will file a report," Tovi answers me, not looking at anything in particular as she runs her thumb along a full and sharp-looking eyebrow. As if waking from a trance, her vision hones in on me watching her. Large, angled eyes narrow at me, and lips—already not very full, though beautifully defined—became a thin line. She *really* doesn't like me.

"That, and we have already used up every single favor we had, traveling by way of Osraed into Erdu unofficially, searching for Lyss ourselves. Next time we pass through the Erdu gate, it would be reported," Beans clarifies, getting down from Ditch.

"Stealth and discretion?" I ask, smirking sideways at Riley, who waggles his eyebrows at me.

"Exactly. We're headed to a small cottage in Nemoris to stable the horses and pick up one more member of our party, before continuing on foot."

I swallow my displeasure that being on foot will mean this will be an even longer journey. I want to ask more, especially about the other person joining us, but Tovi's bored and increasingly hostile expression suggests I cool my curiosity so we can make camp quickly in the waning daylight.

It's been a beautiful cloudy day in Osraed, even if a little cold and windy, as the season dictates. Though it's a pretty cold and windy country most of the time, we've been blessed with a pleasant first evening on the road.

We're on a flat plain away from the main road for privacy. A few massive ollie trees are dotted around, the wind making a rustling sound through the endless canopies of leaves and branches. You can stand at the base of an ollie tree and not see the sky for how dense they are, but their branches don't actually start for easily twelve or fourteen feet up the trunk. I wonder what they're trying so hard to hide in there. Are the rustling of their leaves actually the whisper of secrets?

Tovi is tending to the horses, Beans is chopping some

firewood with a massive axe, and Riley is making some food over a basic fire.

This useless, retired assassin-nanny is standing awkwardly doing nothing but imagining the conversations of fucking trees.

CHAPTER SIX

It's not long before we're relaxing by the fire with a bowl of extraordinarily plain stew in our hands. The other three are eating with such gusto that I'm left to wonder whether these people don't have any taste buds or they're just *that* hungry.

"What, uh, what are we eating?" I ask as I tip the gruel from my spoon back into the bowl, allowing the chunky sludge to drip and plop back on itself.

"Bean and donkey stew," Riley says with a mouthful, staring me down, forcing me to avert my eyes to my food.

"Uh huh. Is it literally only beans and donkey or are there other ingredients?" I grimace. "For flavor?"

Tovi is unsuccessfully trying to hide her laughter behind her hand with a mouthful of food, while Beans is grinning in what looks like sheer delight between me and Riley. This group is fucking weird.

"It's food that you didn't have to make, and you're complaining?" Riley's indignance is mildly amusing.

"All I am saying is that a little flavor wouldn't hurt. Thanks for the food though. Cheers!" And with that, I shove another disgustingly boring mouthful of Riley's stew in my mouth and lift my bowl in salute.

Tovi and Beans also salute with their bowls before Riley tells us all to go fuck ourselves, and stalks off into the sunset, which has both Tovi and Beans snickering.

I AWAKE to the sounds of birds and their morning songs. Laying there listening, I can hear shuffling about. Riley is returning, presumably from relieving himself, which triggers my need to do the same.

"Morning," I whisper, to which he nods a greeting and lays heavily back onto his bedroll.

The early sun is already starting to cause steam to rise from the grass, so it'll be a foggy morning. Beans and Tovi are both awake when I return, chattering happily about their good sleep. Riley glares at them with dark circles under his eyes.

We have a quick breakfast of chewy fruit and grain bars that Beans' mother made for the trip, and get on the road before the sun has fully crested. I resist the urge to ask him how his *mother* made them. He's a Patron who shouldn't— *couldn't*—know who his family are. Perhaps this woman is not his birth mother?

When I try to saddle Applemint, she dances and prances away. I chase her. She stays still long enough for me to think it's over, before springing into the air and taking off in circles around me.

I look at my three travel companions for help, and all three of the assholes shrug and go back to their own tasks. Remembering the applemints, I retrieve them from my pack and dangle them toward the naughty horse. She trots back and snorts in my face with impatience, as if this is what she had wanted the entire time.

The day is dull and never-ending, a gloomy fog surrounding us. Beans and I speak about everything he and the various teams have done and what intel they've been able to source. Tovi and Riley speak in whispers and laughter, randomly chasing each other or having stick fights from horseback.

During a lull in a particularly long and boring stretch of road, I notice Riley has a giant axe like Beans'. I ask if it's purely for chopping wood. Riley *laughs* at me as if I'm a child asking a silly question. This starts a discussion about other countries and their preferred weapons.

I was unaware that all Nemorisborn are taught to fight with the axe as well as the sword, Beans himself only learning after he was purchased by the Nemoris crown. I'd never paid attention to what weapons countries—except Mieva—preferred because I encountered them so little. Most targets were dead before a weapon could ever be raised toward me.

"I prefer the Erdu metal short swords now," Tovi says, gesturing to one holstered on her person and the other on her horse.

"Can you fight with both? One in each hand?" I ask, to which I get a grunt of affirmation that ends the conversation.

She would be fun to spar with if I could find a way to protect the blades of my hatchets. Well, protect *other people and myself* from the blades of my hatchets. They're far too dangerous of a weapon to spar with. I shudder at the memory of the one—and only—time I carried them holstered on my belt. I run my finger along the scar of my left wrist where I almost mortally wounded myself. The closest I've ever come to meeting my Divine end, and it was a careless brush of my wrist against my own blade. Another shudder skips down my spine at the memory.

After three more dinners of bland stew, I offer to cook. Not only does it allow me to contribute, but also to eat something that doesn't look and taste like dirty dish slime. With my ferments and pastes, I'm able to get creative.

By the time everyone returns from their respective duties, I'm soaking a few pieces of the salt-brined donkey, cooking wild rice, and patting dry some pickled onion and carrot.

Now, I have an audience. I fry the now much less salty donkey with the pickled carrot and onion. I add a heaped spoon of my fermented black soybeans, sending a silent prayer to the Divine that it won't end up *too* salty. I serve it to everyone on the wild rice with some swordmint.

Riley stares at me while he eats with an unreadable expression, always with that constant smirk simmering at his edges. I hold his gaze for a moment before looking away, but his eyes bore into my skin for the rest of the meal.

After dinner, Tovi offers to take my plate, doing the washing up for everyone.

Unfortunately, I underestimated how much food the three of them eat, especially Beans. They all end up having some crusty bread and hard cheese as well. Despite not cooking enough, I am officially appointed the travel cook. Riley is banned from ever cooking again, much to his apparent relief.

AFTER A COLD DAY OF TRAVEL, Riley gives me a full smirk and asks if I'm making sure there's enough food tonight. "Flavor is not a substitute for substance," he announces, as if I can't cook enough food for them that *also* has flavor.

"Riley, I promise that if I don't cook enough this time, you're welcome to take over." I hear a resounding chorus of "no" from all three of them, and chuckle to myself. Something tiny thaws in my chest as rage swirls low in my belly.

I cooked far too much this time, making enough for breakfast too. Yet again a delicious meal. I offer a smug look at Riley during breakfast, and he gives me a lazy wink as he reclines. I'm not even sure what that means.

He's not wholly unattractive, though his smirk definitely is. Certainly not a *pretty* man by any means—he's rough and sharp. Pale skin with a smattering of red freckles across his nose and cheeks, with full lips in the shape of a perfectly defined bow.

He catches me watching his lips and raises an eyebrow. I poke my tongue out *like a bloody child* and then frantically busy myself with packing up camp.

I replay that moment in my head over and over all day, cringing internally every time. I can never speak to him again, it's the only solution.

Crossing the Osraed gate onto the Nemoris bridge proves to be more of an issue than when I'm alone. Details must be checked for all four of us to confirm we have permissions on record to enter Nemoris and exit Osraed. I cannot pass through here again without explicit written approval from Queen Neoniri Ofnemoris.

I never had an issue with my sanctioned movements when traveling for assassinations. I was barely asked any questions as a Patron then. This time, fellow Patrons—fellow Nulls—treat me like a prized horse being taken to her new owners.

One of the jobs assigned to Nulls is peacekeeping. Stationed at all the gates in and out of Osraed, Peacekeepers report anything that doesn't align. They're also the people who come after you if you defect, usually with a Gifted captain who can force you in some way if needed.

The bridge into Nemoris is *enormous*. I'm in awe every single time I cross it, which has been only a couple of times, and not recently. Made entirely of wood from the Nemoris elomak tree. It would fit four large horse carriages side by side in width and takes us ten minutes to walk from one end to the other on our horses. Large elomak branches have been used as decoration on the sides. Intricate patterns and designs in the sand-colored wood with a burgundy red grain, spanning the entire length of the bridge.

The horses are able to travel much faster after crossing the bridge, galloping at a breakneck speed and requiring a good rub down in the evenings. Like our travels along the busy roads in Osraed, we don't bother to set a watch here on the well-traveled roads directly into Nemoris. With the horses tethered nearby, they would let Beans know if something was amiss, or so I'm told.

I muse on what his Gift could be. Perhaps the ability to communicate with animals, or horses specifically. It would explain why he barely ever holds Ditch's reins. *That* is a Gift I would've liked to have been blessed with. Or shifting into a horse to run free with them. I've only ever heard of a handful of Patron's being able to shift their entire being, and every single one has been a various breed of horse. There hasn't been one in years though, and there are none currently living.

I've realized the reason for Riley's dark circles and bad moods every morning. He's been drinking himself into oblivion every night. Last night, I watched him stumble into a tree, land on the ground with a grunt, and lay there unmoving for a long time. I looked at the others, but besides an eye roll from Beans and Tovi muttering "drunken wanker" under her breath, they didn't seem to care.

Applemint is still as cheeky as ever. She pinched my bum, again, because I dared to leave it within striking distance. I discovered she could undo her tether at will when I found her shaking one of my bags upside-down, emptying its contents. The other three were not surprised. If I'm not careful, she still dances away from me until I give her an applemint.

One evening, while waiting for water to boil for dinner, I ask, "Where does the name *Beans* come from?"

"Come on, Daddy *Beans*. Show us your *beans*," Tovi purrs, then pokes out her tongue through her teeth at him.

Riley casually puts his arm around my shoulders, and I stiffen at the unexpected touch. Trying not to notice the heat, or the muscles, or the smell of him, I fail and notice *it all*. While looking at Beans, he loudly whispers to me, "So, Beans' Gift is that his *beans* are so…"

He ducks behind me, using me as a shield and yelling his surrender, as Beans throws small projectiles at him, and one hits me in the shoulder. I look down, and amongst the leaf litter are a bunch of pale green…*beans*. I pick one up and confirm that it is, in fact, a fresh bean. We have no beans. Beanstalks do not grow here. I'm still staring at it when I hear Tovi pissing herself laughing.

"Children," Beans growls, and I look up to see him glaring at the other two, though a smile is tugging at the corner of his lips.

He waves me over to where he's kneeling beside a tall weed growing in the large wells of a tree's roots. On the weed, are a couple of bean pods that *shouldn't be there*. I laugh uncomfortably, throwing a questioning look at him. He gently grabs the stalk of a different weed, staring at it intently. To my complete and total fascination, three bean pods rapidly grow from the weed.

He pulls one off and hands it to me. I break it open and find six, small, ripe beans inside.

"Can you do this to *anything*?"

"It's not easy through bark, but any vegetation still rooted to the Divine earth will grow my beans," he confirms, shooting a side-eye at Tovi's snicker. "Except grass for some reason," he complains.

Beans grows a heap of beans for me to cook with and I try not to burst into laughter the entire night whenever I think about it. Even as I drift off to sleep, the thought that the commander of the Nemoris army—their *Gifted* commander—is able to grow beans, is about one of the funniest things I have ever heard.

CHAPTER SEVEN

Our walk to the training ground takes longer than it should, as though she's been walking in circles all day. Perhaps today is the day we never arrive; the day it finally changes.

Pasha.

The sight of him transforms me into a beast barely contained. All claws and fangs. Fire and flames. Rage and ruin.

But I'm frozen solid in this prison.

"Where is everyone, I thought it'd be a group?" she asks the weapons master when we arrive for lessons a few minutes late.

"Just us. Gave everyone the morning off as I knew it'd be your first day since…you know." Pasha makes a weird gesture toward our lower half.

"Right. Okay then," comes the sarcastic reply.

Immediately, I try to make her apologize, to beg for forgiveness, but our mouth and body don't respond.

She cannot hear me. She never can.

"I'm not in the mood for your attitude today, Mika," he spits.

I scream at her to run, go, escape. But she stays, unaware of the seconds ticking down to the moment our life changes irreversibly.

"We're practicing how to disarm someone with a knife. Move into the barn."

Confused about why he's red with anger, she follows him. But his anger fuels me, sharpening my teeth and claws. It feeds me.

"Right. Try to get my knife," he instructs, as he throws his knife from hand to hand, dropping into a defensive position. His skin—so pale it's almost translucent—is going pink from the cold.

She steels herself and advances, focusing on his knife and his body language. We've been learning how to do this since we were five and Jaena saw us winning scraps against the older boys in the children's compound. She thought perhaps it was our Gift, but it wasn't. We are good, very good—especially for our age—but not Gifted.

There's nothing special about us.

I try to stop her. Dull our skill, be meek, anything to stop what's coming. But she disarms him easily, his face sweaty as he demands the knife back.

"Again," he tells her, and she swiftly disarms him with little trouble.

"Am I doing something wrong? Isn't this exactly what you want me to be doing?"

Pasha is Gifted, not in weaponry, but in teaching, and he just so happens to be adept at weaponry. We're better though, even at thirteen.

"I thought you'd be grateful that I gave you more one-on-one training instead of having to deal with a full group for the first time. Instead, you're showing off and giving me attitude."

Pasha was always a bit odd, maybe a little creepy, but never nasty. A decade our senior, we thought he'd enjoyed teaching us one-on-one for the last three revs. But finally, today, we were supposed to be with the rest of the kids in secondary, learning as a group instead of being hidden away.

"Here, take the knife, and I'll disarm you and show you how it's supposed to be done." He hands us the knife, and she prepares to attack so he can defend and disarm.

"Do it badly, don't win, let him disarm you!" I try to yell, *but nothing stops her from pinning his arm behind his back and holding the knife to his throat.*

She releases him and hands his knife back, which he snatches and moves in so close that she's stepping backward to keep some distance from him. Every step, every time, fuels me. Sharpens my claws, lengthens my teeth, just that little bit more.

"You really do think you're better than me, don't you, Mika? I thought maybe once you were sterilized, some of that fire would be extinguished. But no, you're just the same arrogant little bitch you've always been."

Right now, this is when she realizes. We're backed against the wall of an empty stable.

RUN.

But she doesn't run. She still doesn't truly understand the danger. She still trusts him. Still believes he won't hurt us.

Even afterward, when he leaves us broken and bleeding on the empty stable floor, she doesn't understand. We still don't.

Why didn't she fight back?

Why didn't she fight back the next time?

Or the next?

Why did it have to be me?

I never did get to join the group.

I know I can never change the sequence of events. I know yelling and screaming at myself does nothing. But still, I try, and still, I wake up gasping for breath. The revolting memory of Pasha's touch still caresses my skin. Over a decade of this nightmare and it's still as raw as it was back then.

I catch Riley's eye, awake in his bedroll, as I have the few times I've woken from a nightmare. He doesn't sleep long either, or much at all for that matter. He's often carving wood, but something about the time of night and the hushed silence stops me from asking what. I calm my breathing and

let the nightmare-fueled memory wash off me until I fall
back to sleep.

WE REACH a beautiful old cobblestoned cottage surrounded
by all sorts of trees and vines with a massive stable around
midday the next day. It's beginning to drizzle, and the
pluming smoke from the chimney gives me hope that the
inside will be warm and dry.

The cottage is reminiscent of the small parts of Nemoris
I've seen. With only two assassination assignments in
Nemoris, I haven't seen much of the country at all.

The two men I was sent to assassinate, one Laguzborn
and the other Erduborn, both hid in cottages like this.
Though the assignments were two revs apart, the similarities
were uncanny. Both knew I was coming and accepted their
fate as soon as they saw me waiting for them. I was instructed
to kill them brutally, painfully. I did neither. They sat on a
couch and a kitchen chair, respectively. And didn't fight back.
Both hung their heads, waiting. I slit their throats. Then, when
I knew lifeblood no longer ran in their veins, I brutalized their
bodies. No one would know they weren't tortured.

Come to think of it, I've only been tasked to assassinate
one Nemorisborn—a Gifted man able to change the
temperature of water. He was my first assassination in
Sadori. I spent weeks in that Divine-forsaken hot country
before vowing I would never return.

Just as our horses enter the gate, a person sprints out to
greet us. It's a long way to the house from the gate, so it will
take a moment for whoever it is to run to us.

"Bitty!" calls Beans, with a paternal look of affection on

his face. "You're on their horse, by the way," he leans back to say to me.

"Oh?" is my eloquent response.

As Bitty nears, I recognize them. Their coming-of-age was less than a revolution past, though Nemoris had *pre-purchased* them. It's the first and only time I've ever heard of this happening. I remember seeing them around, their pitch-black straight hair tied in a small bun, revealing a shaved undercut. Big eyes with long lashes, square features and a wide nose, and the typical blemish-free sun-kissed bronze skin of a Laguzborn. They're closer in height to me, just a couple of inches taller. Slim but a fit build. Most stunning was the enormous smile across their face, all dimples and teeth.

I hadn't known Bitty's name and we hadn't interacted. They were the infamous Laguzborn who wasn't admitted into Osraed until they were four or five revs old. Lost in Laguz on one of the tiny non-country islands and never reported, as the gossip goes. Adding to the infamy was—though everyone tried to force them—they were not suitable to live with the other children in the compounds. No one ever knew why, only that they lived outside of the compound borders. It wasn't until they aged-up that they moved into secondary and continued life as a normal Gifted Patron. That is until their coming-of-age when, despite there being no official announcement, they were sent straight to Nemoris.

Out of breath, Bitty greets us all and we're formally introduced. I jump down from Applemint, offering her back to them to ride. They reluctantly accept, not wanting to make me walk, but I insist. Once they're up, Bitty's smile is incandescent, and Applemint looks just as delighted.

We continue toward the house with me on foot. Two Nemorisborn women stand on the veranda of the cottage, both *clearly* related to Beans. That bright, fire-orange hair must be a family trait.

When Ditch spots the two women on the veranda, he bolts toward them. It looked like he was about to bowl them right over, but he stops in time, neither woman even flinching. Beans is getting down as Ditch is cuddling and nudging at the two women, desperate to touch them both at the same time. He seems more like a snowwolf pup and not a fully-grown horse. It's adorable given how huge he is in comparison to these *normal heighted women*. While the three are obviously related, these two are not giants like Beans.

"Tall father," Riley whispers down to me, nodding toward them and smiling conspiratorially. I pin my lips together, trying not to laugh.

"And what's your excuse, you overgrown toddler?" Tovi asks Riley, causing Bitty to snort. "Your *entire* family is a normal height, while you grew like a thick, red weed."

Riley tries to push Tovi off her horse and the result is them—yet again—chasing each other. Bitty, Applemint, and I are left alone.

"Are they always like this?" I ask Bitty to break the silence, as it starts to drizzle.

"Yes," they laugh. "Unfortunately."

Bitty tips their head as if listening to something, and I look around on high alert. "Can I be rude and leave you here?" they ask. "Mama is trying to convince Beans to leave me behind!"

I nod and wave them on. It takes me a few moments to register their words and realize that Bitty's Gift must be enhanced hearing. And that they're likely the one joining our party.

Walking alone isn't so bad, though the drizzle quickly becomes heavy rain. I startle when Riley rides up behind me on his horse and reaches his hand out to me. I look at his hand, and then his face, and back to his hand, not taking it.

"Do you want a ride to the cottage, or would you prefer to catch your death in the rain?"

I reluctantly grab his hand, putting my foot in the stirrup he's left available for me, and he yanks me up behind him. I have less than a second before we're galloping, and I'm groping all over him for something to hold on to. He reaches down and grabs one of my hands, pulling it around his waist and holding it there, riding one-handed. His clothes and leathers don't do this man's physique any compliments. He's *ripped*. Pure, unadulterated muscle is rippling under my touch.

His hand is hot. Actually, everything is hot. I'm hot. Why is it so hot? My rage flutters and swirls inside my chest, getting feisty. It's not until we arrive with a screeching halt into the barn behind the cottage and he lets go of my hand, that the rage goes back to sleep.

I slide off his horse with ease. Riley's bags are already in a pile next to one of the stables. He must have dropped them off and come back out for me.

"Thanks for the ride."

"No worries. Mama and Frankie would have castrated me if I'd left you out there," Riley says, grunting as he lifts his horse's saddle.

"Wait. Whose mama is she?"

He lets out a little chuckle. "Everyone's. Yours too now. Prepare yourself to be smothered by the two of them."

I must look the way I feel because Tovi walks past and says, "Don't look so horrified, Mika." But then adds slyly, "Riley isn't *that* ugly."

He whips his head up to look at Tovi and then me. "Geez. Give a girl a hand, and she repays you with uninhibited disgust," he says with exaggerated offense.

I make a stuttered sound to defend myself as both of them cluck their tongues, walking away, shaking their heads in fake disappointment. Leaving me alone in the barn to wonder what the fuck just happened.

Inside the cottage, I am greeted with so *much* that I am instantly overwhelmed. The heat of the roaring fire in the center of the room slams into me. Booming laughter from Beans and—I assume—his sister, can be heard down the hallway directly to my right. Tovi and Bitty are playing a card game at the far end of the room that seems to require lots of table slapping and celebratory whooping. Riley reclines in a massive sofa seat, a drink in his hand, watching me with an intent stare. The smell of food cooking sends my stomach into a frenzy.

Drifting toward the kitchen, finding a smaller, wrinklier, more feminine version of Beans. Standing awkwardly, I try to sniff out the ingredients that might be in the giant pot she's stirring. Red meat, onions, garlic, and something earthy that I can't identify.

"Mika! You're so quiet, you nearly scared an old woman to death!"

"I'm sorry, I was drawn to the smell," I try to apologize as my nose keeps sniffing toward the pot. She laughs and flaps at me with her apron as if to shoo me away.

"Can I do anything to help?

"Come give this a stir then, while I check the bread."

I eagerly take the spoon from her and begin to stir the pot of chunky meat stew, which is interspersed with all kinds of wilting leaves I don't recognize: wide and bright green, small and yellow sword-shaped with pink edges and spots, and curly, dark green ones. Amongst the wilting greens, I see chunks of white kumara and what looks like pieces of young fern stem, prompting my stomach to give a hungry growl.

While I'm mixing, the older woman takes the two

massive loaves of bread out of her little fire oven and sets them aside. Disappearing for a moment, she returns with some dried seed pods and starts grinding them to a powder before tipping them into the pot. An earthy, minty smell wafts up toward me.

"What's the meat?" I ask her.

"Mutton, dear. Our old lady had enough of this life, so we eat her in celebration and thanks."

I like that, and I smile to myself.

"Taste it, will you, and tell me what it needs?" she calls, rummaging in a large butler's pantry.

I quickly look for a small spoon and dip it in the pot to get some of the gravy. The pepperiness punches me delightfully in the face, along with the sweetness from the kumara and earthiness from the greens dancing across my palate.

"Honestly, just a tiny pinch of salt. But a salty buttery bread would be enough."

She returns from the pantry with an approving look, laden with seven bowls and side plates in her arms.

"Good girl. Beans said you could cook, but he eats the slop that Riley cooks, so I wasn't convinced," she says wryly as we hear a *"hey!"* from Riley in the next room.

"Make yourself useful, boy, and set the table before you're too drunk," she calls out to Riley.

He does as he's asked, and everyone else comes to help, and before long, we have a giant table loaded with food and drinks. There is even a spiced pear cider in jugs for us to share. It's a fun meal with stories and laughter, mainly at Riley's expense. It looks like they enjoy deliberately goading him until he explodes. But he gives it back just as good as he gets, so I think he secretly enjoys it.

Frankie—Beans' sister—pulls me aside after lunch to ask if I have leathers. Ofnemoris predominantly wear leather vests or harnesses, leather sheaths for weapons, leather boots, and even fingerless gloves. I have none as Nemoris leather is expensive.

We're in a massive room with sewing machines and piles of fabric and leather. I show her my straps with equal parts pride and embarrassment after seeing the quality of her work.

"You made these?" Frankie asks, and I nod. "These are so clever. Do you mind if I take the measurements of the designs? I'll pay you back with anything you want. I was already going to sew you some leathers anyway, but maybe there's something extra you'd like?"

I have to shut my gaping mouth and restart my brain. Unable to reply yet, I strip off all the different straps. Pulling out weapons from their hiding places but keeping some hidden. By the end, I have the straps from two small flat wrist blades of varying sizes, two longer ankle blades of different widths, the sheathed knife inside the cut of my left pocket, and two straps of throwing knives of different lengths. It was Frankie's turn to be gobsmacked before her laughter boomed, not unlike her brother's.

She grabs out a measuring tape and begins taking measurements of my body, instructing me to lift my arms, stand straight, or take off my current, ratty old boots.

"Do you carry a sword?"

"Oh, yes I do—it's on a belt with my belongings. Should I get it?"

She nods at me, and I look for the room I'm to share with Riley and Tovi. Grabbing my sword and belt, I hesitate. The edges of a soft leather wrap peek out from my bag, giving me an idea fueled by hope. I return to Frankie.

"Would you have any idea how I could holster these?" I ask, almost pleading, as I show her my hatchets.

She takes them from me with awe, being so gentle. She

looks closely at each one and strokes them like a lover. I like her. This is the exact respect and love my hatchets deserve.

"These are *stunning*, Mika! Where did you get them?"

I describe the market stall and the lady who sold them to me, though I don't think I've ever seen her again.

She takes a few more measurements from me, asking if she can keep the hatchets with her while she works, and I agree. I leave all of my straps with her so she can make patterns, feeling oddly naked and vulnerable without them.

CHAPTER EIGHT

Riley is asleep in a chair, and Bitty and Beans are outside, huddled together under a blanket, pointing at the stars. The stars. I hadn't realized it was so late. It makes me a little sad to think of leaving in the morning. Bitty and Beans' casual affection catches me off guard. Not that Beans doesn't seem the type, in fact, something about him screamed paternal even before I'd seen him with Bitty. But his big hulking mass and deep voice are at odds with the small, whispered giggles and relaxed cuddling.

"Would you like a cup of tea, my sweet?" asks a hushed voice.

"That would be lovely, uh, sorry, I don't actually know your name?"

"You can call me Mama Beryl, or just Mama," she says, winking at me and giving my arm a squeeze.

When we're both settled on the opposite ends of a sofa—Riley softly snoring, Bitty and Beans' whispers drifting in, Tovi laughing with Frankie while she sews—we sigh in unison. The slight crackle of the fire, the only light in the room, makes it all very…homely. Especially with a hot cup of tea in my hands.

"Thank you for opening your home to me," I say quietly, not wanting to disturb the peace.

"Oh child, you are welcome here anytime. I mean it, if you're ever in trouble, you come here." Mama is so insistent and waits for me to agree, so I nod.

"Can I ask how you found Beans, or if he found you?"

Mama smiles ruefully, setting her cup aside so she can speak animatedly with her hands. "I knew when his coming-of-age season would be, so we waited and waited to see the announcement, but it never came. His father and I thought he must have died. Of course, we didn't know what he looked like or what his name was, but we attended every single sale of a Nemorisborn man.

"Then one day, during a market while Frankie was selling her leatherwork, we see him. He was carrying a small Laguzborn Patron in his arms. The kid wouldn't let go of him as he ambled about the markets buying different wares."

Mama wipes a tear on her sleeve and reaches for my hand to hold it. I contemplate snatching it away but…I don't. Her hand is soft, and I let her hold it as she continues her story.

"Frankie saw him first, and she went as white as a ghost, her wild orange hair looking like gold on fire. When I finally see what she's looking at, it's a man with the exact same hair, the exact same features, but as tall as their father. I sobbed, and so did Frankie. We stood there watching him move about with little Bitty clinging to him.

"We were whispering to ourselves that it's him and how much he looks like Frankie and their father when Bitty's head pops up and looks directly at us." She laughs, opening her eyes wide and shaking her head.

"Bitty heard you!" I hiss with excitement.

"Yes, but at the time, and actually for many more revolutions, we didn't know that their Gift was hearing!" Mama says with a good squeeze to my hand, continuing. "Bitty somehow communicated to Crissy to be let down and then tugged him to us. His face when he saw us…He knew straight away, just as we did." I hold back my smile at Mama's nickname for Beans.

"We informed Queen Neo, and she submitted a bid for him, angered that he was never announced despite his Junky status. Both he and Bitty moved in here. Crissy joined the army after a couple of revs, while Frankie and I helped to raise Bitty. Crissy only came home for a few days each moon. The only time Bitty spoke in those first few revs was when he came home. It was a bittersweet moment when Bitty went back to Osraed as a fully-fledged young Patron. Our queen promised that a deal would be made for them at their coming-of-age. To return home to us."

It's such a beautiful story, but I can feel myself getting sleepy. The side of my head rests on the back of the sofa, my eyes heavy, and I'm toasty warm.

"Come on. Let's get you to bed, child." Mama drags me up, shows me where I can wash, and says she will leave some fresh bedding out for me. I thank her and do as I'm told.

Crawling into bed, my eyes are barely open. Tovi is already out cold, and Riley is still asleep in the sitting room. I'm asleep before my head hits the pillow.

A DIP in the bed startles me awake, and I sit up, reaching for the weapons I'm no longer wearing around my wrists. But it's only Riley, crawling into my bed, drunk.

"Riley, this isn't your bed."

He's sitting on the end of the bed and turns to look at me, like *really* look at me. He reaches toward my face but falls forward because I'm too far away. Slumping along my legs with a weird, breathless chuckle.

"You have a—mmn...face," he slurs.

"Yes Riley, I have a face. Now get out of my bed."

Rolling onto his back, head now in my lap, he looks up at me. He reaches out and twirls a piece of my hair around his fingers. I'm staring down at him frozen, confused, and slightly too warm. The swirling flutter of rage begins to beat around my rib cage telling me to kick him off. He drops his hand, humming slightly, before closing his eyes.

And he's asleep instantly. In my lap. I try to shove him off to no avail. Managing to at least get out from under him, I take my pillow and climb into his bed, throwing his pillow back at him. He doesn't even flinch.

It turns out we need another day. We have to replenish our supplies and reorganize ourselves to travel on foot. I currently don't have any boots because Frankie is modifying them, so I stay behind with her and Mama while the others go to a nearby market.

The three of us have breakfast together, a delicious meal of oats and fresh pink currants. Simple yet divine, especially with a hot cup of birch leaf tea. We sit in companionable silence, eating and drinking as the fog rolls over the mountain ranges and through the dense forest. I would have liked to have seen one of the black sand beaches, but they're too far west from here. Next time, I hope.

The rest of the day is spent being fitted for all of Frankie's leather creations and helping Mama to cook and bake. The women cackle constantly, clearly enjoying each other's company. Riley was right—I'm being mothered and smothered and yet…I don't hate it. Their forced affections set my teeth on edge and rage uncoils in warning, but otherwise, it doesn't feel…wrong.

They both have the same dark green eyes, so dark that it's almost hard to distinguish between iris and pupil. And, like Beans, they're covered head to toe in freckles on slightly pink skin. If Beans is in his early forties, it means Frankie must be in her mid to late forties. Mama must be in her sixties, though she looks and moves as if she's still her daughter's age.

Lunch is smoked mutton sandwiches—from the same sheep as yesterday—with a thick spread of butter on dark bread. And apricots. I almost fall over when Mama asks if I want to pick the apricots. I eat six straight from the tree and then sit down at the base to eat one more while truly savoring it. Apricots are my favorite fruit, and I haven't had one for so many revolutions. I'm not even sure why.

I set the basket of apricots on the kitchen table for Mama just as Frankie calls me into her sewing room. On top of her table sits a pile of leather and my interest is immediately piqued.

"Here, try these on," Frankie says with not a small amount of childlike excitement, handing me some new boots, recycled from my old pair. They fit comfortably, tying up to the middle of my calf. It means rearranging the way I carry the knives strapped to my ankles, but it's worth it.

Next is a rogue underbust corset, laced up in the front for ease with small pauldrons on the shoulder straps. The leather is soft and comfortable and—despite the tightness—breathable. The best part is that all of the hidden sheathes and pockets for my throwing knives are much more accessible now.

Lastly, Frankie grabs a strange pouch that supposedly connects to the straps of the corset. Looking at it, I don't comprehend its function. It's thin and soft, with a divider lengthways through it, creating two pockets. A flap covers the center portion leaving the edges open. She turns me around and shows me where the attachments are hidden under the pauldrons. It's comfortable, and I can barely feel it.

Until she sits something heavy into it.

"Reach both your hands back over your shoulders," Frankie instructs, with excitement coloring her voice.

I reach back, and my hands hit the distinct wooden handles of my hatchets. Gripping on to one in each hand, I lift them up and out with ease. The flap moves out of the way so the hatchets don't clang together, and both are quickly in my hands and ready to fight.

"We have a sturdy tree outside…" Frankie says, with a mischievous glint in her eyes as she waggles her eyebrows in suggestion.

"Yes, please!" I squeak, as I spin on my heels. Frankie's chuckle follows me as I sprint outside.

I practice, over and over. Pulling them out faster, while running, standing, or only one-handed. I almost scream when, during a forward flip, I pull them out of the pocket and lodge one firmly into the tree I was aiming at. Frankie claps for me and blows me a double-handed kiss before leaving me to play with my new toys alone.

Eventually going inside, I find Frankie back in her sewing room.

"Thank you. Thank you endlessly. I don't think I can truly express my gratitude for this. How can I repay you?" I ask.

"Your strap patterns are innovative Mika. If you're sure I can have them, I'd love to release a new line of products named after you, based on your designs."

"They're all yours!" I beam. I'd give her a thousand strap designs for this.

"So…I wasn't finished…" Frankie says cryptically. I look at her and then at the pieces of leather in her hands, once again not comprehending. "Pull out your hatchets and I'll show you."

I place both weapons on the bench beside her. She grabs one piece of the leather and slides it over the dangerously sharp edge of one hatchet, and then over the butt, snapping it closed with a small clasp. Guards. They're leather guards. I pick up the newly guarded hatchet, shaking it about, swinging it, and hitting it into myself gently. It'll still hurt, and I'll have to temper my blows, but now I'll be able to spar without mortally wounding anyone or myself.

It's almost too much. Frankie is watching with pride written all over her face at her work, as she should. But I don't understand why all this effort. For me.

"Why?" I ask her, trying to swallow the emotions bubbling up that I don't understand.

"Why *not*, Mika?" is all she says before kissing me on the forehead and walking out the door, yelling, "You're welcome!"

So much forced affection. Yet it might just be the best day I've had in revolutions. I can't wipe the smile off my face.

Just as I decide to head inside, the gang arrives back from their trip to the market.

"Is that big smile for me, or my package?" Riley asks me from behind his armload, a smirk on his lightly freckled face. I drop my smile and roll my eyes dramatically, putting my hands out toward Bitty to relieve them of some of their haul.

I HELP Mama prepare dinner again, and afterward, she tells me wild stories of Frankie as a kid while I help with the dishes. When everyone else has gone to sleep, Mama tells me how her husband died in a tragic logging accident that devastated the community. Fortunately, it was a couple of revs after they reunited with Beans, so they were able to have some time together.

She forces me to bed, yet again, and I can see why everyone calls her Mama. I sleep spooning my guarded hatchets, just because I can. I am not plagued by nightmares, and Riley stays in his own bed.

In the morning, Tovi is yanking on my foot asking if I'm washing my hair today since it's our last morning here. Which, of course, I am. What I didn't realize, was that *Mama washes everyone's hair.* All of us. One after the other. With a delicious honey-smelling soap. Bitty gets their undercut tidied up before getting their hair washed too. Beans' head is shaved last, along with a tidy-up of his beard and mustache.

I look at Riley in wonder and confusion while we towel our hair, and he simply shrugs his shoulders with a smirk, mouthing, "I told you so." He tries to hold my eye for far too long, and I look away not wanting it to reach an abhorrent peak. Plus, I can't read him. At all.

He's freshly shaven, highlighting the strong jaw on that square face of his. Chiseled. What a cliché way to describe someone, but that's what he is. Jaw, nose, arms…I wonder if the rest of his body matches, having not yet seen him undressed. Yet? Thinking of him undressed sends my rage into a flurry which propels me to standing, earning myself a quizzical look from Riley. Great. The memory of me poking my tongue out at him bubbles up uninvited, and I leave the room for fear of further embarrassing myself.

Tovi and I sit in the sun to let the wind and warmth finish drying our hair. She's stiff and not one for conversing with me, but I try my luck anyway. "What's your Gift? Can I know?"

I assume it's something impressive—a Gifted fighter, fast runner, or something equally important—that would make Nemoris bid in for her purchase and for her to join this mission to save the princess.

But to my surprise, she says, "Object empathy."

"Object empathy?" I repeat back to her in confusion, like it's one of the old languages I never learned.

"People leave feelings on objects. I can feel what the last person to touch an object felt."

My mouth gapes open. I pick up a rock and hand it to her.

She rolls her eyes. "It's not a carnival trick, and I don't need object empathy to know you're surprised and curious." She doesn't even take the rock, before getting up to leave me by myself. I'm an idiot. This is what I get for being a recluse. Though what kind of assassin would I have been if I had wonderful people skills?

I give Mama most of my jars of ferments and pastes to use, unable to take them with me when I'm reducing down to one bag. Thankfully, I'm able to leave my other bag here with the rest of my belongings. In return, Mama hands me two little bags: one has a heap of dried apricots, and the other contains fresh ones.

"Why is Mika getting gifts?" Riley complains, peeking in the bag and stealing an apricot as Mama smacks his hand away.

Tovi and Bitty round the corner in a jumble of words, asking about gifts and who's getting them. Mama threatens them with a spoon, and they run out squealing. Like children.

"Thank you, *and Frankie*," I raise my voice so she can hear from her hiding place in the pantry. "For all your hospitality and your generous gifts. This has been some of the…It's been so lovely. Thank you." I struggle to finish.

Frankie comes out and pulls me and Mama into a group hug where I'm the meat in the sandwich. "Is this a bad time to point out how much I hate being touched?" I squeak out.

They laugh and hug me tighter.

And I let them.

CHAPTER NINE

The addition of Bitty and traveling on foot has not really changed the dynamic of our group. Riley and Tovi are still sneaking off together, everyone exercises and trains when they can, and I cook, but now Bitty is here too.

We can't cover as much distance each day as we can on horses, but I start to see why we're on foot immediately after leaving Mama's. The terrain is rough. A horse would break a leg trying to move at the same pace we are walking, let alone be able to move swiftly.

Freshwater streams, either small and gentle or large and loud, are our constant companions, either walking alongside one or crossing them at any given point of the day. The air is fresh and crisp, and I love it, though I do miss the Osraed breeze. Fallen trees are everywhere, rocks slippery with moss, and inclines and declines so steep we're climbing on all fours at points. While it really is beautiful, it's exhausting to traverse.

We break through the dense forest onto a well-traveled

road and the air is buzzing with excitement. We're *so close* to a tavern; I swear I can smell the food.

After finding the tavern and agreeing to meet for dinner in two hours, we split up to check into our rooms upstairs. Bitty and Beans are sharing a room, so are Riley and Tovi, and I have a small one to myself. I take the opportunity to bathe and wash my clothes.

Downstairs, the tavern is so full of people that it's almost cramped. It's clean and cozy, much like my room. Dark wooden panels cover the ceiling, floor, walls, and every piece of furniture. The amber light from the lanterns gives the illusion of warmth, despite the chilly sting of cold outside.

I'm the last to arrive for dinner, but they've waited for me to order food. A beer is already waiting for me, though I don't intend to drink it, so I move it to the side instead. Riley, however, is clearly not on his first drink.

We all order the special, and special it is. The pie is spectacular. Big chunks of rich beef so tender you barely need to chew. Chunks of carrot, potatoes, and peas, with a meaty and tangy gravy. All encased in a flaky pastry that's buttery and crisp.

"So, when do we get to see the fighting skills Nemoris bought?" Riley slurs, slightly too loud for how close we are at the table.

"Don't worry Riley. I'm well worth the gold," I respond without looking at him.

Riley snorts. "Maybe you should demonstrate," he vociferates and then laughs as if he made a joke.

"I can kick your ass anytime Riley, if you'd like a *personal* demonstration."

Beans puts his hands up between us, interrupting Riley's response. "I think that's enough beer for you tonight."

"Oh, get fucked, Beans. I was just having some fun,"

Riley grouches as he stands up and stumbles away toward a table of women.

Tovi rolls her eyes. "Red dickhead," she mumbles with a slight groan, rubbing her eyes.

An hour or so after Riley leaves the table, Bitty yawns and announces they are off to bed. Glad I wasn't the first, but happy to be the second, I announce that I am also retiring. We bid the rest of the table goodnight, Beans offering a grin that springs his mustache out, and Tovi gives a nod and a wink as she grabs for my beer.

"Next camp, do you think we could spar?" Bitty asks me, halfway up the stairs.

"You want to fight with me?" I ask, surprised. "Of course we can."

"It was actually Riley's idea, but I wanted you to feel settled first. I think that nonsense tonight was his *very* unsubtle way of trying to get us to spar together."

"He's about as subtle as a brick to the face. Anyway, I live and breathe the fight, Bitty. I probably would have settled in faster if you'd asked me sooner," I joke, as we reach Bitty and Beans' door.

"Don't hold back though. The others refuse to fight with me properly when we spar, and I hate it." Bitty's dimpled smile widens, and they enter their room waving a polite goodnight.

I shake my head with a small, incredulous laugh. I'm not sure I've been asked to *not* hold back before. Not since I was maybe eleven. I'm mulling over everything I can teach Bitty as I fall asleep like it's a children's story lulling me into slumber.

A loud slam wakes me with a jolt. The knives at my wrists are already in my hands before I remember where I am. I sit up, listening to what's going on before returning my knives. I can hear a man and a woman's voice in the hallway. I unlock my door and crack it open silently to sneak a peek.

It's an incredibly drunk Riley and a tall Nemorisborn woman, clinging to each other, stumbling down the hallway. Riley trips and the couple slam into a wall, laughing and shushing themselves as they continue. They pass Riley and Tovi's room, and I have to open my door a bit wider to see them as they go further down the hall to what I assume must be the woman's room instead.

I close my door quietly. I'm so confused, are Riley and Tovi *not* together?

In the morning, I head downstairs to find Beans and Bitty are already eating breakfast and they wave me over to their table.

"The eggs are delicious Mika—you should get a plate before they're gone," Beans suggests, and Bitty nods enthusiastically.

I move to the bar to order a plate of whatever the two of them are eating and quickly return to the table. "Have either of you seen Tovi or Riley yet?" I ask, slipping into one of the chairs.

"Not yet, but I've heard them both. Riley is, no surprise, hungover and going to be a miserable travel companion," Bitty complains.

"When is he *not* a miserable travel companion, Bitty?" Beans laughs with a mouthful of egg and toast.

Then why is he here? I want to ask, but I hold my tongue instead.

My plate of food arrives at the same time Tovi and Riley do, who both order a plate of eggs as well. Riley has a scowl and Tovi looks like she finds his hangover incredibly amusing.

The scrambled eggs are spiced with something peppery, and they taste excellent, especially with the buttery toast.

Riley hasn't said a word, but the other three are chatting away about how much ground they hope to cover today.

IT's no surprise that we don't cover nearly as much ground today. Riley says his headache has nothing to do with the hangover but none of us buy it. He even seems more annoyed than the rest of us that we didn't travel as much as we had hoped.

It doesn't help that we're constantly dodging a beautiful, but incredibly poisonous flower today. Each flower is probably the size of my head and hangs around seven or eight feet in the air. Dark, almost black, green petals in a bell shape facing the ground, with a long and fluffy purple stamen hanging down a few feet. It looks so soft that you'd almost be tempted to run your hands down the feathery-looking thing. At which point hundreds of hair fine spikes would embed into your skin, causing such a serious allergic reaction that—unless you manage to chop off the affected limb in time—is fatal. Stunning plants to look at though.

We stop in a well-wooded area with the tiniest of clearings. There is enough room for a small fire and our five bedrolls, with Tovi and Riley to my left, and Beans and Bitty to my right.

Taking advantage of the early stop, I ask Bitty if they want to spar. I barely have time to finish my sentence before Bitty is up. They're bounding toward a slightly bigger clearing we passed earlier but was too sloped to camp in.

Bitty is quick, but not as quick as me. Though they're stronger, I am never the stronger one, so this doesn't surprise me. Their moves are predictable and clearly based on choreographed steps.

"When I said, 'don't hold back,' I didn't mean, *absolutely annihilate me every single time!*" Bitty announces, panting.

"You basically write your next move on your forehead before you do it—you really are quite predictable," I tease.

I let Bitty get a few good knocks into my ribs, a kick to my thigh, and graze my face with their elbow, so they're not *totally* discouraged. But after two hours, they call it quits.

"Next time, let's actually practice, and I'll give you tips on how to be less predictable. You need to trust your intuition more and rely less on the steps you've been taught."

Bitty grins and nods, wiping sweat from their brow. We head toward the stream nearby to rinse our faces, and I spot Riley sitting a short distance from where Bitty and I were sparring. I didn't realize he had been watching.

After a quick dinner, Beans advises that Bitty is on the first watch, followed by himself, Riley, and me, and then Tovi is on last watch. I decide to make some swordmint tea while Tovi and Riley go for a walk together, Tovi's arm around his waist. Bitty is telling Beans all about our session, sparing no details.

Later, when Bitty goes on watch, Beans thanks me.

"Both Tovi and Riley are too scared they'll hurt Bitty, and I already have. But it's counterintuitive because, without training, Bitty is more vulnerable. I usually shove them up a tree during a fight, since they're good with throwing knives," Beans says with a grimace.

"Bitty didn't get training in Osraed?"

"No. It was deemed unnecessary as they had other things to learn, and they were already behind."

"Why does Bitty come along if it worries you so much?"

"If they're with me then I can look after them. But they need to be able to defend themselves because it's the 'if not' that keeps me up. And they've followed me one too many times to bother leaving them behind. I know it makes about as much sense as waiting for Bitty to go on watch to talk about them when I know they're listening to every word. In any case, thank you again."

"They're quick. And fearless. They'll be kicking my butt in no time, *Daddy Beans.*"

"Mika," Beans growls, so deep that it sounds like thunder.

He tries to keep a stern look on his face, but I erupt in laughter which causes him to crack.

Knocking me over with his outstretched foot, I lie there laughing as he sighs dramatically. "Forever surrounded by children. I thought you were different Mika. A kindred spirit. You've dashed my hopes and dreams."

"Whose dreams are dashed?" Tovi queries, as Riley crawls into his bedroll without a word.

Beans laughs and gestures at me lying on my back where he'd pushed me over. "Mine! You two are already a bad influence on Mika."

"I'm sure she's plenty *bad* all on her own," Tovi says sweetly, sucking on a finger as she gives me a conspiratorial smile with mischief sparkling in her violet eyes. And then promptly shoves her wet finger in Beans' ear. He howls and tackles her. Tovi's laughter is like a beautiful song echoing through the forest.

CHAPTER TEN

I wake up slightly disorientated. The moon is further along in the sky than it should be for my watch. My rage squeezes around my heart as I sit up and count the sleeping forms around the dead fire. Riley is missing. I get up and tie my boots on before searching for him with my knife in hand.

I find him asleep. The fucker stinks like alcohol, and a slight snore escapes his nose as he's slumped against a tree with arms folded. I move my knife to my other hand, and I punch him. In the face. *Hard*.

He at least reacts immediately, though sluggishly, as he falls to the side and tries to kick my feet out from under me in some feeble attempt to fight back. I'm too quick for him, and I pin my knife to his throat.

"And you're dead. So is every single other fucking person in this camp. Because I'm a mercenary or an assassin or skin trader who found an unsuspecting group of people asleep and no one on watch," I angrily whisper at him. I was too angry to be amused by the fact that *technically*, I *was* an assassin.

I snort at him in disgust as I stand and sheathe my knife. He lies there leaning on his arm and watches where I put my knife with detached interest.

"Nothing to say?"

Apparently not, because he stands up, dusts off his pants, and leans down to grab a bottle of alcohol that I hadn't noticed was resting against the tree. I kick it from his hand, and it goes flying off into the forest.

"What the fuck is your problem, Mika?"

"Oh, I don't know. Maybe it's the drunk who was supposed to be on watch, who decided to put us all in danger instead?"

"We're still in Nemoris, and it's safe—it doesn't even matter!"

"If it didn't matter Riley, then why do it at all?" I hiss back, trying not to wake the others who are hopefully still sleeping. "Your selfishness is astounding."

Riley grumbles something unintelligible and stomps after his bottle before returning to the camp and slumping onto his bedroll. The asshole is snoring within moments. I hate him. My rage is a roaring beast that slams inside my ribcage, unwavering and unwilling to calm.

I start my perimeter checks, looping wider and wider before turning around, crossing right through camp and out the other side, and then looping in the opposite direction back toward camp. I do this a few times, stopping and crossing back through the camp at different intervals.

I don't bother to wake Tovi for the next watch because the sun is already starting to peek over the horizon. I do one final sweep of the area, tiptoeing through the dense Nemoris forest. Satisfied all is well, I go in search of some of the fresh herbs I'd seen while checking the snares we set last night.

I find an *enormous* bush of honeysuckle simply because I can smell it. I pull a good handful of the flowers off, using my untucked shirt as a makeshift bucket. When I find a cluster of milkear mushrooms hiding between two fallen trees, I emit a little squeal. I had always instructed the children I looked after in the compound *never* to eat anything you don't recognize when foraging, especially mushrooms. But I could spot milkear from a mile away and I hope I continue to find more.

Swordmint is growing wild everywhere, so I grab a few bunches to replenish my pouch. Excited, I see a rosemary plant and break a few stalks off to tie together to dry.

Pleased with my little haul, I return to camp to relight the fire Riley had let go out. Luckily, there were still a couple of embers I could use to get it going. I fill up our pot from the stream nearby and put it on to boil, throwing some of the honeysuckle in to brew.

Tovi is the next to wake up and looks bewildered. "Why didn't you wake me for watch?"

"It was a short night, so I let you sleep," I reply, not wanting to tell her what Riley did.

As Tovi goes to relieve herself, I begin making breakfast for everyone. First, I rip up the milkear mushrooms. I dig out a brown onion from the bottom of my bag and dice that up too. I pull some embers out of the fire so I can set the teapot to the side to keep warm.

The pan is heating when Bitty wakes up, bleary-eyed but smiling. I can't help but smile as well when I throw the mushrooms and onion into the pan and hear that satisfying sizzle. While they're cooking, I chop up some of the dried sausages we have (since the snares remained empty) and throw them in as I go.

"You can never leave us, Mika. Travel food has never been so good," Beans growls with his unused morning voice.

Once the mushrooms, onion and sausage are done, I remove them so I can add the corn millet into the pan with water and salt to cook down. Finally, it's time to add the other ingredients back in with another pinch of salt. My stomach is making loud announcements of hunger, which has Bitty laughing.

"What is this tea?" Tovi questions in a whisper.

"Honeysuckle. There's a ridiculous bush growing back south a bit—I can't believe we didn't smell it as we were walking."

"Might be my favorite yet," Beans says with his eyes closed, large hands engulfing the metal mug. Bitty and Tovi both agree.

Bitty crawls with their tea, into Tovi's bed roll. Tovi wraps her arm around them, resting her head on top of Bitty's. I'm not sure if I imagine the protective, almost possessive look I get from Tovi over Bitty's head. Bitty sighs contentedly, and they watch me finish making breakfast.

Everyone licks their plates clean with sounds of rapture. It's not till the sun is over the horizon that Riley finally stirs. He has his back to the rising sun, so his face is in shadow, but I'm fairly sure he's frowning.

"Mika made breakfast, and there are leftovers in the pan for you," Beans offers to Riley, who grunts his response.

Beans gets up to relieve himself, and Tovi is relaxing on her bedroll, humming a tune to herself. I'm looking at a yellow dragonfly behind Bitty's head when I see their eyes widen looking at Riley, and then look at me and back to Riley.

Riley leans forward to grab the pan. A black bruise from under his left eye down to the top of his cheekbone is clearly visible. He makes a pointed effort to ignore both Bitty and I staring at it with mouths open. "I love milkear mushrooms," Riley states with a husky disused morning voice. "They're my favorite."

I guess we're pretending that last night didn't happen.

Tovi rolls her eyes and mutters a curse I don't quite catch when she sees Riley's face.

After breakfast, surprisingly, everyone announces they have gifts for Bitty. It's their birthday, and *no one* bothered to tell me. I clench my teeth, trying not to make it obvious how annoyed I am that *I didn't know*.

"Twenty-two! You're still a baby," I tease, as everyone else reveals the gifts they hold in their hands. Bitty is not even five revs younger than me yet the age difference seems immense.

"We're assuming that's my age, I really have no idea." Bitty laughs as Beans hands them a gift.

"Technically, this is the date seventeen revs past that I found a teeny tiny Lilleck, passed out from hunger. Damn kid was feral!" Beans jokes, with a smile reserved for fond memories.

Beans' gift is a piece of thin leather rolled up. When Bitty unties it, their face lights up, and they turn it around to show everyone. A picture has been, I assume, tattooed into the flesh of the leather. It's of Bitty, Beans, Mama, and Frankie. Simply beautiful.

"Your name is Lilleck?" I ask Bitty as they carefully wrap up Beans' gift.

"I think so. Apparently, that's the name I eventually gave Beans. I don't remember at all."

"Only took you a week to say something, and even then, it was only your name. You didn't speak again for almost two revolutions," Beans adds, pulling Bitty in for a big hug.

Their affection for each other is sweet. Bitty acts like an annoyed teen whenever Beans fusses over them, but you can see it in the sparkle of their eyes or the small dimple in their cheek that appears, that they love it. It's a strange dynamic to witness, let alone be traveling with.

Tovi hands her gift over which is a new set of lock picks.

"They've been made of the finest metal in all of Erdu, but the best part is that they can be slotted together and made to look like a simple hairpin." Bitty's face is full of wonder as they inspect Tovi's gift.

"So where did the name Bitty come from?" I ask both Bitty and Beans as the former uses the disguised lock picks to create a small bun at the top of their head, exposing their shaved undercut.

Beans laughs. "I started referring to them as 'Lil bit' because they were just a *little bit* of a thing—only a little bit of a Lilleck! And 'Lil bit' morphed into Bitty when they started complaining that they weren't so little anymore."

Bitty punches Beans in the shoulder, rolling their eyes. I can't help but smile at the story, temporarily forgetting my selfish annoyance at being left out.

Lastly, Riley hands over his gift. It's the thing he's been carving in secret, a knife in a leather sheath. The wooden handle and hilt have been so delicately carved with all sorts of Laguz sea creatures, still managing to keep the shape of the handle comfortable despite the intricate carvings.

Everyone gave such thoughtful gifts.

I hate how jealous I am about it.

"My gift is a promise to kick your ass later." I shrug with a smirk, hoping to at least make Bitty smile. I'm successful—Bitty laughs and says they can't wait.

After a long day of travel, I start to teach Bitty some tricks to help with intuitive fighting.

"I don't *have* fighting instincts!" Bitty complains.

"Instinct is not the same thing as intuition. Instinct is reacting and doing what comes naturally, but intuition is learned. The more we do this, the better you'll get."

Bitty gives me a dubious look but moves back into a fighting stance. "Ok, come kick my ass again."

"Oh, I will, but this time, you can't hit me with your

hands." I grin, as I run at them. Bitty barely has the chance to register what I've said before I'm on them.

I can still see everything running through their mind before they move, but they are quicker. Bitty has to rely on what they've learned about fighting in general rather than *exactly* what comes after each move they already know.

I'm about to elbow Bitty to the side of the head when they drop to the ground, twist their legs in mine so I trip, and then pin me by sitting on my back.

"Ok, I got you down, but I was so excited I couldn't think of anything to do next that didn't involve hands!" Bitty laughs as they roll off me, out of breath.

"Is that a usual move for you?"

"Dropping onto my ass? No!"

I nod as I sit up, raising my eyebrows and doing a dramatic shrug with my hands in the air. Bitty beams at me, and then their gaze moves over my shoulder. I turn, and behind me stands Tovi, leaning against a tree. How long she was there watching, I have no idea.

Our day is long and cold. I regret ever thinking I would miss the wind because the Nemoris wind is *awful*. Whenever we're in areas that aren't densely packed with forest, the wind feels like needles, despite the layers.

Only the incredible plant life brings me joy today. There are all manner of plants that I've never seen, or only read about, like a veritable expanse of teeny tiny green leaves with the teeniest tiny pale blue flowers dotted through, creating a carpet of the flowers. I want to lie down and snuggle into the cushion they create on the forest floor.

There are enormous trees of bright green leaves that

start out red. With the sun streaming through, the young, red leaves at the top and at the ends of each branch turn to a bright yellowish green. The smell is intoxicating. A pungent citrusy smell with a woody, almost medicinal tang to it.

I'm not the only one in a mood—Riley's gray pallor and pinched face suggest he's not doing so great. This is further proven when he refuses to respond to Tovi's playful teasing.

As if the long and cold day wasn't miserable enough, the rain then comes in earnest. So much so that after only an hour of straight downpour, we spread out to look for a cave to shelter in. Tovi finds one first, a giant cavernous thing on the side of a mountain, but it's out of the rain and already has a large stack of dry wood. Clearly, we are not the first to seek shelter here.

There'll be no inn for us tonight.

CHAPTER ELEVEN

It's been two nights, and we're still stuck in this Divine-damned cave. The rain is not as bad as it was, but there's no sign of it letting up enough to travel. We've talked through all our plans, including the route and possible scenarios when we get to Erdu City Castle. It seems like breaking into the castle is our only option. But for now, I am sick of going over the same conversation again and again. This is why I like to work alone.

Riley is sitting with his back against a wall staring outside, knees bouncing and looking sweaty. He hasn't said much to me since *that* night. Gone is the constant simmering smirk on his face, the lingering stares, the cheeky comments at every turn. A sullen and gray shell has been left in its place. I wouldn't have been too worried if it wasn't for the fact that the other three have *also* been looking at him with concern.

After lunch, where Riley—yet again—barely eats anything, Tovi is napping, and Bitty and Beans are stretching. Beans is telling Bitty a story of his time before he found them. Riley is back to his position against the wall, looking like he might sprint outside at any moment. Like he's a caged animal, ready to snap.

I'm propped against the wall opposite him as I sharpen my blades, watching. His knees are bouncing again, pale skin still pallid and sweaty. He keeps clenching and unclenching his fists, spearing his fingers out shakily to stretch them. I'm not even sure if he's aware he's doing it. His eyes are glassed over as he stares down the passage. Dark circles under his eyes indicate he's sleeping even less than he usually does, which isn't much. Decided, I put away my knives.

I crouch down beside him, looking outside for a moment. I don't think he has even registered my presence. "Do you want to do some hand-to-hand outside?" I whisper, and he jumps, glaring at me.

Standing without a word, he strides outside. Not waiting for me or looking at anyone. Riley's silhouette disappears, swallowed by the rain. Looking back to Beans, he gives me a knowing nod and returns to his story with Bitty.

Riley stands in the rain with his back to me. We're both barefoot and not wearing leathers, and his thin shirt is clinging to every muscle. Where Beans has defined muscles, cut without a single inch of fat, Riley is pure bulk. I'm still not sure who I'd put money on in a fight: Beans who is taller with muscles on top of muscles, or the slightly shorter Riley and his solid mass.

Riley has put his dark, blood-red hair in a bun, the rain already darkening it further. I watch his hands repeat their clenching before I clear my throat, and he whirls to face me, eyes rimmed in red.

We start with basic training drills to get our bodies moving. There is no force or strength behind the blows, though they get faster and faster. Mud squelches between our toes, the sounds of slapping as our hits connect over and over. We're both covered in mud from head to toe. It's not until Riley slips and connects a punch harder than he intended, splitting the skin over my cheekbone, that we stop.

He rushes forward to grab me before I tip over, grabbing my face in his hands so fast I don't have time to react. And then I don't know *how* to react as his focus is wholly on me. Our breathing is hard, the rain smashing down as he hisses, prodding at my cheek. Hissing as if *he* is the one with a cut face. It doesn't hurt, even as his hot fingers press and wipe at it. He declares it minor, and nothing is broken, before making eye contact with me. Still holding my face.

"I'm sorry," he says in a hoarse voice, eyes flicking back to the cut. *Still* holding my face.

I gently tug myself out of his touch. "It was an accident, Riley."

He nods, dropping his hands, before swaying slightly and running to the nearest tree to vomit up his meager lunch. I stand there awkwardly, not wanting to leave him alone but not wanting to get any closer to him while he's so vulnerable.

When he finally stops his retching and leans against the tree, wiping his arm across his mouth with eyes closed, I approach him.

"Are you okay?"

His eyes pop open. "No."

I nod, that was a stupid question. "What's wrong?"

He lets out a long and steadying breath through his nose as he fixes his intent stare—returned from wherever it had retreated the last few days—back on me.

"I cannot say to you that it is nothing. But neither do I want to tell you."

Oh. Of course he isn't going to tell me what's wrong or why he's not okay. We aren't friends. I give him a tight smile, nodding as though I understand, and turn to leave. He snatches my hand and whirls me back to face him, the heat instantly triggering the rage deep inside me as he circles his thumb on the back of it.

"I just…don't want to burden you." He swallows and leans his head back, giving my hand one more stroke. "Thank you for this." He lets go gently.

I nod, again, as if that is the only thing I can do, and he can't even see it as his eyes are closed again. I leave him to it, returning to the cave. Once inside, Tovi pins me with a withering glare, looking behind me for Riley, I assume.

"Where is he?" she demands.

Raising an eyebrow at her tone, I gesture with my thumb behind me. Off she stalks, into the rain to see for herself. I frown and look over at the other two, who give me shrugs and wide eyes. It's not long before Riley and Tovi return, changing from their wet clothes as I did when I came back. The silence from everyone is deafening.

FINALLY, after two more nights of extreme downpours, sunshine breaks through, and we're back on the move. The sun sparkles in the sky, a perfect blue with not a cloud in sight.

Riley looks good. The dark circles under his eyes are not as dark, and his hands no longer shake, nor do they clench with every breath he takes. Tovi won't leave his side, so I don't go near either of them. During our stop for lunch, he gives me a nod and a small smile, trying to hold my eye before I look away. I have not been alone with Riley since our sparring session, Tovi is making sure of that.

Later, while the other three are preoccupied, Tovi approaches me. "Riley told me what you did for him the other day," she states matter-of-factly.

I pause, crouched on the ground in front of a patch of fresh mint, and raise an eyebrow.

She clears her throat, looking over my head. "Thank you," she says with reluctance, clouding the sentiment.

"Why?" I ask. Why is *she* thanking me for helping Riley?

Her eyes narrow at me, the violet of her eyes looking every bit Divine with their ethereal glow. I don't get an answer.

WE STOP for camp the next night, and Riley asks if we can spar. I don't even get a chance to respond before Bitty excitedly answers yes for me.

It's different than the time by the cave. *Riley* is different this time. Without weapons—and at seemingly full capacity —he's hard to beat. He's much stronger than I am, and it doesn't matter how quick I am, I can only take a few hits from him.

I get a few decent kicks in that are stronger than my punches. His lip is split, and so is mine, neither of which stops the fight, thankfully. I force Riley to the ground a few times, but he doesn't stay down for long, though he never manages to knock me off my feet.

Fighting to win instead of fighting to kill is hard. I know many ways I could have beaten Riley by now, but I lose the fight when I swing a kick at his head in frustration. Not only does he manage to stop it, but he holds on. As soon as I see the smirk bloom on his face, I know exactly what he's going to do. He yanks my leg up so hard that my other comes off the ground, and I am dangling in the air upside down.

"I'll save you the further embarrassment of dropping you

on your head, *Firecat*," Riley purrs at me. He puts me down gently.

"Who are you calling Firecat?" I spit.

"You. Definitely you. Small, deadly, and mostly annoying. Basically, a teeny tiny bag of claws and teeth that spits fire. *And* you even have the same color hair as firecat fur!" he says in triumph, as if that proves his point.

I'm still sitting on the ground so I trip him, and he lands on his backside. I have a blade to his throat before he has a chance to move.

"I'll show you a Firecat," I growl. My rage starts bubbling in my chest as if Riley had summoned it by speaking its name.

"You just proved my point, I think," Riley says, with not even a shred of concern about the knife I have against the lifeblood line in his neck. "This was fun. I'll have to fight Bitty—*figuratively,* of course—to spar with you each evening."

TRUE TO HIS WORD, every night, I spar with one of them. Even Tovi and Beans get in on it. The five of us stop an hour —sometimes two—early each day so we can all spar before it gets dark enough for someone to go on watch.

It turns competitive of course. Weapons are introduced. Beans was right—Bitty is excellent at knife throwing, so it's always one of us two who wins. Watching Beans and Riley fight with swords is exciting and terrifying—I hope I am never on the receiving end of their wrath.

Almost every fight ends in them wrestling each other on the ground, hollering and yelling. Once, when the day was unseasonably warm, they trained without shirts—their rippled muscles glistening with sweat—and it was a show of pure and unadulterated testosterone and strength. I had to stop watching as the swirling low in my belly triggered my rage.

Riley and Beans also spar with their axes, leaving the leather bindings over the heads to be safe. It takes a lot of control to fight to win, but still hold it back so you don't seriously hurt anyone. Which is exactly what I have to do, every time I have a weapon in my hand. The rage wants to take over and cause pain, no matter who is on the receiving end.

One evening, I decide to spar alone with my hatchets. Their lightness is conducive for me to flip and jump while having them safely in hand. *I fucking love them.* Breathing hard, and grinning to myself after a particularly enjoyable sequence, I yank one of the hatchets out of a tree.

"Are you deliberately trying to prove me right?" Riley asks, leaning against a tree not far from me, giving me a heated look up and down with his classic smirk.

I point at him with one of my hatchets and narrow my eyes. "Don't tempt me," I threaten half-heartedly.

Riley puts his arms up in mock surrender. "I was coming to tell you dinner's ready, Firecat."

I throw a hatchet to hit the tree above and to the right of his head as he ducks and runs back to the camp. "She's an angry little thing!" he yells in a sing-song way.

My lips twist as I resist the urge to grin.

AFTER A COUPLE of weeks with no inn, we're all a little testy. Strangely, Riley is in the best mood of us all. We travel in single file, Tovi in front, then Bitty, Beans, me, and Riley bringing up the rear. I spot the back of a blue deer briefly during our silent march through the countryside. Although it is not *actually* blue, the deer's coat is just so dark and inky that it almost looks blue. They camouflage so well in the forest, looking like the dappled bushes that overtake the understory.

After so many hours of silent travel, and the other three slowly pulling ahead, I am startled to find Riley walking beside me. The sun glows through his hair, highlighting the dark blood-red color in all its glory. He catches me watching him and the smirk is back, warming my cheeks. Maybe the smirk isn't *totally* unattractive.

"Want to play a game?" he asks.

"What kind of *game*?"

He waggles his brows. "You bring up a topic about yourself, I try to guess the correct answer. If I get it wrong, then I have to answer instead."

"Okay…" I drawl. "Example?"

"Favorite weapon. Now you guess what mine is."

I study him, wondering what the trick is, as he uses his shoulder to gently shove me. "Your hands," I guess, and his eyebrows go up.

"Yes," he laughs. "I thought you'd guess my axe, though I know your answer would be your hatchets. Now you pick something for me to guess, and if I get it wrong, I'll answer it."

I think on it, wondering what I would like to know about him, that he couldn't guess about me, but coming up with nothing. "Favorite food," I suggest, weakly.

"Apricots," he says within a heartbeat of me finishing the words.

Damn it, I was too obvious with Mama.

"Favorite season in any country?" he asks.

How the fuck would I know that about him. He only has

a small smattering of freckles, so I don't think it's any of the hot seasons, which leaves three choices.

"Cold and dry?"

"Nope! Now you have to tell me," he says, with a sparkle I've never seen in his eyes before.

"I would've said the cold and windy season, but Nemoris is making me doubt that."

This goes on for a few more rounds, while we learn unimportant and silly things about each other, though I learn more about him than he does about me. I now know he hates being tickled and loves the sound of rain and the smell of fresh bread.

"Siblings."

"*That* is cheating, Firecat. I wouldn't be able to guess correctly unless you know. *Do* you know?"

I shrug, giving him a wicked grin that he shakes his head at as he spins to walk backward in front of me.

"Sneaky. Fine, since there's no point in guessing yours, two younger sisters and an older brother. Favorite color," he demands pointing at me with narrowed eyes, like it's the most important question and not giving me a chance to ask anything about his siblings.

Knowing I have to take a stab in the dark, I try to think of something he *might* like. "Yellow? A buttery, creamy, *sunshine* yellow?" I flail my hands about, gesturing vaguely at the sun, and finish with a smile as I bite my lip. Riley stops in his tracks as he watches me, and I almost bump into him. I won't admit it, but this is fun.

"Yes," he breathes, looking at me in disbelief.

I squeal like a child. "I got it right? *That's* your favorite color?"

"I can think of no better."

My stupid grin becomes self-satisfied, especially when he demands, almost in a whine, "What's yours?"

"Oh, you'll never know, because *I was right.*" And I dance off, spinning around to poke out my tongue. I don't even cringe this time.

CHAPTER TWELVE

We reach Teorann a few days later, slightly behind schedule. Teorann is sprawling, yet somehow doesn't have much to offer except for the pier with a massive inn and tavern on either side of the Teorann waters.

The pier has a barge that ferries people across during the day, which is the only way to cross between Nemoris and Erdu. The neighboring countries named their towns Teorann on both sides of the river, working cooperatively to ferry people across.

Unfortunately, we missed the last barge across for the evening, so we will have to wait until the morning. Wanting to be on the first one across, Beans suggests it would be best if we camp on the edge of the forest. We wouldn't be the only ones. Many people crossing between the two countries choose to camp instead of staying at the inn, which is often full.

Another good thing about the Nemoris side of Teorann is their enormous supply store, which is run out of the tavern. It'll take a few hours for our order to be ready, so we sit in the back and share a quick meal.

Beans, Riley, and Tovi are still in the tavern when Bitty and I leave to set up the camp for everyone. We finish our cups of tea as Riley and Beans arrive.

"Anyone want to come back to the tavern for a game of cards? A group of Erduborn claim they're the best at Talamu," Beans says mischievously, his freckles making him look particularly roguish in this light. He winks at me but is clearly directing the invitation to Bitty.

"Let's go kick some Erduborn ass," Bitty responds, rubbing their hands together.

Riley is already reclining on his bedroll. Not wanting to be alone with him, I follow the other two. We pass Tovi, who nods at us as she continues toward camp.

In the tavern, a group of four waves at Beans to join them in the back. They offer to find me a partner, but I politely decline, only wanting to watch. The place is dark, despite the dirty-looking lanterns dangling precariously above the tables. All four are Erduborn, three men and a woman. The tavern itself is mostly Erduborn, with a handful of Nemorisborn. A table of Patrons, a mixed group like us, are the loudest here.

Beans and Bitty weren't being cocky—they do in fact annihilate the other four at Talamu, several times each. I had trouble even following along. Bitty leans over to me and whispers that they're going to let the others win a couple, so they don't start a fight. I can't help but laugh.

The sun has set, and our supplies surely can't be that far off, so I say goodnight to everyone at the table and enquire about our supplies at the front bar. The man behind the counter says they'll be a few more minutes, but he will bring them to me if I wait here. I thank him and then have to stifle a yawn—I'll be going straight to sleep tonight.

"You're that little Silent Assassin, ain't ya?" I hear a drawling drunk say from my left.

I don't even bother looking at them. "I have no idea what you're talking about," I say, reining in my surprise at being recognized by a group of non-Patrons, in the middle of nowhere.

"Sure, ya do. I seen ya with the big reds, they're taking you to King Oferdu, right?"

"What the fuck are you on about?" I spare a look over my shoulder at his table of five, all invested in our little chat. They're Erduborn brutes with lanky brown hair and beards, with cheap-looking metal jewelry all over them. The man harassing me snorts and spits onto the floor before an ugly smirk shows his teeth. Teeth that are stained a greenish-brown color from chewing what I assume is drogalyf. Chewing the herb instead of smoking is said to result in a more sustained buzz.

"Ya. King Stol has wanted the cute assassin Null as a doxy for revs, but Osraed always said you weren't for sale. He worked out some deal with the reds and boom, here ya go!" He looks around until his entire table laughs and bangs their table like he told the best joke they've ever heard. When he joins them, his laugh sounds like a duck quacking, and I have to resist the urge to laugh at him, choosing silence instead.

They must take my silence and the slight curl of my lip as an invitation to continue. "Didn't you wonder why ya got the moteliest crew of losers as ya official escort?" another man says.

I narrow my eyes at him before calmly saying, "I still have no idea what the fuck you drunks are talking about." Then I turn back to face the bar and continue waiting for our supplies. I drum my nails on the counter. Sometimes, I wish it was socially acceptable to beat the living snot out of people for no other reason than because *I* think they deserve it.

The original man tries again to continue the conversation like I haven't made it clear I wasn't interested. "Ya ya, you got the weird Laguzborn kid, the Erduborn bitch, and the Ofnemoris drunk prince! I mean, at least they gave ya the commander so they could actually close the deal with ya still alive, even if he *is* only a Junky." Everyone at the table laughs again. One man, with a piece of stew stuck in his beard, devolves into a coughing fit.

The Ofnemoris drunk prince. Riley. Riley is the fucking *prince?*

I'm not entirely sure if the rest of what they've said has any truth to it, unless Beans and Riley are the only ones who know it's a ruse. It could explain why Riley has been such a pain the whole time, not taking anything seriously.

Before I could finish my thought, the barkeep returns with the package I was waiting for. "Here you go, love. Big Red's already settled the account. Do you need a hand with it?" He throws a wary glance toward the table of men, before looking back to me with an unspoken offer of support.

I politely decline the need for any help, thanking him, and pick up my heavy load to rest on my shoulder. I spare one last look at the stupid Erdu drunks, most of whom are grinning at me.

"You know, if I really was the Silent Assassin, it's pretty bold of you to be making yourselves such obvious next targets," I say sweetly. The men look slightly stricken, one swallowing visibly. Except the man with the duck laugh, who lets a smile of triumph spread across his face.

I'm boiling with barely checked rage. I should have realized Riley was the Prince Ofnemoris. It means that he's also the kidnapped princess' *twin*, although they did not grow up together because of her status as a Patron of the Divine.

The seething snake of anger in my veins becomes even more dangerous.

I've almost made it back to camp, making the short trip in no time because my brain is entirely spinning with thoughts: *has the princess even been kidnapped? Is this all a fucking lie?*

Riley and Tovi are lounging by the fire, and a small spark inside me is grateful that I haven't walked in on something awkward. I dump the package with a loud thud to grab Riley's attention. I get a surprised look from Tovi, who looks around as if to wonder where I materialized from. Riley raises an eyebrow in my direction.

"You're the fucking *prince*, Riley?" My voice is loud but higher pitched than I wanted. "Are you selling me to the King Oferdu? Is your *twin sister* even in any danger?" I emphasize the words *twin sister* with as much venom as I can.

Tovi immediately stands up making a stuttered sound, gesturing toward the tavern, and makes a hasty exit. Leaving me alone with *him*. Riley also stands, though with significantly less urgency.

"Is this all a joke to you?" I step so close to Riley that he has to tilt his head down to make eye contact with me. He looks amused; the heat rising from my chest to my face like a flame about to engulf the entire match.

He hasn't said a word. I shove him in the chest with both hands. The fucker barely moves—it's like trying to shove a tree.

"You done?" he says with a slight chuckle.

"No, I'm not fucking *done*, answer my questions!"

"You're not making sense!"

My blood boils. He seems to be having a grand old time and is not taking me seriously one bit.

"Are you, or are you not, the Prince Ofnemoris?" I grate out.

"I am."

I don't care about the rest of my questions right now because I need to unleash the beast raging in my chest. I swing. He leans back and ducks forward, and to my utter embarrassment, picks me up and throws me over his shoulder like a sack of potatoes.

"Put me down, you stupid red fuck!" I bark, too busy being indignant that I'm dangling over his back to produce a better insult.

He slaps my ass like I'm a naughty child and shushes me. *He fucking shushed me.* And spanked me.

I don't want to use weapons, so I try to punch him in the kidneys a few times—again, not even a flinch! I know realistically, if I really wanted to, I could get down. I just don't know how to do that without bloodshed, and I'm not entirely sure I want that. Yet.

"Where are we going?" I demand angrily before I am plopped unceremoniously onto the ground. I look around and realize he's taken us deeper into the forest. We can still see the camp, but we can't be seen by anyone else.

"Oh, is this where I get on my knees for you, *Your Majesty*? Or is this where you show me how much of a tough guy you are? Don't like being called out on your lies?"

"We haven't lied to you. What the fuck happened tonight?"

"You're telling me the queen sent her *drunk son* and a merry band of Gifted fucks to save her daughter from a king, who no one else has any idea is even missing?"

"Yes, Mika. That's exactly what we told you—*and* the council, might I remind you—because that's exactly what is happening," Riley says, exasperated. After a slight pause, he tilts his head. "Gifted fucks?"

The way he looks at me when he says that weakens my resolve a tiny bit. He looks genuinely disappointed that I would think his friends—wait, no—his *subjects*, are anything but fine people.

Well, they *are* fine people, but I'm trying to get a rise out of him.

I shove him again, but he is still an immovable wall of muscle. He's far too close to me while I'm backed against a massive tree, and his breath is hot, even in the warm air. It doesn't smell like alcohol, which surprises me since we're near a tavern. "Why aren't you drunk?"

I might have given him whiplash with the subject change. He grabs his face and rubs hard upward until his hands are gripping his hair in handfuls.

"Because I haven't had anything to drink tonight." My momentary shock is flattened when he follows with, "Are *you* drunk?"

He's still far too close to me. The heat is radiating off his body. My anger is dissipating slowly. A small—and I mean, *tiny*—part of me, wants to lean into that heat and put my hands on his hard chest.

What is wrong with me? Focus, you creeping lunatic.

"Why didn't you tell me you were the prince?" I sigh, no longer yelling.

He releases his hair and lets out a slow breath. "I didn't want to come. I was ordered to by my mother." He's waving his hands to punctuate his words and not even looking at me.

"That doesn't really…"

"Oh, Divine fuck, Mika! The only reason I agreed was if no one else knew who I was, besides the people who already knew me. I am essentially being dragged along like a child because I am of absolutely *zero* use in helping to save my sister. But my mother can't have me anywhere near her and lose *another* child. She can barely look at me." He steps back, looking at the sky, breathing hard.

I know the queen lost a son fifteen revolutions past—Riley's older brother—in a tragic accident at the age of twenty. I don't understand what this has to do with Riley, but I do believe him, or at least I *want* to.

"So, you're *not* secretly selling me to King Oferdu as a doxy?" I add to the silence.

Riley gives me a wild look, mouthing the word "no" with incredulity and a dramatic throw of his hands in the air.

I want to trust him. "Okay."

"Okay?"

"Okay."

"…Okay."

At some point after our ridiculous four-word agreement that everything was, in fact, *okay*, he'd stepped back to being almost on top of me. His typical Riley smirk is back.

"And what the fuck is that look exactly?" I hiss.

The smirk cracks into a full-blown smile, and I've temporarily forgotten how to breathe. Blinded by the most beautiful thing I have ever seen, it's like seeing a red sunset glowing through the horizon for the first time. I'm dazed and confused.

He leans closer—I'm unsure how that's possible considering not even an inch of space is left between us—with both hands against the tree behind me, his arms framing my head. He's looking down at me with unguarded desire smoldering in his eyes.

"Is the offer to get on your knees still on the table?"

I can't stop my jaw from dropping, heat rising in my face…and elsewhere.

"You know that is *not* what I meant by getting on my knees, you pig. Or should I say, Your Majesty? Prince Ofnemoris? Sir? Royal Dick?"

That last one has me blessed with a full-blown, head-tipped-back laugh. I don't think I've heard Riley laugh before, at least, not like *that*.

"Royal Dick does have a nice ring to it." His smile drops along with the arms framing me. "Why are you looking at me like that?"

I have no idea what my face is saying that he should be so concerned. "I haven't heard you laugh before."

"Oh. I laugh. Beans' jokes are funny sometimes," he says as he shrugs like it's no big deal.

"Not like that. Well, maybe not around me then."

I hate myself when the last part comes out strangled, so I clear my throat to hide it. He probably does laugh like that, but of course, not in the presence of the Silent Assassin.

Riley lifts his hand toward me, to—*I don't fucking know*—but I flinch. Instinctively. I don't know why his hand would go so near my face! He's looking at me like *this* is the most insulting thing I've done so far. He steps back, moving entirely too far away, the space between us a black void that triggers an involuntary shiver through me.

"Do you think I would *hit* you, Mika?" The hurt I hear in his voice is…*unpleasant*. I would rather he hit me.

"Riley, it's instinct. It's not you specifically, it's a lifetime of being taken advantage of. Being caught off guard is dangerous. Men in particular have found great *joy* in taking whatever they want from me."

He closes the distance between us in a flash, still not as close as before, but leans down so I don't have to crank my neck up to make eye contact. "Firecat," he purrs. "I would never force you to do anything you didn't want to do. If there's any *joy* to be had, I want you to give it to me with enthusiasm."

He runs the side of his fingers from the outside of my thigh slowly up my body. And I mean *slowly*—so slowly that it's leaving a trail of fire and ice, stopping at my ribs. His thumb reaches around and gently caresses the space beside my breast that my leather corset doesn't cover. He's making gentle circles with his thumb as he leans in closer. His warm breath caresses the side of my neck.

I'm frozen solid, unable to breathe, unable to move, not even sure if I can blink.

"I'll wait for you to want it, Firecat." Then he drops his hand, turns on his heel, and swaggers back toward the camp.

I'm left with a puddle between my legs from one slow brush of his fingers to the side of my body, and a raspy whisper to my neck. *What just happened?* I...hate him?

"Just promise me you won't fall in love," he calls back over his shoulder.

I probably shouldn't laugh as hard and loud as I do. "You sure have a royally high opinion of yourself if you think *you'd* be the one to find a heart where it doesn't exist."

He shakes his head as he continues to walk away.

Yes. I hate him.

CHAPTER THIRTEEN

I'm so sick of people thinking I am something to conquer, something to achieve. Riley is no different, even if his words and his touches are smoother; it's all the same because it's not about me, it's about them.

I'm pacing back and forth in the forest, and it takes me a moment to realize that I am so worked up, I'm shaking. I take a deep breath and try to calm the never-ending tornado inside. Steeling my shoulders and straightening my back, I stride back to camp. Everyone is back and getting ready to settle down.

"There she is, we thought maybe you'd gotten lost!" Beans tries to joke while throwing an actual bean at me.

"Oh, I was just checking around to see if I was the only person here who didn't know Riley was the Prince Ofnemoris," I respond with fake brightness as I hurl the bean back at him.

Beans looks contrite and stands to offer me his seat by the fire. I wave him off and sit across from him in front of the fire instead. Riley starts to chuckle before I cut him a death glare that has him turning it into a cough instead, trying to hide his smile.

"Am I being played for a fool here? Should I not trust any of you?" I say to the fire and whoever is listening.

"For the record, I wanted to tell you when you got to Mama's." Bitty's clear voice rings out as they make deliberate eye contact with everyone around the fire.

"Noted, Bitty," Beans says wryly. "It was a calculated risk, and it was ultimately decided that it would be better if you didn't know. You might have felt more pressure with Lyss' sibling around, and perhaps not comfortable in the presence of the royal family who have purchased you. It was the wrong call, Mika. Please forgive me?"

I nod, unable to look at any of them. Beans isn't the one I don't want to forgive.

"Tovi tells me it was a group of Erduborn men harassing you at the bar?" Beans asks with sincerity.

Before I can answer, Tovi cuts in. "I went back to speak to the owner. He said the men you had been talking to had already left."

"They were telling the truth about Riley, so what about everything else they said?" I ask.

Tovi answers me. "Of course we aren't selling you to the king as his sex slave. We aren't so sophisticated to have told you this *entire* strategic plan and discussed it daily for it only to be a ruse."

"So, the princess *is* missing?" I venture, needing further confirmation.

"Yes." Riley's change in demeanor at the mention of his sister is instant. And the fire that was burning so hot inside of me only a moment ago extinguishes just as quickly.

And it occurs to me that it's no wonder he's been drinking. His sister has been missing for *months*.

THE SUN RISES FAR TOO EARLY the next morning. My mood is tempered dramatically when Beans and Tovi arrive with a breakfast of two giant, freshly baked, and still steaming loaves of bread.

One loaf is savory, with spicy pork mince woven through it and a sharp cheese browned on top. The other is the deep brown color of cacote, and much to my delight, has the nutty and sweet flavor to match. Beans cuts the bread into big, healthy-looking slices for us, and we all eat greedily, polishing off both loaves by the time we're ready to leave.

Despite the early morning, Teorann is a hub of activity. We obviously aren't the only ones hoping to be on the first barge. With our packs on and trudging toward the beach, the dirt gives way to sand, and the large trees of the forest begin to thin.

I smell them before I lay eyes on the bright pink and yellow flowers of a tree I don't recognize. The air is filled with a rich and sweet scent, like honey, but with more spice and slightly fruitier. The perfume alone was enough to have me looking around in glee before I spotted the flowers themselves.

The trees are tall with big curly leaves and thin branches drooping downward. The flowers cluster together along the branches, slightly swaying in the morning breeze, and the five-petal blooms have a soft velvet look to them. They are mostly white and then ramp up the color to a warm yellow in the centers, some with a magenta pink along the edge of the petals.

I stop and reach up to run my hands delicately along a branch. The flowers caress my skin and bees dance in and out with heavy bags of pollen on their legs. A big hand reaches up and plucks a flower from the branch I'm staring at in rapture.

"Frasteria trees in full bloom are spectacular," Riley whispers, sniffing the flower he picked.

"I didn't even know they existed," I say with wonder as I look around to see the rest of the group has left us behind, and Riley's giant presence is far too close again.

I look at him. I mean I *truly* look at the man in front of me, with the new knowledge that he's the prince and we are trying to rescue his sister. His face goes from peaceful and perhaps slightly amused to deflated and dejected as he sees me studying his face. My rage responds with a slam into my throat.

"I'm sorry, Firecat. I didn't lie to you, and I never will, but omitting the truth of who I am was still a deceit. One that I had convinced myself was better for you. This is no excuse, and I truly hope you'll forgive me."

Riley tucks the flower behind one of my ears, moving his hand slowly toward my face this time, so he doesn't cause me to flinch. Instead, I soften. But I'm unwilling to verbally accept his apology when I'm not sure that I can speak with the lingering heat from Riley's fingers brushing my ear.

He then tips his head in the direction of the beach, a wordless reminder we need to hurry.

We reach the edge of the beach and I take one last look at the frasteria trees. We're not the first to arrive, but luckily, we will all fit on the first barge across.

We're waved straight onto the barge and told to sit for safety reasons, joined by a dozen or so other travelers. Two large men climb aboard, one Erduborn and the other Nemorisborn. After receiving a signal from the other side, the men begin to pole us toward Erdu, the large chain through the center making a loud clunking sound as each link passes.

Aware it will take at least half an hour to cross, we chat amongst ourselves about nothing important. My mind still reels that Riley, sitting to my left, is a prince. That line of thought leads me to the next until I land on something that makes me smile mischievously.

The barge is loud, so I know I can speak to Riley without anyone—save for Bitty—being able to hear. I lean closer to Riley and signal for him to lean down so I can say something.

"So, if you're the second Prince Ofnemoris…"

Riley looks down at me, frowning in confusion.

"And the twin of Lyss…" I continue.

His eyes narrow at me.

"The twin of…*Amarilyss*," I say with my smile widening, and he rolls his eyes dramatically.

"That means, Riley, your name is…"

"—Aurelius," he finishes for me, a glint in his eye that tells me I will pay for this later.

"*Aurelius Jasper Ofnemoris*," I say slowly, annunciating every syllable perfectly, unable to hide my smirk. "It's a lovely name, *Aurelius.*"

He leans down, his arm coming around me to lean on the barge's wall along my back, breath hot against my ear. "You might think you're mocking me, Firecat, but I like the idea of my name on your lips."

He pauses in place after his lips graze my ear on his last word, sending fire into my veins. Then he leans back to look at me with heavy lids, stopping at my mouth before returning to face ahead.

"Well," I splutter. "I guess I won't be saying it again."

I let out an angry huff when I see him try to hide a smile as he reclines against the barge.

He knows he won. *What* he won, I'm not sure, but we both know that whatever it was, he definitely won. Asshole.

My cheeks are still burning, his breath and lips still tingling on my skin, when the barge reaches Erdu and we disembark. Not another word is spoken between us.

If anyone else, and I mean *anyone* else, spoke or tried to touch me like that, they would lose their ability to function. Somehow, I clam up and become awkward around Riley. This must be because I haven't had sex in revolutions. I'm starved. That's all it is. It doesn't help that Riley is nice to look at. And to smell. When he's not drunk.

I'm a creep. A sex-starved creep.

ERDU IS a hot and windy place most of the time, but during windstorm season there are days when the wind picks up the sand and uses it to scrub everything raw—including flesh from bone. Luckily, this only happens a handful of times each windstorm season. All gorge and canyon towns are specially designed to withstand them. The native fauna has also adapted to survive windstorms, or they know how to hide.

Early settlers in Erdu tunneled out caves in the ground or the side of unoccupied gorge walls for refuge. When a windstorm is upon you, your best chance of survival is to find one of these and hope that it's not already occupied as they can realistically only fit two people, three max.

I knew all this. What I didn't realize was that we were entering Erdu at the start of windstorm season, the deadly season during which Oferdu people don't usually travel because of the risks.

We sort through our supplies, making sure each of us has everything needed to survive if we become separated from the group. Tovi helps me shift a few things around so my hatchets are still secure but accessible, commenting on their beauty as she holds one.

Riley makes a joke about having to carry some spices and herbs, asking if I'm going to help carry some of the random junk he brought with him. Beans clips him upside the head as if he were a naughty teenager and not a 31-rev-old prince.

"I wouldn't worry yet, there are still too many trees in this part of Erdu to worry too much about windstorms. Best to be prepared though," Beans says.

I'm not reassured.

While not as dense as Nemoris, Erdu still has many trees in the south. As we travel, cracks in the earth and small cliffs begin to appear. The further north we go, the hotter it gets. Standalone mud huts are expertly built around trees for maximum safety against windstorms. Erduborn peer at us from behind curtains as we make our way through tiny towns.

We didn't linger at Erdu Teorann after crossing the waters so early in the morning. Our first night was similar to our time in Nemoris, though we were far more alert during watch. A week after entering Erdu, we finally started to get a feel for the country. The days are hot, and the wind only makes them feel hotter as fine dirt sticks to our sweat.

Jundamara will be our first stay in a bed and breakfast type accommodation. It's an enormous canyon town that was once a riverbed, now mostly dry with pockets of water that remind me of Sadori oases. Jundamara itself is built along the dry parts of the riverbed snaking through the canyon.

The B&B doesn't have a tavern, though it does offer a breakfast basket. For dinner, we wind our way along the pebbled pathways to a surprisingly large smokehouse. Music can be heard long before we see our destination, and the smell of smoked meat makes me salivate.

Inside, we're greeted as if we're old friends and shown to a booth not far from the group of musicians. The place is busy and bustling with so many people and so much laughter. Our server assures us that the best way to enjoy their food is to let them bring out plates of it, and we share until we've had our fill. So, that is exactly what we do. We receive a complimentary beer from the owner, and I take a sip to be polite.

The food comes out on various plates, piled high with various meats atop leafy vegetables. The server explains what each meat is smoked with and how, but I am more interested in watching the musicians. A man and a woman are singing together, and I am riveted.

"They are mesmerizing," Tovi whispers loudly near my ear, watching the musicians with the same fascination I am.

"I wish I could sing or play an instrument," I say back.

Tovi grins and nods, not taking her eyes off them.

The music changes to something more upbeat, and people start dancing in the center. I lean back to Tovi, who is still watching the singers. "Do you want to dance?" I ask eagerly.

Tovi looks at me like she forgot I was sitting there. "No. I don't...don't dance. But thank you," she stammers, looking awkward.

"Well, *that's* bullshit!" Riley yells, laughing at Tovi. "You don't dance well, but you *do* dance."

Wondering if I overstepped the boundaries of our precarious relationship, I let it go. I look over at Bitty across from me and mouth the same offer to dance to them. Their violet eyes light up and I receive an enthusiastic nod as they push Beans out of the way so they can get up.

I take another sip of my now warm beer, offering the rest to Beans, then join Bitty. Something about music and dancing frees me to pretend I am a normal person who can find joy in simple pleasures. We dance and jump around to the beat, laughing at each other and our ridiculous moves.

The musicians slow their tempo down. I lift my hands together in the air as I sway, closing my eyes. I'm twirling my hands when a familiar fluttering begins in my chest. I open my eyes, expecting danger.

There is no danger. However, Riley has joined Bitty and I on the dance floor. He would look large and ridiculous dancing somewhere else, but in Erdu where everyone is giant, it's Bitty and I who look ridiculous. Riley looks at home, despite the dark blood-red hair, pale skin, and green eyes.

Heat slams into my chest the moment Riley catches me watching him as I dance. He holds my stare, a slight smile curling at his lips. I am the first to look away of course, surprised at myself for looking him in the eye for as long as I did. The heat travels down and settles between my legs.

He's dancing with Bitty, twirling them around gently as they laugh and make Riley twirl instead. But his eyes are on me, burning every inch of my skin. He's studying me. Like I'm a creature he's never seen before. I close my eyes again. Swaying with my arms in the air, I slide one hand along my arm to find my skin prickled.

"I'm going to go finish my beer!" Bitty announces, leaving me alone with Riley. Alone—with a bunch of other folk *also* dancing. Still, I find it hard to breathe.

The music changes to a lively jig and Riley grabs my hand and spins me. I can barely stay on my feet as he skips around, flinging me in and out, catching me with his other hand and twirling me with no effort.

The song finishes, and Riley gives me one last twirl and pulls me in, ending with him hugging me from behind as we catch our breath. He holds me and I can't help but laugh, overwhelmed by how *utterly ridiculous* that was.

"You were throwing me around like a doll," I laugh as a new song begins. "I had no idea what to do. I didn't know you could dance like that!" I yell over the music to Riley.

"There are many things you have yet to learn about me, Firecat," he whispers in my ear, before turning me in his arms. The song is slower; Riley matches the music perfectly with his movements. Of course he knows how to dance, he's a fucking prince.

Again, he's watching me, but I stare back as intently. I make note of every freckle on his face, deciding my favorite are the three clustered above his lip on the right side. He's tucked his hair behind his ears, and it shows off his perfectly sharp jawline and proud chin. He's attractive. *Fuck*. I'm attracted to this dickhead.

I didn't realize I had leaned in so close, my hand resting on his chest.

He reaches up and covers my hand with his own, leaning down so I can hear his quieted voice. "I like looking at your face too."

Riley gives me a twirl, then winks at me and walks back to the table.

I follow him, and Bitty tells us that both Beans and Tovi have retired for the evening.

"Another drink, Riley?" Bitty asks, finishing their beer.

Riley hesitates for a fraction. "Not tonight. I think I might call it and go to bed too."

I can see his beer from earlier looking flat and untouched. Bitty looks at me hopefully, and I shake my head. "I'm happy to sit with you or dance some more, but no drinking for me."

"You both suck." Bitty whines with a pout, which makes Riley laugh. He kisses them on top of the head and says goodnight.

Riley's hand reaches out to hold the back of my neck

gently as he leans in. "Thanks for the dance, Firecat." His thumb caresses the top of my spine before he lets go and backs away.

"My name is *Mika*," I manage to say as I roll my eyes at him, hoping to distract from my erratic pulse. He grins, mouthing goodnight with a smoldering look in his eye, spinning around to leave the smokehouse. I mumble goodnight under my breath. My world is spinning way too fast.

CHAPTER FOURTEEN

itty and I don't stay out much longer, both of us
yawning excessively within the hour. We're sharing a
room as there were only four available for the five of
us. In an exhausted silence, we use the cleaning powder to
scrub our teeth and then collapse into our tiny—but
extraordinarily comfortable—cots.

I wake to Bitty opening our door. They're getting
something from outside, and I realize it's our breakfast as it's
already morning. In their arms is a basket, one filled with
double servings of everything: still warm sweet bread rolls
with a twist of sticky cinnamon paste, a small bowl of
roasted faegel berries, a big plate of scrambled eggs with
what looks like chunks of smoked meat through it, and a big
jar of noni juice to share.

I didn't think I would be hungry after eating so much last
night, but Bitty and I *devour* our breakfast, a fight almost
breaking out over the last faegel berry. Sitting on the floor,
rubbing our bellies, we argue over who has to wash first. It's
a trade-off because getting to wash first means you get the
cleanest water, but neither of us wants to get up yet.

In the end, I go first because Bitty claims they got breakfast, so I *owe* them. Our room is small, with only the two cots we slept in and a table with a built-in basin. A fresh jug of water was delivered with our breakfast. The basin has a drain that clears the water down and out of the room, so I pull the chained plug to get rid of last night's dirty water.

Bitty cleans up our breakfast and then rests on their cot while I wash. One of the downsides of sharing a room is not getting to wash my hair because I don't want to sully the water even more for Bitty. There is a light knock at the door and an attendant hands us another jug, apologizing they didn't have enough earlier. I take the Divine hint that I should wash my hair. Bitty is thanking the attendant when I call out to see if they have any shears I can borrow.

"Of course," the attendant says with no hint of curiosity. "I'll be just a moment and bring them back for you."

Giving me a skeptical look, Bitty asks why I want shears.

"Can I ask a favor?" I ask Bitty, grinning.

Reluctantly, Bitty cuts my hair for me, and the relief is immediate. It had grown a bit these last few weeks—moons —traveling, and the Erdu heat makes it uncomfortable.

Not surprisingly, traveling with an inch less hair is much cooler. I can leave my hair out without the back of my neck getting too hot or needing to tie it up and feeling stifled.

"Nice hair," Riley teases, flicking my wild, golden blonde strands and making me jump.

The rest of the group is farther ahead, with Beans leading and Tovi carrying Bitty on their shoulders. Bitty is demonstrating something dramatically in the air with their hands, and though Tovi wouldn't be able to see, her laughter is no less enthusiastic.

Meaning: Riley and I are alone. Again. The thrill sends the rage clawing in my chest into a frenzy.

"You're an incorrigible flirt, Riley," I declare, raising an eyebrow at him.

"Maybe I just like to see you squirm." He leers, adding, "Your hair does look nice though. I like being able to see your neck." He showers me with a handful of yellow petals that I didn't realize he'd been picking.

"*Incorrigible!*" I yell, glowering at his back as he races off to annoy Tovi and Bitty next. I stuff a handful of the petals in a pocket. I'm not sure why.

IT'S ALREADY dark by the time we finish our lackluster dinner. We opt to clean our dishes the next morning so we can get to sleep early. Beans takes the first watch, and the rest of us don't complain as we settle into our bedrolls, exhausted from a long day.

When I'm woken for my watch, it's earlier than I expected. Beans grimaces and leans back on his haunches.

"Bitty is unwell and has been vomiting for an hour. They're alright, but are in no state to stand watch," he says with a quick glance at Bitty's huddled form.

I gladly take their place and extend my watch to cover them.

In the morning, Bitty is still not well. They are queasy and nauseous, so Beans suggests we should stay to give them a day to recover. They spend the morning in their bedroll, only moving to vomit a small distance away.

It's a hot day. Beans takes Bitty to an almost dry creek bed nearby to cool down and wash away the sick. Tovi, Riley, and I throw a sheathed knife like it's a hot potato, trying to cure our boredom while it's far too hot to spar, even in the shade. We keep adding rules to our makeshift game. First, you can only catch the handle, then everything is one-handed, and you can only hold on to it for a second before you have to throw it, and it can be to any one of us.

With lots of swearing and giggling at how silly our game is, Bitty and Beans eventually return, and we settle down. The former still looks green about the gills and immediately returns to their bedroll.

Restless, I announce I'm going for a walk. I walk aimlessly for half an hour, not caring where I'm going, but I keep a clear idea of where I am and how to get back. This is why, when I come across something incredible, I race back to camp easily.

"Does anyone feel like coming to see something awesome?" I ask, breathless and excited.

Bitty gives me a sad shake of the head, and Beans pats them softly and also declines. I look to Tovi, hoping she will come, but she chirps a "no thanks," offering what looks like an actual smile. Riley, however, agrees before I even look at him. Earning himself a pointed look and raised eyebrow from Tovi, he responds with a rude gesture that I catch out of the corner of my eye. So, I lead the way, hesitantly.

"How the fuck did you find this?" Riley asks excitedly, stripping off his clothing and weapons.

Before us—after following a very narrow canyon, more like a wide crack in the mountain—is an oasis feeding into a cave. If you crouch and look along the water, you can see the cave opens up at the top, further down. The water is fed by a small waterfall along the top of the canyon into the open cave. Not waiting for my answer, and already down to his undershorts, Riley dives in. He springs out of the water, flicking it everywhere. Then looks at *me* like I'm the mad one.

"Are you getting in?" he purrs, stroking backward deeper into the cave to reach the open area. The small smatter of freckles across his shoulders sparkle with the water, and the light fuzz on his chest draws my eye. Rage springs into my throat.

This is not a good idea. This is a bad idea. I repeat this over and over, as I strip off my leathers and weapons, taking off most of my clothes but leaving my tunic on. Riley watches me *very* carefully from the edge of the darkness in the cave. His eyes snag on the pile where my pants are, as if he's now deliberately not looking at my bare legs.

I step into the water, not wanting to dive in, and then wade toward Riley. He takes the cue and we both swim deeper into the cave. When we finally reach the alcove, it's even more stunning than I'd imagined.

The size of a small room, a deep pool of crystal-clear water shimmers around us. Every wall surrounding us is immense, covered in all manner of plants breaking through with a handful of short ledges dotted about. Riley has that stunning smile again, and just like the first time, I can't see anything else.

I have to tread water as it's too deep for me to stand, unlike Riley, who is not only standing, but the water is only halfway up his chest. He splashes me without looking and then dives under the water. Despite the clear waters, I don't see him until he's under me and lifting me up and out of the water.

He throws me, and I emit a squeal before I hit the water.

"Bastard!" I splutter, splashing him angrily as his unfettered laughter echoes around us.

He dives down again and I growl, swimming away from his sneaky bulk moving through the water. I can't hide my smirk as he pops up on the opposite side of the pool. Down he goes again, and again I dodge, but eventually he catches me and throws me again.

When I catch my breath, I decide *it's my turn.* I dive and speed swim under the water like an eel. He tries to dodge, but I can hold my breath longer than most, and I slip behind him. I surface with a splash and launch myself up to bring him back down into the water with me by his shoulders.

I dunk him, and he comes up spluttering and coughing, and then laughing.

For the next hour or two, we play this weird game of tag. Not really talking, only exclaiming that the other cheated or whooping that we got the other *best.*

The next time Riley catches me, instead of throwing me, he pulls me in close, holding my legs at mid-thigh and moving to position himself between them. Close to a ledge, my back bumps into it, before he steadies me against it.

My hands brace against his chest, rising and falling with his heavy breathing. Mine is likely the same, especially as the familiar crashing begins against my ribs, so hard I'm sure he would be able to hear it if he listened. He lifts me slightly, so we're face-to-face, my legs around his waist in his grip.

"What would you do if I kissed you right now?" he asks huskily, eyes flicking between my eyes and my lips. His long, dark lashes still sparkle with water droplets.

"Probably headbutt you. Perhaps a knee to your favorite appendage. Might bite you. Fucking *anything* to stop you, really," I say in a fast whisper, hoping my voice won't betray me.

My hands now grip his lightly freckled shoulders. A smirk spreads across his face, and he leans further against me as his hands slide along my thighs, stopping before his fingers reach my ass.

"I'd almost risk it. For one taste." He leans closer, and

closer. "But I'll wait," he says to the place where the corner of my lips meets my cheek. His lips brush my skin as he speaks. "It'll be worth it."

He throws his body back in a splash, taking me with him. Again, I come up spluttering curses at him as his laughter trails off down the cave to the exit.

Tovi curses at me when we return as Riley describes the swimming hole. "If I'd known it was something like *that*, I would've come!" she says, her violet eyes blazing.

I laugh, reminding her that I *did* say it was amazing.

She huffs in derision. "I thought you had just found the beetleberry bush and gotten all excited. You are often strangely excited by food and plants."

I narrow my eyes to argue, but… "Wait, you found a *beetleberry bush*?"

Tovi rolls her eyes and signals for me to follow her in a dramatic display, feinting a punch to Riley's ribs as we pass.

"Beetleberries!" Tovi announces in a flourish in front of a huge bush after a few minutes of walking, which earns her a squeal that sounds like it came from a child.

Tovi stands there with her arms folded not hiding the self-satisfied smile on her face, proving her point that I get way too excited about food. But…beetleberries!

They're not exactly rare, but certainly hard to grow. The berries are dark green to red, depending on their ripeness. Earning their name from the shape of the berry, they look like a beetle without legs. The outside flesh is firm and creates a delectable pop when you bite into them.

I fill my pockets and then gesture to Tovi to fill hers as well, which she does reluctantly.

"Divide and conquer!" I tell her, instructing her to go to the other side of the bush.

Well, my intention was to fill our pockets with ripe berries and return to the camp triumphant. That was until Tovi throws an overly ripe beetleberry at me, and it splats directly in the center of my forehead, her musical laughter following in its wake.

"I thought you were nearly thirty! Or was it...thirteen?!" I yell, using berries from my pockets as projectiles and hammering her with them in quick succession.

The shriek and laugh I hear from Tovi make my heart spin, and my rage follows not long after. I ignore them both.

It's an all-out battle, with no winner (or maybe we both won). We return to the camp with only a handful of beetleberries, sticky and overheated.

Riley licks Tovi's face as she struggles unsuccessfully to get away from him. "Delicious!" he announces, as he grabs for me to do the same.

Tovi picks me up and throws me over her shoulders, running toward the creek, screaming. "I'll save you!"

This group is weird, but maybe I'm weird too.

CHAPTER FIFTEEN

Beans gently wakes me, a finger to his lips to keep me silent. I sit up quietly, hoping Bitty isn't ill again, but they are waking Tovi as Beans moves to wake Riley. Once we're all awake and confused, Beans uses the hand gestures he's been teaching me since Nemoris to communicate.

Bitty, who was feeling well enough by the evening, was on watch after Beans. They'd heard approximately fifteen men closing in on us thanks to their Gift. We're surrounded. From what I can decipher with my limited knowledge of the hand gestures, they intend to kill Beans and Riley, taking the rest. They are most likely skin traders looking for new people to force into sex work, though many are just never seen again.

Beans gestures for Bitty to take their throwing knives and climb a tree to the north. He then directs me up a tree to the south with my hatchets, making my bedroll look like I am still in it. The other three move into their bedrolls, their weapons in hand as they pretend to sleep. And we wait. And wait. I am starting to think that maybe Bitty was wrong when I hear the distinct sounds of movement around us.

I make eye contact with Bitty who gestures for me to take the three men directly to my left. If I dispatch them, then I'm to help Tovi. More hushed sounds of people moving about the forest filter up to us. Bitty holds up a hand, slowly counting down on their fingers.

When they finally put their last finger down, chaos erupts.

I throw my first hatchet at a man's neck while jumping onto the back of another, using the blade of my second hatchet to slice his throat. I leap off him, swinging my hatchet at the man directly behind. He blocks with a sword, but on his second swing, I maneuver myself and duck, so his blade is lodged in a tree. My hatchet comes up and around, slamming directly into his eye. He screams, giving me time to flip backward and retrieve my first hatchet.

A man charges me, and I use both hatchets to defend myself against his sword. He's much stronger, but he underestimates my speed, and I slam a hatchet into his sternum with a crack and gurgle. The surprised look on his face as he drops to his knees is replaced by a death stare before he slumps to the ground.

Quickly surveying my surroundings, I fling a hatchet into the back of a man raising his sword at an unaware Beans. I pick up a dropped sword and run it through the man I hit in the face earlier, as he still cradles it, wailing.

Turning around, I find a man trying to climb the tree Bitty is in, and I throw my last hatchet at him. It makes a loud thunk as it lodges into the side of his skull. Gripping the heavy scavenged sword with both hands, I swing it at one of the men Tovi is fighting. He dodges in time and swings his sword at me, but I stomp his ankle and he trips to one knee. I swing the sword and decapitate him easily, but had he been ready to fight me, it would've been tough given his size and the unfamiliar sword in my hands.

The night falls to silence as I move to recover my hatchets. The four of us whip around to see if anyone else is coming. Bitty jumps down from the tree.

"It's over." Bitty points to the man at mine and Tovi's feet. "He's the last one alive," they say with a small grimace.

I stab the sword through his back and end his life.

Seventeen men in total, dead at our feet. The smell of blood and vacated bowels and bladders cuts through the air. Beans asks if anyone is injured, and we all mutter that we're fine. I'm walking toward the hatchet near Beans when Riley laughs breathlessly.

"I knew you could fight, and I knew you were fast—but that was something else entirely, Firecat," Riley says, with another breathless laugh.

"Now I understand why Bitty was complaining about getting their ass handed to them every time you spar," Tovi adds, breathless and wide-eyed.

I pull my first hatchet from the back of the dead man at Beans' feet, wanting everyone to stop looking at me and forget what they saw. Other than Jaena, no one has seen me kill another person, let alone…seven of them, with ease. Eight, if you count finishing that last man with a sword through his back.

"I guess allocating you only three men to dispatch *was* mildly condescending," Bitty says with a grunt, struggling to get my hatchet out of the man's skull at their feet.

"Not at all, Bitty," I reply quietly, heat flaming my cheeks at the way they're all looking at me. I take over the task of removing the hatchet, the awful creaking sound of metal on bone is loud enough to make me cringe.

We drag the men into an area fully under the sky. It's too risky to burn them in windstorm season with this many trees and dry brush around. We're also not going to waste time or honor them by digging holes to feed them to the trees either.

The sun and animals can have their fill until only bleached bones remain.

Unfortunately, some of our belongings are covered in the signs of death. We take everything to the almost dry creek bed to wash off what we can, as none of us want to go back to sleep at this point.

Packed up, we travel a distance downwind and set up camp again. It's still the middle of the night, and much too dangerous to be trekking in the dark with cracks in the earth big enough to swallow a horse.

I offer to take the next watch as I am too wired to even think of going back to sleep. No one disagrees. Beans comes to check on me before retiring for the second time tonight. He doesn't say a word, only rests his hand on the edge of my shoulder, giving it a small squeeze. And then, after a few seconds of silence together, he gives it a pat and gets into his bedroll.

I check our perimeter, and when I'm satisfied that we aren't being snuck up on again, I take up a spot on a high ridgeline with an excellent view of the camp and surroundings.

After a couple of hours, I can see Tovi is awake, and I let her relieve me. Before she passes, she pauses in front of me. Just when I think she's not actually going to say anything, and I make a move to continue back to camp, she opens her mouth.

"Thank you for your help tonight. That could have been a lot worse without you."

"No need. Protecting you all and helping save the princess is what I was…bought for." It comes out sounding bitter, though I didn't mean it like that. "I mean—"

"I know what you meant." She smiles and moves to walk past me, and I feel a sudden slap to my ass. I turn in shock and give her a *what the fuck* look, and she grins and shrugs.

Why does everyone slap my ass?

My mind whirring through tonight's kills, I stretch out in my bedroll, but I'm still unable to sleep.

"Are you okay?" Riley whispers, startling me because I didn't realize he was awake.

"I'm fine. Go back to sleep."

"Why aren't you sleeping?" he says through a quiet yawn, stretching onto his back. He slaps at my foot when I don't answer immediately.

"I'm too good at killing. It keeps me awake sometimes," I whisper, hoping no one else can hear my confession. I disconnect from the reality that is taking a life. Pretend. Detach. Let my rage take over.

Riley is quiet for long enough that I assume he's fallen back to sleep, but then he quietly says, "It would be a problem if it *didn't* give you pause to end someone's life, Firecat."

Contemplating Riley's words, I try to get comfortable. It's a bit chilly, so I put my hands in my pockets. I pull a hand back out, and with it come petals—the ones Riley showered me with. They've lost most of their pretty smell, but they still look beautiful.

Riley, with his head at the end of his mat closest to me, breathes softly. I sprinkle the handful of half-dried yellow petals slowly over his face until his eyes snap open in confusion. And then he's frowning with a grin and closing his forest green eyes, letting me finish.

"You kept them?"

"Never know when they might come in handy. Goodnight, Riley."

"Goodnight, Mika." My name is barely audible through his whisper.

When his breath finally falls into the rhythm of sleep, I quietly voice one last question. "But what if it's not ending a life that gives me pause, but *not* being bothered by it…that bothers me?"

A soft whisper from the leaves in the nearby trees is my only answer. But I have always known the answer. I'm a monster.

"COME ON, *Firecat*. Your hatchets against my swords?" Tovi says the next evening when we stop for camp, using the unfortunate nickname Riley favors for me.

"Only if you promise not to make that ridiculous name a thing," I groan, trying to hide my surprise and delight that Tovi has approached me to spar.

Once again, I'm grateful to Frankie for creating the leather guards on my hatchets that allow me to train safely with someone. Riley and Beans are sparring down by the creek while Bitty watches them, so it will be Tovi and I with no audience.

Tovi is bigger than me, and her reach is much farther, especially with her short swords. Her powerful strikes take everything for me to block with my hatchets, but I am constantly smacking her with the face of my hatchets.

"Bitch, *again*?" Tovi hisses, after taking a leather-covered hatchet to the stomach. She jumps back ready to go again, shaking her head with a smile and showing her perfect teeth —both dangerous and beautiful.

I twirl with my hatchets as if I'm a princess and not a mud-covered slave assassin, flourishing into an exaggerated bow, which causes Tovi to laugh. I grin at her in response.

When both of us are covered in sufficient bruises and cuts, we call a truce (I won, but we weren't technically keeping score…). Lying in the mud and grass as we catch our breath, I watch the Kauri trees covered in Clematis vines. The trees themselves are large, with small almond-shaped leaves dotting their strong branches. Almost no trunk and barely any of the branches are visible, with the Clematis vine covering it entirely. The small white blooms attract thousands of busy bees, the low drone of their buzzing the only sound besides our breathing.

Riley comes to block our view, standing above us with his hands on his hips. "Dinner?" he asks with a wild grin and pink coloring his cheeks.

"Is that an offer, or are you asking where it is?"

"Offer!" Riley announces, turning his grin mischievous. "Beans and I accidentally killed a couple of ducks…"

Tovi coughs through her scoff while I ask, "How do you *accidentally* kill a couple of ducks?"

"When you disarm someone with such force, their axe goes flying into a flock of them." He shrugs as both Tovi and I gape at him and then share a glance.

"Waste nothing. They're on the fire now, almost ready!"

Riley reaches his hands out to help us both up, however, Tovi and I get up without assistance, leaving Riley bent forward holding his hands out awkwardly. Tovi smacks his ass as we bypass him, winking at me as she jogs toward camp, announcing we should wash up before dinner. These two and their ass-smacking.

Tovi reaches the creek before me, and I see her with her hands on her hips and shaking her head slowly. I'm about to ask her what she's doing when I see a literal *blanket* of feathers coating every surface. As soon as we make eye contact, she bursts into laughter, which sends me into fits as well.

Back at camp, I hear a shout behind me and spin with knives ready. Tovi is cackling and trying to hide behind Bitty as Beans scoops handfuls of duck feathers out of the back of his pants and throws them at her. Riley is watching me with a frown, and his eyes note my fighting stance and knives in hand. He cocks his head in a question I ignore.

Later that night, when Tovi is on watch and everyone else is asleep, I watch the stars. It's a mostly clear night, with barely any trees to obstruct my view where we camped. Restless, I roll over to try and sleep on my side instead.

Riley's sleeping form is closest to me, his hands in front of his face obscuring it from view. He has nice hands. I almost laugh at that thought. Since when do I appreciate *hands?* I'm drifting off as I study Riley's hands in the dying light of the fire. Big, attractive hands.

I am afforded a sleep not of nightmares but of pleasant dreams instead.

CHAPTER SIXTEEN

"There's a windstorm coming. A big one," Bitty blurts out, their violet eyes wide.

"What?" I screech. *Oh, Divine fuck, of course there is.* Because nothing else could possibly go wrong on this stupid mission. It's been less than a week since we took on the skin traders. I hate Erdu. Except for Jundamara.

"Okay everyone, start looking for windcaves. Go," Beans says, pointing toward a set of underground gorges while Riley grabs my arm and starts running.

"This is me. Don't die. Bye!" Tovi yells over the increasing wind and disappears into what looks like a crack in the earth.

"You guys can take that one, it looks empty. We'll grab the next one!" Riley drags me along, not waiting to see what Beans or Bitty say.

As the wind starts to really scream and the sand scrapes at my skin, Riley pulls me into him. "There's a cave entrance above us, but I'm going to have to lift you in. I'm going to kneel, and then you climb onto my shoulders, and I'll stand so you can reach. Okay?"

He looks at me in concern, maybe because *I'm* concerned. This windstorm is no joke, and I'm already finding it hard to breathe. He kneels and I climb. "Hold on!" he yells, and up he goes with me perched on his shoulders.

I see the entrance to the cave and scramble in, wondering how Riley is going to fit into the small opening. I crawl through the short tunnel, up and over a short wall, and then have to wiggle my way around another narrow passage to the left. Already, it sounds quieter; I can hear myself breathe.

I wait…and wait…and wait. *Where the fuck is he?*

Then I hear him grunting and dragging our bags. I had completely forgotten about the bags containing our food and supplies when Bitty announced the storm.

Now that he is inside and safe, I explore our cave.

The main area I crawled into has a chimney, airflow going up and out, and a little bit of light through various cracks. A tiny bit of wind and sand float in, but it's nothing compared to the torrent outside. I can *just* stand in this room, but there's no chance Riley will be able to.

An alcove to the left only looks wide enough for a couple of bedrolls—it's almost complete darkness in there and barely tall enough for Riley to even crouch in.

Off to the right is a thin passage with a higher ceiling, and at the end, a privy has been dug out. There is a deep hole to squat over, and when you're finished, a pile of loose earth to throw on top. It doesn't smell half as bad as I imagined it would. Thankfully, there is good airflow in there too.

I come back to the main area where Riley is lighting a small fire. "This is amazing!" I say, plopping myself down heavily.

Riley chuckles. "I'm just happy we found a good one that was left stocked with firewood. The ones lower to the ground are usually first to go, and they don't get treated with the same respect as the ones that are more difficult to get to, like this.

"We actually went past a couple of lower ones, but I was looking for one up high. Didn't want to put you through a week in a cave with me that was just one room for sleeping, eating, and shitting."

"A *week?*" I splutter. "We're going to be here for a week?"

"It's possible. Bitty's face said it all. They were scared, so it must have sounded like a big one. We have enough food and supplies, and the rest of the team are safe. We'll be fine."

WE HAVE a quick meal of dried meat—nondescript, perhaps donkey—with a few dried fruits and nuts, and swordmint tea. Riley digs through his pack and pulls out a clear bottle with a golden-colored liquid. After a long stare at the bottle, he gives it a jiggle in my direction and asks if I want a drink.

"No thanks," I reply. *That is definitely not a good idea.*

"I don't think I've ever really seen you drink—*do* you drink?"

He's taking a swig as I say, "I like being in control, and drinking leads to being…out of control. Do you like letting alcohol be in control so often?"

He wipes his mouth on the back of his hand and contemplates my face, before answering. "Not really, no," he says with a self-deprecating chuckle. "But sometimes it would be nice if I could get a break from the chaos." He points meaningfully toward his head with the bottle.

He tries to hand me the bottle again. "Come on, we're stuck in here. What's the worst that could happen?" I take the bottle. *I can think of plenty.*

After taking a mouthful of the Divine-awful liquid that

burns its entire way down to my stomach, I hand the bottle back with a grimace, and Riley tips it back to his mouth. "Just promise me, no drunken sex. I don't want to fuck you," I say, which causes him to choke.

"I told you, Firecat. I have no intention of forcing you to do anything that you don't want to do."

"Uh-huh," I murmur as I take the bottle for another swig. "Would Tovi be annoyed?" I query, hoping it sounds casual.

Riley lets out a half laugh. "Oh, absolutely not."

"What? I thought you were…together," I ask, not hiding my confusion and not wanting to say the word *fucking*, when it's clear they're not in any kind of monogamous relationship.

Riley's eyebrows couldn't be higher. "Where did you pick that up? No, we're definitely not together. And Tovi constantly tells me I should fuck other people." It's my turn to choke on the drink and Riley chuckles again. "We have been friends for seven revs. A friendship that came with some physical benefits—mutually, of course. Neither of us have wanted anything more than that. We care a lot about each other, but there's nothing there."

"I see." I don't know what else to say to that, so I focus on taking another drink. It doesn't taste so bad now or burn as much. "So, you guys, what? Scratch each other's itch and then fuck other people?" I query, as casually as possible, while I hand the bottle back.

"Pretty much. Though, we haven't for many revs. I hoped she'd find someone to care for her the way I can't. But younger me wasn't above getting what they needed—my itch scratched as you put it." He has a smirk on his face as he takes another sip, watching me.

His eyes hold entirely too much mischief and heat.

Iт's way too warm in here. We finished the bottle of alcohol and were talking about fighting techniques, and then Riley left to use the privy.

I start stripping off my leathers, and my pants. I'm too fucking hot!

"I've set up the bed rolls, but…" Riley stops. "What are you doing?" he laughs.

"It's hot!" That may have come out a little slurred.

"Right," he chuckles. "I've set up the bed rolls, but there's not a lot of room. We can take shifts if you like."

"We aren't taking shifts. Don't be silly." I stumble toward the cave, crawling inside. He wasn't kidding, there really isn't much space at all.

"Well, come and lie down," I demand, flopping down with a sigh. Riley only pauses for a second before crawling in to lay next to me, stiff as a board. "Riley. You're not going to be able to sleep with all of that on," I say while gesturing vaguely at his entire body.

He lets a slow breath out of his nose and shuffles back out to the room he can stand in, where I hear his leathers dropping to the ground. When he comes back in, he's wearing some soft linen pants.

And nothing else.

I clear my throat. "Much better."

I pat the bedroll next to me and lie back. Riley lies on his right side facing me, propped up on his elbow.

After a few moments of silence and letting our eyes adjust to the darkness, I reach up and gently start tracing the lines of his face. He freezes for a moment, then relaxes, and I can see his eyes close in the shadows.

Riley has nice skin, though I wish I could see his freckles in this dim light. I'm alternating between using the tips of my fingers and the side of them to brush and stroke along his face.

I shimmy over so that I'm slightly underneath him. "You should kiss me," I whisper. His eyes pop open as my hand is mid-stroke around his eyebrow.

"No, I don't think I should, Firecat," he whispers back. "Anyway, you made me promise."

"Kissing isn't fucking," I complain, as my fingers move from trailing around his ear to spearing into his hair so I can grip and pull him down onto me.

With his body weight on me, bracing himself on his elbows on either side of me, I release the grip I have on his hair. I move so he's resting more comfortably between my legs, bringing my left leg up to a knee so the fabric of his pants brushes the inside of my naked thigh.

My arm is hooked under his, reaching up his back so I can drag my nails down his skin. I lift my mouth up and place a tiny, delicate kiss on his jaw below his ear, as I scrape my nails downward.

He shudders. "Is this you or the alcohol in control?"

"It doesn't matter," I whisper as I nip a trail along his jaw toward his chin.

"I think you'll feel differently in the morning."

"I don't care."

"I do."

I capture his mouth with mine, and he immediately kisses me back with the same fervor. Pausing briefly for a breath, my tongue flicks out to his bottom lip as he grabs my jaw with his hand, using his thumb to open my mouth wider. Then, he fills me, and I can't tell where my tongue ends, and he begins. Did I bite my own lip, or was that him?

His hand moves from my face and trails down the side of my body, dragging his fingernails along the skin of my bare hip down my right leg. He flattens his palm and grips the bottom of my calf, hooking my leg around him. His calloused skin and the warmth from his hand have the heat between my legs screaming in response.

Riley slides his hand back over my leg and stops as he grips my ass, rocking once into me. I moan a little into his mouth, and I try to arch myself up to press against his hardening length. He grips me harder as he dips his head down to nibble my neck, scraping his teeth across my skin before finishing with a kiss.

I need. *I need.* I reach down to where his hand is still tightly gripping my ass and slowly try to slide his hand around to where I need him most. Riley must understand because he grabs my hand and moves it to pin my arm above my head, shifting his weight on me.

"That is not kissing, Firecat," he growls.

"It's not fucking," I protest.

"You don't think I could fuck you with my fingers?" he says, as his teeth close on my earlobe with a satisfying sting.

His hand moves from my pinned arm, sliding back down and giving my breast a small squeeze which has another restrained moan escaping my lips. With my left arm now free, I use both hands to grip his face.

I'm trying to see his eyes, but I don't know why. I've always hated the way it makes me feel to look into another person's eyes for too long. Like I'm greedy, like I'm trying to take something from them. It's hard in this fucking dark cave, but I do see them. Part of me expected to see a truth not spoken, or the revelation that he isn't really here with me. But it's…Riley, and the relief is staggering.

Relishing in the small intimacy of locking eyes is followed by the pleasure of him gripping my waist and rocking into me once more, his cock pulsing his own need. I consume his mouth again with another kiss, and immediately need his perfectly soft lips touching every inch of my skin.

My left hand is gripping his shoulder while I let the other press against his chest. I swiftly slide my hand down between us, straight into the loosening waistband of his pants. I grip his length, a jolt of shock at the sheer size of him causing me to dig my nails into his shoulder. I let out the tiniest of moans again.

"*Fuck,*" Riley groans softly, breath hot on my lips.

He presses his forehead down onto mine with his eyes squeezed shut, breathing heavily. I stroke his cock fully, a bead of wetness already at the head.

With a hard exhale, Riley extricates my hand and rolls me onto my side with my back to him, then clamps me into a bear hug from behind. "Time to sleep, Firecat," he says hoarsely into the back of my head.

I'm pretty sure I whimper in protest, but the warmth of him wrapping around me and a sense of pure comfort and safety takes over, and I slip into delicious unconsciousness.

CHAPTER SEVENTEEN

here are my pants? Pants. Pants. I'm chanting in my head as I fumble around the empty sleeping alcove.

"The water canteen is against the wall to your left," Riley calls out from the main area.

I'm immediately aware of how dry my mouth is, along with my pounding headache. "Ugh."

I crawl out of the dark alcove, like a monster from a nightmare, squinting at the too-bright light. Crouching on my knees, I glare around at the mess. Why are my clothes everywhere? My eyes widen…

"What happened last night?" I rasp.

"What do you remember?" I can hear the humor in his voice.

Hot. I remember being too hot. Touching Riley's face… he has nice skin. Riley's weight on me…oh fuck! I look over at him in alarm.

He gives me a small smile. "Nothing happened. You were in perfect control." He nods his head toward my pants on the ground as he stirs whatever he's cooking for breakfast. "It's too hot for leathers and thick clothes."

He's only in linen pants and a light tunic, so I grab my own pair of light pants and throw them on before heading to the privy.

When I return, Riley hands me a bowl with a meager portion of breakfast. It's oats with nuts and what looks like some spices swirled through.

I smirk as I take the bowl. "This looks nice, thank you."

"Yes, okay. You were right. Food is better with flavor," he quips with a grin before shoveling food into his mouth from what's left in the pot. We eat in silence as I try to concentrate through the pounding at my temples. The food only marginally helps.

I spot the empty liquor bottle resting against the wall near the entrance. "We drank the whole bottle?" I whine.

"I think it would be more accurate to say *you* drank the whole bottle, but yes, we finished it."

"And how come you look as fresh as a daisy, and I feel like a shriveled-up piece of jerky?"

Riley snorts. "Maybe because you drank three times as much as me and I'm three times the size of you? How's the head?"

I grunt in response, massaging my temples.

"Here." Riley moves forward, pulls my hands away, and starts rubbing his hands together while crouching in front of me. "Close your eyes."

"Why?" I ask dubiously, and he rolls his eyes.

"Fine, leave them open." He places his surprisingly warm and steady hands over my eyes and sweeps them slowly around to my ears.

The only sounds to be heard is our breathing and Riley repeating the actions of warming his hands and softly bringing them back to my eyes and ears. My eyes are closed; this would have been weird—*weirder*—with them open. After only a couple of minutes, I realize that the pounding in my head has stopped.

"How?" I ask incredulously as I touch my ears like I'll be able to sense some kind of Divine Gift he left behind.

He shrugs. "My father used to do this for me when I was a teenager, and it always worked. It just forces you to relax, I think," he says with a small smile that doesn't reach his eyes.

He sits back against the wall opposite me, as I roll my shoulders. "Not your mother?"

"Uh, no. I mean, she used to when I was very young if I had a headache," he says with a small humorless laugh. "But no. By the time I was getting hangovers at sixteen, my mother wasn't coming anywhere near me."

"Wait. Your father was doing this when you were a teenager because you were *hungover*?" I can't hide anything in my voice.

"It was after my brother died. After I killed him."

I'm gaping. Mouth wide open like a stunned pond fish in Laguz. Riley is busying himself using sand and a rag to clean our breakfast from the dishes. "Do you know the story?" he asks quietly, not looking at me.

I don't. I know the first-born Prince Ofnemoris died. I know that it was a decade and a half past, and the young Prince Aurelius was only a teenager. Riley's twin, Amarilyss, was still in Osraed as a Patron and their youngest sister, Nemuel, was not yet born.

But no. Not much is said about it other than it being a tragedy. "I don't know much or haven't heard much. I heard King Dillon had to take over royal duties for a few moons while the queen grieved."

Riley nods. "Lyss didn't even know she had an older

brother when we were able to get her back. It broke my mother's heart all over again to tell her. Perhaps Lyss already realized, but it's different gaining a family only to lose a brother you didn't get to meet. Nemuel didn't get to meet him either. I robbed them both."

Riley scrubs the same part of the pot over and over as he speaks. I want to still his hands, but maybe keeping his hands busy is stopping him from unraveling. I can relate.

He looks at me then, eyes glassy, searching my face. "I killed him, and my mother wishes it was me who died instead," he announces, then he drops everything and stands —well, as much as he can in here—before crawling into the sleeping alcove.

Well, fuck me, what do I do *now?*

I crawl to the entrance of the alcove and sit leaning against the curved wall. I can hear his shuddering breath, but can barely see anything other than a large, silhouetted lump in the middle of the cave.

"I killed someone the season after I turned thirteen," I offer, and then want to smack myself in the head because this isn't a competition. Idiot. Plus, hello? I'm an assassin. *Of course* he knows I've killed people.

"Who?" he asks, clearing his throat.

"Someone I let hurt me too many times."

"*Hurt you, how?*" His voice is demanding though still whispered.

"It doesn't matter now."

"Did you care for them?"

I pause, his shaky voice wreaking all kinds of havoc inside of me. "In a way. Maybe before."

"Do you regret it?"

Well, that's the question, isn't it? Do I? That single act is what started a career of being a killer-for-hire. The catalyst for turning me into the monster I am today. But I cannot regret that he no longer lives.

I'm still mulling over how to answer, chewing on it like a piece of tough meat, turning it over and over in my head, when Riley's voice startles me. "I've spent the last fifteen revolutions regretting everything and wishing it had been me, instead of Dex, who died."

Whatever I was going to say in answer to his question vanishes from my mouth. I crawl into the cave, my hand finding Riley's knee in the dark. I shimmy up next to him, not actually touching, but close enough.

"How did he die? I thought it was an accident?"

Riley takes a long breath in and slowly lets it shudder out of his nose. "I was a terror child and an even worse teen. Declan—Dex—was the cool-headed one. Smart, funny… kind. No matter how much of an asshole I was, he never treated me like the disappointment I clearly was."

Riley takes another shuddering breath, so I use the opportunity to ask, "He was older, right?"

"Yes, by five revs. Never treated me like the annoying little brother though. He was always looking out for me, like he had this sense when I was getting into trouble."

His voice is thick with emotion, though he's as still as stone while he speaks.

"That night, during a Royal Gala my parents were holding, I was angry. They'd just announced to everyone they were pregnant again. They hadn't even told me. I found out at the same time as the vapid cesspit of people they barely ever interacted with. I'm not sure if Dex knew before or not. I never had the chance to ask."

"Pregnant with Nemuel?" I ask.

He hums a confirmation. "I'm more than double her age right now. Dex was old enough to be her father then." Riley sighs with a painful quiver. "He wanted to be king, and he would have been…It's why he hadn't started his own family yet. He wanted to learn and be the very best for Nemoris." Riley clears his throat, taking a deep breath before continuing. "So, I left. Went looking for the kind of trouble that can only be found in the back alleys of Nemoris Castle City. Didn't take too long, of course. I always sought out groups of young men, keeping my identity hidden." He lets out an angry snort. "They don't fight when they know you're a prince," he says with disgust, but I think it was aimed at himself.

"This time was different, too many in the group. I'd picked a fight I wasn't going to win. I don't remember if it was a conscious decision to pick a fight I knew I'd lose. But I definitely didn't know my brother had followed me and would jump in to help."

I'm holding my breath. This story had never made it to the public. Granted, I was still in the children's compound in Osraed when it all happened, but not even the rumors mentioned any of this.

"As soon as he joined the fight with the kids—and they *were* kids—the one I was fighting brought out a knife and stabbed me twice in the gut, and I went down. Dex screamed and took down the rest of the group before turning on the kid with the knife."

I let out the breath I'd been holding, far more audibly than I would have liked. It sounded like a whimper. I don't know if Riley even registered it; his voice now dripped with self-loathing, and he continued without missing a beat.

"All I remember from there is my brother carrying me back to the castle, to our Gifted healer. Flashes of our parents in a panic. The healer arguing with someone. Mother screaming." He lets out a half-choked sob. "I woke up a few days later, clearly healed by Gift, looking around my empty bedroom. My father entered—I assume to check on me—and I asked where Dex was. He crumbled."

Riley's voice changes after a thick swallow. He continues emotionlessly. "Dex had also sustained knife wounds and didn't tell anyone. He knew the Gifted healer would only have enough energy to heal one of us, and he'd chosen me. It wasn't until after the healing that my parents realized the extent of Dex's injuries. The regular healers tried all they could, and they sent for another Gifted healer. But they were too late. Dex died from his wounds not even half an hour after he brought me back."

Riley finishes in a tone so cold that I shiver. "If I hadn't been so selfish, Dex would be alive."

I have nothing to say. What could I say? I move up behind Riley, lying close without touching him. I'm unused to other's emotions, and touch is foreign. Unsure how to provide comfort to Riley, but wanting to do *something*, I pat him. I'm propped up on one arm, gently stroking and patting around his face and down his hair.

His breathing slows, and I'm not sure if he's asleep. We have been lying here quietly for a long time, with only the sound of me patting his head softly. "You didn't kill him. He saved you. They're not the same thing," I say, quieter than a whisper, just in case he's asleep. Just in case he wants to pretend he didn't hear me.

But he wasn't asleep, and he did hear me. He snatches my hand from the top of his head and brings it to his mouth, placing a soft kiss on my palm. He holds it there for a second longer, leaving his soft lips pressed against my skin, before letting go.

Something about the softness of the kiss reminds me of... something. Like a dream you can't quite explain to someone. Like grabbing a cloud with your bare hands only to have it slip through your fingers.

I squeeze his shoulder and then scooch myself out from behind him and move into the main area, leaving him to grieve his brother's memory.

He stays in there most of the day, or what I assume is most of the day, considering I cannot see the sunrise and sunset, and all I can hear is the wind. I make a cold meal of meat, bread, and cheese, and leave some at the alcove entrance for Riley while I eat mine alone, going over his story in my head.

I'm making jasmine tea when I hear shuffling and see Riley emerge.

"Tea?"

"Thank you," he says, taking the mug I offer. "Thank you for the food too."

"I'm sorry."

He looks at me in confusion, but before he can say anything, I follow with, "For pushing you. About the drinking, I mean. I should have been more kind." It sounds awkward to me, so it must sound the same to him.

"You didn't know who I was. I was just some drunk that was making everyone around me miserable. And you were right. I haven't forgotten the words you said to me after you found me asleep, *drunk*, on watch, a couple of moons past."

"I didn't think you remembered."

"Oh, I remember." He touches his cheekbone where there was once a bruise. Something about the memory makes me cringe now. So prone to violence even when someone is clearly hurting. I don't say anything. I know what I said. I'm not sure which part he's repeating to himself, and I'm not about to ask.

"It's hard remembering, I swear the pain is as sharp as it was fifteen revs past. The alcohol makes it easy to forget. Makes it easier to think without feeling too. The thought of losing *another* sibling is…" He clears his throat and takes a deep breath. "But it also makes me feel like I'm asleep…in a constant waking nightmare."

He looks at me then, my rage strangling my heart into a painful ache with the intensity of the pain reddening his eyes. "You have nothing to be sorry for, Firecat. *I'm* sorry."

CHAPTER EIGHTEEN

The next two nights and days are uneventful. We eat, we sleep, we talk about nothing important, and we wait for the wind to die down. In the middle of our third night, rough hands grip my shoulders and I hear someone saying my name.

"What's going on?" I ask in sleepy delirium.

"You were thrashing about—I caught an elbow in the face," he says in a voice I can't quite decipher. "Are you okay? Nightmare?"

Was it a nightmare? I have nightmares often. But…*this* was no nightmare. I remember lips against my neck, strong hands gripping my calf, my hand clawing down a back…Riley's back. That was more than a dream: it was a memory. The rest of it came flooding back in an overwhelming rush.

I do something against my better judgment and reach for Riley. He barely has a moment to register what I'm doing—that I'm trying to undress him while undressing myself, while also trying to kiss him. But in a matter of seconds, he's pulled me on top of him, both of his hands in my hair as he kisses me roughly.

"You lied to me," I breathe, catching a moment without his lips on mine. "You said nothing happened." I have enough room to be half sitting up, straddling his growing bulge through his pants.

"I didn't lie. Nothing happened," he says through a grin while my hands are holding his face, and he's slowly lifting my tunic up, exposing the stretchy fabric around my chest.

He pulls off my tunic as he tries to sit up and remove his own, but I have to help him because the cave ceiling is so low.

"Is this still nothing?" I ask him as he's gripping my thighs, and I grind against him, causing a moan to escape from his lips. He laughs as he roughly thrusts his full erection against my growing wet heat in reply, both of us still infuriatingly clothed from the waist down.

I growl as I grab his face again, taking a moment to smooth the hair away so I can see him properly. I need to see him, see his eyes again. Maybe I *am* greedy. Maybe I do want to take something from him. Or maybe I want to give him something of me instead. Enough light filters in that I can see his eyes, and I lean down to kiss his bottom lip, and then his top lip.

He's reaching up to undo the fabric trapping my breasts. I let him, my heart skipping. He pulls me forward until I'm leaning on my elbows above his face. One of his hands grips my ribs while the other runs a thumb over the small mound and across one of my nipples, which has already puckered in response. He flicks a tongue to the other breast before kissing it fully, pinching the nipple between his lips and teeth, making me gasp.

Heat licks up and down my spine, and I can't catch my breath.

Riley reaches back up to my face and pulls me down so he can kiss me, an intoxicating blend of forceful need and gentle wanting. His other hand is gripping my waist, and my brain is overwhelmed.

I shift all the way back to straddle his thighs, running my hands down his well-defined chest and over his abdomen, caressing every single muscle. A slight fuzz of chest hair trickles down the center and disappears underneath his pants.

Two raised scars an inch long mar the otherwise smooth skin near the left side of his navel. I kiss a line from the middle of his chest until I reach the scars, and I kiss them once each before moving down further toward the top of his pants.

Is Riley even breathing? Am I pushing this too far?

"Are you okay?" I ask, little more than a whisper between kisses.

"No," he breathes. "You've done something to me, Firecat. I don't think I'll recover."

I falter. I can't tell if he means this is good or bad when I can't see him properly in the inky darkness. My mouth is poised to ask when I hear voices.

Beans is calling our names, and that's when I realize I can't hear the wind. It's stopped. *Oh, Divine fuck.* Riley must have had the same thought because we're both *scrambling*, getting dressed, and calling back to Beans. Within minutes we're both dressed, packed, and outside greeting Beans and Bitty, at what looks like the early stages of sunrise.

Bitty.

Bitty with the *Gift of hearing*.

I look at Bitty, trying to discern if they heard anything, but I get nothing.

"Good to see you're both well. It's been a long few days," Riley says, clapping Beans on the back. "Everything okay?"

"Totally fine!" says Bitty a little too brightly, flicking their eyes to me briefly, and I know. I know right then, that Bitty heard *something*. What, I'm not sure, but it's enough that Bitty can't even look at Riley or myself, and they are definitely a little warm in the cheek.

"Uh, so I can hear Tovi just down there and she's looking for us," they say, as if I need a reminder of how good their Gift of hearing is.

I chance a look at Riley to see if he's as mortified as I am, but he's not. He's smiling. Smiling *widely*, in fact. "Well, let's get going," he chimes.

After quickly replenishing our caves with firewood, we meet up with Tovi without incident. Tovi looks even grumpier than usual, which I wouldn't have thought possible.

"I need a bath," she demands. "We all do," she says, as she rumples her nose and looks at each of us.

Can she smell that Riley and I almost had sex? I'll have to make sure I don't let her touch *any* objects from our cave for a while, lest she *feel* something about what was going on in there through her Gift. She uses my shoulder as an armrest as we listen to Beans and Bitty discuss which way to go.

Thankfully, we reach Waadi in less than half a day. We all get individual rooms so we can bathe in peace. Mine and Bitty's rooms are next to each other on the bottom floor, while the other three are spread above on the next level.

I fall asleep for a couple hours after having a thorough wash, including my hair. When I finally wake up, change and wash my clothes, it's dinner time. Bitty and Beans are sitting at a table near a window and wave me over, the colors of dusk in the sky. Tovi has already eaten and retired for the night and neither of them has seen Riley.

Despite the heat, we have the roast special. It doesn't specify the animal, only that it's roast meat and vegetables with gravy. My mouth salivates at the thought. It could be horse or snowolf or even fish, and I'd be happy to eat it. And I really hate fish.

I ask for a second helping of the roast potatoes, and the server kid gives me a knowing smile. A few minutes later, he's back with a *giant* plate of roast potatoes and a boat of gravy. He looks as proud as can be as he sets it on the table for us.

"I hope you're not getting yourself in trouble," I whisper with reproach looking up at him, and he gives me a quick shake of his head, brown hair flopping about. The kid is probably taller than me. I slip him a few sneaky coppers and I am rewarded with his cheeky smile widening to show his two front teeth have only just started to grow in.

We dig into the potatoes, thoroughly enjoying the gluttonous indulgence.

The three of us are nursing our stuffed bellies when Riley joins us. He has the roast special as well and looks to be well-rested. I keep stealing looks at him as the table discusses nothing of importance. A flash of something—possibly my never-ending rage—kicks inside my gut every time I look at him.

Riley catches my eyes on him. He winks, and I turn away quickly as heat instantly engulfs every part of me. The next time he holds my gaze until I have to respond to something Bitty asks me. The final time, he's already looking at me. When I meet his eyes, he smirks, and I squeeze my legs together to ease the desire beginning to burn. I'm flummoxed and excited at the same time.

I'm deliberately *not* looking at Riley when I spot a slimy, greenish-brown colored splotch on the tavern floor. My rage springs to the surface as the hairs on my arms rise. Surreptitiously looking around, I spot the Erduborn man who laughs like a duck from the tavern on the Nemoris side of Teorann—the one who spread the ugly rumor that I confronted Riley about. He's downing the last of a beer, and I try to watch him leave.

He's out of sight, but my rage is fueling my instincts already, and I know I'm going to put my sneaksuit on tonight. It's too late for him to be traveling anywhere, and not much is in or around Waadi. I can't see any of the other men from his table, so maybe it's just him.

The sun had already started to set when I first woke up, so I quickly say goodnight to the table before dashing off. It's not until I'm stripping off my clothes in my room that I remember Riley. I had started to wonder if he would come to my room tonight. Or maybe I would go to his. But I can't now—I *need* to know if it's the same man from Teorann.

Sneaksuit on and kajal blackening the skin around my eyes, I'm relieved to see a moonless sky. I do a full perimeter check, looking for places to people-watch. I note all possible exits and entrances and the roads in and out of town. After an hour of scouting, I settle on the stable as a good spot to wait. I'll be able to see the comings and goings of everyone in the inn and most of the rooms. That is *if* he's even staying here. I haven't seen any sign of him since the first glimpse inside the tavern.

A dark spot at the side of the stable allows me some cover as I climb to the top. Once I reach the roof, I find a comfortable position, grateful that it isn't a Nemoris-cold evening. I have a clear view of most of the rooms on this side and the main entrance into the tavern.

Lots of people are coming in and out, and the clientele is getting drunker and drunker. Beans and Bitty have retired to bed now, both their lights extinguished within a few minutes, and Tovi's has been off the whole time. I haven't seen Riley.

Jaena taught me how to use my rage to focus. I described all the feelings I'd had, and she was the one who said I had to control that rage and use the power it gives me. Most of being a spy, and even an assassin, is waiting. My rage keeps me awake and alert.

I finally locate Riley, but instead of heading to his own room, a stunning Erduborn woman is leading him to hers.

She's exceptionally tall, with tanned olive skin and big, beautiful eyes. Her hair is the color of melted cacote, falling in perfect waves down to her waist. In typical Erdu fashion, she's covered in all kinds of metal jewelry: bracelets and bangles up her arms, multiple necklaces, and earrings, and even some pieces woven into her hair.

Riley is clearly trying to be sneaky, and she seems to enjoy being part of the tryst. Both of them keep looking around to make sure they aren't seen or followed before making a dash up to her room. Fortunately for them, the inn's rooms all have their entrances outside.

He follows her into the room, and I watch as the curtains are drawn so that no one, including me, will be able to see what they are doing. But I know what they are doing.

Why does it bother me so much? Nothing truly happened between us, as Riley said. It's not as though we have made any promises or have had a chance to be alone since. *Though he's found a way to be alone with another woman.*

It was all a game from the beginning.

Yet I still crave—*craved*—his touch.

CHAPTER NINETEEN

I swallow, pushing everything I'm feeling down into the vast void of darkness within me. Everything about this situation, about Riley, about whatever the fuck is going on in that room. I opt for a new vantage point to people-watch instead.

I swing down from my perch on top of the stable roof and land softly on the sandy dirt in my pocket of darkness. Hearing a loud huff, I make the decision to visit the horses. Applemint wasn't with me long, but I miss the companionship.

I sneak in and make sure none of the stable kids are around before sticking my head in the first stall to greet the horse inside. A massive sack of broken carrot pieces had sat at the entrance, so I double back for them, making my way around to feed one to each horse.

Their velvet-soft lips and their spiky whiskers bring me joy for a reason I don't fully understand. After giving each one some attention, I should go, but as I turn to leave, the large chestnut brown pony with fluffy ears nips at my shoulder.

"Sorry, sweet girl, no more carrots," I whisper as I cuddle into her. She rests her head over my shoulder, allowing me to cuddle her, and I breathe in her musky animal scent while stroking down her long neck.

I'm startled by a laugh that sounds like a duck, much closer than I would like. I had been so transfixed by the pony that I was being a terrible sneak. Realizing I won't have the opportunity to leave, I slip into the pony's stall. Crouching behind the partitioned wall, watching through the cracks in the wood, I'm able to see two men enter.

By sheer dumb luck, it's the Erduborn man from Nemoris Teorann with the duck laugh. Was he following us? It surely cannot be a coincidence that he's here, even if he is Erduborn. The two men stand inside, near the entrance to the stables.

"Nah, we can't wait that long," the man—who I have decided I will call Duckhead—says to his companion. "We're leaving soon and need to have that cart good to go. Don't need to be a good one, just needs to get as far as Forsto."

"Mm. Mm. How much we talkin'? I have a single horse cart that'll do the trick," says Duckhead's companion. "It's light. Your pony could pull it."

I hope they don't intend to get the pony right now, as I'm fairly certain my stall mate is the only pony in the stables. The pony tries to nibble and pull at the fabric covering my feet, reminding me of Applemint's cheeky spirit.

"I was going to sell her, but that might work better now I think it. Show me. How much?" Duckhead is muttering as he and his companion leave the stable the way they'd come.

I stay long enough I can no longer hear them before giving the pony a little kiss goodbye on her cheek.

"I hope Duckhead treats you well my little friend. Would you tell me if he was up to something nefarious if you could?" She blows a puff of hot air out of her nose in response, and I chuckle. One more kiss and I sneak out of the stable successfully.

I'm standing in my pocket of darkness—deciding whether to go to bed, try to find Duckhead, report to Beans, or find a new spying spot—when the door to Riley's friend's room opens. A warm beam of light spills out as the woman sticks her head out and looks around. Checking for witnesses, I guess.

With the coast clear, Riley comes out while swinging his jacket on. He kisses the woman on the cheek, and she reaches up with one hand to cup his face and says something softly to him.

Unable to bear the display of affection, or my own volatile emotions beginning to rise, I turn around and melt into the shadows.

I do another perimeter check, seeing if I can find Duckhead or his companion. Seeing what looks like a small, single horse-pulled cart out the front of one of the inn's rooms, I hoist myself up a tree for a new vantage point, with a full view of the room and cart.

The night passes with no movement, and I need at least a little sleep so I'm not useless tomorrow. I'll wake up early and come back. Stumbling into my room, I don't bother taking off my sneaksuit or cleaning the kajal from my face before passing out.

THE MORNING COMES MUCH TOO QUICKLY, though the sun has not yet fully risen. I'm washed, packed, and ready to go, so I leave my bags outside my door as I go to check on the cart. It's gone, along with the pony from the stable. I can't be sure when they left, but I hope it's a good thing that they've left before us.

Beans' lantern light is shining through his window, so I knock gently on his door. Going downstairs together, I decide against telling him about Duckhead. I'm not used to working with a team, and I don't want to tell any of them. The fact Riley would know I was out sneaking and may have seen him with the Erduborn woman is something I want to avoid.

The kitchen isn't open, but they offer us some warm oat muffins and fresh fruit. We happily accept, taking portions for the others, too. Tovi and Bitty arrive next, and Tovi has a scowl on her face until she sees the food. She steals a piece of melon from my plate and sticks her tongue out.

"Everyone sleep well?" Tovi asks with a yawn. "You'd think I wouldn't be tired, seeing as I went to bed before the sun set." At least it won't be too obvious how tired I am with everyone having a terrible night's sleep.

This starts a conversation about how uncomfortable the mattresses were before I'm distracted by Riley sauntering in. He holds my stare, a smile starting to curve his lips before I quickly look away.

"Good morning, my Divine friends!" Riley announces cheerfully as he plonks into the seat across from me.

"Ew, why are you so happy?" Tovi asks in disgust.

With a mouthful of oat muffin, Riley says, "Can't a man be in a good mood for no reason?"

Riley's eyes are on me, though I'm discussing training techniques with Bitty. Tovi and Beans are arguing about something, and Bitty joins in, defending Tovi.

I check, and yes, Riley is still looking at me. He leans forward on his elbows, resting his mouth in his hands, though I can see the smirk underneath. Knowing he's caught my eye finally, he does a double eyebrow wiggle at me, and I frown at him in response. My core is apparently not up to speed about how *not* interested we are in Riley, the heat sending a flush through me.

What a piece of work. I'm not sure if he's really that conceited or if he thinks I am an idiot.

As we all gear up and start to file out, Riley leans over and whispers conspiratorially. "You must have fallen asleep quickly last night." His hand brushes my lower back to try and guide me away from exiting with the others.

"What do you mean?" I ask, confused, moving away from his touch.

"I came to see you…I knocked, but you didn't answer."

Still confused and aware that we are the only ones left in the tavern, I ask, "When?"

He laughs, looking slightly unsure of himself. "Last night. I waited about half an hour after you left dinner, and then…" He clears his throat and gestures at nothing before running a hand through his deep red hair with a sheepish grin.

Last night, when I was doing a perimeter check and wasn't even *in* my room. So, he did come like I had hoped last night. But when he didn't find me, he found someone else instead. Catching me off guard, the crash of rage inside my chest almost buckles my knees.

"I'm sure you managed to find other entertainment," I snap in a whisper, as Tovi yells from outside.

"Are you two dawdling fucks coming or what?"

"Coming!" I call, making a beeline for the door, not waiting for Riley.

THAT NIGHT AT CAMP, after a hard slog in the heat, Riley keeps stealing looks at me. I've avoided his eye the entire time, making sure he and I are never alone together, despite how much he keeps trying to orchestrate it.

"I'll help you cook." Riley offers in front of everyone, while I turn the skinned hare he caught for our dinner over the fire.

I make a sharp sound out of my mouth. "I think we would like to enjoy our dinner tonight, Riley."

"I second that, Mika. Riley, it's not worth it! For us, I mean," Beans adds, clapping the prince on his shoulders, and Riley elbows him in the ribs.

Tovi, not looking at anyone, sighs in agreement. "I hate to admit it, but I don't think I'll ever be able to have camp food that Mika hasn't made ever again. Riley, I can't let you ruin this for me."

"The people have spoken, Riley. You're to stay five to ten feet away from me and my cooking."

"I was just trying to help!" Riley whines, not taking his searching eyes off me.

I exaggerate a grimace at him. "Yeh…" I drawl, "I don't think you *try* hard enough."

Riley's brow furrows as I hold his eye for long enough that he's confused about what we are really talking about before I quickly dash my eyes away. Beans' laughter booms about the canyons below us.

"I'm less disappointed about there not being a Gifted finder or someone to see through walls now—Mika is much more entertaining!" Bitty says, trying to stifle a laugh while poking a stick into the fire.

"*What*." Not a question. A *demand* slices through my teeth.

The jovial air is immediately soured, and all of their

faces have dropped from humorous expressions to bewildered at why I'm glaring at Bitty.

"Uh…I just mean that when they came to Osraed to ask for a finder or someone Gifted with seeing through walls, that I'm glad you and your talents were offered instead." I can see the apprehension and confusion on Bitty's face as they're speaking, eyes darting around, seeking backup and support from the others.

"Was Hastieni unavailable for hire? Or did you want someone permanent?" I'm surprised at how breathless I sound.

Now Bitty's face is confused. "Who's Hastieni?"

Blowing slowly out of my nose and trying not to lose my temper entirely, I explain through gritted teeth. "Hastieni is the Ofosraed Gifted finder for hire. Was he unavailable, or were you looking for someone to purchase and not hire? Why did you ask for me?" Though Hastieni is an item finder, I am sure he would have been of some use.

"We didn't ask for you, we didn't even realize that Osraed had a finder for hire. The council president suggested you specifically, after we explained what we needed," Beans offers in his smooth baritone that suddenly grates on my nerves. He sounds far too calm when a storm is raging inside my chest and ears.

"No. You asked for me, and the council voted to allow the sale." I state this as fact, though I can hear the fallacy of it as it unravels on my tongue.

Silence.

After far too many heartbeats, Beans speaks, softer than I imagined he could with that deep voice. "Mika, we had no idea who you were. President Jaena said she had a Null that was an excellent sneak with exceptional fighting abilities who we could purchase, albeit for more gold than we had planned on spending. She said you had the perfect skill set, even for a Null. We agreed, got the queen's seal to sign the bill of sale, and then said we'd be back in five days to collect you. As far as I am aware, there wasn't a vote."

I don't remember when I stood up. I'm staring at the fire, trying not to look at anyone, so they cannot see the pure and unbridled fury dancing like the flames in my eyes, though my fisted hands would give me away.

"Does this mean you had no idea who you were actually purchasing? The reason *why* I was worth more gold than a typical Null?"

Riley speaks for the first time. "What do you mean 'who'? We knew your name from the bill of sale, and your abilities were detailed by the president. We knew who you were."

"She means you didn't know you had purchased the Silent Assassin," Tovi says, picking her nails with a knife and not looking up.

Bitty openly gapes at Tovi, and then me. "*You're* the Silent Assassin?" Bitty says with an endearing amount of childlike excitement, before whipping their head back around to accuse Tovi. "And you *knew*?!"

The barest of shrugs lifts Tovi's shoulder as she raises one of her sharp eyebrows at Bitty.

I'm pacing. My skin is prickled and on fire. My heart is beating like it's trying to escape my chest so it can self-immolate in the campfire. "You purchased the most hated and feared assassin in all of the Divine world, and you didn't even know it?" I'm not speaking to anyone directly, and every word I say is a sucker punch to my own stomach. "You didn't know. You haven't known this whole time." I'm rambling now, trying to piece together everything while a fog of fury starts to choke me. "I have to…I need to…"

"Do you want to spar?"

I spin myself back to look at Riley, who is already standing, and gives me a nod to direct me behind him.

Beans growls. "Riley…"

"Yes." Without looking at anyone or giving Beans time to throw a wet blanket onto what I know I need right now, I stride directly through them toward the clearing Riley gestured to.

CHAPTER TWENTY

I wouldn't call it a clearing, so much as slightly flattened ground with no sudden death drops in the immediate vicinity. I spin around, rolling my shoulders. I'm far too tense, like a too-tightly-wound string instrument.

Riley isn't far behind and is removing his leathers and tunic, revealing his bare chest. An unnecessary distraction that I cannot fully appreciate. But I do catch a glimpse of his scars, and my heart and stomach temporarily swap places. This enrages me further, and I'm vibrating with the fury I need to unleash.

The rest of the group has taken up positions among the trees to spectate. Beans is standing on the edge of the clearing with his arms crossed, possibly ready to step in if it gets too violent or out of control. To be fair, he did just learn that I'm the Silent Assassin. *Fuck.*

Not giving Riley any more time to undress, I launch myself at him with the frenzied wrath I wish I could aim at Jaena.

Jaena. The lying, betraying, deceiving, cozen piece of Gifted shit.

I swing a fist, but he blocks, trying to land an uppercut in my stomach before I parry out of the way. Riley cracks his neck and then begins to cautiously walk toward me, fists up.

Spinning with a jump, I connect my heel to the back of his head before he has a chance to deflect. I'm a fraction too slow and cop his fist to the side of my face. He's tempering his blows which only makes my rage soar.

"Fight me properly!" I scream.

The fight is similar to the night he was unwell in Nemoris and we fought blow for blow, yet where that was about movement, this is about violence.

They know I am the Silent Assassin.

My reputation is known across the world.

I've had people spit at me when they put a face to the name.

He lands another tempered blow, a kick to my thigh, and I scream with all the rage in my chest. A flurry of my punches and kicks land before his elbow smashes squarely into my top lip. I spin and kick him again, *hard*, and he stumbles into a tree.

Revs. *Revolutions,* I have accepted being the hated one, the feared one. A cautionary tale for some, and a novelty to others. I haven't fucked anyone since my coming-of-age, and I moved into my own apartment. After the second time a man announced while doing his trousers back up, that his friends won't believe he bedded the Silent Assassin, I was done. They stopped trying after it got around I cut off someone's balls. It didn't happen. I started that rumor myself.

Tasting blood, I launch myself in the air to use the trunk of the tree as a springboard. Kicking off and reaching for the lowest hanging branch, I swing myself onto his shoulders. Cutting off his air with my legs while still gripping the branch, Riley becomes a deadweight too heavy for me.

Unable to unwind myself fast enough, I land on the ground with him.

A group of three men were *stupid* enough to think they should "teach me a lesson" a couple of revolutions before I spread the rumor. I let them get close enough that they thought they had me, my wrists held behind my back by two of them. I could've gotten away from them easily, long before then, and not let it get to that point...I didn't need to resort to the measures I took.

But I *wanted* them to try.

As the man who wasn't holding me unbuckled his pants, I attacked. It wasn't slow enough to be wholly cruel, but I made sure they knew their painful deaths were coming. And that I had planned it all along. Three murders that wouldn't be linked to the Silent Assassin.

Riley punches me in the ribs as I try to roll away from him quickly, the full force knocking the air out of me but giving me momentum to wrap my legs around his arm. I pull tightly, knowing this will be the end because his arm will break if he doesn't concede. He taps my leg with his hand calling his defeat.

I release Riley's arm but we both don't move from our tangled position. His arm is still resting between my legs, while my left leg is draped over his chest. He starts to shake. Worried I've hit him in the head too hard and he's seizing, I scramble to sit up over him.

He's laughing. A breathless, throaty laugh with a sparkle in his forest green eyes. I'm still hovering over him, kneeling on one side of his ribs while crouched on my foot on the other. His laughter has me mesmerized until a drop of blood from my lip or nose splashes onto his cheek and surprises us both.

He thumbs my blood off his skin in a sweep and then reaches up to my face to wipe it gently onto my cheek. His warm hand brushes my ear as he lingers, one finger tracing over the shell of my ear.

"You can have that back, Firecat," he whispers, looking at me with something I don't understand. It looks affectionate. His touch *feels* affectionate.

I'm not falling for this again. I stand abruptly, growling. I spin around to stalk off, nearly running into the other three.

"All good?" Beans asks with raised eyebrows and concern crinkling around his eyes.

"I'm going down to the water," is all I manage to croak out, before taking off at a sprint in the direction of the creek.

I'm crashing through the trees and uneven ground, picking up pace. I'm trying to outrun the cacophony of sound in my chest, and I need to go faster to do that. I'm launching myself over the giant cracks in the earth and dead trees felled by the constantly shifting ground.

It only takes one careless foot placement, and I'm thrown sideways, my hip smashing into a log as I tip over it. My body flips and I land on my back with one leg hanging over the log, reminding me of how it hung over Riley's chest only moments before.

I'm heaving, trying to catch my breath, but it's proving impossible. Especially as angry tears sting my eyes. I'm gulping in air trying to stop myself—I will not let the first time I cry in almost two decades be because of this.

"If you can hear me, Bitty. Please don't say anything. I'm fine. Just let me be," I choke out between gasping, tearful breaths.

Fairly sure that I'm no longer going to cry, I drape my arm over my eyes and lay there, the creek forgotten. I've never let anyone get under my skin the way I've let this group. The way I've let Riley. Yet I'm constantly surprised by it. A sure sign of insanity.

I hate him.

I'm going over every meaningful interaction I've had with the four of them, needing to reanalyze it with the new knowledge that they had no idea who I really was. My rage thunders in my chest all the way down to my stomach, making me nauseous. Every secret they trusted me with, every moment of laughter and affection, all based on the wrong truth. I didn't lie, but rage gets stuck in my throat as if I did.

"Are you dead?" Tovi asks in her typical disinterested voice. I didn't even hear her approach—she sure is light on her feet for a woman of six-foot.

"Napping," I reply curtly as I shift my arm so I can make out her leaning against a tree by my leg. She plonks herself heavily onto the log my other leg is resting over, leaning back against the tree again.

She's looking out toward the direction of the water, her beautiful violet eyes scanning the horizon. Her face is calm, not as rigid and harsh as when I first met her. A slight softness in her features contrasts with her disinterested tone. "That was quite a show. The outburst, not the fight."

"I'm here for your entertainment, Tovi."

"At least your sarcasm isn't broken. Your face might be, though."

We sit in silence for a couple of minutes. *Is she making sure I don't run away?*

"So, you really thought we knew?" she asks, to which I gesture with my free hand to indicate I know I'm an idiot. "You should get laid," she adds.

I lift my arm completely away from my face and push myself up, so I can glare at her. "What, and why?"

"Releases tension, and you are…*tense*."

"Thanks for the advice. I'll make sure to ask one of the many suitors lining up."

"I'd suggest Riley, he's usually good for a quick *release*. But he seems to have gone off sex," she says, frowning in what looks like confusion.

I squint at her, not sure if this is a game or if she's actually trying to make me feel better. Did Riley tell her what happened between us? Maybe she picked up on it. I groan internally at the thought. "I wouldn't sleep with him anyway." I plop back down and cover my eyes with my arm again.

"I'll ask him for you!" she chirps as she jumps up, kicks my foot so my leg falls heavily off the log, and starts trotting away.

Sitting up so quickly that my head spins, I yell after her. "Don't you fucking dare, Tovi!"

"Daddy Beans then, Firecat?" she sing-songs as she spins and takes off running back toward camp.

"Bitch better not," I grumble to myself.

Since I'm already sitting up, I get all the way up and head for the water. Hoping I'm not going to have another surprise visitor, I strip off completely and get in. The creek is shallow, but I can almost submerge my whole body if I crouch.

I didn't exactly plan this, so I wash as best I can without soap. I spot a small tree of ritha nuts not far on the other side of the creek. Deciding it's worth the naked dash, I retrieve a couple, along with a large kakahu leaf I spot on the way back. As I get back to the water, I hear a twig snap. I crouch down into the water.

"Tovi?" I call out.

There is no answer and no further noises, so I assume it was an animal. I create some soapy suds with my ritha nuts and use the kakahu leaf as a cloth. I wash my hair too, even though I only washed it last night. The ritha nuts leave me smelling like the forest—nutty, citrusy, and with a hint of honey sweetness.

Satisfied I'm no longer filthy and splattered with blood, I get out. Of course, it's not until now that I realize I have nothing clean to dry myself with. I use my shirt to dry off as best I can and don't bother putting it back on, the leathers will cover enough.

I get back as the sun sets after collecting more of the ritha nuts. Bitty, Tovi and Beans, are all laying on their bedrolls. Riley must be on watch. A plate of food has been left for me, but I can't stomach a meal right now. I hang my wet shirt over a branch to dry. Digging in my pack, I pull out my little black bag with my sneak stuff in it; a staggering reminder of my legacy and who I am.

Once an assassin, always an assassin.

Digging further, I find a dry tunic and my thinner travel pants to wear, as it's far too warm tonight for much else. The sun sets so late in Erdu that I'd forgotten it's probably well into the evening by now. I settle into my bedroll.

Bitty is already asleep. Beans and Tovi are still awake, both on their backs with one arm under their heads and staring up at the sky. Knowing I'm on last watch tonight, I'm eager to get as much sleep as possible. I close my eyes. And lie there. Awake. I hear the soft snores of Tovi as she also succumbs to sleep. While I remain awake.

I sit up, opting to stretch a bit to see if that helps. Beans' violet eyes catch mine as he also lays awake. "You okay, Mika?"

"I'm sorry, Beans. I thought you knew."

"Why are you sorry? Seems to me like we got ourselves a better deal than we realized." I open my mouth to protest, a frown pulling at my brow, but he continues in his hushed voice. "Mika, if it wasn't for you, those skin traders would have been a lot more difficult to dispatch. Bitty wouldn't be nearly as good at fighting as they are now. Riley would still be drinking. Tovi...well, Tovi would be exactly the same." He laughs softly at his own joke, sitting up.

"That's not—"

"And," he interrupts, "we would have food poisoning or have starved."

"But—"

"And." His knowing smirk lifts his mustache. "I would miss you."

We sit in silence for a second, as I move tentatively to speak, unsure if he will cut me off again. "You wouldn't miss me. You wouldn't have known me." I deflect the kind words but cannot help the warmth that thaws my cold bones.

"Not a single one of us would have it any other way. You're one of us. Now stop stretching and go to sleep, little one."

A smirk lifts my lips. "Yes, Daddy Beans." His responding snort fills me with satisfaction.

I WAKE with a gulp of air as someone touches my shoulder. Riley is kneeling beside me. The moon has barely moved across the sky; I haven't been asleep long.

"You were moaning and thrashing about. Good dream?" Riley flirts.

"No."

The tumble of memories from the dream slowly dissipates like fog in the morning sun, but enough remains for me to know it wasn't a good dream. My full bladder makes its presence known, and I tell Riley I'm going to go relieve myself. I don't bother putting my boots on, I'm not going far.

The ground is still warm from the day's sun, the sandy

earth squishing between my toes along with leaf litter and small twigs. I meander a little further than I intended, finding a tree to do my business behind while listening to the soft trickle of the creek nearby.

The creek, which is only about two feet wide and ankle deep in this part, is calming. Moonlight bounces off the tiny ripples as the water cascades over rocks and stones. I crouch to wash my hands and take a few big draughts from my cupped hands.

The ground crunches behind me as I stand up. I whip around toward the noise as a shocking pain explodes at the base of my skull. My body crumbles as I see the feet of at least four men before I hit the ground and darkness closes in.

CHAPTER TWENTY-ONE

T've been awake intermittently for a few hours now. Long enough to figure out what Duckhead's small horse cart was for: *me*. It's been raining on and off. I'm still soaked from one particularly heavy downpour that had everyone stop and run for cover for half an hour. Luckily, I had one of these disgusting hessian sacks to shield me. Or I might have only been wet, instead of wet *and* stinking like a cross between moldy potatoes and rancid grain, with a touch of drogalyf. I wouldn't mind smoking some drogalyf right now.

I wonder if it's the sweet chestnut pony pulling the cart. I hear quite a few men and horses, more than the handful I saw in Teorann all those weeks past. We travel through the night, the light under these sacks starting to turn golden from the morning. I thought that would be a good thing, the sun rising. But after only fifteen minutes of the sun beating down on the sacks, it hits me. I can now add hot, steamy, and musty to my disgusting fragrance.

I've given up pulling at my bindings. I'm hog-tied with rope, and they've taken my weapons. They even found the lockpicks I'd hidden. Or that's what I hope they were doing, since I am no longer wearing the fabric around my chest that they'd been sewn into. Not that I would have been able to reach them trussed up like this and boxed in by multiple heavy somethings.

My hands and feet are numb, my knees and shoulders aching, and my head is pounding. Plus, my wrists and ankles are rubbed raw from trying to pull myself free. I hate the smell of hessian at the best of times, but this soup of foul smells is making me want to vomit.

I'm surprisingly calm. I expected my rage to be thundering around my chest, trying to smash her way out of my throat. But not a flutter or a tingle. It's not because I feel safe, or think the others are going to save me. In fact, I'm confident they *won't* save me, given my circumstances. My rage has deserted me.

I wonder if a weather Gifted Patron is here. Rain wasn't expected, so it was mighty convenient to roll in while I was being kidnapped, washing away all traces of me.

I can see why they thought a small, pony-pulled cart would work better. Less weight and drag means less obvious tracks to follow. Thank the Divine I swallowed my pride and told the group about seeing Duckhead the other night. Oh, that's right, *no I bloody didn't*. They have no idea who's taken me. This, of course, is if they haven't all been slaughtered.

And there she is, my rage scratches at my throat and across my heart. My face is hot, and it's not from the sun hitting the sacks.

My stomach starts to cramp from hunger, thirst, and the need to relieve myself. I'm gagged with a vile piece of fabric that tastes like feet. My mouth is dry, and whenever I manage to produce any saliva, it soaks away into the gag. It's wrapped around my head too, stifling me even more than the hessian sacks. They either can't hear me, or they're ignoring my screams. I'll save my energy.

WE'VE BEEN STOPPED for around ten minutes. All the voices are muffled so I can't understand what's going on. Blinding afternoon light shocks my eyes as the sacks are ripped off me without warning. Hands roughly grab my knees, dragging me to the end of the cart. I have a moment to recognize one of the men from Teorann before he tries to haul me up and over his shoulder. I headbutt him in the nose as a thank you.

I'm thrown unceremoniously. Hog-tied, I have no way to brace myself or catch my fall as I hit the uneven ground. Pain blooms in my shoulder and the wind is knocked out of me.

"What the fuck, Kino?" demands an angry voice. Duckhead.

"Fucken' bitch headbutt me!" Kino says, then spits a wad of blood at me, hitting my jaw and neck. He stalks off and leaves me there, holding his head back to try to stem the bleeding from his nose. I hope I broke the fucker.

Duckhead crouches down in front of me, watching Kino stalk away before turning his eyes on me. He smiles unkindly, and his lip pulls up, revealing a delightful view of his rotting teeth. Adding that to my disgusting list of smells for the day.

"Has it clicked in yet, little assassin? Have you figured it all out?"

I frown at him, unable to respond. Has what clicked? That I've been kidnapped? Because I'm fairly confident I picked up on that within the first few moments I opened my eyes.

He continues, using a dirty rag to wipe Kino's bloodied

spit off me. "I'm sure you recognize me. Thank you, by the way, for stumbling directly into our path. Made it much easier to take you, even if it was the drunk prince on watch. He didn't even notice us slipping away with you."

They're alive. If the mercenaries slipped away with me unnoticed, they must have been left alive and unharmed. At least, I hope so.

He watches me for a few seconds before cutting the bindings around my feet. Hauling me up under the arms, I sag against him a little as I find my numb feet and sore joints are unable to take my weight so suddenly. Not waiting for me to acclimate myself to standing, he roughly drags me into a copse of trees. We're in an area not too dissimilar from where I was kidnapped, if not a little flatter and easier to traverse.

Taking a long rope off his shoulder and tying it around my waist, Duckhead attaches me to a tree. He undoes my hand bindings, and the relief in my shoulders is immediate, except for the throbbing pain of how I landed when Kino threw me. Not given much reprieve, he ties my wrists together in front of me. I have a small amount of give, attached to this massive tree trunk.

Without further word, he leaves me there. Immediately, I take the gag off and out of my mouth, trying to encourage some saliva to generate. The way he's tied me to the tree, the knot is on the other side of the trunk, and my slack is not long enough to reach it, even if it didn't slide around as I moved. A sharp rock will have to do.

A burning need to relieve myself overtakes me and I go behind the tree, as far as my rope slack allows. It's awkward, and I pee on my bare feet, adding yet another unpleasant smell to my collection. I dig my foot into a bit of earth, trying to *clean* it, but it's pointless.

I'm desperately thirsty, and the hunger pains are

escalating. I sit down with my back against the trunk to watch the chaotic situation in front of me. I've counted around a dozen men, all Erduborn, none of them Gifted. Or at least, none that I can see from here. Every man here has their own horse. On the one hand, being surrounded by a dozen men is not a great situation to be in, but twelve men on horses will surely be easy for the others to track, even in the rain, which has started again in earnest. That's *if* they're coming to my rescue.

No sharp rocks or stones are in my reach to use on my bindings, and the tree's branches and sticks are much too flexible to be of use. At least I am able to get some water, albeit slowly. Cupping my hands and drinking small sips of rainwater is a luxury for my parched mouth and throat.

Tents have been erected. All the men are huddled inside out of the rain while I'm out here. Not that it matters when my clothes are still damp from earlier. I sit with my eyes closed and allow the rain to wash away the disgusting hessian sack and other foul smells I've been collecting.

I'm dozing against the tree, trying to sleep away my hunger, when Kino comes stomping toward me. He throws an apple, a chunk of hard cheese, and a slightly moldy bread roll onto the wet earth at my feet. He glares at me, and I smile sweetly at him, pointing to his swollen nose and exaggerating a pout. A kick of mud and debris flies at me before he stalks off.

I eat everything, leaving only the tiny apple stalk behind, not wanting to waste anything when I'm unsure of my next meal. It was all gritty from the dirt, but I was so hungry I hardly even chewed. It wasn't enough food, so my stomach still growls pitifully.

The evening drags on as I'm left in my spot against the trees. I haven't seen the chestnut pony, but I can see a group of horses tied up, so she may be with them. It's a cloudy night and I'm not able to tell what direction we have traveled in because I can't see any stars. It's still raining on and off, nothing serious, some spitting here and there. I manage to weave myself a small bowl from the leaves of a swordgrass bush, and it's sitting under a part of the canopy that has a constant trickle.

They haven't lit a fire, perhaps worried about tipping off their location. Laughter and banter float toward me on the breeze. I guess I'm sleeping out here. My eyes begin to blur, and my blinking slows until I don't remember when I stopped opening them.

A BIG HUFF of warm air wakes me, followed by a velvet muzzle lipping at my ears. The pony from Waadi is staring down at me, and she tries to lip at me again. I stand up so I can give her a cuddle and kiss her nose.

She's trying to play with me, nipping at my shoulder before prancing away. She walks behind the tree and then slowly reaches her head around to nip at my pants as if I couldn't see her coming. I can't help but giggle to myself as I play chase with her. She nips me, and I chase her as far as my rope—and energy—allows.

I'm standing in the dark blue light of pre-dawn, scratching her fluffy ears, out of breath from our little games, when I hear someone calling out. "Arpi, the pony got free and is with the assassin!"

Duckhead sticks his head out of his tent and glares in my direction as I peer at him over the pony's head. Arpi, that's Duckhead's name, then. He stomps out in his boots and undershorts, his hairy belly jiggling with the motion.

"How did you get out?" he growls, reaching for the pony.

She waits until he's about to touch her before bolting, kicking the air as she goes. We watch as she trots herself back to where the rest of the horses are tethered. He shakes his head in her direction before stomping back toward his tent.

"What's her name? The pony, I mean," I quickly ask his retreating form, hoping he can't hear in my voice how much I desire to use his intestines as a skipping rope.

"She don't got one."

BREAKFAST IS FISH JERKY. The absolute worst kind of jerky. Who even *likes* fish jerky? I eat it all and ask for seconds, but Kino turns me down with a sneer. As it turns out, Kino completely lacks any front teeth—and he is probably going to lose a few more by the state of the rest of them. Remembering that he spat on me with those rotting teeth in his mouth causes bile to churn in my stomach.

I now understand the conglomerate of stench in the cart. They weren't all from the hessian sacks, though they still have a lot to answer for. Small barrels and crates of food are taking up most of the space, including the fish jerky. The cart looks too heavy for the sweet pony, and I'm hesitant to get on it. A swift backhand across the face from an Erduborn man —who wasn't with them in Teorann—is my encouragement to get in.

At least I'm not hog-tied. My tree rope is attached to the pony after being wound through some of the gaps in the slats of the cart. I don't have much slack to move, but no gag. I am still covered by hessian, and the Divine fucking stench is assaulting my very last nerve.

We break for lunch and for everyone to relieve themselves. My rope is used like a leash, much to my embarrassment, when the man keeps holding it while I relieve myself. I'm given a handful of nuts and dried fruits, and more fish jerky. This time I'm allowed to have a drink of water, which I guzzle greedily before the rest is confiscated.

The sweet pony tries to get my attention when I'm not looking at her. I wish I had an applemint to give her. I wish I could take her to live at Mama's with Applemint. Duckhead —Arpi—is coming toward me, so I assume it's time to lie down and be covered. But instead, he leans over the side of the cart to talk to me.

"When she said you were the Silent Assassin, I didn't believe her. But then I thought you'd confirmed it in Teorann. Now though, I must say, you're pretty disappointing." He walks away, laughing like a duck.

I'm still staring at him in confusion when I'm covered up. She? Who is *she*?

CHAPTER TWENTY-TWO

We travel for hours without a break, and I curse myself, not for the first time, for not at least asking Beans which direction Forsto was in. Breaking for camp mirrors the night before. I'm tied to a tree and left alone with my dinner thrown to me in the dirt. Though, I'd much prefer to be tied up outside than be cramped in a tent with a bunch of stinking Erduborn men. They're starting to smell worse than I do, and I've been huddled against barrels of fish jerky and covered in filthy, wet hessian.

The pony doesn't wait for night to fall before escaping and coming to visit again. No one notices the small horse-shaped figure sneaking along the outskirts of the camp in the setting sun. I'm still eating my apple when she arrives. Sitting on the slightly damp ground, she comes to stand as close as she possibly can without stepping on me. Her head slowly comes down, inches from my mouth, as I continue to eat my apple. A snotty huff bursts from her nose whenever I take a bite. She throws her head up and down, her lips clapping to show further irritation when I take a *very* slow and *very* deliberate bite making "mmm" sounds at her.

I still have two bites and the core left when I spot Arpi across the camp, a black look in his eyes as he stomps toward us. I quickly feed the pony the rest of my apple and tell her she has to go. She eats the apple with painful slowness, and my rage fires up in my belly. Pushing her out of the way so I can stand, I push her again, encouraging her to leave.

I didn't realize I had punched Arpi in the face until I felt the sting of it on my knuckles. It wasn't a great punch, considering my hands are bound, but the resounding crack was *excellent.* He'd walked up and punched *her* in the head, and she took off running. Then I must have landed the punch, and now Arpi has his hands around my throat, lifting me off my feet. The pain in my neck and head is worse than the lack of air. His face is so close to mine that his nose presses against my cheekbone.

"No wonder the Gifted Erduborn woman paid me to get rid of you, you filthy cunt," he all but screams at me. "I have big plans for you, and not a single one relies on you being whole. Test me again, and I will break you. Maybe I'll break you anyway."

He slams me against the tree by the throat before dropping me, and I crumple to the ground, gasping. Not done with me, he grabs me by the hair and pulls me back up to standing.

"If you still have enough strength in you to throw a punch, I must be feeding you too much. I hope sharing your apple with the fucking pony was worth it—you ain't getting shit for a while," Arpi taunts, spittle flying from his mouth.

He punches me so hard in the stomach that it winds me, and my meager dinner threatens to come back up. Letting go of my hair, he grabs me painfully by the jaw and shows me the knife in his other hand. He pushes it into my side, not enough to draw blood, but enough to let me know exactly which organs are at risk.

And then he puts his disgusting mouth on mine.

I bite my lips together, but he pushes them open with his tongue as he digs the knife in deeper in warning. He tastes like rotten meat, fish, and rancid drogalyf. My fists are balled up and stretching the boundaries of my tied wrists so hard I might snap a bone. He's licking the roof of my mouth, and his dirty facial hair is scraping my lips along with his. Taking my bottom lip painfully between his teeth, he bites and pulls hard enough that I let out a cry.

Letting me go, he steps back with blood on his lips. My blood. He wipes his mouth, and seeing it, he spits at my feet.

"There's more than one way to break a woman, and I know which ways are *my* favorite," he threatens with venom, spitting once more and leaving. I do my own spitting on the ground, trying to get the taste of him out of my mouth, and then my entire meal comes up with a few violent heaves. I'm still chewing on a bunch of wet grass to rid me of the vomit and taste of that vile man when realization hits me.

She.

The Gifted Erduborn woman.

Tovi.

"It was the woman I was traveling with," I say to Arpi as I am loaded into the cart without breakfast the next morning. "She paid you."

"She was most distraught when our first attempt in Teorann didn't work. But this has worked out *much* better," he says, as his eyes look me over appreciatively before covering me with hessian for the day.

It can't be true.

It took her a while to warm up to me, but she's my friend. She wouldn't risk the entire mission or the lives of the others. Why would she hate me that much? This is a mind trick meant to derail my confidence. He must've heard things and repeated them. Exactly *how* he knows so much information about me and the others gives me pause. But still, I cannot believe that Tovi would betray me, let alone Riley, Beans, and Bitty too.

When we stop for lunch, I'm not even given the chance to relieve myself or anything to eat. I push the hessian off me so I can breathe in some fresh air and find a moment of relief from the stifling heat. Kino barks at me to lie back down and covers me again. I wait there, seething and fuming for another ten minutes before the cart starts moving again.

As promised, I'm not given dinner, and I haven't had a drink of water since lunch yesterday. My sticky mouth and pounding headache are worse than the cramp in my stomach. There is no rain, just another cloudy night with no stars. The temperature has dropped dramatically tonight, and it's getting colder by the minute. The light tunic and pants I'm wearing are not enough, especially without boots and being stuck outside in this damp valley.

The lights in the tents have been out for hours, but still, I am awake. I'm shivering too much to sleep even though it's all I want right now. I'm huddled in a ball at the base of a tree with my arms tucked between my chest and knees to protect them from the cold wind. The tell-tale signs of soft hoof beats reach my ears moments before I see the beautiful little pony coming to visit me again.

I untuck my arms to reach up to pat her nose as I whisper, "You shouldn't be here, sweet girl. I don't want you to get hurt again."

She huffs, before sprawling ungracefully on the ground in

front of me. I lean forward a little, giving her a pat. Heat is radiating from her body, and I lean against her, stroking her whole body with my bound hands as I steal some of her warmth. The shivering finally stops.

The pony wakes me as she moves to get up. There is no sign of the sun, but I can hear the first songs of a morning bird, meaning it's near dawn—I must have fallen asleep. I stand with her, giving her kisses and massaging her ridiculously fluffy ears.

When I escape, I'm taking her with me. She's too good for them. Too good for me. Mama and Frankie will love her and treat her right. I whisper all of this to her because even if she can't understand what I say, the Divine can hear my vow.

Kino brings me water for breakfast. Still no food. The water only makes my hunger worse, rousing it instead of helping to satiate it. I spend the day in the cart in pain, nausea rolling off me in waves. I'm allowed to relieve myself when everyone else does at lunch, but nothing comes out. I'm an empty, dried-out husk.

The next three nights and days follow the last so closely they blur into one memory. Tied to a tree outside. No dinner. The pony sneaks out when everyone is asleep to lie with me until sunrise, waking me as she sneaks off, and I still have no idea how she's escaping. A few mouthfuls of water in the morning. The chance to relieve myself at midday with no success. Rinse and repeat. Rinse. Repeat.

I miss the others. All of them. I've never really friends before, and I thought maybe these four…A large lump forms in my throat at the thought, and my eyes sting.

Tovi couldn't have done this. I'm still angry at Riley and the weird game he's been playing with me. But I'd give anything to have the warmth of his touch right now.

I fall asleep thinking of him, my thumb brushing over my three favorite freckles.

On the fifth night of cuddling the pony even though it's no longer cold, I name her. I've been thinking about it for days and can't think of anything better than calling her my sweet girl.

"Sweet Girl?" I whisper, to see her reaction.

Her furry ears turn to me, and she lifts her head.

"Is that your name? Can I call you Sweet Girl?"

She snorts her hot breath at me and drops her head back down.

"I'll take that as a yes, Sweet Girl," I mumble into her fur as sleep takes me.

ONE OF THE men takes pity on me, or perhaps Arpi has changed his mind, and I'm offered some food with my usual breakfast of water. I can barely stomach the handful of nuts and dried fruit, forcing them down requires concentration. My body tries to reject the food immediately, and the sip of water doesn't help. I sleep the entire time in my dirty hessian tomb, not waking for lunch, unsure if we even stop. When I awake in the early afternoon, Arpi tells me, "We're here."

Here is a dusty clearing on the edge of the forest, with the side of a long canyon—more like a cliff—looming over us. In the wall of the canyon cliff is a well-worn cave entrance. Sitting in the cart, I watch Arpi's men carrying things in and out of the cave. Some readymade structures sit to the left of the cave entrance, worn too, like they've been here for a while.

"Is this where you all live?" I ask Arpi in a croak, my throat painfully dry.

"No, we'll be here a few days before moving on."

His rough hands drag me off the cart and I'm tied to a tree on the edge of the forest with a full view of what they're up to. Sweet Girl is taken around the corner past the structures that I can now see are full of tables and chairs. The men periodically go into another small cave I assume must be their privy.

I'm given an apple with a cup of tea for dinner. Kino gave it to me with a wink, pushing his finger to his lips in a shushing motion. I'm not sure what to make of it, but I savor the tea anyway. It's not until I finish that it occurs to me it could be drugged.

Fires are dotted around the area, the men sitting around singing and laughing. Some men are at wooden tables and chairs eating or playing card games in the structures.

Sweet Girl doesn't visit me tonight, and I miss her. My rage sluggishly uncoils from its sleepy position in my belly, a gentle flutter in my chest. It's only the fact that I can't see *any* of the horses that I don't let it consume me. They had intended to sell her before getting the cart. Surely, they wouldn't put her down—they'd at least sell her. But I wish I could confirm that she's okay with my own eyes.

Kino fills the metal cup that I had tea in last night with water. Someone else takes me to the small cave entrance to the right, confirming that it's the privy. It is the most revolting one I've ever been into; I would have preferred going next to my tree. I swear I'm dirtier coming out than when I went in.

Tied back to my tree, I slump to the ground and sit. The earth is cool as I dig my toes down into it, a sandy type of soil squishing between them. Something sharp catches my toes and I pull my foot back with a wince. I dig around to find the sharp object and discover what looks to be a piece of broken ceramic. It's pointed but not overly sharp, having been out here for a while. But it *could* be sharp again.

Finding a flat stone, I move to sit beside the tree. I gently scrape the small piece of ceramic, the size of a gold coin, along the stone, sharpening an edge. I haven't decided if I'm using this to kill someone or cut my binds. Hopefully both.

Arpi comes to retrieve me not long after I'm satisfied the piece of ceramic is sharp, already testing it against a small bit of the rope. Without a word, he undoes my leash, leaving me only bound at the wrists. I'm holding the piece of ceramic as inconspicuously as I can as he tugs me toward the cave entrance. Inside is a winding tunnel with small cave alcoves dotted along it, eventually opening into a larger cave at the end, shaped like a peanut. To our left is a low table with cushions strewn about, and to the right is a dirty mattress with pillows and a blanket. A bed.

Arpi takes me over to the bed, and the fluttering that began in my chest at the entrance of the cave turns into a roar. Near the ground on the cave wall is a metal bracket, and my wrists are bound to it. No one else is here but him and me. I can't reach him with my hands bound to the ground like this.

"Since you won't be with us much longer, I thought we could get to know each other a little better." His voice sends shivers down my spine. He reaches out to trail a finger down my calf where my pants have gotten caught up and exposed the skin.

I kick at his hand and snarl. "Don't touch me, you disgusting fuck!"

He lunges forward with a growl, grabbing the hem of my pants and yanks them off roughly, scraping my skin with the awkward way he pulls at them. He is panting, looking at me with undisguised hatred in his eyes as he clutches my pants, when Kino comes in.

"Uh, sorry, sir. The men are outside, ready for you." His eyes dart to the pants in Arpi's hands and then to me briefly, looking straight back up to Arpi.

They both leave, and Arpi takes my pants with him.

CHAPTER TWENTY-THREE

As soon as they leave, I maneuver my piece of ceramic into position and begin working on my bindings. While I only sharpened one side of it for this purpose, the other edges are cutting at my fingers with the pressure and movement. Not wanting my blood to give me away, I growl in frustration as I try to be more careful. I get through one piece of the rope, but the way I'm bound, I'll need to cut through two more to be free. I'm working through the second piece when I hear someone coming. I shove the piece of ceramic between the folds of the rope and relax against the wall.

Arpi stomps in, making a beeline for me. He grabs my ankles—though I try to kick him away—roughly pulling me down and flipping me onto my stomach. His knife scrapes along my hip in warning. I have to stop fighting. My bindings are not near enough to breaking, and my tiny makeshift blade is no match for Arpi's knife. I have to stop fighting.

Once. I can survive once. I let Pasha violate me weekly for moons before I killed him.

Let. As though I had a *choice.* There was no choice until I killed him. *That* was my choice.

Next time, I will kill Arpi before he has the chance. Next time.

My underwear is ripped to the side as he spreads my legs and kneels behind me. I look at my bound hands once more, struggling to breathe, and close my eyes. It's like when I kill. Disconnect from reality, pretend it's not me. Except this time, the one dying is me.

Pressure nudges at the entrance between my legs, his fingers or dick, I'm not sure. It's as dry as the rest of me down there. I hear him spit and try to use it as lubricant. This is it. I don't need to be here for this part. My rage buzzes loudly through my veins, trying to drown out all sense so I can't hear him. Can't feel him.

The sounds of clamoring and screaming override my buzzing disconnection, and I can only assume Arpi hears it as well because he's fumbling as he stands, pulling up his pants. With a frustrated growl, he grumbles about not being able to shove his—half limp—*"dick, inside this dry as dust cunt".* Moments later, he's readied his sword.

The entrance to the cave darkens as an enormous figure fills it, and my rage wars with uncertainty at the intense size of him. Until I realize it's not one of the Erdu men here for Arpi. He's here for *me.*

Beans.

I roll over to my side and catch Beans' eyes. He roars so loudly that dust shakes loose from the cave wall, and Arpi runs at him, the clash of their swords almost deafening. I hastily roll back onto my stomach and work the piece of broken ceramic over the last of my bindings, not caring about my fingers bleeding this time.

The rope falls from my wrists as I hear someone being disarmed. I'm relieved to see it's Arpi and not Beans. Arpi pulls a knife from his belt to rearm himself, as I'm running toward him. My rage is an enormous beast battling in my chest, and I let it free.

Beans sends Arpi's knife flying across the cave to my left as someone else comes crashing into the cave behind him. It's one of Arpi's men with an axe. With not even a second to take in the scene in front of him, the man—who I now recognize is Kino—swings the axe at the side of Beans' head.

The sound of the weapon connecting with its target is horrifying.

As though time slows, I watch blood splatter into the air and Beans tip to his left. Kino, obviously surprised, releases his axe and it flies across the cave in the direction Beans is falling. I can't be sure if I scream.

I drop to one knee, sliding myself across the cave floor toward the carnage. Arpi, standing dumbstruck and unmoving, has a small blade handle poking out of his boot. Still sliding on my knee, I grab the blade and take less than a beat to understand the size and weight before lobbing it into my other hand.

Pressing down, I use my foot to push myself up, stopping the slide and turning it into a forward lunge. I pass Arpi and aim myself at Kino. I bring the blade up with focused speed, directly under his jaw to lodge it into his throat, all before Beans even hits the ground.

Not waiting to confirm the blade killed Kino, and knowing it would be too slippery to pull back out, I use his body as a springboard and twist around to face Arpi.

Arpi—dazed, as if not yet registering anything that's happened since he was disarmed by Beans—is close enough that I reach to grip my hand behind his neck while still in the air.

Using the momentum that I've created, I swing myself

around, using his neck as my counterbalance to land on his back, my grip now on his other shoulder. Looping my arm under his chin, I let go of his shoulder to jam my right wrist into the pit of my elbow. I lock everything in place by gripping the back of his head with my free hand, completely blocking his airway.

I know I don't have strength on my side, so knotting my arms in such a way that I would have to fully relax to be able to untangle them, means that strength doesn't matter here, only time and determination.

Arpi must realize this because after he finally reacts and scratches at my arms, he tries to punch my face. He can't reach, so he changes tactics and goes for the ribs. He gets a few good punches to my side before he gives up and starts stumbling backward.

Picking up speed, it takes me a moment to figure out what he's doing before I'm slammed into the uneven cave wall. I hear, more than feel, the pop of a rib or two breaking.

Arpi steps forward, going for another backward slam, but it lacks intensity. This time though, the lightning bolt of pain momentarily dazes me, and I am grateful that I'm unable to let go accidentally. He stumbles to his knees, and I use the weight pulling him forward to tighten my grip even more.

Arpi finally loses consciousness and falls, and I relax my arms to fall to my left, scrambling for the knife that Beans sent flying in this direction. Two quick jabs with the knife into his neck, and I watch as his lifeblood drains freely.

Kneeling in a pool of blood and struggling to breathe through my broken ribs, I use my filthy tunic to clean the hilt of the slick knife. I crawl to Beans' prone form on the ground. Blood leaks from the wound on his head, but not as much as I was expecting for an axe. His beautiful orange lashes and brows are hidden by so much blood…and my rage threatens to choke me.

After inspection, relief washes through me with staggering intensity. It appears to be a minor injury—he must have been hit by the butt or even the cheek of the axe. But I can't immediately tell if he's breathing, so I feel for his lifeblood, relieved that it still pulses in his neck. I note with slight detachment the dissonance of first draining one man's lifeblood with malice, only to be relieved another's still flows.

Beans grimaces and breathes out a groan, but doesn't rouse when I say his name, which comes out only as a soft croak. Satisfied he isn't in immediate danger of dying, I stumble to my feet to navigate the caves, toward the continued sounds of chaos outside.

One foot in front of the other.

Tight breaths.

Testing the weight and size of the knife.

Calculating which arm will throw with the most accuracy.

Lift arms.

Pain.

Decide I can throw with my right if I hold my breath.

I make it outside to a blinding sun, the stench of death, and the sounds of swords clashing.

Tovi is closest, in front and slightly to my left fighting a man I don't immediately identify. Riley is to my far right with his back to me, fighting two men with deadly grace. I cannot yet see Bitty.

Stumbling forward a few steps, my path is cut off by a small stampede of terrified, unsaddled horses. I see a person raising a sword on my left and brace myself for the fight. But he either hasn't seen me or doesn't see me as a threat because he's going for Tovi. I try to draw in a breath to scream for her, but the pain stops me. She won't see him coming.

The knife flies from my hand before I remember what Tovi might have done, though maybe her presence here means it isn't true.

For the briefest of moments, I fear I have miscalculated the knife and my throw, but it flies true and lodges itself in the man's neck. He drops his sword, narrowly missing the man Tovi is fighting, and reaches his hands up to his throat as he falls to his knees and keels over. Distracted by the display, her opponent makes a mistake and that is all Tovi needs to swing and slice his head clean off at the shoulders.

Tovi spins to face me but looks to my right and then back to me in alarm. I see her scream my name but don't hear it, the pain of being tackled is louder.

I land with a sickening thud, the air forced from my lungs painfully, and I know this isn't good. Now weaponless, I can't defend myself. Tovi is already fighting someone else and can't help me. I'm not even sure if Riley is aware I left the cave.

Fortunately, my attacker is also weaponless, so I'm being strangled. Strangled to death instead of being cleaved or stabbed. *Fortunately.* I find this amusing for some reason and would laugh...if I wasn't in the middle of dying. My consciousness is wavering in and out. The rage inside me is nowhere to be found, it's left me for dead. I'm too tired to care.

The man with his hands around my throat is sent flying with force out of my view. I gasp painfully for air, which has me involuntarily doubling over to my side. I must lose consciousness briefly because I'm awoken by hot breath blowing hard in my face. A soft velvet muzzle with prickly whiskers nudges and lips at my face aggressively.

It's the pony. My Sweet Girl. She lips me once more on the cheek and I brush my hands on her warm face in thanks.

Bitty comes running from the direction the man went flying. They are a sight to behold: their face and leathers covered in blood, black hair down and tucked behind their ears, and violet eyes blazing with an intensity I recognize. Their dimples are nowhere to be found, only a vicious disposition and a concerned crease to their brow. Pride swells within me seeing Bitty full of fight. They help me to a sitting position.

Just in time to see Sweet Girl stumble in front of us.

She wasn't just breathing heavily to wake me up, she had a jagged gash almost the entire length of her side and was bleeding profusely. Syrupy drips are lazily splashing into the dry earth. Despite my ribs and lack of lung capacity, I manage a small scream when she crashes down, and the gash tears open even further, threatening to spill organs.

I crawl to her face, her eyes wide open and wild. She whinnies in terror and pain. Bitty sits behind her head as both Tovi and Riley arrive. Bitty yells at Tovi to help Beans in the cave and she hesitates for a second before sprinting away. Riley has fallen to his knees beside me and is trying to ask if I'm hurt.

My beautiful, Sweet Girl. Everything inside me is screaming in agony as I lie awkwardly on my side, hugging her face. But the agony isn't from my injuries alone.

I'm stroking her from between her eyes all the way down to her soft muzzle whiskers, trying to soothe her, while whispering in her fuzzy ear.

"It's okay.

"Go to sleep, Sweet Girl.

"Thank you for saving me.

"I'm sorry I couldn't save you.

"It's okay.

"I've got you now."

The only sounds are my whispers and her slowing breaths. Soon, I can hear Bitty and Riley's breathing too. The sound of shuffling steps from the cave's entrance increases as Sweet Girl's breathing slows further. Then, she breathes out one last lingering breath. And doesn't breathe one back in.

"I'm sorry, Mika. I can't hear her heart beating anymore," Bitty whispers.

And the breath I didn't realize I'd sucked in and held, comes ripping out of me in a guttural scream that might last forever. My vision goes black while the scream still rings in my throat.

CHAPTER TWENTY-FOUR

I t's night-time, I think. I stare at the roof of a darkly lit room and take stock of my injuries without moving. It hurts to breathe in, but not as much as it did.

I'm not dead then.

A painful throb stings from my knee to ankle on one leg, and I assume this is my reward for skating along a rough cave floor on bare legs. There are various aches and bruises and a pounding headache, but nothing serious of note.

I have no idea where I am, but it's not a cave, and I'm in a real bed. Despite my physical complaints, I am numb. Devoid of rage, empty of everything. A thin sheet covers me. Thankfully, I'm not naked, though I do wonder who changed my clothes.

A snore startles me. Someone else is in the room. The snore turns into the soft breathing of sleep. I wait, listening for other sounds, before turning my head slowly toward the sound of breathing. There, slumped awkwardly in a sofa seat next to my bed, is Riley. He's asleep and likely has been for a while. The lantern next to him on the side table has burned out.

Behind him, there is another bed and side table, and presumably the exit. A table laden with jugs, bowls, and uneaten food is on the opposite wall. Turning the other way, a dark but star-filled night is visible through a giant window, and nothing else. Not even a tree or another building. *Where am I?* I can't even tell what time of night it is.

Sitting up isn't easy, but I refuse to make a sound and wake up Riley. I fail when panting with the effort wakes him.

I see him reach for me, but he must decide better of it and rubs his eyes instead. "You're awake?"

"Apparently so," I reply with a grimace. My throat is a little sore.

Riley refills and relights the lantern on the bedside table. A soft glow illuminates the room, its delicate flicker bouncing around the walls. I've stopped panting, but I haven't moved from my seated position or even turned to look at Riley.

Riley stands and walks to the end of my bed in my line of vision, his arms crossed. Half of his hair has fallen out of the thong he must have tied it up with. He's not wearing any weapons, though I saw his sword next to his seat.

"How long have I been out?" I rasp as he hands me a glass of water, and I nod a small thanks.

"Four days."

I thought it would've been longer. "Were my injuries not so bad then?" I ask, surprised.

"They were bad. We brought in a black market Gifted healer. She wasn't powerful, was only able to fix your ribs so they didn't puncture your lungs, but it helped."

That makes sense. Plenty of Junky healers can only heal cuts and bruises, or something specific like bones. There is an unspoken agreement to not report them for defecting. The general populace doesn't have legal access to Gifted healers, who are usually reserved for royalty and the wealthy.

"You're still badly bruised, and you have a concussion.

Stitches in the back of your head. Your leg is very swollen." Riley's voice begins to sound like he's reprimanding me.

I look up at him, angry he's speaking to me this way. I don't care that he is the fucking Prince Ofnemoris.

He looks *furious*. His face is red, his eyes bloodshot, and a frown creases his brow as his forearm muscles bulge from gripping the bed head so tightly. There is a sheen of sweat on his prickly-looking skin.

I'm about to ask what the fuck his problem is when Bitty crashes through the door. "You're awake!" they cry. They stop short of jumping into the bed with me, but their beaming dimpled smile and glistening eyes say it all. "I couldn't sleep, but when I heard your voice, I thought I was dreaming!"

"Good to see you in the land of the living, Mika," comes Beans' booming voice as he enters the room behind Bitty. "Wouldn't have been able to handle Riley's cooking in your absence." Beans' head is bandaged, his right eye and cheekbone a dark blue.

"He's learned a thing or two," I jest, smiling at the two people I realize I don't mind I've come to care about. I chance a peek at Riley, but his mood is unchanged. Is he annoyed they had to rescue me, or that I woke up?

All that's missing is…"Where's Tovi?" I blurt. I need to confirm. If she's here, then it was a lie. *Right?*

"She was just…" Bitty's voice trails off as they frown toward the door. "Huh."

"You need to get her. Bring her here, right now." My voice is tight and screechy. I'm looking at all three of them, eyes darting between as they stare at me, puzzled and unmoving.

Beans backs toward the door. "What's wrong?" he asks, leaning out and looking down the hall.

"She's not…I can't hear her," Bitty announces, confused, as they move to look down the hall.

Shouting and a crash outside startles all of us. Beans and Bitty run down the hall while Riley lunges for his sword and stands between me and the exit.

"What's happening?" I ask Riley, my voice hoarse and painful. He's either ignoring me or too focused on the commotion to hear me.

Beans walks back in after a few minutes with a frown, Bitty right behind him with a confused and crestfallen look on their face. Beans closes the door and tells Riley he can stand down.

"Why did you want Tovi?" Beans demands.

"What happened, where is she?" Riley asks before I can answer.

Beans doesn't reply, doesn't even look at Riley, his full attention on me.

"They told me it was her. Everything. The rumor at Teorann. The kidnapping. But she was here, she helped save me!" I cry, pleading with Beans, begging to the Divine that he'll tell me they lied.

"She took off on a horse. Her pack is gone."

"Get out," I breathe, not looking at anyone in particular. When no one moves, I shout it over and over until Beans and Bitty leave. Riley gets to the door and closes it behind them, not leaving. The pain in my ribs is a radiating agony.

"Get out, Riley!" I scream into a gasp, unable to suck air into my lungs.

She betrayed me.

I was kidnapped, beaten, starved, and almost raped because of *her*. Beans almost died. Sweet Girl *did* die. Because. Of. *Her!*

My hands fist into the sheets, tensing so hard my ribs

scream along with my rage. I'm holding my breath. I can't cry. I won't cry.

I might have been able to talk myself away from the ledge if Riley hadn't crawled into the bed behind me, his legs on either side of me. One arm circles under mine, gently crossing my ribs as the other wraps over the top. His massive hand rests across my heart, almost spanning my chest and shoulder, too.

He gently pulls me back into him, and I can't fight him. I have nothing left. No rage. No fight. I am a crushed vessel.

Hugging me gently, his breath gently tickles my neck. I'm gasping, as he tightens his grip and cuddles into me. Still gentle enough that it's only my erratic breathing causing me pain.

"I've got you now," Riley whispers.

I unravel.

Two decades of trauma come flooding out in ragged, heaving wails. I scream instead of breathing out. I whimper instead of breathing in.

I cry for the Mika who was told she should never cry again after having to murder the snowolf pup Jaena had given her in some sick empathy lesson.

I cry for the Mika cruelly bullied by her once best friends about the way she looked and her lack of Gift.

I cry for 13-rev-old Mika who was repeatedly raped for being *too much* and deserved to be taken down a peg. I cry because she *didn't* cry each time he broke her and took a piece of her soul. I cry because she *couldn't* cry when she brutally murdered him, her rage not allowing her to feel anything else.

I cry for the Mika who became the Silent Assassin instead of being executed, owing her life to a woman all too eager to have a beast on a leash.

I cry for the Mika who was tricked by a boy at sixteen

and forced into something she didn't understand because she thought he liked her. Spitting his ejaculate in his face and breaking his nose was not enough.

I cry for the Mika with fake friendships turned fake lovers, who had the sick fetish of saying they fucked the Silent Assassin and lived.

I cry for the Mika who so desperately craved touch and affection but only received burning agony. For the revs and revs of killing and isolation. The wall of stone and ice that's been built brick by brick around her heart to suffocate it, allowing herself to be controlled by rage instead.

And I cry for the last few moons with these people I'd deluded myself into thinking were my friends, and that I could be deserving of their love. Sweet Girl. Riley. Bitty. Beans. Tovi. I cry in bitter grief for the loss of them all. For everything that was and could have been.

Every single ugly sob, every single burning hot tear, every single shuddering breath makes whatever was left of my suffocated heart burst into a million pieces. I vow to build the wall higher. Tighter. Colder.

I will give no more—*can* give no more—of myself. I am done.

Nothing is left.

A soft knock on the door wakes me. I'm still in Riley's embrace. Bitty and Beans come in with trays of food, my stomach announcing itself loudly.

They clear the table and drag it over to us with the food. With a start, I realize the warm golden glow in the room isn't from the lantern—it's early morning. Riley held me the rest of the night.

No words are spoken as Beans serves me a bowl of stewed fruits in syrup, topped with a crunchy and crispy mix of fried oats and nuts. Riley lets go of the embrace but also makes no move to leave the bed. I sit up straighter as Beans wordlessly hands me the bowl, and I whisper my thanks. It's fucking delicious. Maybe it's because it's the first proper food I've had in…over ten days.

"I think we should wait a few days before we leave. We can travel on horses from here, but your bruised ribs need to be ready for that," Beans advises me through mouthfuls of breakfast. "That's if you still want to continue…"

"Where are we?" I ask, choosing to ignore Beans. As if what I wanted would make any difference.

"A settlement outside of Forsto," Beans says as he shares a look with Riley.

Bitty clearly notices, and they raise their eyebrows at their bowl and shake their head. "Tell her. She should know."

"Tell me what?"

Riley sighs, and the hot air ruffles the back of my hair. "Do you know what they had intended to do with you? The Erdu mercenaries?"

"No. They weren't really the sharing types."

"They had intended to sell you to skin traders in Forsto," Beans says, loading up a second helping of breakfast. "We don't know much more than that because people got spooked when we started poking around. But people know you are— were—the Silent Assassin. We need to keep watch, we don't know who is going to sell that information now."

I'd assumed as much. Either that or something equally depraved, after Arpi had gotten what he wanted from me first. I shudder at the memory of him touching me. I hate that he's the last person to have touched me like that. It's like he replaced Riley's touch with his poison.

"Is all my gear here?"

"Of course." Beans angrily breathes out of his nose, scratching his beard. "Tovi insisted on carrying most of it herself."

"She was the one who would wake us long before dawn

to keep on your trail, sleeping only a few hours at a time," Bitty adds, staring at their empty bowl.

"And she was the first one to start the fight so Beans could rescue you," Riley says quietly, his hand resting on the small of my back.

I shake my head, still unable to reconcile everything. "Why? *How?*"

No one answers because no one knows. The betrayal further rips open the void within me.

CHAPTER TWENTY-FIVE

After breakfast, I ask to bathe, and fresh water is brought in. Riley refuses to leave until I throw a metal plate at his head. He tells me he will stand right outside the door.

"You need your own fucking bath Riley, you stink!" I spit at him as he closes the door with a slam. My rage takes a nosedive straight into my stomach as soon as the door closes. A sting behind my eyes has me gasping for breath.

I wish I could wash my hair, but unless I admit I need help, it would be impossible. It takes a long time to bathe because I have to keep taking breaks. I pull a wooden chair around and end up doing most of it sitting. The water is tepid by the time I'm done, and I'm exhausted.

Naked, I look down at my body. I have lost weight, and my muscles are no longer as clearly defined. My entire right leg from knee to ankle is bandaged, and it hurts to walk. I have cuts and bruises everywhere, but they're nothing compared to my ribs. I can't see all the way around, but I have dark, mottled bruising on both sides, but predominantly on the side I remember being in the most pain. There's no mirror available, so fuck only knows how battered my face and neck look.

Lifting my pack has me whimpering and Riley calls out to ask if I'm okay, and I bite back that I'm fine. Something in me has snapped. If I hadn't let this group get under my skin, then perhaps I would have had my wits about me when Arpi came. I can't let them—*Riley*—be such a distraction. It's too dangerous.

All of my clothes have been cleaned, and I slide a cropped chemise up and over my hips instead of lifting my arms above my head. With fresh underwear on, I forget about my ribs temporarily and attempt to lift a tunic over my head. Losing my balance, the world tips as the edges of my vision darken.

I must make a pained sound as I hit the side of the bed because Riley bursts in. He's by my side, holding my elbow as I gain my balance and swallow my dizziness. His nearness, though, is just as disorienting: the heat radiating off his skin, the intense stare on his angry-looking face.

"Why are you so fucking angry, Riley?" I growl out as I manage to wrench myself out of his grasp without falling over.

I try to put the tunic on again, but he grabs it, stopping me. He shakes his head and looks at me like I'm crazy. "*Angry?* I'm not angry!" Gesturing at my battered body from head to toe in disbelief, "You almost got yourself killed," his strangled voice bites out.

"Fuck off," I laugh derisively. "*Tovi* almost got me killed. I did what I had to do, to survive."

"It was reckless," he says, in a tiny voice barely above a whisper, "You should've waited with Beans."

Rage. The firecat in my chest is spitting flames, and I hope Riley can see them reflected in my eyes.

"*Reckless*? Oh, so, I should have just waited patiently to be saved by *you* instead? I think I need you to leave me alone before I do something even more *reckless*."

I yank the tunic from his grip and swallow a hiss of pain. Closing my eyes, I wait for the dizziness to dissipate. Riley gently takes my tunic from my hands again and helps me dress as I keep my eyes squeezed shut. I can't be sure if I'm hiding from the pain or my shame at how I'm treating Riley.

"I'm not leaving you alone, no matter how much you hate me," Riley says, gently.

"Maybe I wouldn't hate you if you weren't such an asshole."

I crawl into bed, spreading out so a giant Nemorisborn man with stupid forest green eyes won't fit, fixing a glare on him. Shame? What shame? I am unhinged. Nothing but venom and fangs.

"Retired or not, I'm an assassin, Riley. You don't get to put me in a bubble of your protection like I'm some feeble maiden of yours. I don't need you," I say, trying and failing to curb my hostility.

Riley doesn't reply. He stalks off and strips off in front of the wash basin to use the last of the fresh water. I'm trying not to look. I'm back to hating this man, but by the Divine, he's beautiful.

His dark hair is tied up in a messy, blood-red bun. The freckles on his shoulders are sparkling with the soap and water he's scrubbing on them. He has his back to me so I can't see his chest, but I remember it well enough. His back muscles are rippling with his movements. I hate that I want to slide my nails down them.

He takes off his pants in jerky, angry movements. When he is down to only his undershorts, I quickly avert my eyes. I'm sure he would have preferred to be totally naked instead of having to wash in his undershorts, but fuck him.

Riley uses the powder to clean his teeth, and now the

water is well and truly fouled by the two of us. Dressing quickly, he sets the basin bowl and empty jugs outside of the room to be cleared away.

I'm reclined in bed, still recovering from the exertion of bathing, when Riley plonks onto the sofa seat he was in last night. We sit in the pregnant silence, both of us looking at the ceiling instead of each other.

I remember the thoughts I had of him while I was tied to a tree, cold. How they kept me warm and how I would have done anything to touch him again. It softens me slightly and words rush out, uninvited, "Did one of you hurt Sweet Girl?"

"The pony? I was hoping you wouldn't ask." Riley sighs, and my heartbeat quickens. "No. The Erdu mercs didn't do that to her either. She did it to herself."

"She did *not!* I saw that gash, it...I could almost see organs, Riley."

Riley looks stiff in the chair, his elbows resting on either side of the arms while resting his mouth on his hands. He studies me, before closing his eyes and taking a deep breath.

"She had been contained in a poorly made makeshift stable. I don't know whether it was the chaos or what. Bitty thinks she heard you." He pauses, watching me flinch, before continuing, "She forced her way out. Broke through the fence. We found a jagged piece of metal covered with blood and fur, in the opening."

No. Absolutely not. Someone did that to her.

Riley must sense the panic threatening to overwhelm me again because he gets up and sits at the end of my bed. He holds my foot, of all things.

"Some of the horses that followed her had similar gashes, though not life-threatening. Most of the others didn't even try to force their way out."

"What happened to her...body?" I choke out.

"We buried her. We got you here and then we took turns in twos going back to dig the hole to bury her. We threw the rest of the fuckers in a pile and burned them."

"I want to see her grave."

"We thought you might. It's a few hours' walk, but maybe we can borrow a horse and I'll take you."

"Today?"

"Tomorrow."

I nod. I don't think I could handle a horse ride today anyway, not even a gentle one. Riley is still holding my foot, and it's bizarrely comforting.

One solitary tear slips down my cheek and I use my shoulder to wipe it away, hissing with the pain in my ribs I keep forgetting about. Riley gets up, the anger I could see earlier is beginning to look like something else. Something that looks like pain.

"Were you hurt?"

"No. Not really. Everyone, including Bitty, got a few cuts, bumps, and bruises. But nothing serious."

"Then why do you look like you're in pain?" I ask, watching him pace between the beds.

He sighs, looking at me long enough that my rage begins to swirl deep in my belly. "It's not pain. Or it is, but it's…" Riley gestures at nothing, eventually crossing his arms to stand in front of me, frowning.

Why does *he* look confused?

He lets out a sharp breath, steps forward quickly, and leans down to me. The back of his fingers brush along my cheek until his hand grips the side of my neck and shoulder. He leans down and kisses the side of my forehead softly. "Just promise me, you won't…die," he whispers, leaving his lips against my skin for a moment longer, as he shudders a breath in.

Without saying anything more, he moves away as quickly

as he came and leaves the room. I can see his shadow under the door. The confusion is wholly my own now.

I SLEEP on and off most of the day, Riley hovering and swapping with Beans every now and then. Beans joins me for a lunch of cold roast duck sandwiches on fresh bread with slatherings of butter. In the afternoon, Bitty brings me a cup of hot cacote that I greedily gulp down, finishing quickly.

I'm sick of sleeping but I know it's what I need to recover. I may not have broken ribs anymore, but my body is still battered and bruised. I am also *ravenous*. Everything the trio feeds me, I inhale.

Beans brings a hearty beef stew with crusty bread for dinner. I try to tell him I'm okay to eat alone and that he can enjoy dinner with the other two, but he says he would prefer quieter company.

"Thank you for coming to my rescue," I say to our silent dinner.

Beans gives me a wild look, one eyebrow rising while the other hides under the bandage. "I do believe it was you who saved my life. I think we're even."

"You wouldn't have even—"

Beans sets his bowl down with a huff. "I don't know who or what has made you think that you wouldn't be worthy of your friends coming to rescue you, but I won't tolerate it. I won't tolerate you treating yourself with any less respect than you deserve."

I frown at my food as the rest of the meal is eaten in silence.

A SNORT WAKES me in the morning, and I look over to Riley's bed. He's lying on his side facing me, trying—and failing—to hide the grin on his face. The residue of a snort sits in the back of my nose…it was me. I snorted myself awake.

"Morning, Firecat. Sleep well?" he asks, then yawns through his smile.

"I'm not used to having to sleep on my back," I grumble, addressing the snort though he didn't actually mention it.

"You snore on your side too, so that's a lie," Riley tries to joke.

"I'm not the liar around here," I quip. "When can I see Sweet Girl's grave?"

Riley stretches noisily. "As soon as we've eaten, we can go."

I sit up too fast and then float back down with a groan.

Getting up and eliciting his own groan, Riley scrubs his face in his hands and aims for the door. "I'll check if anyone else is awake so we can get an early breakfast."

An hour later, we're both fed, dressed, and standing at the stables, where Riley was able to hire us a horse. One horse—a large horse, but still, *one* horse.

"Am I going by myself then?" I deadpan at Riley.

"You can't defend yourself, nor will you be able to ride properly yet. And you need a smooth ride. Butters here is the smoothest ride and can carry us both."

The pale cream horse is enormous, just as big as Beans' horse Ditch back in Nemoris. His fur is sleek, and his mane and tail are thin, typical of Erdu horse stock. Butters starts to nibble at one of my sleeves which makes me smile. I am constantly blessed by cheeky equines. My heart constricts painfully. Sweet Girl. Tears threaten to spill again, which triggers my rage. *Stop crying.*

After some logistical issues getting me up onto Butters' back, I am finally seated in front of Riley. He's holding the reins, and I'm holding on to the front of our two-person saddle.

The ride is comfortable, even though I have to relax and lean back into Riley as we ride. It doesn't take me long to fall asleep listening to the soft calls of birds and Butters' clops along the packed earth. With the rocking movements and warmth surrounding me, I had no hope.

Riley has let one hand go of the reins and is hugging me against him. Once he realizes I am awake, he lets go of me and takes up the reins in both hands again.

"We're almost there," he announces shortly after.

Riley steers Butters into a tree-dotted area slightly West of the cave systems, and I am grateful I don't have to go anywhere near them. The ground is mostly even here, with no large cracks. Still, it cannot have been easy to dig a pony-sized hole with the Erdu-packed ground.

I see her grave not far ahead, so I ask to walk the rest of the way alone. Riley hangs back with Butters after helping me down, and I limp to Sweet Girl's grave amongst the Erdu trees.

They marked out the grave with stones, with a large stone at the head. I take out my knife and I use it to carve into the relatively soft stone: *Sweet Girl. My hero.*

"I'm sorry, Sweet Girl, I wish I could have gotten you away from here. I would have loved for you to meet Applemint, and I think you would have liked to live with Mama and Frankie. I'll never understand why you did what you did, but I hope you did it with purpose and courage, and not in fear."

A few hot tears drip onto the stone as I say my final

goodbye. I let the grief of her loss war with Jaena's lessons about not crying over something as pathetic as a death. *"I won't cry for you,"* she once told my 7-rev-old self.

I sit there, breathing, watching the trees and the small animals scurry amongst the dry brush. A stunning hot pink beetle scuttles over Sweet Girl's headstone. I listen to the sounds of new life. A ground-dwelling bird I can't recall the name of, calls for its mother. I let it all wash over me like a soothing balm.

Not wanting to repay Riley's kindness by making him stay out here all day, I say a final goodbye to my sweet girl. Riley's sitting on the ground leaning against a tree carving something small and pale. Seeing me limping toward him, he tucks his carving away and comes to help me get up on Butters again.

I spend most of our slow journey back absorbing the landscape. The further north we travel, the more it reminds me of Sadori, and although it gets very dry in the northern tip, Erdu isn't as barren. Sadori has some beautiful oases that are lush and fertile, but they're only for those high up in the tribal hierarchy. Erdu is still beautiful in its own way, especially the dramatic cliffsides and gorges, I just can't seem to find it in me to appreciate anything about it right now.

"What will happen to me when we rescue your sister? I ask to break the silence. I can't see him, though his tension is evident as he stiffens behind me.

He starts to say something but seems to change his mind before starting again. "I don't know. Obviously, my mother sent us to get a Gifted Patron, and we sent a falcon to let her know we had…purchased—" Riley clears his throat, "—you, getting her official seal for the council. That's it. There's no plan for *after* the rescue. I assume you could probably have any position you wanted in our court after we get Lyss back," he finishes quietly.

"How will the queen react to the news of who I really am?"

It wasn't often that I'd get to know who requested the assassinations and why, but I usually knew if it came from one of the monarchies. Unless the queen had sent an anonymous request, I don't believe I ever performed an assassination on behalf of the Nemoris crown. I suppose one of the others could have, but I was Jaena's favorite, so it's unlikely.

"I can't answer that. But you have us to vouch for you. You are not your reputation."

But I am.

We continue in silence for a while. My eyes begin to glaze over with sleepiness when Riley's deep voice startles me.

"What would you want to do? Back in Nemoris, I mean."

I open my mouth to say that I wouldn't even know, but instead, I say, "I was a nanny. In Osraed, when I wasn't busy being an assassin. I worked in the children's compound teaching them how to forage and cook." I shrug very lightly, trying to play it off like it was no big deal, but my throat constricts painfully. I miss those kids.

Riley speaks quietly, gently, as if he can sense I'm still fragile. "You could do that. Or something similar. You wouldn't have to…I'd make sure you weren't…*used*."

Dumbfounded, I can't speak for a long time. And when I can, I am unable to respond to *those* words.

"Thank you for taking me to Sweet Girl's grave, Riley."

Riley sputters as if he wasn't expecting my not-so-subtle change of topic. "We—well not me specifically—but my family could find your family. If you want, that is…to find out who your parents are…" He sounds more uncertain as the words tumble out.

"I know my mother's name already."

"You found her?" he asks in a sudden burst that causes Butters to flatten his ears.

"No. I haven't looked for her. But I know her name is Sehna Ziemia. I'm…not sure what I'll find if I look any deeper. Or if I want to know," I finish in a whisper. *She was probably executed.*

Thankfully, Riley must sense my emotions on this topic and doesn't push further. Instead, his voice drops low, and he brings his lips closer to my ear. "Mika Ziemia Ofnemoris is a beautiful name."

The use of a family name lodges in my throat. I am a Patron of the Divine. I do not have a family name…nor do I deserve one. But that name spoken by Riley replays in my mind like music for the rest of our silent trip.

CHAPTER TWENTY-SIX

After another three days of bed rest and light stretching, Beans declares me well enough to travel if I can prove I am able to get up and down from a horse unassisted.

A medic was able to visit and remove the stitches in my head, though the bandages on my leg are required for another week or so, and I was told to monitor for signs of infection. Getting dressed and putting on my weapons was a strange experience, almost as if this is a different life. As if I'm a different Mika. But it's not, and I'm not.

My boots are uncomfortable, and I have to wear the laces loose on my injured leg. But, despite all my complaints, I'm ready to go when everyone else is.

"Where's my sneak bag?" I ask the three of them, noticing it wasn't with all my stuff.

"Sneak bag?" Bitty asks.

"Small black bag with my sneaksuit and other paraphernalia I use for sneaking in it."

The three of them give me blank looks, so I add, "It was with all my other stuff. Before…before they took me."

"Sorry little one, it must've been left behind in the frantic pack-up to go after you. We can try to replace it in Erdu Castle City." Beans apologizes, his heavy hands on my shoulders as he looks down at me with remorse. Like it's his fault.

Rage chokes me. "Of course. There's no need to apologize. I'll make a new one." I slide out from under Beans' affection, the rage threatening to burst through my skin.

I notice Tovi's absence as soon as we start traveling. It's palpable. I still haven't come to terms with what she did, though I have gone over it and over it in my head. The other three have steadfastly avoided the subject, so I can't even talk to them about it. I don't blame them. They've known her for revs.

My horse for the journey is a black and fawn colored gelding named Snooze. No surprises where the boy got his name because he is *slow*. He moves faster than if we were walking, and I appreciate the smooth gait, but the pace is excruciating.

I tried to spur him to go a bit faster, but he clearly doesn't enjoy it, and his gait is definitely rougher the faster he goes. Beans, who is riding Butters, laughs at me and encourages me to accept my fate. I give him a rude hand gesture which only makes him laugh harder.

They're assholes. All three of them. They keep sprinting off and coming back. Not all at once, obviously. My precious self cannot be left alone for one second. I even have an escort when I need to relieve myself.

The next time Riley and Bitty take off, I ask Beans why no one seems upset about Tovi. They're playing around and acting as if none of it happened.

"Mika, if we constantly let the awful things that happen darken the sun, then we would never see the light again." His tone is gentle. Caring, even. "We are all desperate to find Lyss. And we all love Tovi and I hope one day we find out what happened. I know what's in that girl's heart, just as I know what's in yours. There's no evil. And I can tell by how feisty you're being, that you're as brokenhearted and confused as we are. We don't have the whole story. I'm not excusing what she did by any means, and I wouldn't blame you for hating her. But we have a job to do, and Divine damn us if we won't live our lives while we do it."

"I'm not being feisty," I mutter, distracted by his words about my heart.

"You are the epitome of feisty, little one, and I wouldn't have you any other way."

I snort, saying nothing more. Not sure when he decided I was *little one*, especially when it's more like he's *big one*. I let my feisty retort slip away instead.

AT OUR CURRENT PACE, our estimated time to the outskirts of Erdu Castle City is at least three weeks. A couple of smaller towns are dotted through, but mostly we're staying away from main roads and going off the beaten tracks as much as we can, though it's clearly chaffing Riley to be so far behind schedule.

Riley has been keeping his distance, barely speaking to me unless he's changing my bandages. I hate that I miss him. He makes me so angry, and I lash out at him. But when he isn't around, it makes me angrier. I'm exhausting myself.

We travel as far as we can until, apparently, my breathing changes, and Bitty signals that I am in too much pain to continue. It's uncanny how accurate they are, as much as I despise being spied on.

I'm back to my regular cooking duties, much to everyone's delight. There haven't been many herbs for us to forage in the barren Erdu countryside, however, the fruit trees and bushes have been plentiful. We've been eating a lot of berries and plums in our breakfasts, and bush bananas for snacks. I even found a patch of desert sweet potato that we were able to forage.

Most nights are a stew of sweet potato, Beans' beans, various dried meats unless we are able to hunt or trap something (which is rare), and the last of whatever dried herbs we have. Garlic grass seems easy to come by, so that has been a welcome staple. We were able to buy some black and green tea leaves before we left town thankfully, as there has been nothing to use along our way. I'd kill for some jasmine or honeysuckle tea from Nemoris.

Whenever we make camp, I lay down and rest while Bitty tends to the horses, Beans chops wood, and Riley gets a small fire going to boil water for tea, then changes my bandages. Everyone sets up their bedrolls early, and we go in pairs to wash if we're lucky enough to be near a water source.

Beans helps me stretch, doing low and slow exercises that will help me rebuild my strength and flexibility without causing too much pain as I heal. I'm getting stronger every day.

I watch the three of them spar. Beans still goes way too easy on them, but Bitty is getting *good*. Beans has had to start *actually* defending himself against the enthusiastic Laguzborn. Riley has been training with Bitty the way I used to. It's been nice to watch, though more often than not when they're sparring, he ends up making them laugh until they make a mistake, and he wins.

The skin traders we fought when we first got to Erdu and my kidnapping might have put the reality of Bitty not being able to defend themselves into perspective. Though Bitty did hold their own during my rescue, fighting hand-to-hand after using all their throwing knives. It was Bitty who finished off the man Sweet Girl kicked off me. Sweet Girl. Tears sting behind my eyes, and my throat swells. When does it stop? When will I think about her stupid fluffy ears with joy and not a wrenching pain in my gut?

I can't wait till I am well enough to get back into training and sparring with everyone, but until I can take a hit to the ribs, I'm staying well away from all three of them.

At night, Riley sleeps directly beside me. He doesn't try to touch me. In fact, he barely says a word to me at all. I wanted to push him away, and now that it's worked, it makes my rage scream and thrash through my entire being. I can't even talk to him about it because I don't even know what I want from him.

They won't let me stand watch yet, not until I can fight. We're down Tovi too so they are all on long watch shifts. The darkness under their eyes and constant yawning during the day is growing worse.

It's been eight days since we left Forsto. Bitty announces they can hear what might be a small town nearby, but we can't be sure because we aren't using roads. The thought of being able to sleep in a bed and have someone cook a meal for me sounds like pure bliss.

Bitty wasn't totally off the mark. It's definitely a *small* town. One inn, and fortunately, two rooms are free. There is a stable for our horses as well, though it's untended. The main issue is they barely have any provisions for us to stock up on. They only have traveling merchants come through once a moon because of how remote they are.

We get what we can, including some more staples like cured and dried meats, some grains and legumes, and emergency feed bags for the horses. We have been fortunate enough that the horses have been able to graze so far, but we can't rely on that.

Beans gets our room keys, and we head there straight away. The elderly Erduborn woman said she will get her boys to bring us a couple of jugs of warm water for bathing in an hour. Dinner is served in two hours: soup. What kind of soup? *"A bit of everything."* I shudder as I think of the woman's toothless smile as she said it.

It's no surprise that Riley and I are roommates. What surprises me is *there is only one bed in the room.* We were not informed of this. Riley and I stand in the middle of the small room with sad peeling wallpaper, staring at the singular bed.

"I can sleep on the floor," Riley announces, grabbing a pillow and one of the blankets off the bed. He throws them in the corner of the room and starts digging through his pack. He didn't even wait for me to say anything. Does the idea disgust him that much?

"Divine help me," I mumble under my breath. Riley raises his eyebrow, though he doesn't look at me. "Riley, we're both adults. I think we can safely share a bed," I say in exasperation.

"Wouldn't want you to think it's a bubble of my protection, Firecat," Riley states, continuing to dig around in his pack with his back to me.

"You are infuriating, you know that?"

"You're easily infuriated," he rebuts, to which I can only growl in response, proving his point yet again. "Look, if you desperately want to share a bed with me, then I'll be happy to join you tonight," Riley manages to say, with only a hint of sarcasm. *Still,* not looking at me.

Letting an angry breath out through my nose, I temper my voice. "You can continue to do whatever the fuck you want, *Prince Ofnemoris.*"

Not waiting for any response or reaction, I leave the room. I need fresh air and to be anywhere that Riley is not.

I'm in the stables patting Snooze within minutes because nothing else is around. I hear the squeal of children playing somewhere close by, and I stick my head out of a window in time to see two Erduborn children dashing about, giggling freely.

I miss my kids in Osraed. I miss getting to be silly and happy and not have the weight of the Divine on my shoulders. Both kids have wavy brown hair to their shoulders, with eyes almost the exact same color as their hair. It's been a while since I've really looked at any kids with an eye color other than violet.

Snooze is dozing, with his head resting on my shoulder. Another wave of pain rolls through me at the thought of Sweet Girl. I snuggle into Snooze a bit harder, hug him a bit tighter, and let the smell of him calm me until I'm ready to face Riley. Returning to the room, I hope the attendant has brought water for us to bathe.

I swing the door wide open and catch Riley in front of the wash basin. Completely naked. With the door wide open, unmoving, I stare at him.

He slowly reaches to cover himself with a towel. "When you've finished ogling, would you mind closing the door, Firecat?" Riley laughs. "I mean, you can continue if you want, but the whole Divine world doesn't need to see."

I attempt to say something like "*I wasn't looking*" or "*I don't want to look*," but what I actually say is: "I was want look… ing." And then frown at the nonsense. I turn and close the door and rest my forehead on it. Divine help me, this man will be the death of me.

I face the door until Riley announces he's decent. His smirk is back, and my heart rapidly plunges into my stomach.

It only reminds me of Riley waking me the night I was kidnapped.

How did those men kidnap me when he was on watch?

I don't think he had anything to do with it. Though, I thought the same about Tovi and look where that got me. But still, it's not that. I'm not safe with him, my rage has always warned me of that.

Sitting on the end of the bed, Riley inspects my leg with gentle fingers. Each touch sends my rage into a frenzy, heating me from the inside out. He declares I no longer need the bandages anymore, and a small amount of disappointment curls through my veins as I realize it means he'll no longer touch me like this. This is quickly followed by disgust at myself that sounds a lot like Jaena's voice telling me I should not need or want anyone.

Riley gives me privacy so I can wash my hair, and I'm a new person. Well, I'm still full of rage and slightly unhinged, but at least I'm clean.

After dinner, Beans calls for an early night as everyone is exhausted. In the room, Riley starts getting himself ready to sleep on the floor.

"Please sleep in the bed, Riley. You're exhausted from long watches, and we've been traveling for moons. Just sleep in the Divine-damned bed with me."

Without argument or another word, Riley gets into bed with me. Despite my assertions that I can't trust him, I have the best sleep I've had in a long time. Since the windcave.

CHAPTER TWENTY-SEVEN

The bed dips and wakes me up. Riley is sitting on the edge of the bed with his back to me, hands on his knees. His hair is a sleepy mess, sticking out at funny angles like mine does.

Birds are beginning their morning song, though it's still dark as the sun has not yet peeked over the horizon. Riley doesn't move from his position on the edge of the bed.

Being alone with him like this, in such close proximity, rouses my rage from its slumber. Back at the inn outside of Forsto, I was recovering, and it was different to be alone with him. This silence and warmth…It's too much like the windcaves. I'm embarrassed by how much I want to reach out for him. I could. I would be able to reach. Slide my hands along his warm skin.

I remember how soft his lips were on mine. How he still smelled and tasted delicious even though we had been stuck in a cave for days. His rough and hot hands on my skin. My eyes close as I remember the weight of him on top of me, his hard body against me…

"Firecat?"

My eyes shoot back open. Did I make a sound?

"You alright?" he whispers, turning back to look at me.

I clear my throat. "I'm fine. Why are you awake so early?"

"Just keen to get going. Feels like the longer we take, the more danger everyone is in, and the less likely we will find my sister," he says, standing up and rubbing his face. The urge to reach out for him is almost too much. *Almost.*

Apparently, he isn't the only one, Bitty knocks on the door after hearing us awake to ask if we're good for an early start on the day. The tavern hasn't opened for breakfast, so we eat hard cheese and dried fruit as we tack up our horses.

We're able to travel marginally faster now I'm not in so much pain, though Snooze still refuses to do anything beyond a slow canter. But I can grit through an uncomfortable faster pace for the sake of being able to travel further each day.

Beans thinks we're making good progress and that, at this pace, we should be at the edge of Erdu Castle City within ten days. This only serves to further my resolve to ride harder through the pain. We continue to discuss our plans for Erdu Castle City as we travel, though by now, I could almost recite them verbatim.

After a few days, I'm finally allowed to be on watch. Though I would prefer not to take a hit to the ribs, they're recovered enough that I can move freely. My leg has a nasty scar healing with patches of scab, but it no longer impinges on my movements.

After my usual loop and spiral perimeter checks, I find a perfect vantage point at the top of a dead tree that is at the lip of a gorge higher than our camp. Relieved to finally be alone, I relish the time I'm on watch.

The moon is almost at the point in the sky where I need to wake Riley, so I do one more loop. Everyone is still asleep as I tiptoe to Riley's bedroll. Usually, he wakes up easily. Not this time. I gently grab his shoulder with a small jiggle, but he grabs my wrist and yanks it across his body as he rolls flat onto his back. A knife at my throat before I even have a chance to say his name.

"Riley!" I hiss. "What the fuck?"

Riley drops the knife and my wrist immediately. He gulps air a few times before sitting up. I'm sitting on my knees, rubbing at my wrist, looking at him in bewilderment.

"Sorry," he breathes, shaking his head.

He looks down at my wrist, which I've cradled absentmindedly. He takes it gently in both hands, massaging it with his thumbs.

"I'm sorry I hurt you," Riley whispers.

I know he means my wrist, but something in my throat imagines him apologizing for other things. I take my wrist back with a snatch.

We don't say anything further as I crawl into my bedroll. I hear Riley's footsteps recede as he leaves the camp. It takes me a little while to fall asleep, but eventually, I slip into darkness. Unfortunately, I don't get a reprieve from nightmares.

It's not real. None of this is real, I repeat to myself, trying to wake.

I wade through the blood, warmth seeping into my pants, the copper tang in my nose and on my tongue.

There wasn't this much blood, I try to remember. There wasn't this much.

Blood rains down the walls; laughter echoing.

Streaming from his eyes, his tears the color of his ruby blood as he pleads for his life.

The laughter is in my throat.

I lose count of how many times I stab him.

Over and over. Over and over and over.

This, I wish, was an embellishment. Only a part of my nightmare.

Over and over.

But my memory of this is as vivid as the nightmare that plagues me. Over.

And over.

My blood mingles with his as I cut my fingers on the blade, so slippery from his blood.

I don't stop until the blade is bent and useless.

Then, when I can no longer stab, I rip. I rip and claw and scrape at his face, screaming until my throat is as raw as the open wound where my soul used to be.

I cannot remember if this part is the monster I am or only my nightmare. Do I dream about doing this because I did it, or because I wish I had?

The sound of my heaving breath and the gushing walls of blood are my only companions now. I sit, waiting, pleading for the blood to fill the room.

For the release of my own death as I drown in Pasha's blood.

A FEW DAYS LATER, Beans and Riley are bathing in a nearby creek while Bitty and I hang back at camp drinking tea. It's a pleasant day. The sky is cloud-free, and we have enough random trees for shade, even if the wind is a bit hot.

"Does Riley usually…startle? When you wake him for watch?" I question Bitty tentatively.

"Since you were taken? Absolutely." Bitty laughs without humor. "I've learned to wake him by kicking his boots to keep far away from the knife he sleeps with."

Frowning, I don't reply. I'm not sure why I asked or what the answer means to me. I know I should be talking to Riley, but it's awkward with Beans and Bitty around, especially with Bitty and their Gifted hearing.

Beans and Riley's laughter can be heard long before we see them coming back from the creek. They're both barefoot and shirtless, only wearing their pants with axes swinging on their hips as they carry the rest of their clothes and boots. They make a gorgeous pair of Nemorisborn men. Riley's hair is wet and so is Beans' beard. Chests and shoulders glistening with water. Beans' skin—so pale it's almost translucent—is covered in dark freckles, and just like his beard hides the freckles on his face, so does his chest hair. Riley's freckled shoulders can barely be seen from this distance, as pale and sporadic as they are.

Bitty clears their throat, and I reluctantly tear my eyes away from the red-haired giants and look back. They raise an eyebrow with a smirk, one dimple appearing as if to mock me.

"I don't know what that look is, Bitty, but you can stop right there," I say, with fake reproach.

Bitty laughs loudly while gathering their things for our turn to bathe. We find a good spot and bathe with our backs to one another for privacy. Once we finish getting ourselves clean, we stay soaking together in silence.

Bitty snorts. "Your horse has broken free and managed to nibble on Beans' weapons harness. He's sternly telling the creature off, but I get the feeling…"

"…Snooze gives no fucks?" I finish, and we both laugh.

After a long soak, we begrudgingly leave the water. To my disappointment, both men are fully clothed when we return to camp. Actually, my disappointment lies solely at the feet of *Riley* being fully clothed. That slap of realization makes my cheeks flame.

The terrain continues to change the further north we travel. There are fewer trees, deeper cracks in the earth, and flatter plains. Long stretches with no trees, only brush bushes dotted all over and the sides of the giant canyons and gorges for shade. Some of the gorges are so large and deep, with beautiful rivers through them. The immense amount of water passing through is slightly terrifying.

"Erdu Castle City is made up of four enormous gorges with dwellings built into the walls. Have you been there before?" Beans asks me one afternoon.

"I haven't. I've had a couple of...jobs in Erdu, but none in Erdu Castle City. I've also never been very far west in Erdu—the most I've seen are the mud hut villages or the settlements at the foot of the gorges in the east."

"Beans took me to West Erdu once and it is *spectacular!* The canyons face out onto the beaches, so getting to stay at inns that have been cut into the side is incredible," Bitty tells me dreamily.

"Ah," I say. "This will be why Erdu has a standing agreement to have the first bid on any earth and rock Gifted Patrons."

"That is quite likely, little one," Beans agrees.

"Erdu castle itself is built into the side of an enormous canyon near the border of Sadori. Behind the castle is unlivable terrain that just ends in death drops. Then the beaches of Sadori begin," Riley adds.

Without trees, we only have shade at certain times of the day from the walls of whatever gorge we're in. The sun wants to fry us to a crisp. Except for maybe Bitty. Their Laguzborn skin has tanned an even deeper bronze. Beans and Riley have developed a few more freckles, and I am uncomfortably pink.

I'm finally fit and healthy enough to spar again, though everyone is still being gentle for fear of hurting me. It won't last long because I keep handing them their asses, and every single one of them is getting annoyed. Without weapons, my chances of winning are usually just over half with Riley and Beans due to their sheer size and strength.

One good thing about the long canyons is it's much easier on watch. There is no need to set a watch until the sun has well and truly set.

That evening, near sunset, Bitty and Beans are sparring, and he finally gives in to Bitty's demands to be treated fairly. Riley and I are reclining on the ground next to each other, listening to the distant sound of weapons clanging. I'm not sure who is avoiding who lately, but we have barely spoken a word to each other.

So, of course, the first thing that comes out of my mouth when we're semi-alone is: "How was I captured when you were on watch?"

I've wanted to ask him for weeks but haven't known how to bring it up. I'm so angry at him, but I am also always on the edge of *crying* because I miss him. How can I miss someone who was never mine? *Pathetic.*

He doesn't answer for the longest time, and I start to wonder whether I imagined saying it, or perhaps he's ignoring me.

"I don't know." Riley sighs and then grimaces at his own response.

I nod, looking away from him, willing away the sting of tears. I have to bite my cheek, beginning to panic that the tears are going to overwhelm my lids anyway. This whole crying thing better be temporary.

"It's not like I didn't do a perimeter check. I did multiple. Not a sound or movement out there. We couldn't figure it out," Riley says quietly, squinting at the setting sun. "I did get distracted, though. You were making sounds and I thought maybe it was a nightmare, so I came back to check on you. Then when you left to relieve yourself…after my bad joke…I went in the opposite direction to give you space." Riley is analyzing a bunch of small pebbles in his hands, the sounds of Beans and Bitty training filling the silence as I wait for him to continue. "One of my biggest regrets is not going with you that night. I'm truly sorry. For everything," Riley says with a noticeable quaver.

Grateful he isn't looking at me, I discreetly wipe my falling tear. "Maybe they were already there," is all I can say back, unable to look at him either.

"What do you mean? You think they were waiting for you?"

"It's possible. Could be why you never heard them, if they were already in position before you went on watch."

"Did they say something to make you think that?" Riley asks, clearing the emotion from his throat.

"Sort of. But also, when I was bathing that day, I remember hearing a twig snap. I thought Tovi—"

"That was me," Riley blurts, cutting me off. "I didn't mean...I wasn't *spying* on you. Beans sent me on watch, and I wanted to check on you, and I didn't expect you to be..." Riley gestures vaguely, and I assume he means naked.

"You could've said something."

"Fuck no, I couldn't have! I already loathed the idea of you thinking I'm a creep as it was. Announcing my presence after diving into a bush because I didn't realize you'd be naked, sounded like the worst idea." Riley's horrified face as he says this is enough to make me laugh. I'm holding it in, but the heat is rising in my face, the harder I try.

"I had to lie there, knowing you were naked in the creek, unable to resume my perimeter check, just so you didn't think I was a pervert!"

I burst, unable to contain my laughter anymore. "Why are you telling me now?"

"Because I don't want you to think those assholes were watching you!" Riley shouts, his face bright red, but a smile emerges when he sees me laughing.

"Maybe they were! Maybe you were all just hiding in the

bushes watching me bathe together!" I cry, holding my ribs because the laughter is too much.

Stifling his own laugh, Riley protests. "This isn't funny, Mika!"

"Oh, but it is. I'm imagining you diving into a bush to hide from me, right next to my kidnappers!" Tears are streaming down my face from laughing. I have to lie down to relieve the pressure in my ribs. "So, you just sat there and *watched* me bathe?"

"Yes—No!" Riley's flustered response only fuels my hysteria.

Beans and Bitty come over to see what the two of us are yelling about, so I tell them an exaggerated version, much to Riley's continued embarrassment.

"I hate all of you," Riley announces with no malice. He stalks off smiling and shaking his head, as the three of us continue to howl with laughter.

CHAPTER TWENTY-EIGHT

We're due to arrive in Erdu Castle City in a few days, but we come across a small tavern along the road after bypassing Lyngby. There is no inn, but designated camping areas are available, with metal drums provided for fires. A few groups are already camped, and we claim one furthest away from everyone, appreciating the flat ground and rush of the nearby river in the gorge below.

For a small tavern in the middle of nowhere, it's bustling with activity. This might be the most diverse gathering of people I've seen, including the most Patrons I've seen in one place since Osraed. Laughter and hollering, music and singing, the clashing of dishes and glasses—the sound is overwhelming. I can't help myself as I stride straight toward the musicians, ignoring my hunger for now.

Beans creeps up behind me and offers his hand to dance with a slight bow. I laugh and take it. We dance, and it's less chaotic than it was with Riley in Jundamara, and certainly less...angsty. The result is the both of us laughing, the crinkle in his eyes the obvious reason for the slight wrinkles he's developing.

After a dance, we join the table where Bitty and Riley are arguing over the merits of washing your hair when you're cold. I can't follow either of their logic, but both are very passionate about their stance. Beans and I vehemently decline to pick a side, and we order food instead.

The tavern is old and worn. The tables and chairs are creaky and rickety from use. Every window has been covered in curtains, every lantern flickering. No fire heats the hearth as it's much too warm already.

I'm leaning against the bar after dinner, people-watching while I wait for service, when a Sadoriborn man catches my eye. His yellow eyes of the sand are a stark and beautiful contrast to the burnt umber of his skin and black hair braided into locs and falling almost to his waist. He smiles in my direction, causing the pale wood piercings that stick out of his nose to jiggle. I frown in confusion and look behind me and spot an equally gorgeous Sadoriborn woman approaching behind me, smiling back at the man. They share a short embrace and move to a table.

Next to where the Sadoriborn man had been seated is a rather short-looking Erduborn man covered in beautiful jewelry. His eyes are closer to red than they are brown, and he has a wide smile that I'm sure is aimed at *me* this time. He registers my attention on him and raises a glass in offer.

I look at my travel companions, who are all engrossed in conversation. Why not? It's a drink with an attractive man who doesn't know who I am. I nod with a shrug, and he moves down the bar to me.

When he reaches me, the man leans in. "How much?" he asks, close to my ear.

I hear a snicker from behind him as I take in his two companions, trying to contain their laughter.

"Excuse me?" I say with deadly calm, stepping back to assess the situation better.

The first Erduborn man, failing to contain himself, repeats the question which sends his friends howling. It's a dare or something. Ask some unsuspecting woman how much she's worth for the night. Insinuating that, one, I am a lady of the evening for hire, and two, there's something offensive about the profession.

I'm about to say he couldn't afford me when his eyes widen, as do his companions behind him. All three track their eyes up behind me. The swirling flutter inside my ribs and the heat skipping across my skin tell me who is behind me.

"Why is it that you look scared of *me*?" Riley's deep voice rumbles dangerously.

His giant hands rest on my shoulders as the rest of him steps close behind me, and I make note of every part of him that touches me.

"It's my girl here that would have you three pissing into your boots as you cried for your mothers. I just came for a beer." Riley leans forward, takes the man's glass, and downs it in one, slamming it back down with a loud thud.

The three of them stand abruptly and mutter their apologies, still confused. But I watch as their eyes slowly take stock of all the weapons visible on my person. Their faces pale before they trip over themselves getting away.

Riley's hands continue to rest heavily on my shoulders, his heat searing my skin through my clothes and even my leathers. I make no move to pull away, and neither does he.

"Your girl?" I ask, during a lull in the chaos of sound around us.

"Thought it was better than 'my assassin,' but it's a work in progress."

I laugh despite myself because he's not wrong. I *am* his assassin. He's the Prince Ofnemoris, and the crown owns me. My laughter catches in my throat as his hands slide in from shoulders to around my throat, his forefingers lifting my chin so I look back and up toward him. His intense gaze looks down at me.

His chest is rising and falling in short succession as if he's trying to calm himself. "I know you don't need my protection, Firecat, but I'll be Divine-damned if I allow anyone to treat you as anything less than the fucking glorious woman you are. As much as it might have turned me on to see you annihilate those cockheads," he finishes huskily, a curl to the side of his lip.

His eyes flick to my mouth and I think, or dread, or hope, he might kiss me. He strokes my throat and lets me go gently, walking back to the table. I wait there, alone, catching my breath. Correcting the equilibrium in my brain, and the white-hot heat inside me that's warring with the searing cold absence of Riley's touch.

Later, in my bedroll, I am yet to calm down. My logical brain is relieved we're not at an inn and instead camping out in the open. But my slutty brain, located between my legs, is yelling her disappointment as I struggle to fall asleep. I can't even let my hands wander for relief. I fall into a frustrated sleep at some point, waking just as frustrated the next morning.

The rest of our journey to Erdu Castle City, while difficult with our lack of supplies and dwindling water, was almost enjoyable. Fortunately (or unfortunately, I change my mind daily, hourly even), Riley and I share no more close interactions, and no further heated looks or touches. It's like old times, pre-kidnap. Except for the gaping hole where Tovi should be.

KING OFERDU WILL HAVE spies all through Castle City, and it will be reported immediately if any of us are spotted. This means we're unable to go to any of the nicer inns located closer to the castle.

We sell the horses off at a stable and I swallow a teary goodbye. I knew we wouldn't be able to keep them, but it still sucks. I give the stable hands a lot of my coins to ensure they're well looked after, and then we head into the city center.

A dilapidated looking nighthouse is bustling not too far from the castle. Unsurprisingly, gold pays for discretion, and we're able to rent a single room with twin double beds and its own washroom for us to share. Ladies and men of the night attend to their clientele in private rooms, and luckily it seems to be soundproof so far.

I can't keep my eyes to myself as the professionals parade around the halls and common areas with barely any clothing on. My three companions don't seem fazed in the slightest. Though scantily clad, the workers freely move around, chatting to everyone. Bitter jealousy coats the back of my tongue at their ability to make people feel welcomed instead of uncomfortable. They're all so friendly—even though we are surely disturbing them—and I make a mental note, adding nighthouses to my list of pleasant places to stay in the future.

Only Bitty and I can explore the city discreetly. Beans and Riley are far too memorable, being giant Nemorisborn, one of them not a Patron. Both have already been reported in the city.

Beans whips out some Oferdu pins for us, red diamonds

with fake Patron numbers in black rhodium. Beans tells me that not too many Patrons mill about Erdu Castle City, so it will be best to keep our hoods up and eyes down, bringing as little attention to ourselves as we can despite the small security of having fake Oferdu Patron pins. The numbers obviously won't match our tattoos, which requires both of us to ensure they're fully covered.

I rub my tattoo with the memory of getting it. It's like being slapped over and over with a switch while simultaneously having a pin scraped along raw flesh. A blue-black set of ten numbers in thick bold writing is tattooed from one side of the widest part of my left forearm to the other.

Some people get tattoos for pleasure or cultural significance, like anyone Oflaguz. Assignments to that country were always fascinating, as I saw how people had permanent pictures inked into their skin and wondered what made them decide on their designs.

I suppose freedom of any kind, including freedom of expression or bodily autonomy, would be fascinating to someone who has none of their own.

Ofosraed people don't tie themselves to any one country or culture, no matter where it might look like you're born. Leian doesn't have Laguzborn tattoos. In the children's compound, the Sadoriborn head cook, Mastudo, doesn't have pierced skin with bone or wooden embellishments. Nash, the stablemaster, isn't covered in jewelry like someone Erduborn.

An exception to this might be Dell, who is Erduborn and the current commander of the Ofosraed peacekeepers. Dell was always decked out in Nemoris leather regardless of whether they're on duty or not. To be fair, Nemoris leather *is* the best leather.

We're faceless, shapeless, ready to mold into whatever country bids to own us.

It's not often I've seen a Patron who fully embraces any one culture, not the one they're born of nor the one they are sold to. But I recently saw a Nemorisborn Ofmieva Patron draped in extravagant furs—the preferred attire for the Ofmieva people—and it was a sight to behold. I loved it, they looked spectacular. Adding to the allure I suppose, was the fact he was an Ofmieva Patron despite that country's reluctance to purchase Patrons of the Divine.

Bitty and I make a good pair for the task at hand. They listen for anyone who begins to gossip about us, or if the peacekeepers stationed around Castle City begin to talk. I know how to be a sneak, spotting the best places to hide or disappear as needed. Plus, I can disable someone quietly without them realizing, which unfortunately does happen more than once.

We leave most of our Nemoris leather back in the room as it would have brought too much attention. Being in a hooded cloak while everyone else is in the Erdu style of soft, light fabrics—not to mention that we have no jewelry—is already a risk. Fortunately, we're rarely given a second glance.

Three times we have had to lure men and women to dark pathways so we can deal with them following us. I knock them unconscious and steal any gold or weapons they carry. Better to make it look like a random act of theft than anything else.

Eventually, a man recognizes me. Apparently, he has an acquaintance who pointed me out to him during a bi-moon market they both work in Osraed. The acquaintance told him I was the Silent Assassin and that if he ever saw me, I was up to no good. *Asshole.* He's correct of course, but still, what an asshole.

Bitty says his wife doesn't believe him, however, he has plans to go to peacekeepers in the morning and let them know. We need to tell the others, and since it's getting late, we head back to our rooms.

I ditch Bitty before they even walk through the door.

We would have had to discuss what to do, debate, and decide, risking the man changing his plans and going to the peacekeepers early. He needs to die; that's all there is to it. What is the point of a discussion when I know the result will be the same? We cannot risk him alerting the peacekeepers and losing our chance to find the princess.

Murdering an innocent person is not something I want a witness to, nor do I want the man's blood to be on any hands but my own. Chances are this man has a family, further requiring a monster for the job.

I'm already a monster. What's one more piece of my soul so the three of them can keep theirs intact?

I'm sitting on a roof—*not* in a sneaksuit since I haven't had a chance to replace it—watching through the window of their little mud brick house. No children, thankfully. I'm still mulling over if I need to kill his young wife when I see him grab her by the hair and yell in her face. I can see the spittle fly from his mouth onto her.

The wife gets to live.

The moon is bright and far enough along the sky that I'm uncomfortable with the amount of time left to do this. I make my way undetected toward the back of their house, which is in the moon's shadow. He's inebriated and angry that she doesn't believe him about me. Of course, she's saying she believes him now, though it doesn't matter to him. I can hear his slurred shouts and her whimpers, my blood boiling and rage thrashing.

I have some knives and blades stowed, but using them would raise suspicion, or cause the wife to be the one arrested. It needs to look like an accident. He's large, as all Erduborn are, and if he could fight, my plan wouldn't work.

I kick a few things in the back alley, making sure that something hits their back door. Hoping that none of his neighbors are interested, I hide beside the steps, waiting in the darkness. My first problem is that the lazy fuck sends his wife. She opens the door and stands with her arms folded. After a few seconds, she steps down and out, and I grab her.

With a hand over her mouth and a blade to her neck, I whisper in her ear, "You have two choices. Scream and die. Or stay quiet, and your piece of shit husband has *an accident.* Nod if the second option is more appealing to you."

The woman gives one shaky nod, and I let her go. Wide-eyed, she turns back to me, her eyes scanning over my silhouette. Tears welling, she melts into the darkness of the alley, and my rage flares as I note a fresh bruise already blooming across her young face.

This whole time, he's been yelling her name and asking what's going on. She remains silent even after I let her go. It's a risk. She could be going for help. But something in her eyes as she backed away tells me I answered a Divine prayer.

Eventually, he stomps to the back door looking for her, grumbling threats. Standing on the top step, he looks out. His wife must be hiding around the corner now, and he hasn't spotted me right beside him. I need him to take another step down. One step forward.

Go one step forward, you bag of moldy dicks. Tovi would have appreciated my insult. My heart seizes briefly at the thought of her.

When he takes the final step forward, I kick the back of his knees. I lunge onto the top step behind him, jumping to grab the door frame, as my arm hooks around his neck. I let momentum and my weight drag him back, using the force from pushing myself down from the door frame. The resounding crack as his head hits the sharp edge of his concrete step is loud enough to cause me concern about his neighbors.

But no one sounds the alarm. The only sounds are from the man gasping softly as blood gushes from his head. I pull my hood back slightly as I stand over him, making sure he sees me. His eyes widen a fraction. I look up at the sound of soft footfalls. It's the wife. When she comes closer, she's shaking, staring in shock at the man who was her husband. I look back down, and his eyes are unfocused. He's dead.

"What a shame. Your drunk of a husband slipped and fell," I say pointedly, slipping back into the shroud of darkness, ensuring I am fully cloaked by my hood.

"Yes. Such a shame. Too bad I was already in bed asleep and didn't notice until the morning," she replies with a steady whisper.

"Do you have work?" I can't help but ask, as she stands frozen in place, staring at her deceased husband's body.

"I'm still an apprentice midwife, but I will be able to start attending births myself in the next moon. That'll bring coin."

Further relieved that I haven't fucked this woman's future entirely, I start digging in my pockets for the gold I've been accumulating from ambushes. I hand her a gold and a few silvers to tide her over until she's earning her own.

Staring at the coins in her hand, she asks, "Who sent you after him?"

Containing the unhinged bubble of laughter in my throat at the thought of this man being worthy of the Silent Assassin, I answer. "No one. Call it a happy coincidence." Turning to leave, she whispers a small thank you, and I disappear into the night.

The bakers of the city are starting to wake which means dawn must not be far. I slip all the way back to the nighthouse without incident, Bitty swinging the door open before I even have a chance to turn the handle.

All three of them are awake and waiting for me.

CHAPTER TWENTY-NINE

Beans growls for me to get inside. I put my head down in contrition, but I'm trying to hide my smirk at the fact I'm about to be reprimanded like a naughty child by *Daddy Beans*. The mirth is completely extinguished by yet another unwanted thought of Tovi tonight.

"The man will no longer be a problem, I assume?" his deep voice asks stiffly.

"Correct. Nor will he beat his young wife anymore," I reply, looking up into his eyes. I stay there for as long as I can before the revulsion gains traction, and I look away. I'm frustrated that it looks like weakness when I do that.

Bitty pouts. "We could have gone together," they say, earning themselves a glare from Beans.

"You're part of a team Mika. We should have discussed and planned this together," Beans is saying as I glance at Riley, who is looking at everything but me.

Once an assassin, always an assassin.

I walk toward the washroom to clean my face and rinse my mouth as I reply with exasperation, "Agreed. But then murder would have been on four sets of hands instead of one, and if we delayed, we risked him blabbing to people who believed his story."

Bitty had already debriefed the other two on our slightly successful day. We learned of the new royal gardens on the edge of the castle, which are in view of the western part of Castle City. We plan to go there tomorrow—*today*. The first glow of sunrise has reached our window.

"I'm going to get a couple of hours of sleep before we head out," I say through a yawn, unlacing my boots.

"Sleep as long as you like. Bitty and I will go out today. Rain is predicted, and I can wear a jacket and scarf to hide my Nemorisborn features," Beans says, the last words trailing off as I slip into sleep.

"KILL HER," the older woman instructs while pointing at a snowolf pup wriggling with excitement in front of them.

Fear shoots into the heart of the little blonde girl. Tears fill her eyes before spilling down flushed, pale-skinned cheeks. She doesn't protest or beg. She knows it would be futile.

In the blink of an eye, the pup is dead, mutilated beyond recognition.

With the almost unrecognizable body of Anerea in front of her, the little girl looks at her hands, covered in blood.

"No!" she screams in confusion. "I didn't do that to her!" She stands on shaky legs. "I didn't kill her like that, did I?" she asks in disbelief.

Uncontrollable sobs escape her throat, as she struggles to understand, while confusion and fear bloom to a painful crescendo. "This isn't what happened," she pleads to no one.

Jaena approaches with vicious precision, reaching to take the knife from the little girl's blood-stained hands. She lets her.

Briefly, for a tiny, soul-crushing moment, she thinks the older woman will cuddle her this time, comfort her instead of scolding her for crying. But Jaena stabs the 7-rev-old girl in the abdomen.

"Do not cry for the dead," the older woman says as she slices the little girl's throat. "I will not cry for you."

Jaena continues to mutilate her beside Anerea's desecrated body while she screams in agony, the little girl knowing she deserves every bit of it.

I fling myself to a sitting position, a knife in my hand as I look around, the remnants of a scream in my throat.

"What happened?" I ask Riley, breathless as I will my rage to get back into its cage. The memory-twisted nightmare coats the back of my tongue with bile.

"I'll assume your thrashing and scream means it wasn't a good dream then?" he asks, peering at me from the floor. Shirtless and sweaty.

"No, not a good dream. What are you doing?" I return the knife to the place between the wall and the bed.

"Trying to keep some semblance of fitness while being confined to a room." He grunts, resuming the push-ups I must have interrupted. "There's breakfast on the table."

I get up and shove some ham and pea egg-slice into my mouth before going to the washroom to clean away the nightmare still fresh on my skin. The nighthouse may look dilapidated from the outside, but the running water and stone basins make it lush compared to everywhere else we have stayed. I suppose when they have to entertain high-paying clients with discretion, an inconspicuous outside and lush inside makes sense.

Fresh as a daisy, I exit the washroom to find Riley looking out the bedroom windows, still topless.

"Sorry if I took too long in there."

Without a word, he turns around and walks straight past me.

"You're angry at me again," I accuse him.

He sighs, pausing in the doorway. "No. But worrying about you constantly is exhausting, Firecat."

"Well, stop."

"We can't all just turn off our feelings like the Silent Assassin," he bites back, immediately growling and looking at the ceiling. "I'm sorry. I didn't mean that. I'm feeling like a caged animal, but I shouldn't have lashed out."

Riley turns and leans against the doorway, his brows creased and sweat glistening over his naked chest. Distracting me. Causing my rage to start raking its claws from my throat downward, splitting me open.

I turn my back to him. "*Go away. Go away. Go away.*"

"Go where?" Riley asks, annoyance in his voice.

Realizing I've spoken the words aloud, I groan. "Not you." I grimace and scratch my eyebrow. "I was talking to my rage building up."

Riley remains silent. I turn around to see if he heard me.

He heard me, because his face clearly says, *"keep the crazy away from me."* I steel my shoulders and look him dead in the eye, waiting for the moment I will need to look away. But it doesn't come because he shakes his head and backs into the washroom. My rage drops like a hot stone into my stomach, turning it to acid.

AFTER CHANGING INTO CLEAN CLOTHES, I set out my weapons and begin to sharpen them one by one—except for my hatchets which *still* don't need sharpening. Riley eventually comes out of the washroom and joins me at the small table in the corner of the room.

"I didn't...I didn't realize that I...e*nraged* you," Riley says quietly, not taking his eyes off his hands in front of him at the table.

"I never said you did." Riley opens his mouth with a look of protest as I continue. "*My* rage. Mine. It's inside of me always, constantly trying to break free. Sometimes, it's only fluttering. Other times, it's clawing my insides." I do not want to mention that I had likened it to a firecat long before he gave me the nickname.

His brows shoot up, and he finally looks at me. I hold his eye, wanting to show I'm not ashamed, despite knowing it's quite the opposite. His eyes search mine. As if summoned, my rage begins to flap about, my heartbeat increasing. But the need to look away doesn't come.

"I'm sorry."

"Why are you sorry?"

"So many reasons, Firecat. If I list every single one, do you think you would hate me a little less?"

I pinch the bridge of my nose between my eyes, willing away the tears beginning to sting. Worried I might be unsuccessful, I gather my now sharpened weapons. "For the record Riley," I say, as I carry them to our bed. "I try to hate you. I *really* try." I grunt, pulling my bag out from under the bed, putting my knives in it, and shoving it back under. "But I can't," I say, the last words a whisper, and then my breath hitches.

He's standing right beside me. Looking at me like no one ever has before. I've had men and women leer, I've had them look at me appreciatively, or even possessively. But this is something else.

"Why do you look at me like that?" I ask as I try to maneuver around him. His hand juts out to capture me at the hip before I can pass.

"Like what?" his deep voice asks, caressing my skin in

such a way that I have to resist the urge to shiver in response.

I put my hands on his chest, applying pressure to push him away, as I try to sidestep him again. "Like you want to kiss me."

The hand gripping my hip pulls me closer while the other pulls my chin up, forcing me to look at him. "Maybe because I do want to kiss you, Firecat!" he growls.

"Kiss someone else."

"I have thought of kissing no one else but you for moons."

I let out an angry snort, accompanied by an ugly laugh. "A lie or a waste."

"It is neither. We haven't had a chance to talk about the windcaves," he says with his familiar smirk. The smirk that confuses me on so many levels. Exciting me beyond measure and devastating in its reminder that this is all a game.

I step back this time, trying to create distance between us. The lines are blurring and getting dangerous, and my rage is giving its warning. "Nothing to talk about. It was a mistake, or it would have been if anything had happened."

In the blink of an eye, Riley steps forward, his hand on my hip moving to my lower back and the other down my leg. He uses both as leverage as he turns and sits heavily on the bed, pulling me to him. One of my legs kneels on the bed beside him, and my other stands directly between his knees.

"So, if I kissed you now, like I kissed you in those caves, you'd tell me to stop?" he all but whispers.

His hand has left my leg and grabs my neck, a thumb caressing my throat. The sound I make couldn't be confused for anything but the breathless moan that it is, and he chuckles.

"And if I told you to stop?" I ask, out of breath, trying—and failing—not to lean into his hand.

His thumb leaves my throat and traces the line of my bottom lip. "I'd stop. So, tell me. Tell me to stop."

I can hear his smirk as he speaks, which widens into a grin when I glare at him. I open my mouth to reply, but he puts his thumb into my mouth, running it along the top of my bottom teeth. He bites his lip, and it's not until he breaks eye contact to look at my mouth that I realize how long I held his eye.

"Are you going to headbutt me?" He moves his thumb further into my mouth, my tongue licking it involuntarily, causing him to hitch his breath.

Wanting some control back, I suck on his thumb. I can play this game too. Can't I?

But he's better at this than me, and when I bite down on his thumb enough to cause him a tiny bit of pain, I am straddling him entirely. Too focused on the hand at my mouth, I hadn't realized his other hand had moved down to the back of my leg where it was an easy adjustment for him to lift me into straddling his lap.

"Is that what you meant when you said you'd bite me, Firecat? If I'd known that, there's a lot more I could have put in your mouth." His thumb slips out of my mouth, and he leans back on the bed with that arm. Devouring me. Looking smug.

My hands scrunch his tunic into my fists, one at his shoulder and the other low between us. Some part of my brain remembered to keep us separated slightly, and my eyes flick down to see just how close we have gotten. My eyes flick further than my hand, straight down to the strain against the crotch of his pants.

He sees my line of sight and laughs, letting go of me to adjust himself and giving me a wink.

Nothing. Absolutely nothing has happened here, not even

a kiss. But I know my own arousal rivals his, surely soaking my underwear by now.

I need him, need his touch. I need to taste him. I pull him roughly to an upright seated position again. My hand lowers slightly to grip the edge of his pants between us. Both of his hands grip my hips now, and he grinds me into him, despite the space I tried to keep.

I put my mouth on his and he opens it to kiss me. Instead, I suck his bottom lip into my mouth and bite it until he growls, and I lean back with my own smirk. The scent of him is overwhelming my every thought and sense. That fresh mint and pine mixed with *him*. Riley.

Obviously sick of waiting for me to kiss him, he fists a hand into my hair and pulls me toward his mouth, a rough kiss of lips and teeth. He tastes better than I remember, better than my dreams of him. I hook my arm around his neck for leverage so I can kiss him deeper as he grinds me against him again. His moan reverberates through my skull and down to my core, and I am addicted. I need to hear him make that sound again. Hear him lose control because of me.

I had forgotten—*thoroughly* forgotten—what an enormous cock Riley had in his pants. I am reminded as I trace the thick outline of it between us, gripping it to hear him moan again. It would be proportional to the size of him, of course, but my mouth dries at the thought of him fitting it anywhere inside me.

I'm scraping my teeth along his neck as I use the heel of my hand to rub his entire length, giving the area where his balls would be a slight squeeze before sliding back up and using my thumb to rub the head.

Riley's thunderous heartbeat and uneven breathing are not enough, so I move faster and harder. His fingers dig into my skin where he holds my hips as he kisses me with such wild abandon that a groan sounds from the back of my throat. I'm grinding against the back of my own hand, needing the friction and pressure for myself.

All at once, my hand is removed from between us. Riley interlocks my fingers in his. "When you make me come, I want to be inside you," he finishes with a pant as he tries to kiss me again.

"That won't be happening, I told you I don't want to fuck you."

He laughs as he kisses my jaw, then dips down to lick the column of my neck. "Then why are you touching me like this, Firecat?" he asks, voice husky.

I know exactly what to say to get the power back. "Just scratching an itch."

He grinds me down into him, causing me to suck in a breath of pleasure. "Nothing else?"

"What else could there be, *Prince Aurelius?*"

A look flashes across his face as his grip loosens, and the way he dodges my kiss with a smirk lets me know that I hit my mark.

And I despise myself for it. This was what I wanted, to keep him from getting too close. It's all a game, all supposed to be fun. So why do I feel so shitty about it?

He growls, standing up quickly and setting me on the ground. I look up at him questioningly, but he's looking toward the door.

"Perfect timing," he bites out, as I hear Beans' booming laughter in the halls. "This situation cannot be hidden."

I look down and see the very obvious outline of his cock straining against his pants and resist the urge to touch it. I turn, making a beeline to sit at the table before they arrive, assuming he's behind me.

But Riley is reclined casually on the bed, the corner of our blanket bunched across his lap. It looks effortless, like he's relaxing, and not hiding a raging erection.

CHAPTER THIRTY

Beans and Bitty burst through the door, both beaming and dripping wet. They found the garden unguarded because it's a *shared* garden. The area where the royals sit is indeed guarded, but the garden, as a whole, is not.

But the best part is that they were able to follow the young Prince Eryn Oferdu after they found him lounging in the gazebo during a break in the rain. They now know which room is his because Bitty was able to follow his footsteps through the castle. This makes them feel very proud of themselves, as they should. This is an excellent result.

We plan, as a team, how we're going to sneak me in with Bitty on the lookout. First, we need to find me a uniform of a Patron on staff, which has me tingling in anticipation as I'll get to sneak and steal one from the royal launders.

But the rest of our day is uneventful. It starts to rain again so the next part of our plan is postponed. We spend the afternoon eating and playing Talamu (I suck, which surprises no one), and we have an early night.

Rolling over in bed, I see the naked body of a man. It's Riley's pale, freckled skin glowing in the sunbeams of a new day. I stroke his chest, and he grabs my hand, flattening it against him roughly, as he pushes it slowly downward.

He flaunts his cheeky smirk and smoldering eyes that unleash immediate desire within me. My bare nipples harden almost painfully as I clench my thighs against the heat pooling in my core. When our hands reach their destination, I grip him, and he covers my hand with his. He guides my hand along his shaft, lazily pumping him to a full erection.

Unable to wait any longer, I hook my leg over his waist to straddle him. I slide myself along every delicious inch of his cock, coating him with my slick arousal. He holds my neck with one hand as he rolls my nipple between his fingers with the other. I arch and buck against him with the painful pleasure.

I'm guiding him to my entrance, when a sound catches in my throat, waking me from my dream.

I let out a very angry, very frustrated breath through my nose. The moon—not the sunrise—is streaming through the window, and Riley and I are most definitely clothed.

Riley's sleepy voice startles me. "You okay?" he says, reaching for me.

I look up—I've managed to scoot down the bed so I am facing his chest. "No," I say, causing him to sniff and sit up on his elbow, rubbing his eyes.

The room is still dark, the moonlight only illuminating the back of him, keeping his front in a shroud of darkness.

"Nightmare?"

I let out a breath, dragging my word. "No."

"If it wasn't a nightmare, why aren't you—oh," he says, as I capture his hand and drag it down my body.

"Just scratching an itch," he says, a statement, not a question.

I pull up the long, sleeveless tunic I was sleeping in and confirm. "Nothing else."

His hand moves to my hip, gripping and dragging my underwear down with a delicious scrape until it reaches the point where I can kick them the rest of the way. Hooking his hand under my left knee, he moves it to spread my legs.

"As you wish, Firecat," he whispers down to me, stroking the shell of my ear with his other hand.

With painfully slow swirls, his fingers caress my inner thigh. I reach down to hurry his hand, but he grabs it with a growl, passing it to his hand beside my head to restrain me.

"If you want me to do this, I will do it my way."

Apparently, he is waiting for a response as he hasn't resumed his movements. I breathe the word *"okay"* at him. His hand slides along my thigh so quickly my breath catches, only to have him stroke the skin *next* to my core, where it meets the edge of my thighs. While he keeps my left hand restrained, my other is wedged uselessly between us.

I lean up to kiss him, but he dodges me. I don't have time to wonder why, as he slips his fingers into my wetness and slides it up my slit.

He sucks in a breath. "You're so fucking wet. What were you dreaming about?"

"Daddy Beans," I tease, licking up the column of his throat, since that's all I can reach while restrained.

He releases my hand and growls softly. "Then why don't you ask *him* to scratch your itch?"

"Maybe I wi—"

Riley slides a finger inside me, cutting my words short. The room is silent, and I stifle my moan so the two people on the other side of the room stay asleep. The slick sounds of his finger's rhythmic movements are amplified in the silence, especially as he adds a second finger. He pumps in and out with deliberate strokes, and I muffle my ragged breath into his throat.

With my hand free now, I slide it down his torso, aiming for his pants. I need more, I need to touch him at the same time. I reach his waistband and slip my hand under it. He leans down to my ear. "I will not be able to remain as quiet as you are if you touch me, Firecat," he whispers.

I grunt my frustration, nipping at his ear as I hold his hip instead. He slides his fingers deeper and brings his thumb around to stroke the bundle of nerves at the apex of my thighs. As his fingers slide out slightly with a curl of pressure inside, his thumb slides downward. Fingers sliding all the way back in while his thumb, now slick, slides up and over my sensitive nub.

He must realize I'm close, because he cocoons me entirely under him, all while his fingers slip in and out of my core and the heat of his thumb caresses along my slit. I buck and arch my back, holding my breath against him so I don't make a sound. My nails dig into his hip as I quake with release. I pant as quietly as possible, trying to return to even breathing as my body continues to quiver and shudder with aftershocks.

"I can still feel your climax fluttering around my fingers," Riley whispers, fingers still inside me. And then he laughs quietly as his words cause my walls to clench around his fingers in another wave of pleasure.

Finally able to breathe normally, I relax onto my back, and he gently removes his fingers. I reach for his face, but he rolls off the bed to stand. The moonlight streaming through the window reveals the silhouette of exactly what I was missing between his legs. He hands me my underwear quietly and moves like a ghost into the washroom.

Never have I been able to climax with someone else's

fingers, proving how wound-tight I really was. I consider following Riley into the washroom, surely he could be quieter in there. I want to taste him, feel him in my mouth. I haven't done *that* since the time I was forced to, and I thought I'd never want to again. But I do, if it's Riley. I must fall asleep thinking about him fucking my mouth because he startles me awake, crawling back into our bed, erection gone.

"I'll scratch your itch next time," I promise.

"No need, Firecat. I just wanted to prove I could fuck you with my fingers. Goodnight."

THANKFUL FOR A MOONLESS SKY, I'm climbing the outer walls toward Prince Eryn's room the next night. Unfortunately, I am still only wearing a black hooded cloak instead of a sneaksuit. It's risky and dangerous to be doing this so exposed, but we have no choice. Part of our plan is to kidnap the young prince and get him to tell us where the doxies are. Then tomorrow, hopefully before anyone realizes he's gone, I'll take my new uniform for a tour.

For a tyrannical king, it's far too easy to get to his son's room. Bitty is nearby and will cause a diversion if they hear anything to suggest someone has spotted me, giving me time to get away. But so far, so good, there is not a single guard around.

It's the middle of the night, and Bitty said they've heard nothing since the prince went to bed a few hours after sunset and has heard nothing since. Praying to the Divine this isn't a trap, I silently open his window and slink into the room, closing it behind me.

Crouching under the window, I allow my eyes to adjust to the darkness and survey the prince's room. My heart skips a beat before realizing the three faces looking at me across the room are only a realistic painting. The large and gaudy frame takes up most of the wall, and as my eyes continue to adjust, I make out the super detailed faces of who I assume are the king, his deceased queen, and their son, Eryn.

Yet another tragic royal death. Queen Jasi broke her neck falling off a horse a decade past. Though I do remember there being something in the rumor mill about it, so there may be more to the story than what was made public. But I had my own shit to deal with at the time—learning to become an assassin in exchange for Jaena cleaning up my mess and avoiding the inevitable execution she promised I'd receive otherwise. I didn't really care what was happening to a royal family across the world.

I quickly survey the room. There is a bedside table and a large canopy bed to my left, with another bedside table on the other side. Along the left wall is a large dresser toward the far wall. The far wall consists of an open door to what looks like a washroom next to the painting, which sits above a long cabinet that runs almost its entire length. Two sofa seats are to my right, next to what I assume must be the door to exit. A plush rug takes up the empty space in the room, and a cold shiver overtakes me, looking at how bare the room is of personal belongings.

I can hear the soft snoring of sleep, and I crawl forward to see the tousled hair of a 16-rev-old boy in his bed. Fortunately, he's alone.

I crawl further into the room, so I can stand without casting a shadow in his window. Taking both blades from my thighs, I pounce on the kid, using one hand to cover his mouth and the other to hold my knives in his view.

He doesn't make a sound as I keep my voice low. "Try to scream, and you'll be dead before it leaves your throat." He nods.

Sitting on Eryn's chest, I move a blade to his ribs and one to his throat. My knees keep pressure on his arms.

"How many guards are outside your door?"

"None. Well, not directly. They're stationed outside my sitting room next door," he whispers, not even a tremble.

"I don't want to kill you, but please do not misunderstand. I won't hesitate if I have to, Prince Eryn."

"What do you want? My father will not pay a ransom. He would sooner send the Silent Assassin to kill me before rescuing me."

I blink at him. No love was lost between the prince and his father then. I file that bit of information away to share with the others. "You look resigned to death either way?"

"Well, if you cannot ransom me, what else is there?"

Letting a long breath out of my nose, I look at the kid. He's surely over 6-foot, and not so wiry that he wouldn't be able to overpower me if he had been taught. He'd likely still die at my blade but is it not better to die fighting than to not try at all? It disappoints me that the king did not teach his son to defend himself or even post sufficient guards.

"Where does your father keep his doxies? Have you seen the Gifted Princess Ofnemoris recently?"

Eryn's face changes, to almost…excited? Happy? I cannot tell in the darkness, but his voice is quick and punchy. "You're here to rescue her?"

"So, you know that she didn't go home?"

"I saw her once *after* my father had said she'd left two weeks prior."

I sigh, relaxing my blades slightly. "This is the first good news we've received since…well, since she went missing."

"The doxies are in an entire wing in the East. *Their* windows are guarded, though."

"Thank you. Knowing they're in the east wing is already

a massive help. We can figure it out from there. Why are you helping me?"

"Besides those knives aimed at me?" he laughs nervously. "She was always nice to me and helping her get away from my father is the least I can do."

This boy is either an exceptional actor or... "Do you want to be kidnapped anyway? I have it on high authority the Silent Assassin won't kill you."

"Why?" the prince drags the word out slowly, inquisitively.

I shrug, slowly pulling my knives away from their threatening position. "To get you away too."

"He would find me, somehow. How do you know the Silent Assassin wouldn't kill me?" he asks, studying me.

"Retired," I say as I put my knives away, getting off him gently so he can sit up.

His face lights up. "You're *her!*" he hisses.

I rub my face. The last few nights of shitty sleep are catching up to me. "Yes. But as I said, I'm retired." *Why did I just admit who I am to this kid?* I adjust my hood to ensure my features are still hidden.

"I thought you'd be scarier. *I'm* bigger than you!"

I snort derisively. "And yet you didn't try to overpower me, my darling prince."

"Rude," he says, feigning indignation.

I watch him for a moment, his innocence and enthusiasm reminding me of Bitty. He stares back at me pleasantly, not acting in any way I would have expected a first-born Prince Oferdu to behave.

It also isn't the first time that someone has realized *I* am the Silent Assassin and reacted...differently. I'm so conditioned to the Osraed response of spitting on me or being obviously disgusted by me as a person. This...

excitement? I'm not sure which makes me more uncomfortable.

Standing to stretch my back, I ask him, "So how do I trust that you won't go running to your father the moment I leave?"

He moves to sit on the edge of his bed. "You'll have to trust my word, as I'll trust yours, that you're here to do exactly what you've said and nothing more."

"There's the Royal backbone I was looking for," I tease.

Walking to the window, I peer out to make sure it's clear.

"What's your next move?" Eryn asks.

"I wouldn't be the *Silent* Assassin if I told everyone what my plans were, kid," I chuckle.

Out of the corner of my eye, I catch a projectile heading toward me. Throwing myself back into a flip and unsheathing both knives, I land in a crouch, poised to throw.

As a pillow hits the sofa seat, plopping softly onto the ground.

Eryn's face is stricken; he holds his hands up in panicked surrender. "Sorry! Sorry. I was...I didn't think!"

I glare at him from my defensive crouch, letting him sweat a bit. My hood has fallen back and—*of fucking course*—the light through the window has illuminated me. He can't help it. He's already studied my face and hair before I realized he could. I stand, sheathing my knives, giving myself a moment to decide what to do.

I should kill him. It's bad enough that he knows the Silent Assassin is here and could tell his father, but now he can identify me too. I'm still weighing my options as I stare at him when he slaps his hands over his eyes dramatically.

"I didn't see you. Were you Sadoriborn? Nemorisborn? Couldn't tell. Couldn't pick you from a crowd, that's for sure."

The prince's word vomit finally comes to an end, and I

sigh. The Silent Assassin is getting soft. Or I'm just really fucking tired. Probably both. "I'm going to go now before I accidentally—*or deliberately*—kill you and your pillows. I'll see you around, prince. Or not."

I slink out the window I came in, cascading down the reinforced gorge walls that make up the front of the castle. Reaching the bottom, I pause, waiting for an alarm to sound. Looking back up, I spot Eryn watching me from his window, and he gives me a tiny wave. I awkwardly wave back.

What a strange kid.

CHAPTER THIRTY-ONE

B itty meets me halfway back to our accommodations. Apparently, the prince and I were quiet enough that they couldn't catch everything said. I'm still impressed and slightly horrified by how excellent their hearing Gift is. No wonder they evaded discovery as an abandoned child until they passed out from hunger and were found by Beans.

Waiting until we are safe from prying eyes and ears, I tell the three of them what was discovered and discussed. They are all equally baffled by the prince's relationship with his father.

Riley puts his head in his hands, breathing a large sigh of relief when I get to the part about the Prince Oferdu seeing his sister *two weeks* after she had supposedly left. Beans makes a quiet, celebratory "fuck yes" gesture and strokes his mustache one-handed while pacing. Bitty flops back on the bed they share with Beans, thanking the Divine.

Their collective relief is contagious.

I crawl into the bed next to Riley after a quick wash. They're double beds, but Riley is double the man. His presence is imposing on the bed at the best of times, but more so after the adventures of last night that haven't been spoken about. Riley and I have our backs to one another, and Beans extinguishes the lantern as we all say our goodnights.

I lay awake listening to the slow breathing of three people falling asleep. I roll onto my back to stare at the ceiling. *Why can't I sleep?* I'm considering getting up to stretch on the floor when Riley rolls over in his sleep to face me. Shifting myself down and onto my side, I look at the man who keeps sending me and my rage into volatility. It's too dark to see much more than vague outlines.

My eyelids are getting heavy while I'm facing him. I close my eyes for a second to imagine his freckles, those endless— almost black, blood-red—lashes, and his perfect lips. When I open them again, I'm facing the wall instead of Riley. The room has lightened, and the birds of dawn are singing their song. Sounds of the city beginning to wake drift through the window and under our door.

Riley twitches his hand in his sleep. He is gently gripping the top of my ribs, while his heavy arm is draped over me. His body is pressed along the length of my back and legs. Moving my head slightly, I feel his other arm above my head, across the pillow I'm not even using, again.

I listen intently for the sounds of breathing from Bitty and Beans, but they're still asleep. Savoring a small, stolen moment of affection, I try to focus on every part of me that Riley is touching. His knee is resting on top of mine, spooning the back of my other knee. The weight of his draped arm is a comfort, and his chest rises and falls against my back, soothing me.

His hand falls to the bed but moves quickly to pull me closer, like a reflex. I freeze. Is he awake? His heavy breathing suggests otherwise. That's when I notice it. The distinct hardness of Riley's erection against my backside. My stomach rockets into my chest, causing me to shoot forward and into a sitting position.

Riley wakes with a startle, looking at me blearily. "Nightmare?" he asks me in a concerned whisper. His hand reaches up to grab my neck, using his thumb to stroke the bare skin. My skin immediately prickles in response, and I turn to respond. But his eyes are shut, breathing already returning to the rhythm of sleep.

In confusion, I watch this enormous man fall back to sleep, while still half stroking the back of my neck. I can't help myself; I look at the tent in his pants. I didn't know that men could be aroused in their sleep too. What does Riley dream about?

Riley sniffs, giving my neck a squeeze as he sits up and rubs his eyes, oblivious to me objectifying him in his sleep.

"Good dreams?" I ask, facing the wall as I stretch to hide my knowing smile.

Riley's unused voice crackles as he tries to whisper. "I don't often get to remember them, Firecat."

I turn to look at him, not bothering to hide my stupid grin. "*You* might not remember, but something else thinks you had a nice dream."

He frowns for a moment before looking down and jolting to cover himself. He grabs his pillow and wallops me with it. "Now who's the pervert?"

I laugh softly, falling to my side and throwing my pillow at him as he stands. He shakes his head smiling and mouthing *"pervert"* at me as he walks to the washroom, with the sounds of Bitty and Beans waking up as I reach for the pillow I threw.

Riley offers to get breakfast with Bitty, going stir-crazy at being inside this whole time. Unfortunately, the nighthouse doesn't have its own tavern, so we're limited to supplies that don't require cooking while we are here.

When they're both gone, Beans checks in with me. "You are not alone Mika. Please stop taking the entire Divined world on your shoulders and let us support you."

"I'm trying. I promise. But you can't help me with this beyond Bitty being a scout and keeping an ear out."

"That might be true, but no unnecessary risks. I'm not sure how sober Riley is going to stay if you keep giving the poor kid a heart attack every few weeks. Or me, for that matter," he says, laughing. I'm frowning at the side of Beans' face as he makes their bed. I don't want to know what he means about Riley, I need to focus on today. "You've already aged me more than Bitty ever has, little one, and I don't think Mama or Frankie would forgive me if anything happened to you either."

I swallow the lump in my throat, unable to speak. At some point in this journey, Beans' terms of endearment have latched onto the last pieces of my soul, and I'm not sure they'll ever let go. Or if I even want them to.

Finished making the bed, Beans engulfs me in a giant hug and kisses the top of my head dramatically. He holds me for a few breaths before letting me go and ruffling my hair. Touching. Always with the touching.

Without thinking, I suddenly wrap my arms around the giant Nemorisborn man from behind as he begins to walk away. Over his arms, I can't make my hands touch in front. It's only a few seconds. Beans doesn't turn his head when I release him. He stands frozen for a beat before clearing his throat and striding into our washroom, leaving me with my rage to remind me of the dangers of getting too close.

During breakfast, the four of us go over the plan. After lunch, the king will be hearing from his people, so the castle gates will be opened and I'll be able to blend in unnoticed.

Slowly, I'll make my way toward the eastern end while Bitty stays a safe distance away to monitor and relay information to Beans and Riley.

Time is flying, and my rage is a consistent buzz keeping me on edge. Ready for action. This type of waiting makes me nauseous. I'd rather be waiting on a rooftop alone than pacing in a bedroom going through the plan over and over.

Bitty and Beans leave to get lunch, but I won't be eating, as an empty stomach will keep me focused. I get changed into the uniform and ask Riley if I look okay.

He adjusts my collar as I fiddle with the waistband of my pants. I still haven't decided how many weapons I want to take just in case I get caught. Fighting is unlikely to be the best course of action, so best to only take one at my thigh.

I'm mulling it over when Riley finally answers. "You look resplendent." Looking into my eyes, still holding my collar, one of his thumbs reaches up to stroke my cheek. "And beautiful, as always."

I clear my throat and move out of his grip. "Stop that," I say, my voice hoarse.

"Stop what?"

"Playing games."

"What games?" His frustration shows in his voice as he grabs me by the waist and pulls me toward him roughly, his back against the wall.

"Go and say those things to someone else, Riley," I whisper as he leans right in, his lips barely an inch away from my own.

"I don't want anyone else. I only want you. And I know you want this too."

We stay like that for an eternity or more. Riley's hands on my waist and my hands on his muscular forearms. Our breath is the only thing between our lips. Neither of us makes to move away. I stare at my favorite freckles on his face and the curve of his lips.

I want to kiss him. *Desperately.* I want him to kiss me.

As if he read my last thought, he closes the distance, his lips colliding with mine. He pulls me in tighter against his body, heat spreading across my skin like wildfire. I open my mouth slightly, and the kiss deepens. I taste his tongue and dig my fingers into his forearms.

"Stop," I whisper against his mouth as I break the kiss.

He freezes, letting me go but only slightly as he looks down in confusion. But I can't do this with him, I can't. I don't want to scratch each other's itches with some kind of transactional sex. But I can't offer him anything more, and neither can he return it. So, I let go. But he doesn't.

"I said stop."

"I have stopped. Tell me why."

My rage is circling like a predator around its prey. "Because I don't want to, is that not enough?" The tone in my voice makes the hairs on my arms rise.

"You truly only want my fingers, and nothing else?"

I growl and buck against him, and he releases me further but keeps his hands on me. "I want nothing from you!"

He hisses, looking at me like I've lost my mind. And maybe I have.

"Why are you so bothered that I won't play the game, Riley? Is it because I haven't yet returned the favor?" I reach aggressively toward his crotch. "Take your fucking pants off, and I'll do it now."

Before I even get there, his hand snatches mine, bringing it up and flattening it on his chest. "Why are you being like this? Is the Silent Assassin scared of feeling something other than rage?"

I try to knee him in the crotch, but he blocks it, using the force to pin me against him. He half slides down the wall, caging me in his legs so we're face-to-face.

"Say you feel absolutely nothing for me, and I'll let you go, Mika."

I open my mouth with a sneer to lie, but he grips my face and brings me to his lips. Stopping before his lips touch mine, only for a second, giving me that time to say it. But I don't. Then, softly, he kisses me. My eyes prick with tears as I kiss him once more, vowing to the Divine that this is the last time. His lips are so soft against mine, his thumb stroking my cheek again, his thundering heart under my hand. *The last time. It has to be.*

I push myself off him and step back, and he lets me. The shattered pieces of my heart blow away in the wind from the distance I create between us. He reaches for me again, and I step further away. With my hand against my lips, I close my eyes, relishing the taste and feel of him before I close the door on us for good.

"Don't. Don't ever kiss me again, Riley," I plead, my voice barely a whisper.

"Firecat," his deep voice croaks out as he reaches for me again. And again, I dodge him, leaving his hands hanging in the air. "*Mika…*" He says my name as if it's a plea.

The unhinged tone of my voice forces my rage to scream louder, and I grimace in pain as I beg. "Promise me. Promise me!"

All I get are those red-rimmed eyes and a strained look on his face. So, I leave, slamming the door behind me. I have everything I need for today and I'm not eating lunch. I'll wait for Bitty downstairs.

Please let there be a breeze outside to calm me.

CHAPTER THIRTY-TWO

The streets of Castle City are buzzing with activity. To avoid suspicion, I look for other Patrons in uniform and follow them while they line up to enter the gates. Bitty assures me that it's to stem the flow of people going in and not that they will be checking who I am.

As promised, I am able to pass through the large gates into the castle's surrounds. Once inside the main foyer, I am immediately swept up in a throng of clamoring people. It's chaos in here. People are everywhere, fighting to be first in line to be seen by the king. I manage to get away from the hordes of people and into a corridor with many passages. I pretend I belong here.

I'm slipping down corridors and checking random doors as I go, trying to get as far east as possible. I pass few people, and any I do see, pay me no mind until I come across a handful of guards who direct me to go *"back that way"*. Knowing I hadn't come across any other way east from this level, means I am going to need to go up a floor and try again.

I'm striding down a wide corridor back the way I came

when the king steps into view with his royal guard. Not able to slow my step without making it obvious to the people and guards behind me, I keep my pace. That is, until the king turns around.

King Stol Brud Oferdu has violet-colored eyes.

Several people bump into me, causing a small scene. Recovering myself, I apologize and try to slip away, but a guard roughly grabs my arm.

"I don't recognize you. Show me your tattoo and state your position."

"There's no point, it won't match my pin." I huff in resignation, hoping this unexpected admission brings the least amount of attention.

I am fortunate that the king doesn't miss a step and continues on, unaware of the scene unfolding behind him. I crane my neck to follow him around a corner of glass and confirm that he does indeed have the eyes of a Patron.

My mind reels as the guard roughly drags me toward the dungeon. I assume. I hope.

I'm thrown into the arms of a woman in a small room, with stairs leading down to the dungeon. The putrid smell wafting up makes my eyes water.

"Strip," the guard who brought me in orders, leering.

"Fuck off back to your post, Gomi," the woman snaps at my Erduborn guard, revealing a large gap between her top front teeth.

Alone with the woman, I try not to react. She's a Mutt. A few inches taller and wider than me—and exceptionally muscular—she legitimately looks like she could snap me in half. And maybe she can. She has the violet eyes of a Patron too.

"Unfortunately, I do need you to strip and give me any weapons," she says, closing the door to the hall we came from.

I pull the knife out first and hand it to her. Not knowing what her Gift is, it would be a foolish risk to fight her. To distract myself from the task at hand, I study the woman as I undress.

Her skin is burnt sienna, but her nose, cheeks, and even her full lips are covered in dark freckles. Her medium-brown hair has a distinct orange hue to it, and she wears it free in a lovely mass of kinky curls coiling very tight. It doesn't reach her shoulders, but if it were straight, I imagine it would be quite long.

Sadoriborn and Nemorisborn. How does that even happen when they're almost at opposite ends of the world?

Not many records still exist from before the Divine Intervention, but Divine Law was introduced to keep the peace. It became forbidden to live anywhere other than the country of your eye color. Sadoriborn all have the yellow eyes of the sand, Mievaborn all have the gray eyes of the mountains, and so on. Osraed became the central country where the Gifted were sent, and the Patron of the Divine Council was established, not having anywhere else to belong.

People who had the physical features of one country but the eye color of another were treated little better than thieves. Someone who *looked* like a Laguzborn but had Oferdu brown eyes of the earth would have to live in Erdu; the Oferdu people believing they stole from the earth. They wouldn't be able to live in Laguz because their eyes were not the blue of the water, despite their otherwise Laguzborn appearance.

People stopped having children with anyone outside of their own country for fear of having a child they couldn't keep. The countries became monolithic, and Mutts became more obvious and subjected to cruel punishments and violence for the rest of their lives. Parents abandoned children or even outright murdered their infants at birth.

The Gifted didn't become slaves right away. It wasn't until Osraed had become an entire country full of Patrons that they realized the concentration of Gifts made them a threat to the other five nations. A war ensued where countless lives were lost.

Divine Law was then updated to what it is today: A Patron can never have agency over themselves and will be the property of the country that owns them. We are chattel.

"You done gawking, prisoner?" the guard asks with a tone that suggests it happens often.

"Sorry," I mumble, naked, as she checks the pockets and hems of my clothing for weapons and lockpicks. Unfortunately, she finds my lockpicks and gives me a smirk, removing them from the fabric. She gives me a quick bodily inspection, but thankfully, nothing invasive.

I eye my knife on the table beside her. Maybe I could grab it and dash out. Naked. *What a great idea.* The woman is looking at me from the corner of her eye. "Go ahead. I will punch you through the wall before you have the chance to stab me, girl."

"I'm naked, not exactly a great escape plan."

A small laugh. "What's your name?" the woman asks, handing my clothes back.

Getting dressed, I reply, "Mika," answering truthfully, but leaving out the *Ofnemoris* part for now. It will take them a while to submit a Patron number check to Osraed, and maybe I can get out of this before then. "What's yours?"

"Liesolette. Down you go. Don't bother holding breath for the smell, it only gets worse."

Liesolette hadn't exaggerated. The air is thick and humid. The further down we go—and we go a long way down—the worse it gets. Lanterns are lit periodically down the stairs.

Reaching the bottom, the stench of feces, urine, and

unwashed bodies is unbearable. I'm trying not to think about the fact that I can taste it in the air. Too late. I gag. There is not a single window for fresh air. Liesolette huffs and pulls a kerchief from her pocket, wrapping it around my head and under my nose. It smells like jasmine.

"You'll get used to it, but this will help until then. I want it back, though."

Baffled by her kindness, I thank her sincerely.

"Far end and to the right you go," she says, pointing.

I wasn't given back the cheap, laced shoes I'd bought on our first day here. The sludgy ground, covered in old pieces of hay and nondescript lumps, is squishing through my toes as I walk to where I was directed.

Liesolette opens the cell door and locks it behind me after I step inside. She lets me know that the channels of running water through the middle of the cell are my toilet, along with the discarded waste passing through from everywhere else in the castle.

"Oi, you still alive in there?" Liesolette calls into the cell on the left of the back wall, an empty cell between us.

"Unfortunately, Lottie," calls a voice that sends a hot knife into my spine.

Unable to make my body do more than breathe, I listen to the sound of the guard moving up the stairs leading out of the dungeon. I can't take my eyes away from the prone form huddled on a metal bed with a straw mattress that matches the one in my cell.

"Tovi?" a voice says. It's my voice, but it's disconnected.

The head snaps up and looks at me. It's her. Her once beautiful brunette hair hangs in lanky clumps around a filthy, slightly sunken face. But it's her. She stands and comes closer to the bars. Her clothes are loose and filthy too, having lost a bit of weight in the moon since she ran off.

I take off the kerchief covering my face so she can see me.

"Mika?" the familiar voice asks, gripping the bars as she tries to look at me. "How are you here?"

"Attempting to rescue Amarilyss, remember?"

She flinches as if stung. I'm still frozen in place. She looks like shit.

"Is getting jailed part of the plan?"

"No. How are you here?" I rasp in disbelief.

"Got caught looking for Lyss myself."

"How long have you been in here?" My heart is racing, trying to beat faster than my rage running circles around my stomach.

Tovi shrugs. "I have no idea, but I've been fed seventeen dinners, I think."

A gushing sound followed by trickling and dripping interrupts us. I have the pleasant experience of watching someone else's shit and piss come down a pipe and travel along the open channel at my feet. It eventually turns and connects with a main channel that all cells feed into. The main channel empties out noisily into a hole in the ground that I can only assume leads outside somewhere.

I immediately put the kerchief back on. The stench is overpowering me, and I'm glad I didn't have lunch. Tovi is pacing, periodically looking at me before frowning and focusing on her hands.

"Why?" I ask in a small voice. There's no need to clarify, she must know what I'm really asking.

"The Silent Assassin murdered my brother."

CHAPTER THIRTY-THREE

My knees buckle and I land heavily on the bed. *The Silent Assassin.* Tovi had said it as if they were a different person to me. But it *is* me.

"Who?" I croak and have to repeat the question. My mind is running through the list of Erduborn men I've assassinated. Out of the almost forty sanctioned assassinations I've had, fifteen have been Erduborn, and thirteen were male. Unless he was part of a group of mercenaries, then I wouldn't even remember him. My stomach acid begins to churn at the sheer number of people I've killed. Yet I remember every single face of the men and women I've been paid to assassinate.

"It was eight revolutions past, his name was Koly, but you wouldn't know that. He wasn't your target." Tovi's voice is getting sharper and meaner. Her breathing is increasing, and she fidgets as she paces.

"I'm sorry, Tovi. I don't remember. If he wasn't my target, had he been caught up with mercenaries?"

"No! He was fifteen, and *you used him* to assassinate a

farmer in his hometown of Vavabora," she screams, tears beginning to stream down her face.

Vavabora. That's in the far northwest of Erdu, which I've never been to. Almost all of my Erdu assassinations were on the east coast or in the southeast, and a handful were in central Erdu. Not to mention I've never assassinated an Erduborn *farmer.* Cautiously, I ask, "How do you know this happened?"

"My father told me before he died. By the time Queen Neo helped me find him, he was dying from the drink. My mother had already killed herself, after Koly was murdered."

Taking a deep breath, I ask again differently. "How did your father know it was the Silent Assassin?"

"After it happened, the royal guard came to tell my parents, officially," she cries, her face hysterical.

"Officially? What does tha—"

"Koly was the farmer's hand. The Silent Assassin, *you*, asked him to let you into the farmer's house, and he refused. So, you forced your way in, using him as a shield. Koly was stabbed, and then you assassinated your target. You left my brother to bleed out and die!"

"Tovi, listen to that story. Does that *sound* like me?" I say calmly, but she's not having it. "You've seen me fight! I wouldn't need to use a child as a shield. Also, *why* would I be assassinating a farmer? My targets were always highly influential people or big problems for influential people. It sounds like this farmer owed taxes, and the king wanted a scapegoat. Your poor brother was collateral."

I pause, waiting to see if she's going to respond but she's hysterically sobbing as she paces instead.

"I didn't kill this farmer, Tovi, and I certainly didn't kill your brother."

Tovi collapses into her bed and screams into the straw mattress. How many other murders am I being blamed for?

Eventually, she crawls into the bed properly, resting her back against the wall, heaving, and trying to catch her breath.

"I have never even been to Vavabora. I have never killed anyone except the intended target during an assassination. I have *never* had collateral deaths. I could find the paperwork in Osraed to prove this—all sanctioned movements into countries have to be documented," I ramble at her.

"You have to have done it," she sobs quietly. "Because if you didn't, then…"

"I didn't do it." I'm mirroring her position in bed against the wall with my knees against my chest, hugging them tightly. "Tovi."

She looks me in the eye briefly and then resumes staring at the ceiling. I can't look at her when I begin to speak. "Did the others know…did they know you thought I murdered your brother?" The last few words barely scrape over the lump of shame in my throat.

Silence. Long enough that I think she isn't going to answer, so I look back to her. Her head is still tipped back but her eyes are squeezed tightly.

"No," she says as she gulps in air, trying to contain herself. "They didn't even know you were an assassin, remember? But it *is* the reason I volunteered to join them. I couldn't let you betray them."

"But it was you who betrayed them instead." The words hang heavy in the air, and I regret them immediately, wishing I could grab them and shove them back down my throat.

"I know!" Tovi fists her hands to her eyes and lets out an anguished cry as she breaks down into heaving sobs once again. I open my mouth to speak, but Tovi's voice cuts me off. "I regretted it instantly. The moment Riley woke us to say you were gone I wanted to rescue you, even though I knew what it would mean for me." She's looking at me now, almost pleading, wild. The whites of her eyes are wholly visible.

"I knew Beans was a lost cause from the moment he met you. So, I started trying to convince Riley that you couldn't be trusted. That he should cut you loose. But he liked you and had started to believe you could help rescue his sister."

I'm in a daze as my brain tries to understand the words as she says them.

Tovi takes a shaky breath before she continues. "Then I saw the mercs in Teorann and had the idea." Her words are coming out fast now, like a runaway horse that she can't rein in. "I paid them to make you *leave*, with half up front and the rest when you'd left. I didn't care how they did it. I gave them a rumor, about you, about our journey. But you came back to confront Riley about it instead, and I panicked. I couldn't let the team find out what I had done, so I went back to them and said the deal was off. They laughed at me!" she bites out, and then tries to catch her breath.

"With Bitty and Beans nearby, I didn't want to make a scene. So, I told them that they'd get no more gold from me, but that they better not fail if they tried again."

I'm shaking. I knew she had betrayed me, orchestrated this, and wanted me gone, but this is more—this is *so much more*.

"Time passed, and I was stupid enough to think that they'd just taken my gold and moved on."

But of course, they tried again. Now they knew I was the Silent Assassin. Worth far more gold than you'd given them.

I didn't say it. I wanted to. I wanted the venom to coat my tongue and let it lash out on a whip. But I bite my tongue until I taste blood instead.

She laughs, an ugly sharp sound with no humor. "But everything I did, it wasn't until you'd been *taken*, that I realized." She angrily wipes the tears away from her face as if they were the ones doing the betraying. "I wanted my brother's murderer to pay, and I let hate fuel my decisions. I just realized too late that I didn't hate *you*, Mika."

I think she pauses after that to finally let me speak if I want to. But I don't want to. Or I can't. Or I don't trust the words on my tongue yet.

"I knew what it meant that they had taken you, not run you off. I didn't think about the risk of that before, but it was all I could think about after. Especially when Bitty..." Tovi pauses to swallow and take a breath. "When Bitty said we had to charge because of what was about to happen in the cave," she says with a raw voice.

Her eyes are on me, so I tilt my head forward enough to see her properly. She looks wild, with tears clearing paths down her dirty face, revealing red and angry skin. Her eyes beg me to understand, and maybe I do.

"I knew when you woke, that I would have to leave. I was a coward, one that couldn't face any of you, not after you fucking *saved my life*," she croaks with desperation.

"So, I prayed to the Divine that you would wake, that you would be okay. Not for me, not to assuage my guilt, but because I just wanted you to live. And then you woke up."

"How did you even know who I was?"

Tovi takes her time answering me, clearly struggling with her words. "I came to find you *after*...after I found out about Koly. I never saw you up close, only found out your name and that you were Mievaborn. Then, I'd seen you from a distance.

"I was originally only supposed to be an escort for whoever we hired or purchased, swapping with Bitty and another Gifted Patron in Nemoris. But then Beans had said your name while sending the request for Queen Neo's seal of approval. I wasn't sure if it was you when I asked to join the rescue, and no one batted an eye because they knew Lyss and

I were friends. But I recognized you straight away. Though I didn't expect you to be so…small."

"Why did you risk the entire mission for this? Why not just tell Beans and Riley straight up?" I ask, my voice raw from unshed tears.

"I wasn't thinking logically, or even about Lyss anymore. You'd been this big bad monster of my nightmares for so many revs. But then I met you, and you were this…tiny creature that made everyone laugh, and you had this lost look about you. I recognized it. But the need to make you pay and get you away from the people I love was too strong. It was obviously a shitty plan."

"Fuck, Tovi," I scream. "You think?" I don't even care if the guard comes down to see what is going on. I haven't been down here very long, and the desperation and hopelessness of being in a dungeon has already crawled under my skin. What hope did Tovi have when she's been in here for weeks?

"I thought you murdered my brother!"

"But I didn't. I know I'm a monster, but I wouldn't have killed a child, much less used one as a shield," I say quietly, no longer yelling. My rage quietly reminds me that I've killed a mother and her unborn child, though. *I am a monster.*

Tovi goes back to the hysterical sobbing. I'm furious at her, but I cannot find it in myself to hate her. Despite everything she has done, I care about her. I'm definitely going to punch her in the tit when we get out, but that's it. Beans' words about knowing what's in her heart play in my head.

"Tovi, stop. Please." I'm standing up against the bars, as close as I can get to her with the empty cell between us.

"I'm the biggest monster in this room Mika, not you. I deserve to rot away in here."

"Stop."

At least she's no longer hysterical, but she's hitting the back of her head against the stone periodically.

"You need to stop crying and save what little hydration you have left."

Tovi snorts, mumbling. "What's the point…"

"Because we're going to need every bit of strength to escape."

We sit in silence for a long time. I replay every word she's ever said to me, every interaction. I can see it now. The way she kept her distance, the wariness whenever anyone else was alone with me. She was worried about her friends. Worried about the reputation I had crafted and let run wild. It doesn't matter that what traumatized her is a lie.

"I used to pick up your things constantly, you know," Tovi says into the murky light that is neither darkness nor daylight.

"What? What do you mean?"

She barks a laugh that causes her to cough. "Whenever you put something down, I'd pick it up. See if you were feeling assassin-y or devious or something."

"And?"

"Nothing. I didn't get much from you at all, really, which fueled my suspicions. It was like you knew how to cover everything with a blanket of noise."

I'm trying to formulate a response. A question. Anything.

She answers me, though I didn't articulate a question. "It was like a fog, but also a storm. Sometimes it was really clear: happiness, humor, compassion. But I'd get these flashes of… rage, fury, *fear*, and loathing. Just a flash. And then I wouldn't be able to feel it again, like feeling it once was the only taste of it left. I've never experienced anything else like it."

I let out the breath I'd been holding. "I don't know what any of that means."

"Neither do I. Though I wish I knew then that it didn't mean you were trying to hide nefarious intentions."

"Me too."

Interrupting us, a guard brings us some kind of gritty gruel with chunks of…*something* mixed in. It's not until we're eating that I realize Tovi and I aren't alone down here. Only a handful of the cells are empty. Not a single one of them stirred while Tovi and I were screaming at each other.

After our meal, we settle down to sleep, but it eludes me. The sounds and smells are a barrage on my senses and my rage won't leave. I'm exhausted, yet it's like I'm still adding fuel to the fire that's keeping me awake. I replay the conversation with Tovi about her brother, and the weight of it is crushing. Though I didn't kill him, being blamed for his death still makes me complicit. The legend I created for myself was used as a coverup.

My last moments with Riley also plague me. His refusal to promise not to kiss me again. I didn't want him to agree, yet I was still furious when he didn't. *Fucked up* doesn't even begin to describe me.

I fall asleep indulging in the fantasy of Riley holding me, imagining his smell and the warmth of his skin. Jaena's voice tells me I'm pathetic, whispering alongside my rage.

CHAPTER THIRTY-FOUR

I can see why Tovi isn't sure how long she's been here. The lanterns, hanging from the ceiling outside the cells and not illuminating much, never seem to run out of oil. With the guards upstairs, we don't get to see a scheduled guard change to mark the time either. It's only when Liesolette comes ambling down the stairs that I assume at least the evening has passed.

She comes straight to me with a small paper bag in her hands.

"I'm only helping because he said it was truly life and death, and you are here on behalf of the Queen Ofnemoris. But this is it. I won't pass anything else between you," she says in her strong, but hushed voice.

I gratefully take the package. "Why are you helping at all, Liesolette?" I ask as I hand over her kerchief with a smile of thanks.

"You can call me Lottie. Regardless of who *owns* me, I know Nemoris blood runs through my veins. Maybe Queen Neoniri will offer me a boon for this, or maybe you will use this as leverage," she finishes, eyeing me carefully.

"Who was it? Who gave you this?"

She shrugs. "Nemorisborn man. Intense. A little broken looking and desperate."

Leaving me with my small package and Tovi pressing her face against the bars of the cell between us. I consider who she meant, as I watch Lottie go up the stairs.

"What's in the package?" Tovi hisses at me.

I glare at her impatience and open the bag to see two fresh apricots. I tip them out into my hand, looking in the bag for anything else, spotting writing inside. Ripping the bag open, I see the words, *"Sit tight. We have a plan."* They are written inside a crude drawing of flames with cat ears and whiskers. *Firecat.* I smile as I crumple the bag tightly and drop it into the sewerage line.

Tovi hops from one foot to the other, picking her lip as she tries to see what's in my hands. They don't know she's here. The thought of leaving Tovi behind to rot or be executed by the King Oferdu hurts more than her betrayal ever did. There must be something so pathetically wrong with me if I will cling to the hope of her friendship even after she betrayed me. Leaving without her is not an option.

"Here," I whisper, gesturing to Tovi that I'm going to throw her something.

She catches the apricot with ease, her breath hitching as soon as it lands in her hands. I start eating mine straight away. The smell and taste is pure bliss. I hope the bitch appreciates the apricot. Giving away my favorite fruit while locked in a dungeon is madness.

Tovi hasn't eaten her apricot yet. Turning it over and over in her hands, inspecting every inch of it. "If you don't want it, then give it back," I say, sucking my pip clean and throwing it into the drain.

"I want it," she snaps. She closes her eyes with a frown. Taking a deep breath and opening her eyes again, she peers at me. "Why don't you hate me? And why do you think you are pathetic?"

Fucking object empathy.

"Just eat the stupid apricot, Tovi."

ANOTHER BOWL of gruel marks the end of our day, just as revolting as yesterday's. I hope *"sit tight"* means their plan will come to fruition soon, because dungeon food is a form of torture all on its own. I sleep in short bursts, constantly waking myself up with the ghosts of my memories.

Nothing happens all day. No visit from Lottie, no rescue from the team, no conversations with Tovi. Another bowl of gruel. If I have a few weeks of this, I'll be as unstable as Tovi. *More*, considering how unhinged I already am. A small giggle pops out of my throat, and Tovi's head snaps in my direction. I have to bite my lip to stop from giggling more, and Tovi looking at me like I'm insane is only making my delirium worse.

The next morning, a procession of guards, including Lottie, march down the stairs. Tovi and I look at each other in alarm. I mouth at her, asking what this is, and she shrugs, her panic as wild as the rage inside of me.

One by one, each prisoner is brought out of their cell and manacled to a chain. Tovi and I are at the end of the long chain of about fifteen prisoners. I look at Lottie to ask what's going on but as I open my mouth, she gives me a cutting glare with an almost imperceptible shake of her head.

Manacled together, a guard addresses us all with his booming voice. "Today is the scheduled day of the moon for crime sentencing. You will be brought before the king and judgment will be passed immediately."

Tovi squeaks in front of me and takes a step back, stepping on my toes and I bump forward into her. Maybe this is part of the plan, and I whisper to Tovi not to panic as we're marched up the stairs.

Reaching the top of the stairs is unbelievable. The fresh air tastes sweet and clean. Now I can see everyone clearly, Tovi and I are the only women and the only Patrons. I am the only non-Erduborn.

Men are crying, some with what looks like relief as they breathe in fresh air, some with desperation as we're marched toward our sentencing before the king. Tovi hasn't made a sound since we started marching. I grip onto her filthy shirt, partly to let her know I'm here with her and partly because I need something to ground me to the Divine earth.

"I'm sorry, Mika," Tovi whispers frantically. "I'm sorry for what I did to you, I'm sorry for everything. I'm sorry." A small sob punctuates her final word.

"Don't you dare. This isn't the end, stop it!" I whisper, digging my fingers into her back to make my point. "Don't give up now."

The fifteen of us are lined up in front of an empty dais and told to kneel. The chain connecting us is removed but our manacles remain. Most of the guards leave along with Lottie, with a few remaining to station themselves between us and the dais, their swords drawn.

The king's violet eyes are all I can see as he enters the room and sits down on his throne with feline grace. He doesn't look at me; he doesn't look at any of us. He looks bored and annoyed. Covered head-to-toe in jewelry, a large and gaudy crown sits upon his head. Multiple rings, necklaces, and the buttons on his clothing are all jeweled.

Standing to the king's left is an older-looking Laguzborn

Patron with short-cropped gray hair and a thin frame. *He's looking* us all over, and I quickly avert my eyes before he sees me staring.

I'm staring down at my hands as someone else comes into the room, and the original guard starts speaking. "You will be heard one-by-one and sentenced immediately. You," he points to the man who was first on the chain. "State your name."

The man does as he's told, and I look up to see the guard shuffling through papers on a table in front of him. He's reading out the man's transgressions as my eyes lock onto someone sitting to the king's right. My heart slams into my spine and down into my stomach painfully. Prince Eryn.

I hear the king's voice for the first time, and it sends chills down my spine. He asks a question and the prisoner responds, but I miss the entire exchange. My focus is locked on Eryn. I can see he's struggling to breathe normally, his eyes becoming bloodshot. I look around in fear of being seen locking eyes with the prince, but everyone important is staring at the wailing man being led away. Flicking my eyes back to Eryn, I mouth, *"It's okay,"* and try to give him a small smile. His lips turn into a thin line, and his jaw twitches.

Listening to the ridiculous reasons these men have been imprisoned and their equally ridiculous pleas is already hard enough, but hearing the wails when the king declares their punishment is death, fills my stomach with lead.

On the tenth man, the Laguzborn man standing next to the king tilts his head to the side with a frown, watching above the prisoner's head. Once the man finishes speaking, the Gifted Laguzborn whispers something to the king that has him sit forward with a smile full of malice.

"Dion, you should know better than to lie," the king says, sounding *excited.* "Now, I do not know *what* to believe. Perhaps you really *did* pay for the loaves of bread. But now that Lylle has told me you have lied, I am going to have to assume the truth is much, *much* worse.

"Dion, you are sentenced to death by hanging today, as the sun sets. Guards, escort him with the rest," the king orders, returning to his bored look and sitting back on his chair.

The next three men are also sentenced to death. And now it is my turn.

"State your name."

"Mika."

"Charged with trespassing in the Royal Castle. Found impersonating a Gifted Patron Oferdu."

"Father," Eryn interrupts before anything further is said. "May I sentence the last two? You said you wanted me to start taking on some duties. Allow me to practice?"

Eryn stands but doesn't look at me, thankfully. A small bolt hits me in the chest at the risk the young prince is taking. He shouldn't be doing this. The king stares at his son, a small smile curling at the side of his lips as he side-eyes Lylle, raising his eyebrows.

"Sure, my son, have *fun*," the king purrs, looking at Tovi and me.

The prince sits back down, brushing his pants and steeling his face with cruelty. He looks good. He has a small crown, not as hideous as his father's, and a few rings—a particularly pretty one that he's wearing on his pinkie. I recognize it from the painting in his room as belonging to his mother.

"Mika, what is your reason for being in the castle, and why were you impersonating a Gifted Patron Oferdu?" he asks me, one flick of his eyes at Lylle. A warning: I cannot lie.

"I was looking for someone. The easiest way to move about without detection was in a uniform. My friend," I gesture to Tovi, "was in the dungeon the whole time. An unlikely coincidence." My rage flutters like an angry bird, but keeps the claws retracted. I didn't lie.

If Eryn is surprised, he doesn't show it. My gaze looks to my right, and I see Lylle looking disinterested, with no hint that he detected a misdirect in the truth. I am somewhat emboldened.

"You, state your name," Eryn directs at Tovi, eyes wide as she darts her eyes between me and Eryn, giving her name quietly.

Eryn's next question is directed at the guard handling our paperwork. "Xavi, what are her charges?"

"Caught moving about Castle City with no official permissions. Resisting detention and assaulting a peacekeeper."

"Tovi, what is your reason for being in Castle City without permission, and why did you resist detention, assaulting a peacekeeper?" Eryn's cool voice asks her, the only sign that he's anything but *cool* is the fast and bulging pump of the lifeblood line in his neck.

"I, too, was looking for someone. The person I love. I had traveled here alone in shame after...after I betrayed my friend here," Tovi's voice catches as she gestures to me, and continues with a wobble. "I had barely eaten for days and was delirious by the time I reached Castle City. I thought what I did was the right thing, but I know now that it wasn't. Please forgive me?"

Lylle's head tips slightly as he stares above Tovi. The king whispers something and he looks back, chuckling and going back to his disinterested look. Whatever he saw, it wasn't enough to flag Tovi as a liar.

"What are your Gifts? I see you're both Patrons of the Divine."

"I am a Null, sire," I answer quietly.

Tovi follows. "And I am a Junky, with object empathy."

The king's interest is piqued, a smile that I could only deem venomous slowly spreading across his lips as he looks me over. He doesn't look me in the eye once, only assessing every inch of my body instead. My skin crawls.

"Lylle, do both of these women speak the truth?" Eryn asks, not looking over at the living lie detector.

"I see no lies, Prince Eryn."

"Thank you. Mika, Tovi," Eryn addresses us both, making eye contact with calculation beyond his sixteen revs. "Both of your crimes are punishable by death."

CHAPTER THIRTY-FIVE

My mouth drops and Tovi sucks in a hard breath, but Eryn isn't finished.

"However, I think you both understand the gravity of your offenses. Your punishment is life." Eryn makes eye contact with his father briefly before taking a breath and delivering the rest with so much cruelty that I could almost believe it was true. "Life, as Royal doxies. Guards, take them to the doxy wing."

Tovi screams. "No! You can't do this!"

I put a mask of horror on my face as the tears fall from my eyes. But they are tears of relief. That sneaky little shit. He's a king in the making, after all. I can't tell if Tovi's terror is real or also a mask. It sounds real enough, but surely she realizes that this is exactly where we need to go?

"If I may, son?" the king's voice interjects and my hope, already balancing on a precipice, wobbles dangerously.

"Guards, please take them to the healing wing for inspection first. Divine knows what they have picked up. And keep them in the guest chambers next to the doxy wing. My son's doxies will need to be kept separate," he says with as much emotion as if he were talking about a horse, switching his indifferent face to his son and giving him a benevolent smile.

The guards pull us up by our manacled hands as the king leaves the dais, followed by Eryn and Lylle. We're being marched at sword point down a hallway, Tovi muttering tearfully to herself.

"I can't do this, Mika!" she says with a voice dipped in panic, pulling away from our guards.

"Yes, you can. Think of your lover," I say pointedly, hoping to get through to her. "Think about whether they would prefer you dead *or as a doxy*."

"Hurry up royal whores, we don't have all day," one of the guards bark, shoving Tovi's shoulder.

I'm not sure whether she's clicked yet, but she remains silent for the rest of our trip.

Tovi and I are awaiting a healer, both strapped to reclined chairs and unable to move. It's been at least half an hour since we saw the guards after they strapped us down and left the room. Tovi and I haven't dared to speak to each other, not knowing if we could be heard.

The healer arrives—an ordinary man—not a Patron of the Divine. He doesn't even speak to us; he only washes his hands and then begins inspecting me. Tovi stares intently at me, not taking her eyes off his hands and where they begin to touch me.

"Open your mouth," the healer orders, in a voice gentler than I was expecting.

"Tilt your head.

"Look left…look right.

"Lift your chin."

With my face and neck inspected, he begins massaging under my arms and breasts. Tovi's breath hitches, and I look over to her and mouth, *"It's okay."* She's not convinced. Hysteria tickles my throat. It's the second time I've mouthed those words in as many hours.

After inspecting every inch of my skin, which unfortunately also involves my clothes being cut from me, I lay completely naked. I'm okay. Tovi is not. He hasn't even inspected her yet, and the tears are tracking down her face, eyes closed.

My body has not been my own for a long time, if it ever was. This healer's inspection barely registers compared to other violations inflicted upon me over the years. Perhaps I'm more broken than I thought. Empty and hollow.

"I'll be right back," the healer says, not looking at either of us as he dips out the door.

Deciding this wouldn't be an unusual thing to say if we are being eavesdropped on, I risk it. "Tovi. We can do this. It's clinical—" Tovi cuts me a look, shaking her head. "—and I'll be here with you the whole time."

The healer comes back with what looks like a torture device, and my rage responds. Angry flutters beat against my ribs as he washes his hands again. He gives me a small—not unkind—smile as he spreads my legs apart and uses the device to inspect me *more thoroughly* between my legs. It's uncomfortable, and had Tovi not been here, I might have made it more difficult for him just for the sake of it.

"You're all done. There's a set of clothes here for each of you. Do I need to get a guard while you get dressed?"

I shake my head and he undoes my bindings. Tovi has begun to pant, the anticipation that her turn is next is overwhelming her.

"Can I...can I hold her hand while you inspect her?" I

plead softly, before grabbing my clothes. I open my mouth to plead more as I dress, but he agrees, and I snap my mouth shut.

I'm dressed in plain cotton underwear and a set of light gray silky pajamas. I wish I could have bathed first. The pants are cuffed at the calf, and the shirt is short-sleeved. Another set is ready for Tovi. The healer has waited for me to get dressed, busying himself washing his hands and the torture—*inspection*—device.

Tovi's eyes are pleading with me, and I give her a small smile. "It's not too bad. He's gentle."

He inspects her face and neck first, the same way he did with me. I hold her hand, and she grips me fiercely every time he touches her. I note that he's touching her less, instructing her verbally more, and only touching her when he *has* to. His voice is softer as he speaks to her, and he pauses every time her panic looks about to overwhelm her. For all he's not Gifted, he seems to be in tune with her emotions.

He's tall, as all Erduborn are—even taller than Beans— probably close to seven feet. He's older than us, maybe late thirties, with a few creases around his eyes that suggest he likes to smile. His hair is a dark brown, almost black, and kept a similar length to my own. Typical Erduborn brown eyes of the earth against tanned skin, closer to caramel in color than olive. He isn't unattractive, and his soft demeanor only helps.

The healer warns her when he has to start inspecting her physically. And then he asks her whether she would like to remove her clothes instead of them being cut off. She nods. He allows her to be unbound at the arms to undress her top half, herself.

Once he inspects her top half, he gestures gently to the silky pajamas while looking at me. I hand them to Tovi to dress her top half before she undresses her lower half. I stand over her while he inspects the rest before he gets to the internal exam. She stares at me, and I hold her gaze for as long as I can. But inevitably, the repulsive strain becomes too much, and I look away. And I hate myself that I can't even help her with something as simple as eye contact.

She hisses and lets out a shuddering breath, and he apologizes while doing the internal exam. It wasn't painful, it's definitely uncomfortable and invasive, but not painful. He doesn't linger, only doing the barest of inspections before removing the tool that allows him to see inside. He nods to me, indicating I can give her the pants now.

With his back to us, he washes the gloves and tool while humming to himself softly. And—I realize—he is giving Tovi more time to regain her composure. Her breathing is still erratic, and a sob escapes periodically. Once she sounds calmer, he returns and sits in a chair facing us. His brow furrows as he writes something in a folder in his lap.

His dense, almost black beard is kept short. His nose is slightly hooked, and he has a broad mouth with full lips—lips that he chews on every now and then.

"What're your names?" he asks us, catching me studying him.

"Mika." I wait for Tovi to offer her name, but after a moment when it's clear she isn't going to, I answer for her. "And this is Tovi. What's your name?"

"Otto," he says with a smile, which reaches his eyes. The reason for those creases.

Otto blows out a breath, reading his notes, and then studies Tovi for a moment before giving me a sympathetic look. My rage—which I hadn't even realized was asleep— perks up a little. Does he have bad news?

"You're both in perfect health," he says, then leans

forward to whisper with an exaggerated grimace. "Unfortunately."

Tovi snaps her eyes up at him then, finally looking at him for the first time since he walked in.

He continues. "You're both healthy enough to be Royal doxies. And as you're both Patrons, I don't have to warn you to drink the tea to prevent pregnancy. I do, however, have a different kind of tea. If you need it. Ofori…" He looks at both of us to see if we recognize it. I do, but Tovi doesn't.

"It makes you…care *less*, Tovi," I say, nodding to him in thanks. With the way she's behaving, it would be odd if we *didn't* accept the tea, even though we won't actually need it.

"You usually get an hour or two warning. That should be enough time to drink the tea. Even cold-brewed, it'll be effective," Otto adds, getting up to search cupboards, grunting as he digs around. When he finds it, he holds it out to Tovi, who doesn't take it, and then hands it to me instead.

"Do you two need more time…before…" he says softly, gesturing to the door.

"Tovi?"

"No. Let's go," she says with a detached voice that sends a chill into my bones. Somehow, she is looking stronger than I've seen in days.

"THANK YOU," Tovi says to me when we're deposited into some guest chambers.

I had tried to take note of our location as we walked, but it was impossible with so many winding corridors. The doors to our guest chambers were small, opening into a tiny receiving room where only a chair on either side would fit.

Then the set of large ornate doors into the chambers themselves were opened.

The sitting room is large. Tovi and I sit in oversized sofa seats that face a massive window, looking out onto the city. As suspected, we're in the east wing, but it's hard to tell which floor from our vantage point. The window doesn't open, nor do we have a balcony.

There is one big bedroom at the end of the room with two large beds, a washroom for us to share, and a giant wall of windows along one wall of the sitting room. The sun is setting, a beautiful sunset baking the horizon with golds and reds, warming the colors of our chambers.

"You're welcome," I finally reply. "How are you doing?"

"Sick to my stomach. What are we—"

I hold a finger up to my lips to silence her question and she frowns. I point to my eyes and ears and then around the rooms. She nods. We both search the room: every picture, corner, and wall for any kind of holes or ways to spy on us.

Nothing. I quickly scan the ceiling and floors, but nothing obvious stands out. Releasing the breath I had been holding to keep my rage in check, I yell, *"Fuck me!"* and then laugh, an edge of hysteria in it.

Tovi whips around, looking at me like I've lost it entirely.

I give her the biggest, dirtiest, scheming grin I could possibly muster and run at her. She takes a step back, still looking at me like I'm crazy, but a smile tugging at her lips when I shake her shoulders.

"He's with us, Tovi. The prince!"

"What? *How?*"

I shake my head, still not quite believing it. "We—*I*—broke into his rooms a few nights ago. We had a half-cocked plan to kidnap him and force the king's hand. But then the prince…was not who we expected."

"He looked as fucking expected to me!" she hisses.

I laugh softly, full of pride for the little prince. "I know. He did *so* well. This wasn't planned, he didn't even know I'd been captured until we saw each other. He said he would help to find Amarilyss. It seems she was nice to him when they met, and so, we trusted each other."

"You are trusting a complete stranger. Well, that's a Divine miracle, isn't it?" Tovi drawls, shoving my shoulder gently as she sits down.

"He didn't know about you either because I didn't know you were here. The kid did all of that on his own."

"You're sure this isn't some sick game? That he hasn't just fucked us over *royally*?"

I scrunch my face and shrug. "He looked pretty sick about it to me."

"You mean 'menacing and vicious,' right?"

A knock startles us both, and an elderly Patron ambles in with a trolley of food. All discussions are forgotten as the smell of real food hits us. I am famished and my stomach is growling, but Tovi looks positively *delirious* at the sight of real food.

"Careful," I warn. "You might make yourself sick."

"Worth it." She grins, already shoving a buttered bread roll into her mouth.

The Patron gives me a courteous nod as she leaves, her violet eyes a reminder. I watch Tovi stuff her face, gravy dripping down her chin, while I pick at my food.

"Are you going to eat that?" she asks, pointing at the chicken drumstick I haven't touched.

I pick it up and take a massive bite out of it, then with my mouth still full, lick the gravy off the other side in one swipe. I offer it to her with a smirk. I nearly choke when she shrugs and takes it from me and continues to eat it where I left off.

She's chewing open-mouthed through a smile, and I narrow my eyes at her in question.

"You didn't think I'd take it. Suck shit. *Object empathy*, remember," she says, spinning the half-eaten leg between her fingers.

"Hope you felt how stupid I think your face is too."

She sighs, giving me a side eye as she puts her plate to the side. "No. But I *could* feel that you're anxious about something. Something you want to ask me but don't know how."

"All that from some chicken? Sheesh." I try to joke but earn myself a kick in the shins instead.

I groan, this isn't going to go down well. "What color are the king's eyes to you?"

"Brown," she says, as if I'm stupid. "Brown like the Erdu earth. *Why?*"

"Okay. What does he look like?"

She raises her hands in the air in an exasperated half-shrug. "Tall. Dark brown hair kept short on the sides with a —" She gestures at the top of her head. "—floopy bit up here. Roundish face, large and wide nose, no facial hair. What in the Divine, Mika?"

She's describing the king, except for his eyes. I see those violet eyes, and she doesn't.

I open my mouth to say it, but I can't. Maybe I didn't see his eyes properly. It's not like I *really* looked at them.

Tovi flicks a pea at me. "Tell me," she demands, pointing at me with the chicken then taking another bite.

Taking a deep breath, I hold it for a few seconds, then let everything out in a rush. *"I see his eyes as violet like a Gifted Patron of the Divine but I see him as everything else you describe except his eyes and maybe I didn't see them properly but I'm pretty sure I did and what if I just found out my Gift is that I can see through glamors or something and there's someone masquerading as the King Oferdu?"* I finish with a squeak and then take a deep breath. "Tovi, am I insane?"

Eyes and mouth wide open, she stares at me, her eyes flicking off to the side periodically. Swallowing her mouthful of chicken and squeezing her eyes shut. "What? Repeat that again, *slowly*."

When I'm finished, she looks no different than when I said it the first time.

"*Tovi!*" I whine when she still hasn't said anything.

"I'm thinking!" she hisses back. "No one has said anything about him having violet eyes before."

"I know."

"Not even a *whisper* of a rumor."

"I *know*."

"We—Riley, Beans, Bitty, and I—have been here so many times and none of them have ever said anything either. They would have if they saw it too…"

"*I know!*"

"No wonder the chicken felt anxious."

I growl and push her with my foot, digging my toes into the side of her thigh until she slaps at me.

"You should ask the prince when you see him. Surely if dear old daddy Erdu is acting differently, he would be the one to know?"

CHAPTER THIRTY-SIX

W e sleep most of the day away, not waking for breakfast. Someone is clearing our untouched breakfast plates and leaving lunch when we finally wake. Again, we gorge ourselves on the food. A giant tray of fresh fruit, spiced yogurt, and a jar of honey. Plus, some kind of hot drink that I haven't had before that's darker than tea, with a bitter yet slightly fruity flavor.

Tovi and I are stretching on the ground together after dinner, coming up with wild reasons why I can see violet eyes on the king when a maid enters.

"Mika, Prince Eryn has requested your services tonight in one hour. Please prepare yourself and get changed into these." Without waiting for a response, the woman places a pile of fabric on a side table and quickly leaves, her short brown hair the only thing I actually remember about her.

"Interesting," Tovi says as she examines the pile. "You're *sure* the prince isn't trying to fuck you, Mika?" she chuckles with slight concern crinkled around her eyes.

Tovi holds up a tiny nightdress that shimmers a dark

green shade, and a small bit of beige-colored lace in the other.

"What is that?" I hiss.

"Your outfit, apparently. At least there's a large, black cloak to go with it."

I groan as I snatch the clothing and head for the washroom.

After a quick wash, I put on the *outfit* I was given. The small bit of lace is underwear that barely covers anything in the back *or* front. The nightdress turns out to be sheer, with a thin underwire to support my breasts. But it's see-through. My nipples can be seen perfectly. The nightdress has no sleeves, thin straps, finishes at mid-thigh, and is very form-fitting. For Tovi's sake, I am relieved that my still slightly bruised ribs are hidden.

"Well, I certainly *look* like a—" I begin to say as I stroll out of the washroom to show Tovi, expecting a fit of laughter at how utterly ridiculous I look. Stopping mid-sentence, I tilt my head and raise an eyebrow.

"Uh." Tovi continues to look stunned while eyeing me up and down.

I reach for the cloak, self-conscious and wanting to cover up. "Is it that bad?"

"I mean, *bad* because it's going to waste. You look *hot!*" she exclaims. "Once again, I must ask, if you're *sure* the prince is helping us?"

"I highly doubt this outfit is his doing unless it's a requirement of all doxies." I pause. "I'm 99% sure he's helping us."

She gives me a dubious look and helps to fasten the cloak around me.

I'm flanked by six guards, escorting me to the prince's rooms for our evening: one in front and one behind, with two flanking either side of me. My heart is hammering in my chest because I know this isn't the direction of Eryn's rooms, but I can't ask because I shouldn't know where they are.

My escorts and I are waiting outside a set of enormous ornate doors, my toes curling under me in trepidation. The doors swing inward, and the guards move aside for me to enter. As soon as I see the Gifted lie detector, I know I'm about to speak to the king, but I'm not sure if the lie detector's presence makes me feel better or worse.

"Hello again, Mika." King Stol's voice greets me as he sits comfortably behind an enormous wooden desk littered with papers and other paraphernalia. I curtsy in response.

The lie detector closes the door and takes up their position standing beside the king, looking bored. Both pairs of violet eyes watch me closely, neither speaking a word. At least avoiding eye contact with them is easy when I'm supposed to be a cowed prisoner.

"Mika. I thought we could have a quick chat before you see my son. Lylle here is just to keep you honest of course, but nothing to worry about."

"Of course, sire," I politely respond, not wanting to speak more than necessary.

"Right, I will jump straight in. I know that this position is not exactly what you had in mind, but I am sure it is better than execution," he says sweetly, but I sense the thinly veiled threat in his words. "I am surprised though, why my son chose you first. Mievaborn." He taps his pen against his lips.

Not wanting him to muse any further, I quickly offer a reason. "Tovi, the Erduborn woman, is still recovering from her time in the dungeons. Your son seems like a kind and fair man." I hope that the two separate facts I state are close enough that the king infers my intended meaning, but not so close that Lylle would see the disconnection and know it's a lie. I smile sweetly at the king, looking at his mouth. I flick my eyes to the lie detector quickly, but he still looks bored.

"Indeed. Perhaps he is curious too. This is the first doxy he has requested. Truth be told, I had become concerned that he was not showing any interest." The king's eyes are still boring into me, but I offer no response for fear that agreeing with him could be seen as lying.

"This will also be your first time as a doxy—a Royal doxy, no less. Usually, more training is given in the art, however, you are being thrust right into it. You do understand what is expected of you?"

"Yes, Your Majesty. I will do my very best to satisfy your son." I dip my head in submission and hope again that Lylle can see that I'm not lying about making Eryn satisfied, I just don't intend to do it sexually.

"Mhmm. It may take some *encouragement* on your behalf."

"If I may be honest, sire?" I ask, rather redundantly, given the lie detector standing beside him. "I'm not going to do that."

The king raises his eyebrows at me. "And what do you mean by that?"

"Your Majesty, I mean no disrespect, and I am not saying that I will hide in the corner or not go anywhere near the prince. But I believe he should remain in control. Perhaps the *encouragement* could come from seeing him more often, perhaps every couple of days?" My heart is slamming against my chest. *Did I show my hand?*

My gamble pays off, and the king smiles widely. "I like the way you think. He *does* need to learn to take control. I do, however, want him to see the Erduborn woman as soon as she is fit and able." He nods at his own statement and then claps his hands.

The doors behind me swing open.

"You may go," he says as he lifts his hand and gestures toward the door.

"Thank you, sire," I say as I curtsy and turn to leave.

"Oh. One thing Mika. Your cloak. My men will escort you into Prince Eryn's sitting room, at which point you will take off your cloak and give it to them. They will keep it with them outside the doors, awaiting my son to come back and get it when he is finished with you." A feral grin spreads across his face as he speaks.

I curtsy once again and leave before he can say anything else.

I'm mentally mapping the way to Eryn's rooms from King Stol's office in relation to mine and Tovi's rooms. Thankfully, the prince's rooms are much closer to ours than his father's office, albeit on a different floor. I am still not sure where King Stol's rooms may be, and whether they're located in the same place as his office or not. I hope they're not near his son's rooms.

The guards do indeed take my cloak and exit the sitting room. "Prince Eryn?" I call softly as I look around for him.

I poke my head into his bedroom and see him standing with his back to me, looking out the window. I walk in and close the door, wanting to keep another layer of sound between us and possible listening ears.

As soon as the door snips shut, Eryn runs at me, enveloping me in a hug and almost throwing me off my feet.

"What..." I manage to get out before he's apologizing desperately.

"I'm so sorry, Mika. And your friend. I didn't think. I panicked. I wanted to help. I'm so sorry. Is she okay? Are you okay? Please, I hope you're okay." The words are tumbling out of his mouth at rapid speed while he clings to me.

I push him off me gently to see his red-rimmed eyes and panicked face. He's genuinely distraught. I keep my arms on his shoulders, partly to keep him from hugging me again, and also to give him a modicum of comfort.

"Eryn. What are you talking about? You not only

stopped me *and* my friend from possibly being executed by your father, but you have given us the best chance we have to save the Princess Ofnemoris. Your father believed every word, and you fooled Lylle, too."

Eryn's eyes start to well with tears, so I pause what probably sounds like a lecture. I close my eyes and take a deep breath. Now is not the time for rage. When I open them again, one of the tears escapes and tracks down his face, and he looks down, a slight tremble in his lip.

I'm not sure why I do it—something about this kid has burrowed its way under my skin— but I use one hand to wipe his tear and the other to lift his chin. He won't meet my eye right now, though I realize distractedly that the reluctance I usually have is absent when I look into Eryn's eyes.

They're kind eyes, the reddy brown of a hot sunset in Erdu. Eryn's olive skin is a little pale, like he needs more sun. Dark brown lashes, long and full, are glistening from the tears he's so ashamed of. He's a good-looking kid, with a strong brow and jaw, a wide mouth full of straight white teeth, and a small, pointed nose. It's all wrapped up in an innocence so endearing that it's slightly concerning.

"You know you're my hero, right? Eryn, you saved my life," I say softly, trying to get through to him.

He gasps because he's been holding his breath. "I just felt so guilty. I couldn't do *nothing*, but I didn't know what to do!" he says through hiccups.

"You did everything right." I smile at him. He pulls me into another hug, and I let him. He grips onto me and I hold him until his breathing returns to normal, and he eventually loosens his embrace.

"I'm sorry," he says, and I'm about to admonish him again when he follows with, "I mean, about this, my reaction. Is the Erduborn woman okay? Is she really your friend?"

Grateful for the change in subject, I walk us over to his bed so we can sit down.

"Yes, a strange coincidence that ended up working out well. She's okay, *now*, once I was able to tell her that you were my friend."

"We're friends?"

"Do you often risk your life and then snotty cry on people who aren't your friends?" I tease as he side-eyes me with a little smirk. "Though she wasn't convinced when she saw my outfit for tonight."

"Oh Divine, you're basically naked!" he says with legitimate disgust, finally looking at me. "Gross!" he finishes and throws a blanket at me.

That did it. I laugh so hard tears begin to overflow, and I have to lie down on his bed to breathe because it's hurting my ribs.

"Thank you for the confidence boost," I reply between gasps of laughter.

"Not to add insult to injury, but you seem unhinged today."

Wiping my tears, I nod. "Oh, I know. The hinges fell off many revolutions past, I'm afraid." Eryn widens his eyes, shaking his head. Finally calming down from my hysterical release, I add, "Have you told anyone about me since that night?"

"You mean, the night you came to kidnap me and then almost killed me because I threw a pillow at you?" I feint a punch to his ribs, which earns me a lopsided grin. "No. Not even my ex-boyfriend who I tell almost *everything*." I relax, the part of me that thought perhaps this young prince wasn't savvy enough to keep a secret, relieved. "Now you have a secret of mine, so we're even," Eryn adds to the lengthening silence.

"Your father doesn't know you prefer men?"

"I don't actually have a preference. Boy, girl, both, neither. But he certainly wouldn't have approved of me having a boyfriend." He shrugs.

I narrow my eyes at him. "Why then, young prince, am I *so* disgusting?"

"Because you're old?" he replies, with a look on his face that suggests I asked a stupid question. "And you're my *friend*, so I don't want to see—" he gestures at my body, "—that."

"Smooth recovery," I say wryly. "What about his male doxies? Is the king that much of a hypocrite?" I ask, getting the topic back on track.

Eryn looks at me like I've grown another head. "He doesn't have *male* doxies. He once caught two stable boys kissing, and they weren't even on duty, but he cut off an ear each and sent them to opposite sides of the country to work."

Shocked at the brutality, I don't want to bring up the purchasing of male Nulls to yet another person who denied their existence. Either the king is so ashamed of being with men that it's a secret even from his own son, or something else more sinister is at play. I fear it's the latter.

"I look forward to the day that you won't need to hide who you love. If that's what you want," I say as I sit back up with only the slightest of groans.

"You're so sure that day exists?"

"I have to be. Speaking of which, I need your help to find the rest of my friends."

My friends. My *friends*. The *rest* of them. Every part of that thought is a strange sort of thud in the chest, like my rage kicking in tune. They're my friends, even Tovi. And I miss them.

Eryn is sitting up as well, hugging his knees and leaning against the headboard, looking so young. Rage churns in my stomach that I'm risking his life even more than I already have.

"How?"

"Are you able to spend time in the gardens without it being out of the ordinary? You could sit out there and quietly say their names—one of them is Gifted with hearing."

"Oh, that's cool! But how will they know I'm helping you?"

"Two things. One, be eating an apricot. They're my favorite fruit, and they—"

Eryn cuts me off. "Apricots are my favorite too! At least it won't be weird for me to be eating them." He beams.

"That's because they're the superior fruit," I declare, and he nods in serious agreement.

"And the second thing?"

"When they approach you, they'll ask you a question, and you just have to respond, *'Mama Beryl'*. It's a secret code we already have in place that no one else will understand."

I give Eryn their names, and he promises to start tomorrow. It's been long enough that I should head back now. We decide on what we can truthfully say to his father if his personal lie detector is around and agree to meet again in two days.

I stop him before he gets to the door to get my cloak. "Thank you, Eryn. You are truly, incredibly special. You'll make a great king one day. Please stay safe." He gives me one quick nod before swinging open his doors, and I return to Tovi.

CHAPTER THIRTY-SEVEN

Tovi is still awake when I return from speaking with Eryn. I start answering her questions as I strip off my cloak to hang on the wall, and without thinking, I take off my nightdress. I Immediately regret it when Tovi sees my bruised ribs.

"Oh Mika. I'll never be able to make up for the pain I caused you." She's not speaking to me but to my ribs, not taking her eyes off the bruises.

I sigh, wrap a blanket around myself, and sit on the couch next to her.

"I don't forgive easily. I never have. In fact, I can't remember the last person I forgave for hurting me in any kind of way."

Tovi is nodding as I'm speaking, chewing the inside of her lip.

"But you must know by now that I've forgiven you. I've made sure of it. Both with my words and my actions, but also, you know what I feel, Tovi. I can't lie about that, can I?"

"No," she says softly. "But I don't deserve your forgiveness."

"Isn't that for me to decide? Please, Tovi. It's time to forgive yourself."

She reaches out for my hand and gives it one squeeze before taking a deep breath. "Tell me everything about tonight." And so, I do.

Tovi's favorite part is how disgusted the young prince was by my outfit, especially when he called me *old*. She was, however, annoyed because I'd forgotten one of the main things I was supposed to talk to the prince about: his father's violet eyes.

For the next two days, Tovi and I train to get her strength back up. She's returning to herself more and more, cracking jokes and being a pain in the ass again. Though I still see the dark shadow behind her eyes whenever she catches a glimpse of my ribs.

Over one of our meals, I blurt out, "They'll forgive you too!" I try to keep it light, but she's not convinced.

It's almost time for me to meet the prince again. Time for me to find out if he was able to locate the others. Sitting in the bath, I'm replaying my conversation with Tovi in my head, annoyed that I can't seem to be tactful or reassure her.

My lamp flickers softly. Eyes wandering, I stare at the cabinet taking up most of one corner in our washroom. With no natural light in here and on the furthest wall from the door, it's *hideous*. This thing is monstrous. Both in its gaudy design and size. It's entirely too fanciful in a washroom, of all places.

I sit up, splashing water everywhere. *What is that outline on the ceiling?*

I slosh my way forward to the end of the bath, trying to get a better look at the ceiling in the corner, shrouded by the cabinet. Still unable to see clearly, I splash back to the other end for the lantern. Standing, I step out of the bath and walk directly to the corner holding the lamp up to light the corner.

"*Tovi…*" I call distractedly, then clear my throat and say it loud enough for her to hear.

Tovi stomps in. "What are you…*Why* are you naked, Mika?" she whines.

"Tovi."

"There's water everywhere!"

"Tovi!"

"What?" she vociferates, and I point to the ceiling.

"*Look.*"

Her mouth drops open, and she walks toward me, slips a little, glares, and then stares back up at the ceiling. "Is that a *door?*"

"Looks like some kind of hatch. Person sized."

Tovi and I share a look of triumph before she looks down and remembers I'm stark naked and shakes her head. "I'll have a look while you're gone, but *you* have to get dressed. They'll be here to collect you soon."

I look at her and growl with a pout. I want to be the one to explore, but she's right. I deliberately stomp my feet so the water on the ground splashes her as I reach for my towel. I hear Tovi mumble *"bitch"* under her breath, and I smile to myself.

"Do you think they will have made contact?" she asks as I'm getting dressed into another doxy outfit, this time with black lace underwear and a champagne-colored sheer nightdress.

"I hope so. This sitting around and not knowing and not

really doing anything is wearing thin—almost as thin as this stupid dress!"

Tovi chuckles as she helps with my cloak again. "You're just jealous that I get to look in the hatch before you. Make sure you ask him about his father this time."

Annoyed but admonished, I give her a nod before knocking on our doors so the guards can escort me to Prince Eryn's rooms. I send a silent prayer to the Divine for no detours this time.

Fortunately, I'm taken directly to the prince's rooms, and after the guards take my cloak, I find Eryn in his bedroom like last time.

"Hello, my sweet Prince," I tease.

"Ugh. I think this outfit is worse than the last. Here," Eryn says with exaggerated disgust, as he throws me a blanket, smirking. I smile and shake my head as I drape the blanket around me like a cloak.

With a heavy sigh, Eryn tells me that he hasn't made contact with the team yet. "I wasn't able to go to the garden at all yesterday because of the rain, and then today it was only for an hour because my father had me parading around in front of some important people playing the dutiful son of a loving father."

"Well, that's a shame, but hopefully soon. We couldn't expect it to be that easy."

"I'm not done with the bad news, unfortunately. I asked my father when you two would be moved in with the rest of the Royal doxies, and he said you wouldn't be. That wing is for *his* doxies only, and if you were to move there, I couldn't see you again."

Reminded, I excitedly tell him about the strange hatch we found in the ceiling of the washroom. "We hadn't noticed it because it's a rather dark corner of the space, and there's also a large ornate cabinet in the corner blocking it from view. Do you know if there is some kind of crawl space between other rooms?"

Frowning, Eryn gets up to look in his washroom. "Maybe. Could also just be storage."

We analyze every nook and cranny of his washroom ceiling, and we find one.

"What does this mean?" Eryn asks distractedly as we both glare at the outline of a hatch, with me still wrapped in his blanket.

"It means that we may not need to be moved in with the rest of the Royal doxies."

Finally understanding the enormity of the discovery, Eryn almost skips back to his bedroom. "He grilled me about our first meeting, by the way," Eryn says, changing the subject. "I told him, *and his lie detector*, that I wanted to see you more but that I wasn't ready to sleep with you, which is *definitely* not a lie," he exaggerates with a lopsided grin.

I try to laugh at his cheekiness but I'm sobered by the mention of his father. I know I need to ask him, but I don't want to sour the mood.

"Your father…" I ask tentatively. "What do you see when you look at him?"

I watch Eryn from the corner of my eye, and he tilts his head as if he doesn't understand what I'm asking. I'm about to elaborate when he surprises me in a small voice. "Not again."

My heart is doing backflips. "Eryn. Does he have violet eyes like a Patron of the Divine?"

"Yes."

I'm not sure when I stood, but I'm up and pacing the room. Blanket forgotten, I'm holding my head with my fingers in my hair, trying to maintain steady breathing.

"You can't say anything. To anyone. Ever. Mika, promise me!"

"What do you mean? I'm trying to figure out what the fuck is going on!"

Eryn has fear written all over his face, so I sit back on the bed and take his hands. My mind wanders for a moment at how easily I can touch Eryn when I barely know him.

Working as a nanny in the children's compound involves a lot of touching. Kids are very physical, and I would never deny comfort and affection to a child who wants it. But once they leave, once they're out of the children's compound, the season they turn thirteen, something shifts in me. I'm completely averse to ever touching or being touched by them again.

Eryn sniffs, and I snap back to the here and now. "How long have you been able to see violet eyes?" I ask.

"As long as I can remember. At first, I didn't know anything was wrong. Until I started asking my mother why his eyes were different from everyone else's. I hadn't really seen any Patrons of the Divine at that age, so I didn't know what it meant, only that they weren't the same color as ours.

"She brushed me off for a couple of revolutions, but then I think she must have realized it wasn't just a child's wild imagination, and she told me to keep it a secret."

He trembles, staring at our hands as he speaks, and I give them a small squeeze of encouragement.

Eryn takes a deep breath. "When I was six, I remember her asking me specific questions about whether I had seen other people with violet eyes sometimes, but other times they were normal. I didn't know what she meant at the time, so I couldn't answer.

"One night, as she was putting me to bed, she told me to pack a bag, and she'll be back in an hour because we're going on a secret trip."

His breath is shuddering, and he's having trouble speaking, so I tell him we can take a break. He nods and focuses on my hands in great detail, like he's trying to memorize every line and crease.

After a few minutes of silence, when his breathing has returned to normal, he speaks again. "I waited for her to come back all night. I sat there with my bag packed and hidden under the blanket with me until morning, but she never returned.

"The next morning, my father came to tell me my mother was dead. People had seen her kill her brother, and then run away on a horse. They found her by the side of the main road toward Osraed with a broken neck. *Fell* from the horse."

He looks me dead in the eye. "I knew it then at the age of six, and I know it now a decade later. There is no way she would have killed my uncle, she loved him. And she wouldn't have left me behind."

I'm reeling. This is so much more awful than I was anticipating. This is no longer the case of someone hiding in plain sight—he is murdering people to keep the secret.

"So, you see, you can't say anything. I can't let him hurt you too."

Choosing my words carefully, I gently check in with him. "You know it's not your fault, right? Eryn, you can't blame yourself for what happened. You didn't 'let' him do anything."

"I know that, I do. But afterward, I vowed to never speak about his eyes again. Speaking about them was a death sentence for the only person who ever loved me."

"Well, I see them too, and I promise that I will do everything in my power to make sure he never hurts *anyone* ever again."

He gives me a weak smile. My heart aches for him and how lonely he must have felt. That's too much for such a little person to go through. It's no wonder he unraveled the other night when he thought he put me in his father's path.

"I don't understand. Why can only you and I see them?" he asks.

"Honestly, at first, I thought maybe I had discovered my Gift. That I could see through tricks of the mind, but that doesn't make sense anymore. Not that it ever really did, to be honest."

"Do you think there are other people who see them but don't say anything?"

"Perhaps. But I don't think so, or rumors would eventually surface and run wild. What I wonder is: how long he has pretended to be the king…"

Eryn's eyes widen, his gloomy demeanor finally starting to lift again. "You think he's someone else, like a shifter?"

"Yes, exactly. He could have changed himself to look like your mother so that everyone would see her kill your uncle too."

"But there hasn't been a shifter like that in…*centuries.*"

"That we know of. The chance to be someone other than a Patron, to live a normal life…I might hide that Gift, too," I say with a grimace. "Not everyone would immediately think of murdering to become a royal."

Eryn finally releases my hands and scrubs at his face aggressively. "This is so confusing!"

"I know. I'm not sure if it makes it better, or worse, but he might not actually be your father."

"*What?*"

"Patrons of the Divine have a procedure in the season they turn thirteen that prevents them from ever being able to have a child. It is said that the Divine curses children born of their Patrons with afflictions of the body and mind—and you do not appear to be cursed as such."

"Worse." He grimaces.

"Fuck. Sorry Eryn. I just thought you might've felt relief at not being related to that monster, but having your biological father murdered, as well as your mother and uncle, is much worse."

He barks out a laugh. "No, I hadn't thought of it like that, though I am now, thanks," he deadpans. "It's just, I was starting to think of a reason why you and I are the only ones who can see him."

"Oh, and what's that?"

"He's your father too."

CHAPTER THIRTY-EIGHT

I laugh. It's an awkward and ugly sound. I know it's covering the panic that's triggering my rage to awaken, so easily roused and now slamming against my ribs.

"I'm Mievaborn, Eryn. It's impossible," I say dismissing him, the memory of my paperwork in Osraed booming in my head like a warning bell.

Unknown/Unclaimed Father.

I finally look at Eryn, and he's giving me a disbelieving look. He glances pointedly at my exposed skin and hair, then looks me in the eye with a raised eyebrow. "Well, what's your theory, *purebreed*?" he asks, using the slur that, historically, Mutts used to insult anyone born of two parents with the same citizenship.

I try to glare at him, hold his stupid eyes, and intimidate him, but I back down first, not wanting the unpleasant hold to wash over me, not with him. I don't want that with Eryn, I have no desire to take something from this kid who has already given me so much.

Aiming the rest of my glare in the direction of the door. "I don't know. I haven't had a chance to think about it yet.

Why would jumping straight to being related even be on your mind?"

Eryn shrugs. "We do look kinda similar. The same nose."

"The same nose," I repeat, flatly.

"Yours is *infinitely* cuter, of course."

I roll my eyes. "You *do* have a wild imagination, kid. I'm sorry, but it's impossible. If I had an Erduborn father, I would at least look like a Mutt—" I cut him off with a glance when he opens his mouth to protest. "I've seen Erdu-Mieva Mutts, and they're obvious. That dark hair is much too strong of a trait." I mess up his wavy dark tresses to annoy him.

"And you'd be pretty damn short for an Erduborn," he agrees, slapping my hands away.

Sighing, I change the subject. "Tovi should come next time. Your father wanted you to see her as soon as she recovered, and we can't deny that she isn't well anymore."

"What's she like?"

"Bossy. Arrogant. Annoying. Bitchy. Snarky. Sarcastic—" I start listing off on my fingers.

"And this is your friend?" Eryn cuts in.

I shoot him a look for interrupting me. "—Strong. Protective. Righteous."

We sit in silence for a few seconds as the word *loyal* rings in my mind, but I can't say it. Not yet. She *is* loyal, just not to me. And why would she be? I'm the assassin of her nightmares. Before Eryn says anything, I continue. "Caring. Funny. Silly. Smart as a whip, and believe me, she will whip you. And yet, she's also fucking stupid."

"What was the strange coincidence that worked out?"

"It's a long story. First, she betrayed me, but it got out of her hands, and she ended up risking all of us. But I wasn't her friend then. And she had…valid reasons, albeit misinformed. Then she ran away and got here first. Came looking for the princess, hoping to save her but was caught instead."

"*Betrayed* you?"

"I forgave her. Please make sure it's clear to the others when you find them. I have forgiven her, and they should give her the opportunity to explain."

"Is she in love with the princess?"

I look at him, blinking in response, connecting the dots that she can't have lied about looking for the person she loved.

Tovi is in love with Amarilyss?

"You have spider webs in your hair," I say to Tovi, hanging my cloak.

"Put on some clothes that cover you so I won't see what you had for breakfast, and come check out the ceiling hatch. It's too small for me, but I think you'll fit."

"What I had for…Oh Tovi!"

"That lace barely covers you. If you start climbing, I'm going to see more of you than I ever need to. Hurry up!"

I grab the set of silky shorts and shirt we were given, putting them over the lace underwear and sheer nightdress for now. When I come out, she's already moved into the washroom, so I follow her in.

"You know, you're going to get your own set of doxy clothes too. You're going to see Eryn next time."

She gives me a dark look and gestures to the hatch impatiently.

It's lucky this ugly cabinet is large, as we can climb it easily. I pop open the hatch, and it's pure darkness inside. I turn to ask Tovi for a lantern, but she's already standing on a chair and handing one to me.

Inside are what look like tunnels, only big enough for someone to crawl on their stomach and elbows.

"There are pipes, and they're hot, so try not to touch them," she says as I look inside.

I see the pipes she's referring to, going up into the floor of the next level. I push the lantern in first and crawl all the way in, trying not to shudder at the spider webs tickling me. Pushing the lantern, I pull my body along on my stomach and hope I'm not making my clothes filthy.

I pick a direction and make sure I'm keeping track of where I'm going so I don't get lost. After crawling for about ten minutes, I find what looks like another hatch. I rest my ear on it, trying to listen, but I can't hear a thing.

Still, I'm excited at the prospect. This could lead us to the doxies or at least to other rooms. And I backtrack, hoping I haven't gotten lost. Seeing the open hatch is a relief, and when I stick my head down into it, Tovi blows out a loud breath of air.

"It's dark and a fucking maze in there, but I found at least one more hatch." I grin at her, and she grins back.

"Now, did you remember to ask about the king's eyes?"

All excitement from the hatch is immediately sucked out of me. Climbing down awkwardly, I tell her everything except Eryn's speculations. Tovi tries to speculate as well but falls short of anything beyond it being a random coincidence. I cannot think of any reason why Eryn and I can see them, but no one else. If *anyone* else had seen them, there would surely be stories. Too many stories for him to silence.

"We need to try and map the tunnels out," I say to our brooding silence. "You should ask Eryn for some paper and charcoal when you see him in a couple of days."

Maybe Tovi wasn't lying when she said I looked hot in my doxy attire, because, standing there in her own, she looks incredible. I whistle at her, waggling my eyebrows in appreciation as she does an exaggerated twirl, finishing with an offensive gesture. I roll my eyes, and she leaves.

Alone, I run myself a bath.

Soaking in the slightly *too* warm water, only a dripping sound to distract me, my mind wanders all the way back to Petia, Katla, and Niesha.

They were normal little girls, who liked normal little girl things. I liked all those things too at first. But those girls certainly had no interest in fighting with boys in the mud or having competitions to climb to the top of the tree first. Unlike me. Their bullying didn't start in earnest until we went through puberty.

The children's compound had many communal bath houses, and we were all forced to go to one together. One day, while I was in one of the more private baths, the girls busted in. We're all naked, and Petia points to my newly growing pubic hair and screams, "I told you so!" to the other two.

While Mievaborn are blonde, it varies from white blondes to light golden blondes. The three girls loomed over me with their budding new breasts and light blonde pubic hair beginning to grow, laughing at me mercilessly.

I tried to cover myself, but it was obvious that my pubic hair was not light blonde and was a much *darker* blonde than theirs. Neither had I even begun to grow anything that would resemble fuller breasts, like them. Turns out I never really would.

"It's just as *dirty* as the rest of you!"

"You're in a bath, but you're still dirty."

"Do you rub dirt all over yourself, or do you never actually wash?"

Their awful taunting was relentless, and my anger festered. Jaena forbade me from fighting anyone outside of the training grounds. Usually, you don't even see the training grounds until you move to secondary. However, Jaena had me training separately for a few revs by then.

I could have beaten the snot out of all three girls easily, but I still wanted to impress Jaena. So, I let them get away with it. For *revolutions*, they taunted me, and for revolutions, I allowed it. No wonder Petia isn't scared of me, even knowing I'm the Silent Assassin.

It wasn't only my pubic hair that was darker. My blonde hair is much darker at the roots, which fed their unwashed narrative. Their skin is typical Mievaborn porcelain, whereas I am a shade darker. I am still pale, just not as pale as them. My skin looks slightly darker on some of my joints, like my knees and elbows, further proof that I was dirty.

I scrub myself raw before I get out of the bath.

Tovi should be back soon. I think it's been as long as I usually take. My rage has been simmering and bubbling low in my belly the entire time she's been gone. What if the king made her detour? What if the prince *still* hasn't found the others? What if they hated each other and killed one another? What if—

The telltale sounds of an escort pop my bubble of panic. Tovi makes a grand entrance, spinning her cloak off with a flourish, throwing it onto the nearby side table, and brandishing her wrists at me dramatically. And now I understand the shit-eating grin across her face: she has two blades strapped to her.

"How in the Divine?"

"He found them, Mika! Or they found him and his weird whispering to himself. Bitty gave over their two wrist blades so we could have *something* on us."

My mouth gapes open, and tears prickle my eyes as she undoes one of the blades and gives it to me.

"They're okay?"

"Apparently. Annoyed that we *ruined* their grand plan to break you out of the dungeon, but glad you're okay. Surprised and thrown a little into disbelief that I'm here or…that you have forgiven me. Eryn asked about how much exploring we've done, and—fuck—I forgot to ask for paper and charcoal to make a map. I told him we hadn't explored much more than the entrance so far."

I raise an eyebrow at her, not missing the irony that she couldn't believe how I *forgot* to ask Eryn about the king's eyes. "Did he tell them about the king?"

She rolls her eyes at my raised eyebrow and tone. "Yes. Confirmed they see what I see, what we all see, except the violet eyes. They're going to do some subtle questioning, planting seeds that he started acting *weird* a decade past, and see what grows."

I blow out a breath. This is all so much. We need to explore, but I'm loath to do so without some way to know where I'm going. "The knives!" I exclaim. "I can use the knives to mark my passage, so I don't get lost. When is Eryn meeting them again?"

"In a couple of days, let them rustle some shit up first. And yes, good idea. Want to get in there now?"

Yes. Yes, I do. I get changed into the silky clothes I wore the other night that I've already ruined. Again, Tovi hands me a lit lantern when I climb in, and off I go.

I spend about two hours in there and find four other hatches, each one silent, and I don't try to open them. I wish they were mapped, but at least I know how to get back out and how many are around. It's hot in here and I have a slamming headache. Calling it quits for the night, I vow to do more tomorrow.

CHAPTER THIRTY-NINE

T he rage inside is building, getting battle ready for a fight. I'm not supposed to be meeting Eryn yet, and I fear something is wrong for him to ask for me days early. Impatient with the guard taking my cloak, I snap at him to hurry and not make his prince wait. I gently run to the bedroom, about to call his name and ask if he's okay.

Riley.

"Riley."

Riley.

Standing next to Eryn in the middle of the room, is Riley, with an unreadable expression, looking me over.

Eryn looks from me to Riley and back to me with a stupid grin on his face. He all but skips toward me and leans in for a quick and unreciprocated hug, whispering conspiratorially. "Well, I bet *he* doesn't think you look gross." And then the prince saunters past me to his sitting room door. "I'll just be in here, pretending I don't exist for a bit." He closes the door with a self-satisfied chuckle.

Riley looks tired. His hair is a little longer, hitting his shoulders and tucked behind his ears, but he's freshly shaven.

He's wearing his light tan colored linen shirt with most of the buttons undone and sleeves rolled up, exposing the corded muscles of his forearms. His leather weapons harness sits empty. His trousers are black, fitting snugly *everywhere* and I'm certain they're new.

He's still staring, taking in every inch of me, exactly as I am doing to him. I am wearing the beige lace underwear and the champagne dress, so no doubt he can see absolutely everything they *don't* cover. The urge to hide myself barely registers.

I'd left my hair out, which I recently had one of the servants cut for me. It's still a crinkly mess from trying to dry it quickly with a towel. I wonder if I look tired. Because I am tired. Deep into my bones and the darkest depths inside me.

I'm frozen in place. I can't decide what I want to do as the rage dances around my ribs. Do I run to him, or walk and take a seat by Eryn's window? Do I reach for him, or ask him how he is? Do I miss him, or do I miss what could have been? Do I hate him or only want to hate him?

The decision turns out to not be entirely mine as he races forward, picking me up with one hand by the meat of my ass, so I am forced to wrap my legs around his waist while his other arm wraps around my back. The momentum of the action has us spinning, or maybe it just feels like it.

I've tangled my arms around his neck and over his shoulders while burying my face down by his ear. I'm not sure how long we stay like this, clinging to each other. It may be hours or no time at all.

"I thought you were...*again*," he murmurs into my neck. "I had to see for myself that it was really you."

"I'm okay."

I unwind my arms from around his neck, releasing us both so I can face him. I stop when he turns as I pull back, and our lips graze. He looks my face over as if trying to commit every corner to memory, stopping on my lips a few times. He's breathing as hard as I am.

"Can I kiss you?" he whispers in question, tightening his grip enough that I dip closer to his face.

"Ye—" But before I can get the full word out, my mouth is already on his. It's a hurried, frantic, desperate kind of kiss. Both searching with our lips, exploring with our tongues—he tastes *so* good. I miss his touch so much it hurts, my rage hurtling inside of me so violently I'm dizzy with it. When we stop for air, our breaths are heavy, lips bruised.

He's walking, carrying me, and I look to see that we're almost on the far side of the room, away from the door to where Eryn is. When we reach the wall, he adjusts his grip from around my back so he can press me into it and cups my face. I close my eyes and turn into his hand, ignoring my rage still battling to be free. I just want to feel him.

His thumb brushes over my swollen lips and he leans in for another kiss. This time it's slow, as he presses his body into mine. The kiss is soft, but his hardness rubbing between my legs is sending heated signals all over my body. Grinding into me, swapping soft moans, the kisses turn rough and demanding before becoming slow and delicate again.

I'm almost shuddering at how much I need his touch. The hand cradling my face slides down to hold the side of my neck as he begins to kiss down the other side to my collarbone.

"Don't think I didn't notice what you're wearing," he says huskily between each slow, tiny kiss. "I like it."

My hands, still tangled in his hair, pull his head back roughly. "What I'm wearing has nothing to do with you."

It only makes him grin.

But it disappears just as quickly, and I remember our last interaction, what I tried to make him promise, and the way he refused.

I don't care that I can't have more than his touch, that he can't give me more than this. I reach down and fumble to undo his pants. His confusion and then realization is apparent when he almost drops me.

"What are you doing?" he asks in a quick whisper.

"Obviously, I want you to fuck me, Riley," I say with an edge of exasperation, getting frustrated that I can't undo his pants fast enough. I want to do this before I remember all of the reasons why I shouldn't. Maybe if I get this out of my system, I'll feel as dirty and debased as I usually do after sex. And then I won't crave his touch anymore.

Despite the hesitation and the confusion on his face, he helps me to undo his pants, and I look between us as his erection springs free. I grip him firmly, and he shudders as I stroke him. He whispers my name. My *name*. Not Firecat. *Mika*. It sounds like a promise on his lips, one I might want him to keep. Forever.

Something about hearing my name on his lips tips me over the edge, and I guide him between my legs, moving the stupid scrap of lace out of the way.

"Are you sure?" he whispers, as he tries to make me look him in the eye.

Refusing to answer or look him in the eye, I slide the head of his hard cock up and down my slit, coating him in my wetness. He exhales hard, whispering my name again. I finally look at him, a needy moan escaping me as I continue to stroke myself with his cock.

"Kiss me instead of making that sound."

So I do, because I cannot wait any longer. I nudge him only slightly inside me, and light on fire. Slowly, he begins to ease himself deeper, my entrance stretching to accommodate his cock that's as big as I'd feared it would be. I whimper into his mouth, my fists clenching around his collar.

He stops. "Are you okay?" he whispers while concerned eyes search my face.

I nod a yes and grab his hips to thrust him toward me as I buck into him. But he doesn't budge. "Slowly, or I'll hurt you."

"I don't care," I growl.

"I do."

He moves *slowly*, edging in only a fraction more. Again, I try to force him deeper, knowing that even now he is stretching me painfully. But the rage is screaming, and I need to drown it out.

"Don't use me to hurt you. If that is your aim, we can stop right here," he says, grabbing my face to force me to look at him. I lock eyes with him long enough that it should be unpleasant, but it's the opposite. My rage calms a little.

He moves out and back in gently, keeping eye contact with me, until finally, he fills me. I breathe heavily, savoring the fullness of him inside me. Then he moves more rhythmically, harder. I kiss him, trying not to make a sound, but I still make a throaty whine of pleasure, albeit muffled against his mouth.

I'm bouncing against the wall, our muffled breathy moans rivaling each other. He pulls the strap of my dress down to expose my breast, and I arch up to meet his mouth. I cover my mouth with my hand as he licks my nipple and then teases it between his teeth.

"*Riley*," I whimper into my hand.

He pulls my face back to his mouth, and I kiss him hard and forcefully. I'm reaching a pinnacle. Overwhelmed by the taste of him, the scrape and slide of our lips, and his tongue against mine, the pressure inside me continues to build.

He adjusts me in his grip and now I'm more exposed and open for him. With one hand on his shoulder for grip, I slide the other between us, desperate. Our eyes lock again as I circle my fingers around his cock as it pumps into me, squeezing the base before sliding back up to play with myself too. His tempo increases and I'm panting as my back begins to arch involuntarily.

My climax is intense. My knees grip tightly around him. Sounds become muffled and distant as heat explodes from my core and takes me over entirely. My hand has dipped under his shirt to hold onto his side, the other digging nails into the back of his shoulder.

Riley's hand has come up to cover my mouth. "Shh, shh," he laughs between pants of his own.

Following closely behind with his own release, Riley empties himself into me as I continue to clench in pleasure around him, his moans muffled between my breasts.

As my ecstasy slowly fades, Riley moves his hand from my mouth and back to my ass to hold me up, my legs no longer clamped around him with such a vice-like grip. I move his hair out of the way and hold his face, my thumbs stroking along his sharp jawline. The need to see his eyes is coursing hot through my veins. His eyes—eyes I don't understand how I ever thought were *regular* and *normal* green.

Yes, Riley's eyes are the green of the forest as a Nemorisborn, but they aren't *just* green. They're a dark evergreen of dense forest, dancing with an outer ring of colors from the waters of a silent beach. Speckled with warm light through young leaves, and golden hour warming their center. His eyes are breathtakingly beautiful, and I cannot believe I have never truly *seen* them until now.

"What are you looking for?" he asks with curiosity.

I look at him a little longer, wanting to bask in this moment with him before I allow reality to set in. It's already circling like carrion birds waiting to descend.

With fully dilated pupils, Riley leans in to kiss my neck

and whisper. "You have no idea how long I have waited for you."

Like a bubble popped, the rage is back and screaming in my ears, if it ever stopped in the first place. I can't do this with him. What is *wrong* with me? Held prisoner for the second time in as many moons and allowing lust to take over like some horny teenager. Disgusting. I am playing with fire, and I should know better, *be* better. This was silly at best and dangerous at worst.

Hate. I need to *hate* him. I'll make him hate me instead. Make him hate me so much that he will never risk touching me again. It shouldn't be too difficult.

"I'm just looking for you, Riley. Trying to find something real." He leans back to look at me, confusion creasing his brow as I continue. "This isn't real. We aren't real," I say sardonically, almost taunting. My skin prickles, and my heart rate increases wildly as I struggle to breathe evenly.

"What do you mean, 'we aren't real'?" he questions, trying to move closer to me against the wall, even though he's *still inside me.*

"Us. You and me. This isn't real. It's just sex," I say, out of breath, getting agitated and lightheaded.

"You don't get to decide what's real for me. This was never *just* anything, Firecat."

I'm trying to push him away so I can get down, but I'm struggling against him. The rage I've barely kept inside is becoming louder than I can bear. I'm biting the inside of my cheek and tasting blood as I continue to struggle in his grip.

Trying to get me to look at him, he pleads. "Stop. What just happened?"

"Let go of me!" I hiss, staring him straight in the eye.

He lets out an angry breath, holding my gaze for another moment before gently easing me off him and releasing me to my feet. I try to move around him as I straighten my dress. The giant mountain that he is, captures me as I try to go around. He lets go immediately but still won't let me pass as he tucks himself back into his pants.

"This is more than scratching an itch, and you know it."

"You said not to fall in love with you!"

His eyebrows go up. "And you said your heart didn't exist."

"It doesn't!" I hiss again as I can't seem to whisper. "This is all just a game. You can't care for me!"

Riley finally loses his temper at my antagonizing. "Stop twisting my words, that was about Tovi! And this has never been a game to me, even though it clearly is to you." His words are like a hot knife into the haggard pieces of what's left of my soul. It's the reminder I need: I am a monster. So, I will fucking act like one.

"And the other women?" It's a low blow and I know it, but I'm losing the will to push him away, to fight. I need him to *hate* me.

"What other women?" he angrily whispers.

I try to get around him again, but this time he grabs my face in his hands, engulfing my head easily. Before I have time to struggle away from him, he's leaning down to my eye level, and gently repeats himself. "What other women?"

"I've *seen* you with them. Sneaking into their rooms in the middle of the night."

He makes a frustrated sound. "Yes, okay. *Once*, but that was before. I won't apologize for being with women before you." He frowns, using his grip on my face to bring me closer to him as he straightens up, maintaining eye contact. "As I told you in that cave, you've done something to me."

The memory of him leaving the room of the beautiful Erduborn woman in the middle of the night, as she held his face after he kissed her cheek, crashes hard inside my chest along with my rage. I want to scream until I have no breath left in me and my throat is raw. My rage reminds me how pathetic and weak I am for letting him get this close again. *Closer.*

Jaena's cruel laughter echoes in my ears.

Shaking my head, as much as I can when two giant hands are holding it, I say, "Not just *before.*" I grab onto his empty weapons harness to push him away. "So, you're a liar too. Let go of me, Riley."

I slam against him with my fists holding the harness to push him away from me, but his hands only drop to my shoulders as he opens his mouth to say something.

"It doesn't matter anyway!" I get in first. "We aren't bonded. I don't have your heart and you *don't* have mine. We're nothing. You can lie, sneak around and fuck everyone else. Just continue to do whatever you like Riley. I. Don't. Care. You're just the drunk prince and I'm the monster you *bought.*"

I try to give him the most hateful and vicious look I can, as I'm not sure how much more of this I can take. My heart feels like it is just vibrating now, not even bothering to beat.

He falters for a moment, a flicker of emotions scrolling over his face. Our eyes are still locked as he starts shaking his head. "No. I don't know what this is, what you're trying to do right now, but *no.*"

I snarl like the beast I am. I can't breathe. The edges of my vision are swimming.

"I have never lied to you!" he says, his voice beginning to rise.

Snarling again, I go for another shove. "Then who was the Erduborn woman you snuck around with in Waadi, mere *hours* after trying to fuck me? Or is that considered *before?*"

Confusion and then recognition dawns on Riley's face as I hear a rap on the door. It quietly begins to open, with Eryn chanting, *"Please don't be naked,"* with his eyes firmly squeezed shut.

CHAPTER FORTY

Eryn opens one eye to look around the room and sees us near the wall beside his bed. "Thank Divine," he breathes, before tiptoeing in and closing the door behind him.

I look back to Riley, who still has hold of my shoulders and hasn't looked away. I let go of his weapons harness and push his arms away. This time he doesn't resist. Wrapping myself in a blanket from Eryn's bed, I walk toward the young prince.

"Sorry to interrupt, but I don't think we should take much longer as we still need to decide what to do about the hatches. Did you discover anything else?" Eryn says to me in a normal tone but with a confused and concerned look on his face. As I'm about to answer, Eryn mouths, *"Are you okay?"*.

I give him a tight nod and launch into a brief update on what Tovi and I found.

Riley apologizes to Eryn, clearing his throat. "I'm sorry, Eryn, I really thought you were making shit up when you said both Tovi and Mika were here."

Eryn narrows his eyes at Riley, apparently not believing I'm okay and correctly assuming that Riley has something to do with it.

I speak quickly, not wanting an altercation between these two males. "Tovi doesn't fit, so it's just been me exploring. It might just be something to do with the water piped through to each washroom. I can try to find the doxy washroom, but it's hard to hear if anyone is in the rooms of the hatches I find."

"Bitty," Riley offers. "Bitty is closest in size to you, and they'd be able to hear exactly what's going on."

"Maybe we can get...?" Eryn fumbles over which pronoun to use as both Riley and I say "them" in unison.

"Right, thank you. Maybe we can get them here and try to find a way down to you from my rooms?" Eryn finishes, not taking his narrowed eyes off Riley.

"I think that could work!" I say a little too cheerfully.

I risk a peek at Riley, as I've kept my eyes on Eryn the whole time, only to find that his intent gaze is on me. I'm embarrassed by the immediate sting of tears in my eyes, and I hope Riley doesn't notice. Or Eryn, for that matter. I have to get out of here right now. The need to break something, snap something, punch *anything*, is beginning to overwhelm me. My skin itches painfully with tension.

"I have to get back to Tovi. You're right, Eryn. It's been too long," I say far too quickly. Eryn tries to say something, but I keep going. "You guys work it out with Bitty, and I guess we'll know if they can reach us when the Laguzborn is jumping into our washroom," I finish with an awkward laugh.

Not able to spend a moment longer with the raging tornado in my chest, Eryn's concern, or Riley's...Riley-ness, I march for the door.

"We need to talk, Mika. Please," Riley pleads, and I

catch him trying to reach for me in the corner of my eye, so I take a quick step to dodge him.

"We're *done*, Riley," I say coldly.

I swing open the door and charge through with Eryn hot on my heels to get my cloak. It's not until I'm standing in the middle of the sitting room I share with Tovi that the rage finally leaves me. When it does, I'm completely and utterly empty. Devoid of everything. Barely the husk of a beast now.

Tovi must be asleep in our shared bedroom, so I allow myself a moment. I sink to my knees, my face in my hands on the ground, my cloak covering me, and the hood falling over my head.

I'm not sure how long I weep, but once I start, I cannot stop. It's like I lost the ability to stop myself from crying when I allowed the floodgates to open after Sweet Girl. Thinking of her makes it worse. How do I have this many tears to shed when nothing remains of me but a darkness so complete it could suffocate the Divine world?

Tovi is digging into the cloak, trying to uncover me and find my face. "What happened? Are you okay?" she cries as she starts pulling me up to sit, grabbing my hands away from my face.

She gasps, or hisses—I'm not sure which—but I must really look like shit. "I didn't hear you come in. I fell asleep waiting."

I clear my throat and try to fix the hair stuck to my face in my tears. "Everyone is okay. I'm sorry to scare you, nothing is wrong. I'm just…" *What?*

An emotionally volatile, rage-oholic? Stuck replaying every awful thing I've ever done in my head to remind myself that I don't deserve to be loved? Confused about what to believe, so I choose to believe the worst? Sick to death of how weak and *useless* I become whenever Riley touches me, so I erupt in brutal anger and lash out? Hating that I *willingly* gave him a hold over me, and now I am terrified I can't get it back? Not wanting to be used by him and turning into this ugly creature that uses him first?

"Get up," Tovi demands.

I let out a distinguished "Huh?" in query.

Tovi pulls me up, takes off my cloak, and orders me to lift my arms. I do as I'm told, and she pulls the nightdress off, then pulls me by the hand into the washroom.

"Sit," she orders, pointing to the wooden chair against the wall.

Tovi disappears for a moment and comes back with a clean tunic, gesturing for me to lift my arms again so she can slip it down over my head. Tovi wets a cloth and cleans my face of crusted snot and tears. The last thing I remember is being led to the bedroom and bundled into bed. *Bossy.*

USUALLY, I'm up and awake before Tovi, but not this morning. I'm just a used rag that's been rung out until it ripped. Tovi is nudging me awake, getting progressively rougher as I ignore her.

"Mika. Breakfast," she whispers before repeating herself louder and louder.

I mumble that I'm not hungry and snuggle down into the blankets, pulling them over my eyes to hide. I haven't tried to open them yet, but they feel heavy and swollen.

A heartbeat later, Tovi is repeating this dance, but saying lunch is here. Again, I say I'm not hungry, but this time I roll over to face the wall so my back is to her. In the time it takes for me to fall asleep again, I tell myself how pathetic it is that I'm hiding in bed.

Instead of trying to wake me gently for dinner, Tovi pulls off my covers without warning.

"Get up right now, or I will carry you."

I glare at her, but not wanting her to pick me up, I stand. I glare at her some more for good measure. The foot height difference means I'm angling my face up, and suddenly, I feel like a small, petulant child. She gestures for me to follow her to the washroom.

"Get in." She gestures to the steaming bath.

I'm already glaring so I let out an angry snort of frustration to let her know how bossy she is. I strip off, throwing the underwear I was still wearing into the bath to wash as well. The water is a perfect temperature, oils dancing along the surface, and the steamy room is filled with a spicy scent.

"Thank you," I say, smirking at her.

She reclines herself on the wooden chair, using the edge of my bath as a footrest. Apparently, I'm not getting any privacy today.

The bath isn't big enough for me to stretch out. Made of wood, the big round tub is only deep enough to just cover my breasts. But inside is smooth and pleasant, and I sink into the water with a groan.

I clean my underwear first, hanging them over the edge of the bath. Then I wash my body, scrub my teeth, and clean my face. I don't worry about my hair; I washed it yesterday and can't be bothered today, even if it does have dried tears and snot in it.

Tovi has her arms behind her head while she reclines, her eyes closed and face relaxed as she hums a soft tune. She found me in a messy puddle on the floor, and I couldn't even begin to explain why. But she looked after me anyway. My stomach curdles.

The silence is too much. It's inviting my brain to think of Riley and the sex…Rage flashes through me like lightning and my cheeks flame. Never has my rage responded to *sex* before. I thought I wanted a quick release and that I could use Riley for it. Combine them but keep them separate. The fact that I *needed* Riley's touch, and *he* was the reason I needed a release in the first place, unravels my logic. I've made a grave mistake thinking I could keep them separate.

It wasn't *just* sex to me, and the overwhelming realization begins to choke the air from my lungs, reminding me that I accused the same of Riley.

He hates me, and I hate him, I try to convince myself.

I can't…*breathe*.

He *hates me*, he has to.

I hate him.

He's a liar.

I'm a toy, something to take, something to play with.

He wants to use me.

I don't deserve more than that. And certainly not someone like Riley.

He deserves better than a monster like me.

I hug my knees, resting the side of my head on them, and attempt to distract myself by asking Tovi a question I've been trying to ask the last couple of days: "I'm not ready to talk about last night. But maybe you could tell me about Amarilyss?"

Tovi's eyes snap open, and I can see the decision warring behind them as she raises her eyebrows. She moves her arms from behind her head to cross them over her chest as she takes a deep breath.

"Lyss? Uhhh…I think there's a similar age difference between you and I, as Lyss and I," she begins, her eyes lighting up and cheeks warming.

"I knew her well. We hung out a lot in secondary." She

shrugs, but the smile on her face belies her attempt at nonchalance. "I was eighteen or nineteen, and her coming-of-age season was approaching, so I was getting nervous. We hadn't ever really talked about guys. I'd been with them before, but it just wasn't a topic *we* spoke about. I didn't even know if she was into girls. But I thought this was going to be the last I ever saw of her."

She laughs and rubs her face. "I kissed her! And it was *awful*. She laughed! Mika, I cannot tell you how hard she laughed." Tovi shakes her head, still grinning. "You're probably wondering whether we talked about it, right?" she says but doesn't wait for a response. "Well, we didn't. We pretended like it was this funny thing that happened. Then she was gone. Sold to Nemoris."

"You didn't know how she felt?"

"I wore gloves all the time back then. Feeling everyone's feelings *all the time* was overwhelming, so no. But even then, if I was ever *not* wearing them, I made sure not to touch anything she'd touched recently. Because I didn't *want* to know."

Tovi continues her story with a little less humor now. "A couple revs later, my coming-of-age season was upon me. I wasn't exactly a Junky, but I also didn't have a desirable Gift. They sent the notice out for me at least, but I didn't think there'd be any bids." Tovi leans forward. "But there was one from Nemoris."

"Did you know she was a princess by then?" I ask her.

"No!" she laughs. "I had absolutely no clue. But I was excited to maybe get to see her. And off I went."

The water is getting too cold, so I let it drain and step out to dry off. We pause the storytelling so I can get dressed. I meet Tovi in our sitting room to eat dinner, and she continues.

"So, I'm brought into their receiving hall where I can see the royal family up on the dais, right at the end of the impossibly long room. I keep my head down as I walk toward them. When I reach them, I curtsy and look up. Mid-fucking-curtsy, I see Lyss sitting there next to the queen, *beaming* at me! She squeals and runs at me for a hug." Tovi laughs, shaking her head. "I panicked a bit, trying to see what Queen Neo thought, but she was smiling and said it was nice to finally meet me. That's when I learned she was a fucking princess."

I laugh at how fantastical it all is, like a children's story. Tovi's demeanor changes, and a darkness descends around her. We finish our dinner in silence in the dying light of the day, but I raise my eyebrows at Tovi after a while as a subtle prod.

"Okay." Tovi takes a deep breath and holds it, letting it out slowly before she continues. "I was doing odd jobs for the crown, like seeing if people had ill intentions by touching their cutlery after dinners. I'm pretty sure it wasn't of any real help, and I only had the position because of Lyss. So, I had a lot of free time. Lyss and I spent all of it together, and it was wonderful. Until I fucked up."

Tovi groans. "We slept together. And instead of being with her, like I actually wanted, I panicked and asked the queen if I could take a position in her army."

"You *what?*"

She nods. "I bolted. Didn't even talk to her. Left to go and train with Beans almost immediately. I mean, *eventually*, we talked. She said I broke her heart, and she didn't know if she could forgive me."

"Oh Tovi…You idiot!"

Tovi laughs. "Yes, I am aware of that, thank you. We managed to be friends again, and she allowed me back into her life, though she keeps me at arm's length. It probably didn't help that I started sleeping with her brother." She grimaces, scratching one of her sharp eyebrows.

The silence hangs heavy, and I don't know what to say.

Tovi blurts into the long silence. "Mika, she's the most beautiful woman you will ever see in your life. Not because she's gorgeous on the outside, and believe me when I say she *is*. But she has a light about her, she makes everything around her feel magical. She's wonderful and caring and…" She chokes, unable to continue.

"We'll get her back, Tovi. Then you can apologize and tell her you love her. Or I will punch you in the tit like I wanted to the other week."

"You wanted to punch me in the tit?" she asks incredulously, a smile tugging at the corner of one lip.

I wave my hand at her, scrunching up my nose. "Yes. For that whole betrayal thing."

"That's it?" she laughs. "That's all you wanted to do?"

I shrug. She's got big tits, so it would definitely hurt. "It might be an idea to stop sleeping with her brother, though," I say as nonchalantly as I can, ignoring the jealousy that roars in my ears with my rage.

"I haven't slept with that wanker in revs. Too cold and broody," she laughs.

"What about while we were traveling? You guys snuck off together…"

Tovi makes a loud "ha" sound and goes to say something, but then her face crumbles. "We weren't going off to fuck if that's what you're suggesting. But we *were* trying to get away from the rest of you for some peace. He's my best friend, and…it's nice to be alone together, just existing. But I *was* using that time to convince him you were not to be trusted." She winces, and we fall into silence again.

We tidy up our dinner plates, which are almost licked

clean. Even though it was cold, royal meals are always delicious. Tonight's fare was roasted quail stuffed with lemon and tarragon brown rice, a side of honeyed carrots, and wilted greens with butter. Two small, sweet custard tarts sit uneaten, as neither of us wanted dessert.

When someone knocks on our doors, we assume it's a servant to collect our dinner plates. But the man says Prince Eryn has requested my company again tonight, and I am to be ready within the hour.

I'm dizzy. It's not only rage in my chest, or at least not as it usually is. I don't know what this feeling is, but it's telling me I *cannot do this.*

"Tovi, I can't," I plead. "I can't tonight. I can't go. Just in case..."

"Just in case what?" she demands with narrowed eyes, knowing I'm keeping something from her.

"I promise I'll tell you. But I can't yet. None of it makes sense." I'm getting jittery, my voice is rising. "There's literally *nothing* wrong!" I yell at myself more than Tovi.

She gives me an unconvinced look and tells me to go to bed. We will say that I'm unwell and that Tovi will happily attend to the prince's *needs* instead.

After she leaves, I try to imagine all the possible scenarios of what will happen when she reaches Eryn's room while I lie here faking illness. Is Riley there, and now he knows I'm avoiding him like a coward? Has Tovi figured out what's going on? Has Eryn figured it out? Or is there actually something wrong, and I'm so selfishly stuck in *whatever this is* that I am risking everything because I'm...sad? Angry? Nothing? All I feel is rage.

Who is this person? I don't recognize myself. Before I left Osraed, I knew who I was. Someone who can kill and not think anything of it. A nanny who cares for children and embraces them freely, sharing the joy that I keep from everyone else. I could, and would, beat the shit out of anyone for any and all reasons. *I didn't cry.* I was only my rage. And I was happy with my solitary life.

Happy.

Was that happiness?

CHAPTER FORTY-ONE

I'm staring at the ceiling in bed while listening to what I can only assume is another windstorm raging outside, as it matches the torrent inside me as I wait for Tovi. When I hear the procession of guards escorting her back, I jump up and peek out of the bedroom door.

Tovi swans in dramatically as the doors close behind her. I tentatively start walking toward her, trying to guess what's happened based on what I can glean from her body language.

"What's hap—"

"What is going on with you?" Tovi demands, whirling to face me with her cold, hard stare.

"Wh—"

"Don't give me the bullshit version, tell me what the fuck is going on."

I close my mouth and raise my brows at her.

"I'll kill him," she spits.

I'm lost. This didn't start the way I thought it would. "Kill who?" I ask with trepidation, unsure of what's been said and by who.

Exasperated, Tovi asks, "What did Riley do?"

"What makes you think Riley did something?"

"Don't dance around me, Mika. Eryn was hoping to see you because he's *worried*. The fact you didn't come has him even more worried." She pauses briefly in contemplation. "He genuinely cares about you, you know?"

My heart somersaults into my throat for a second before I realize who she means. "Eryn? He's a sweet kid," I say quietly.

Tovi, not missing a thing, narrows her eyes at me. "You thought I meant Riley!" she growls. "Has he stuck his dick where it doesn't belong? Because that dickhead has a really good habit of drunk fucking women, and then blowing them off like they're nothing. Most of the time because he can't remember, but sometimes it's just because he's a fucking asshole."

Her voice is aggressive, but she crouches in front of me where I've slumped into a sofa seat. Face full of concern, she grabs one of my hands and refuses to let go. What is it with these people and their forced affections?

"No. He…It wasn't…I mean, I—" *I'm the asshole here.*

An ugly mess of words start tumbling out of me.

First, I tell her what happened in the cave. Then I backtrack and tell her about the night I confronted Riley with the rumor, and the things we said to each other. I mention how I had seen the two of them sneak off together quite a few times before that, and I'd seen him go into at least two women's rooms. I choke when I tell her about the beautiful Erduborn woman whose cheek he kissed after being alone in her room for hours.

She lets me take my hand out of hers so I can use it to wipe the tears betraying me as they slide down my cheeks. She's studying me, but she hasn't said a word.

I tell her about the conflicting feelings and emotions and

signals. I'm starting to get angry, so I stand up to pace. The affection, the way he looks at me, the secrets and the lies. I can't help but let out a sob when I tell her about how he held me after I woke up from the kidnapping.

"It was the first time I'd cried since I was seven, and it all came flooding out." I let out a bark of laughter. "And now I can't seem to stop," I say as I angrily wipe the tears from my cheeks. "The kidnapping and feeling helpless. So close to being raped, *again*—" Tovi flinches, but I continue without pause. "—Being saved, only to watch Beans take an axe to the fucking head!" I'm breathing hard, trying not to yell.

"Fortunately, once an assassin, always an assassin," my scathing voice spits out. "But then..." I growl at myself so I don't cry. "Sweet Girl. I promised her. I fucking promised I'd *save her,* Tovi, and instead, she sacrificed her life for my pitiful existence!"

I know I've started to yell so I pace, clenching and unclenching my fists, grateful that Tovi hasn't once tried to say anything since I started.

"Tovi, when I saw you with the rescue, I thought they'd lied. That they'd spun another rumor. I was *so* relieved. But then you ran. And it was as though it was the last thing holding me together because..." I gesture, unable to find the words. "Then Riley just held me as I broke apart."

It split me open, and all the ugly and vile things trapped safely inside violently spilled out. All the darkness within me, the disgusting shards of my soul, everything dripping in fury and rage. But I can't tell Tovi that part. Especially when I know that I shoved it all back within me again. So, I pause to catch my breath instead.

Tovi nods to me, gesturing at me to keep going, to tell her the rest.

Tentatively, I explain to her what happened after that, how Riley wouldn't let me sleep alone ever again. But it kept flipping from me pushing him away, to him trying to give me space, to me being angry at him, to him looking at me like I was crazy. Rinse and repeat.

I take a deep breath and explain how I *used* him back at the nighthouse, that I tried to play it off like it was nothing but admitting that it might be the opposite. And then the kiss, the one right before I was captured, where I asked him to promise not to kiss me again, and he wouldn't.

"You know everything that happens after that because I got caught in the castle and sent to the dungeons."

"Except for what happened last night," she says wryly, one eyebrow raised.

"Yes. Except for that."

I pace some more, deciding how much to tell her. For some reason, it's not the part where we fuck that I can't say. It's the awful things I said and how I said them. Holding my breath in an attempt to calm myself, I watch the flurry of sand and dust battering our window and am reminded of being in the windcaves with *him*. Where I dared to think life could be different. That *I* could be different.

I blurt it out in a jumble. Not in order, I miss bits and then have to jump back to explain. I don't go into full explicit details, but enough. I relay some of the things I said to him and some of what he said to me. Then with tears in my eyes and shame coloring my face, I tell her what I said to him before Eryn interrupted us. How I said it, and how I looked at him. All while my rage is like a snake wrapping around my airways.

"It was hateful, Tovi. I was vicious. I was *trying* to be. But still, all he said was 'no' like he didn't understand. Fuck, *I* didn't understand, so how was he supposed to?" I ask, not truly expecting an answer.

I'm trying to catch my breath. I've said it all. Tovi

probably thinks I'm a monster. A coward. Useless. Nothing but a heartless assassin.

And it would all be true.

I can't look her in the eye, not even briefly. I know it's because I can't bear to see the truth in her eyes. She's still crouching where I'd been sitting, watching me pace. The silence stretches out before us.

"He was sober?" Tovi's question breaks the silence, catching me off guard.

"What? Yes, *why?*"

She shakes her head, looking confused. "Last night, when you had sex, he was sober?"

I growl, opening my mouth to say yes again, and she holds up her hands in surrender.

"Look, we haven't fucked in revs, like I said. And even then, it was *quick*. Definitely no kissing. The point was to get it done as quickly as possible and move on. He was *never* sober. I don't think he's ever *had* sex sober."

I groan into my hands, fingers digging into my eyes. "It doesn't even matter, Tovi! He's an unbound man who can fuck whoever he wants. I don't get to have a say in that. Especially not after the way I treated him."

"Riley's changed, Mika. Laughing and smiling with *actual* happiness, and not just being a miserable cunt every day. I barely see him drink, at *all*. I thought it was because of Lyss, and maybe it is in part. But I think it might be you."

I make a derisive sound and she cuts me a look, continuing. "He usually tells me about the women he's been with. In *detail*, or as much as he can remember." She's looking at me, pointedly, trying to let something sink in that I'm obviously missing.

"There *was* a woman he slept with in Nemoris, at that first inn after we left Mama's. He was too drunk to remember what happened except that he woke up naked in her room."

I frown, but she puts her hand up forestalling my ugly thoughts and opinions.

"That Riley? The Riley we have all known and loved for revolutions, is not the same Riley you've gotten to know. The drunk and selfish asshole at the beginning of the Nemoris forest was all we knew, and it's the last we've seen of him. We've all tried over the revs, us three and his friends back home, his sisters, but we just came to accept it was who he was. Until now..." Tovi sighs, standing up and shaking her head. She gives me an almost pitying look that has my rage swishing its tail viciously, and I don't know if I can bear to hear the rest of what she has to say.

"He hasn't told me about *any* other women after her. Certainly not some Erduborn woman he kissed on the cheek." She scrunches her nose. "That's definitely not his style. He doesn't *do* affection, not after sex. Even the first time we slept together, there was no confusing anything he said or did with affection," she finishes sardonically.

"I'm not sure that's helping anything. How is telling me what a slut Ri—"

"He never told me about you! In the cave. That is definitely something he would have told me."

"Because nothing happened! Or he was embarrassed," I say, exasperated.

A creaking noise sounds in the washroom, and Tovi and I both move to defensive positions. Someone is coming, the sounds of soft footsteps moving toward us.

A familiar face appears in the doorway.

"Bitty," we both cry softly.

Tovi looks unsure, but Bitty runs at her. They slam into her with force, wrapping their arms around her, Tovi stepping back slightly from the momentum.

They're murmuring things to each other, and I step into the washroom to give them some privacy. I wash my face, trying to cool it down as my cheeks continue to flame. I can hear the soft sounds of Tovi's apologies and Bitty's forgiveness. Despite all of my assurances, part of me worried none of them would forgive her. I hope Bitty's forgiveness is a good sign for the other two.

I waltz back into the room to see Tovi's arm resting around Bitty's shoulder, and they have a matching gleam in their eyes. I give Tovi a knowing "I told you so" look, and she rolls her eyes dramatically. Bitty runs at me next for a hug. They slam into me, enveloping me in their gangly-limbed embrace. I reciprocate, holding on tight. I missed them, more than I care to admit.

No doubt Bitty heard some of what Tovi and I were arguing about, but in true Bitty fashion, they don't speak a word of it. Giving them my cup, I pour some tea, and we settle down in the comfortable sofa seats.

"How did you find us?" I ask, and then wish I had phrased it differently. The answer to that question could easily be: *"I could hear you telling Tovi all of the awful things you said to Riley."*

But Bitty is as diplomatic as usual. "Easily, once I was able to figure out how to move quietly enough. Once I felt I had gone as far east from Eryn's rooms as I could, I tried to find the quietest rooms. I waited half a day to make sure that no one was there. When I finally jumped down, the room was *covered* in dust and spider webs. Took everything in me not to sneeze."

Tovi and I share a look. Whose chambers would be like that? It dawns on me. "Queen Jasi."

"That's my assumption, based on all the dresses and jewelry. It looks like a tomb. No one has been in there for a *very* long time. I was concerned at first, leaving footprints in the dust, but *duh*, no one is going to see them." Bitty frowns. "The doors were locked, *from the inside.*"

"The king and queen didn't share chambers?" Tovi asks.

"Rumor has it the king has terrible nightmares, so he locks himself in his chambers each night." I'm frowning as I explain, another reason forming in my head. "But maybe it's because he can't hold his shift when sleeping?"

Both Tovi and Bitty raise their eyebrows.

"Are the queen's rooms *connected* to the king's?" I ask.

"There was another door that would connect to a room I didn't go into, though I couldn't hear anyone on the other side. There's also a small courtyard that comes out near the gardens and overlooks the ocean. Unguarded. I'd planned to investigate further another time. The door out of the queens' rooms took me to a large hallway."

Bitty excitedly interrupts their own train of thought. "I got to use my lockpicks! I had to use them to relock the queen's doors behind me. I waited an hour until it was clear to be able to do so," they say, beaming.

"Anyway, I found a large staircase and I narrowly missed someone in the hallway at the top. I hid in a small library. There were people in there, but they hadn't seen me come in. Once the hall was clear again, I checked rooms until I found guest chambers that had a washroom with a hatch." Bitty scratches their head, looking from me to Tovi with hesitation.

Tovi looses a sharp breath. "Spit it out, Bitty."

"I found the doxies yesterday. I heard six distinct voices. All women, but none of them were Lyss."

"What the fuck does that mean?" Tovi says angrily to the ceiling, gripping her teacup with white knuckles.

"I didn't mean to—I was looking for you two. But when I found them, I didn't want to waste the opportunity. I listened for hours. They gave no indication that there was ever any more than the six of them. Obviously, I didn't risk trying to speak to them.

"I spent the entire day today scouring the doxy wing to see if maybe there was another room. Nothing. Only the six women. And you two." Bitty's defeated voice is in stark contrast to their earlier excitement when they found us.

I'm lucky that Bitty has my teacup because I would have thrown it against the wall. I still might. The destruction of something the king owns might appease the rage building in my head.

"I've told the others I found the six doxies, but not that I haven't found any more of them, or you. I think it might send Riley over the edge. He's been a mess."

Rage takes a nosedive into my stomach, and I have to stand and pace, exert some unspent energy before I explode. My fists clench and unclench, breathing unsteady.

"Now what?" Tovi's sharp voice cuts through my angry fog.

I make an exasperated noise, flapping my arms up and slamming them down against my sides. *Now what?* What the fuck do we do now? We had pinned everything on Amarilyss being with the doxies.

"They *have* to be somewhere else," I say to myself more than the others. I glance over at Tovi, who's giving me a look like I'm stating the obvious. I rub my face and take a deep breath. "All of them, I mean. Not just her. King Stol has purchased far more than six Nulls. Plus, there's the male Nulls. I don't remember ever seeing the king notifying Records of a Patron death, so there should be *a lot of them*."

"How would they be checking in each rev at the Registry in Osraed?" Bitty asks with a frown, voicing a question I hadn't even considered until now.

Tovi huffs. "Maybe he is impersonating them too?"

"That's a lot of effort. Surely the king disappearing for weeks at a time, multiple times a rev, would raise suspicion," I add, trying to figure it out.

Bitty makes a humming noise that gets mine and Tovi's attention. "He could just have someone at the Registry checking them off. Who would really know they weren't real check-ins?"

Tovi and I stare at Bitty, slowly shaking our heads. I growl and Tovi mutters her hate for the king. Bitty's probably right.

I'm back to pacing. Tovi is bouncing a knee, with a scowl on her face and unfocused eyes. Bitty is reclining in the chair, picking at the hem of their shirt sleeve. They're wearing a uniform like I had been.

We *have* to be missing something. I'm going through every piece of information they've told me, adding it to everything I've learned myself.

"The explosion," I burst out. "Where was the explosion that started this whole thing?"

Bitty and Tovi look at me and then each other in frowned contemplation.

"Was it explicitly said that it was in the doxy wing, or only that his doxies were injured?" I add when neither of them speaks.

"Just that the assailant snuck into the castle and his doxies were hurt. We never sought to ask *where* the explosion had been," Tovi says, standing to pace with me.

Chewing my nail, I say, "So, if we find where the explosion happened…"

"Find the explosion, find the missing doxies, find Lyss." Tovi is muttering to herself, or me, I'm not sure.

If they're still alive. I push away the horrible thought.

"Time to go. Someone's coming, and I need to break the news to the others. I'll check with Eryn about the explosion first though, he might know," Bitty says, jumping up and jogging to the washroom.

We opt to sit, waiting for whoever is coming, listening to the sounds of Bitty climbing, and exiting through the hatch.

If Bitty heard someone coming, they never made it to us. Tovi and I eventually go to bed without a further word.

Tovi and I spend the day going through training exercises, not speaking. The frown hasn't left her face the whole time. Nothing will make this hopelessness any better. The chance we have of discovering where the explosion happened is too small to offer any real hope.

When dinner arrives, the servant advises that Prince Eryn would like Tovi's company this evening and they'll collect her after dinner. When she leaves, Tovi and I discuss the possibility that Eryn *does* know where the explosion was. We grin at each other as we dig into the meal, spirits lifted.

Medium-rare venison, mashed potato, a salad of celery, and a tart red pepper gravy swimming with tiny mushrooms I don't recognize—all piping hot and delicious, as always.

When Tovi puts on her cloak, she curses, pulling a small package out of her pocket. "I was supposed to give this to you last night, but I was so angry, and then we got interrupted. And then I forgot. It's no excuse, though. I'm sorry. I should have given it to you right away."

It's small and wrapped in a square of beautiful fabric, dyed to look like frasteria tree blooms. I look up at Tovi, questioning.

"Eryn gave it to me to give to you. It's from Riley. Eryn didn't know what it was, but he said Riley told him to tell you he wasn't sorry. I don't know if the message has gotten slightly skewed." She shrugs, knocking on the door for the guards to escort her to Eryn's rooms, leaving me entirely alone with a package from Riley.

CHAPTER FORTY-TWO

My fingertips are tingling, and my lips are a little numb. I meander to the bedroom, expecting my rage to make its presence known. *Why has he given me a gift?* The numbness and tingling are spreading. There is no clawing, not even a flutter in my chest. Walking to the bedroom, my legs are full of lead and jelly.

I sit down on the bed, when the doors to our chambers swing open. I thrust the package under my pillow and stand too quickly, catching my head in my hands as everything spins. I'm still holding my head as I enter the sitting room, a chill creeping into my bones.

"Mika. Are you feeling alright?" the king's smooth voice questions me.

I try to curtsy but stumble as the tingling in my feet and numbness spreads through my mid-section.

"Oh, please sit. You look most unwell, dear." King Stol gestures to the sofa as he takes a seat opposite me.

I collapse onto the sofa as the world tilts and sways. The king only watches me, not at all concerned by my behavior.

He reminds me of a snake, ready to strike. Slippery. Poised. Full of fangs and danger.

Snake is a funny word.

Sssssnay-kuh.

I giggle and then frown. Why am I giggling? Stol's face has a vicious, wide smile, and his violet eyes are watching me with delight.

"Have you ever experienced pain, Mika? Real pain. The type of pain you think you may never recover from?"

"What kind of question is that?" I slur. My throat is numb. Everything is either numb or tingly now. I try to stand, but my body won't obey.

"Did you know, that often, Gifts are only trapped? Needing some *motivation* to manifest. I have found pain to be a great motivator." Stol's words sound warped as his grin widens and takes over every corner of the room. Violet eyes swim above me. A laugh echoes through my brain, sounding both like my own and also the king's. Then I can hear nothing at all.

King Stol's smile swallows me whole.

CHAPTER FORTY-THREE

D ripping. The innocuous sound echoes in my brain before I slip back into unconsciousness.

My mouth is very dry, and I'm nauseous. I try to move, but the bindings on my wrists prevent me from lifting them higher than by my side. I'm lying down. It's dark and I'm struggling to open my eyes. They're gritty and sticky.

Someone comes to lift my head gently, pushing a cup to my mouth. Water. I drink greedily. The person takes away the cup before I've had my fill.

"Sorry, not too much, or you might hurl. Those mushrooms wreak havoc on your system for quite a while, unfortunately," says a woman's voice. Soft and kind.

Mushrooms. The gravy. The asshole drugged us. The first rule I teach children is to never eat anything that they don't recognize, *especially* mushrooms.

Is Tovi here, too?

I try to open my eyes through the sand and molasses that must have replaced my eyeballs. My skin is crawling, like millions of tiny spiders are dancing across it. My joints ache, and I groan as I open my eyes a slit. I can see nothing but darkness.

The bed I am lying in clunks and shudders a few times before I move to sitting, the contents of my stomach sloshing around and threatening to come up. I close my eyes again, not that they had far to close. But squeezing them shut helps the intense nausea.

I concentrate on my other senses. It smells damp, and I can still hear the dripping. Hushed voices sound far away, slightly echoed. Within the dampness, there is the smell of rotten eggs and mold. My consciousness is slipping in and out again. Sometimes, I hear the flutter of wings, or is that inside my chest? Footsteps, only one set, mill about.

The next time I wake, I'm less disorientated. Opening my eyes, blinking away the stickiness, I confirm I'm back in a fucking cave. This one is cold and damp, not like the one with Arpi. Not even the thought of him manages to rouse my rage from wherever it slumbers.

I attempt to look around, but all I see is utter darkness or sloped walls. Directly to my right is a low ceiling above gently moving water. Stalactites drip periodically.

"You are awake! Hungry?" the woman from earlier asks.

I try to speak, but I can only croak. The woman comes back with a cup of water, and I finally get to see her as I take a drink. Long, wavy, dark blood-red hair in a loose ponytail to one side. Violet eyes on a pale face filled with freckles. A face full of kindness and warmth. She looks so much like Riley if his features were smaller and softened. She looks to be a similar height to Bitty, but where Bitty is straight and gangly, she's all curves and bosomy. *Amarilyss.*

"Thank you," I rasp, my throat still dry even after the drink.

"Do you think you could stomach some bread with meat paste?" her strong yet sweet voice asks. I scrunch my nose at the thought and she quickly adds, "The sooner you can keep food down, the sooner you will feel better." So, I agree, and she feeds me.

The meat paste is *disgusting*. It tastes like fish, but also raw meat, and the smell is cloying in the air. I eat it all, and through sheer will alone, I keep it from violently erupting back out the way it came. Amarilyss has moved my chair around so I can see where I am. An underground river continues long into the murky blackness, made visible by the low-hanging cave walls that don't quite reach the ground. In front of me are pockets of caves and dark passages with various flickering lanterns.

Amarilyss is chained. It's a *long* chain, but still, she's shackled to the wall with only enough length to reach each patient—prisoner—but not enough to explore. Each pocket of cave that I can see has a person or two strapped to a seat in a similar fashion to me. She flits about and tends to everyone, exercising them as far as their chains will let them, securing only some with their hands back to their seat afterward.

One Laguzborn woman is blindfolded, but everyone else seems free to look around like me. Every single one is a Patron, though I only recognize some faces from Osraed. Maniacal laughter can be heard from a cave that I cannot see.

Amarilyss is as beautiful as Tovi had described, carrying herself with confidence and determination even in this dark and desolate place. She's as filthy as everyone else, with black bags under her eyes and greasy hair, but somehow, she radiates sunshine. Her clothes are loose, and though she's still voluptuous, she must be losing weight. To be honest, everyone down here looks either gaunt or outright sickly.

Crying. Multiple people crying. Either softly or in heaping wails. Some people cry out for Lyss or moan the word "please." I've been lying here awake and alert for a couple of hours, and Amarilyss hasn't stopped. Benches and crates are scattered everywhere. I can see why she looks tired as she purposefully darts between them all.

My stomach rolls, and again it takes some mental bargaining for me not to vomit. My main argument is the food was horrible enough going down. It can only be worse coming back up.

Amarilyss is leaning over a bench writing notes when I call her name softly. She looks up at me, frowning, and studies me. Setting down her notes, she crosses her arms and comes forward.

"How do you know my name?" she demands softly, looking around to see who else will be able to hear our conversation.

"Aside from hearing people calling you that, Riley says hello," I say with a struggle, devolving into a coughing fit.

"Sure, he does," she says, rolling her eyes and turning away.

"Who has the best B&B in Nemoris?" I ask quickly before she leaves.

She freezes, body stiff. "Mama Beryl," she whispers before whipping around, a wild look on her face. "Do not play with me. Who are you?"

"My name is Mika. I came here with Riley, Tovi, and *B&B*. To rescue you." The irony of my situation makes a small laugh escape before I can swallow it.

She looks around wildly, moving swiftly to my side. "Truly?" she breathes, tears welling in her red-rimmed eyes.

I nod. "Unfortunately, me being captured wasn't exactly part of the plan. But at least I found you." I make an exaggerated face of triumph, mouthing *"yay."*

"The king would not bring you here unless you are a Null…" she says, concerned, mild panic building in her eyes.

Of course, the Nulls. This is why *I* am here, and Tovi won't be. "I am a Null. But why does he want them?"

Someone yells, and a loud crashing sound causes others to wail. Amarilyss runs off into one of the dark passages, presumably to another set of caves to deal with whatever that was.

I doze off as I wait for her to return. When next I wake, she is undoing my hand bindings, and tells me I can call her Lyss. I'm still attached to the wall in a similar fashion to her, though my chain is significantly shorter. A chair behind her holds two plates of food, neither of which looks to have the meat paste, thankfully, though it's still a dire affair. A couple of dried berries and a hunk of smelly cheese. I eat with trepidation, unsure how my stomach will fare.

"Everyone is mostly asleep," Lyss says between small mouthfuls.

"What is this place, and why all these Nulls?"

Lyss' hesitation is evident. "He is experimenting on them. Successfully too. Forcing Gifts to surface."

"With pain," I add, remembering the drugged conversation I had with him before I was brought here.

She nods with a slight grimace.

"You're here to heal them so they don't die during the torture?"

"Yes, but also because the pain inflicted is messing with some of their minds. Everyone here is mentally troubled to some degree. Some more so than others. I am here to heal their minds, otherwise he could have any Gifted healer down here."

"You said 'successfully', does that mean his methods have worked?" I ask with equal parts horror and fascination.

Nodding, Lyss continues. "He is trying to build an army of Gifted Patrons. But so far, the *army* is too damaged to be of any use. It is why most of them have to stay strapped down, instead of just chained. They are all likely too weak to do much harm anyway."

Nausea is rising to the surface again, and not because of the food. Forcing Gifts to emerge through torture. How in the Divine is this happening? I close my eyes against the dizziness, wondering where my rage has gone.

"What Gifts have manifested?"

"Quite a few have manifested *something*. But most notable is Renn, an Erduborn man who can increase his muscle mass at will. Grotesquely so, he looks like a monster. It causes an insatiable hunger for him to maintain it for long periods. Then, of course, is the Laguzborn woman blindfolded just over there. She can cause explosions just by looking at something. Lenore's the whole reason I was first brought here."

"There was no mystery assailant. Lenore caused the explosions that hurt the doxies?"

"Yes, she caused the explosion *accidentally*, but none of his actual doxies were hurt. Just—" Lyss gives me a pained look, "—a few of the Nulls. He needs me to *fix* her so she can be stable enough to use as a weapon. It has been so many moons and barely any of them have improved. They are all so utterly traumatized, made worse by being trapped down here."

We both shudder. I'm trying to shake off my own memories of being abused and manipulated. *And here I am again.* Is this all the Divine has for me in this life?

I'M NOT GIVEN long before King Stol wants to *motivate* my trapped Gift. Lyss advises me that it's better on an empty stomach, waking me an hour or so before he's due to arrive. I ask what he will do, but she doesn't know. It's different every time.

"I will be here waiting for you when you return. If it gets too much, go to a happy place and I will meet you there in your mind later," Lyss says in a fast whisper when we hear the tell-tale signs they're coming. I don't understand what she means. What happy place, and how would she meet me there?

Two Erduborn Patrons arrive to escort me. Unaware of what their Gifts are, I comply. The manacle is removed from around my ankle, and both Patrons wrap a firm hand around my upper arms to drag me. While they're both older, maybe in their sixties, they're strong.

I remain calm until they strap me to a chair.

We're in another cave that took us a few minutes to get to, down a long passage that continued into the darkness. The room smells like blood and other bodily fluids. It's the smell of death, and my insides turn to liquid. Something darker swirls dangerously inside of me for the first time since Pasha. I'm an empty vessel barely containing a nightmare.

But I survived Pasha. And then I killed him.

The chair I'm strapped to has my arms laid out along tall, flat armrests. Both hands face downward. There is no headrest, but if I lean my head back far enough, a small ledge will cradle it.

Across my midsection is a wide strap securing me to the chair, and my legs are strapped to flat boards. Part of me wants to fight, to try to get away. But I would put everyone else here in danger. I will not risk collateral damage.

I think of Sweet Girl. The shattered pieces of my heart splinter through my chest at the mere thought of her. I close my eyes, wanting to imagine her soft, whiskered muzzle nudging me. Seeing her prancing about, strutting in front of me, and being a general nuisance.

Here I am again. Captured by a man wanting to break me. To take something from me. To take a piece of my soul, or what's left of it. How many times can you lose a piece of your soul before there is nothing left? Maybe you die. Maybe King Stol will be the one to finally kill the Silent Assassin, and he won't even know it.

CHAPTER FORTY-FOUR

Deliberate footfalls sound in the passage. There is nothing else I can see in this cave except for the running river through the side and the same low-hanging walls. There would be no escape, even if I wasn't restrained.

His violet eyes rouse my rage from its peaceful torpor, like a savage beast roaring an attack inside me, desperate to be let loose. I'm shaking. But the rage has filled the nightmare void within me, and I am going to continue to feed into it for as long as I can.

The king has removed his jewelry, and not a single piece remains. "Hello again, Mika dear. Sorry about all of this. Our last accommodations were suddenly unsuitable, though I find this to be much better anyway." His smooth, venomous voice slithers around the cave. The king looks me over with what looks like glee, almost salivating.

I don't say a word. Let him think I am too scared to speak. He's talking again, but I'm imagining his lifeblood gushing from his neck. I'd like to use a serrated knife for a jagged and messy cut, staring into those devious eyes as his life dims. I've never done that before, but I would for him. The satisfaction of seeing his eyes become unfocused in death—as they see me watching him—would be worth the horror.

The king clicks his fingers and one of the men who was standing sentry outside the cave entrance wheels a trolley in. There is a feral smile on the Patron's face as he sees me. I swallow my stomach as I take in the tools of torture laid out, caked in dried blood. I've felt pain, real pain. This will be no different, and I will not allow him to break me.

"Are we in agreement, Mika?" he's asking me.

Having missed his entire speech, I look up at him. "About what?" I grind out.

"Oh, come now, dear, pay attention. You agree you will try to manifest your Gift, and I will try not to remove anything from your body. Unfortunately, severed limbs do not grow back, even with a Gifted healer," he finishes with a poison-dripped smile.

I don't offer an agreement, I simply stare at his mouth with every bit of hatred consuming me. *May the Divine smite you where you stand, you disgusting excuse for a man. And if not, I promise I will do the smiting, given the chance.*

Instead of grabbing a weapon, Stol comes to stand beside me, stroking my right arm slowly. Watching me. I look away from him, staring straight ahead. The snapping sound seems so silly to my ears, as if it's only a mockery. But the pain isn't far behind, especially as he snaps a second finger. I haven't screamed yet; my moan of pain is half growl as I bare my teeth at him. He caresses the next finger, humming. I don't hear the snap this time, only the blasting pain screaming in my ears. I let loose a small yell that I turn into a roar.

"Anything?" he says with a saccharine smile, snapping the last finger on my hand. At least he has left my thumb alone. Small wins.

I don't even bother to analyze whether a new Gift flows within me. "Fuck…you," I growl and then spit at him. He backhands me, and my head snaps back painfully. Sparkles fill my vision as I watch him pick up a mallet with a solid iron head as thick as my calf.

He gives me a little tap on the knee of my left leg and watches me jolt slightly, my involuntary reaction widening his smile. Something is trickling down my face—blood or sweat, I'm not sure. I let my lids hang lazily, eyeing his face, trying to make a pointed effort to ignore the mallet in his hands. Excitement flitters across his face as he lifts the mallet with both hands, bringing it down on my kneecap.

I scream so hard that the old injury in my ribs protests. Or maybe it's because my body is throwing itself against the straps holding me down. Now I know why Lyss didn't feed me—it most definitely would've come back up. Retching up bile beside me, my throat burns from the scream and now the acid. I'm still writhing in my seat, unable to find a position that doesn't put pressure on my leg in some way.

At least I haven't pissed myself. *Yet.* There's still time.

Putting the mallet down, the imposter king kneels by my mangled knee. He makes an exaggerated pouting face, asking if it hurts *enough*, before poking the mess where my kneecap used to be. Fresh pain alights all down my leg into my toes and up into my hip. My vision sways as the king stands up to watch me.

Coming around to stand behind me, he pulls my head back onto the ledge. A strap is secured across my forehead, and now I cannot lift my head. He disappears for a moment, coming back with that deranged smile on his face.

"Sometimes," he says, leaning over my face with fetid breath. "The horror is enough when you are already in pain. Please do tell me if your Gift manifests. I do not want to be wasting our time."

His cold thumb pulls my left eyelid open and holds it. A thin sewing needle moves into my vision as he slowly pierces it into my eye. It's uncomfortable, and my sight warps as the globe of my eye takes the pressure. My vision swims with red and black before the pain shoots into my head. My broken fingers scream in protest at my attempt to ball my fists.

I'm panting as he leaves the needle in my eye and returns with another. Again, I feel an uncomfortable pressure as he pushes it in, and again, the pain lances into my head as it reaches the intended depth. It takes six needles for me to lose consciousness.

My body launches forward with a scream as I lean over, dry retching. There is not even bile as my stomach cramps in protest and tries so hard to bring up *something*. I fall out of my chair to my hands and knees as my stomach tries again to vomit, my eyes watering from the task. Lyss runs over, smoothing my hair back, clicking her tongue.

Finally, I sit back in a reprieve from the unsuccessful vomiting. My vision is fine, and so are my fingers and the knee that had been smashed to oblivion.

"How did you even fix my knee?" I ask Lyss, rubbing it, expecting some pain.

"Slowly. I had to ask him to allow Zinniani—one of the others—to help me with everyone else while I worked on you. You have been out a whole day." She helps me back into my chair, bringing me some barely warm broth to drink.

I hug the cup in my hands as if it were hot tea, glaring at nothing, planning how I will kill the king. It delights me to think about how *no one will know.* Surely, if he cannot hold his shape while sleeping, his death will be the same. The king will disappear, and a random dead Patron will be left in his place. I'm focusing so hard on how I am going to kill him that I don't notice Lyss speaking to me. "Sorry, what?" I ask after she waves her hand in my face.

"Get some bread down if you can. He will be coming for you again in the morning. Unless…Do you feel any different?" she asks, almost pleading. "He stops when you manifest."

No. I'm exactly the same. I am missing a few more intangible bits and pieces, but I was never whole to begin with. I shake my head and start eating the bread, going back to planning the king's death. I need more time. I need a weapon. I confirm with Lyss that it's always two people who come down with him. I can kill three people. The only problem, besides my lack of weapon, is not knowing what Gifts his men have. Lyss isn't sure what they are, either.

I'll kill them when they try to strap me to the chair. And then wait for the imposter King Oferdu.

UNFORTUNATELY, I'm barely able to stand, let alone fight, when they—the same two men as before—come for me a few hours later. I'm strapped back into the chair, the patch of bile I vomited up still marring the ground. My wrists are bound with palms facing up this time.

"My dear!" the king announces with a flourish as he rounds into the room, not even looking at his two men. The man with the feral smile again brings in the trolley of torture tools at a click of the king's fingers before standing sentry outside the cave doorway—exactly like the first time.

"You are looking well. Lyss says that nothing has manifested yet. What a shame," he says with exaggerated disappointment, a feral delight in his eyes. How much of this is about manifesting Gifts, and how much is *actually* about the torture itself? I *will* kill this man, and I will make it as painful as possible.

He clicks his fingers, and the second man enters. The pig winks, kissing the air once at me. The king grabs a metal fire poker and holds it toward the man, not taking his eyes off me. If he wants to see how I'll react, I'll give him nothing. I can see the action out of the corner of my eye as I continue to stare at Stol's mouth. Not his eyes. I can stand his eyes even less than everyone else's.

The room brightens slightly, the Patron heating the poker with a blue flame from the palm of his hand. When the poker is glowing red, the king immediately stabs it into my left calf. The searing pain is blinding, but smelling my own flesh burning is another experience entirely.

He holds it there long enough while I scream and writhe in pain that the poker has begun to cool. I'm dizzy and trying to catch my breath as he rips the poker away. Some of my flesh rips with it, and I scream again.

He swaps the fire poker for what looks like a thick metal knitting needle sharpened to a deadly point. He traces the skin along my palms up to my elbow and then back down. Those violet fucking eyes watch my face as he stabs the needle through the center of my forearm. I know I'm screaming, but I can't hear a thing as I watch him stab my palm with such force that my hand lifts a little. The needle embeds into the armrest under my hand.

Leaving the needle where it is, he leans down into my line of vision, and I see his mouth ask, "Anything?". I try to say, "*Fuck you!*" but he wiggles the needle around violently while it's still impaling my hand.

This shouldn't be as painful as yesterday, yet the agony is like a chorus. My nerve endings remember the pain from yesterday even though Lyss healed me. I close my eyes. I will not give him the satisfaction of seeing my pain.

CHAPTER FORTY-FIVE

I imagine kissing Sweet Girl's muzzle, stroking her stupidly fluffy ears. Bitty's dimpled grin comes bounding up on Applemint, who starts nudging me for sweets. Beans pats my shoulder, looking down at me with paternal affection in his eyes before going to stand by Applemint. Bitty leans over and kisses the top of the old man's shaved head. Tovi is on the other side of Sweet Girl, and she throws a beetleberry at me, smiling before plopping another in her mouth.

I hear the name "Firecat," and everyone disappears. There is only Riley.

He and I are alone in the Nemoris forest, frasteria petals sprinkling down on us like snow. Tucking a flower behind my ear, he brushes my hair back so he can kiss my neck.

Standing back up to his full height, he looks deep into my eyes, and I into his. I do not need anything more than this. Just Riley. So, I'll stay. I will stay, looking into his—everything but *"just"*—green eyes, forever. For the rest of my life and into the Divine end. I will stay here.

"Mika," a voice whispers, trying to make me look away from Riley. *No.* I will look at nothing else.

"Mika," the voice repeats. "You have to come back."

Riley begins to fade, and I scream soundlessly. I scream for longer than I should be able to. He is slowly fading into nothing. His eyes are the last thing to vanish, and my scream is all that remains.

I am nothing. Falling to my knees, still screaming, I am in a black void. I lie down, hugging my knees, finally stopping the endless, soundless scream. I allow the tears to flow, hoping they will drown me.

CHAPTER FORTY-SIX

"Mika," says a woman's voice I recognize.

I'm still in the black void, but something in the distance begins to illuminate and increases rapidly. Sitting up, I have to shield my eyes until a beautiful sunrise fills my vision.

The sunrise turns into a woman—turns into Lyss—as she kneels before me, taking my hands.

"Will you come with me?"

"No," I say and lie back down. Down into an inky black puddle of my tears, slowly sinking into them. Perhaps these aren't my tears, but the blackness of what's left of my soul, leaking out of the cracks and broken parts of me.

A deafening screech reverberates around us as Lyss looks at me in alarm. "What is that?" she asks frantically, trying to pull me back up.

Large vibrations slam into the ground as the creature stalks toward us and screeches again, "My rage," I answer and close my eyes.

"Mika!" Lyss wails. I open my eyes in time to see an enormous, hideous, black creature bat her away with its giant claws. She goes flying into the blackness, leaving a trail of sunshine. The creature takes flight, heavy wings flapping down and battering me with wind. The ground shudders violently as the creature slams down over the source of the sunshine, and I watch the beautiful light turn red, slowly dimming.

A red sunset. I love a red sunset.

"Stop!" I scream at the creature.

It whips its head toward me, studying me, sniffing as if tasting the air. I stand on wobbly legs, dragged down by the weight of my black river. The creature runs at me, picking up speed as its giant tail swishes violently behind it, the heavy thundering of feet on the non-existent ground beneath us. Lightning cracks loudly in the air. The creature dives into my chest, throwing me back in a heavy splash.

CHAPTER FORTY-SEVEN

Nothing. I am nothing.

No. Not entirely nothing. I can see tiny pieces of me drifting like dust in the wind. I follow the particles. My consciousness floats along with them.

The blackness around me starts to change. The particles form into dense forests. I'm walking now, wading through the endless green. Smelling freshness, I relish the touch of new leaves caressing my skin. The end of the forest opens to a small beach, waves lapping quietly on the black sand shore.

The sun is rising. I look back and see its broken sunbeams filtering through the trees. I watch as the sun rises before it bursts into the sky above me, warming me to the core. I didn't realize I had gotten so cold.

It's as if the day is passing faster and faster. Still, I watch, unable to take my eyes off the sun. With golden rays glowing across the water, the sun begins to set. Gold turns to red, slowly darkening the horizon. It's leaving. Leaving me.

"Wait!" I call. Desperate.

I run into the water, chasing the red sunset. I run until I have to swim, and I swim until I no longer can.

"Wait..." I whisper with the last of my strength, before I slip under the surface.

CHAPTER FORTY-EIGHT

"Mika?"

My eyes snap open, but a light blinds me, and I immediately close them again.

"Lyss?" I ask, my throat dry.

"Oh, thank the Divine," she breathes, pushing a cup of water to my lips for me to drink.

I wince at the memory of the painful brightness. "What's that light?"

"There is no light, Mika, beyond the small lantern. Would you like me to extinguish it?"

I hesitantly open my eyes to find the blinding light is gone. Lyss' concerned face fills my view as the rest of the familiar cave follows.

"I did not think you were coming back. It has been three days…"

The memory of the torture assaults my nerves. I writhe in pain, grabbing my face, which is already wet with tears. Lyss is making soothing sounds, patting my head, and turning my chair back into a bed. I'm heaving in breaths, sweat beading all over my body as the memory stops. I'm alone. Unsure how long I was in that state.

With careful movements, I move to a seated position, but no pain attacks me. I pull up my sleeve, seeing *six* scars along my forearm and the one through my hand. Every single scar has an entry and an exit. Fourteen new scars on my arm in total. I flex my hand and fingers. No pain. I'm no different than before.

I pull up my pant leg. A gnarled burn scar digs into my calf. I suppose the imposter king really wasn't lying. Burned or ripped-off flesh cannot be Divined back into existence, even by a healer as skilled as Lyss.

The memory of pain shudders through me again, less violently this time. But still, I close my eyes and lie back down as tears dribble down the side of my face, wetting my hair and ears.

Holding my hand up, I see the silvery scars sliced across my fingers. I didn't even know I'd cut them on the slippery knife as I stabbed Pasha over and over. Jaena had withheld a healer for days as further punishment for losing control of my rage and because she had to "clean up my mess."

Making a mental tally, I take stock of all my new scars. I almost laugh, hysteria fizzing in my throat. I went from barely a scar a few moons past to being riddled with them.

Lyss comes back in with a plate of food. Crusty bread and hot beans in a tomato sauce. Surprisingly delicious. Either that, or I'm starving. She watches me eat, clearly wanting to say something.

I raise an eyebrow at her. She clears her throat, frowns, and speaks hesitantly. "I tried to heal you…Your mind, I mean." She pauses, contemplating my face before continuing. "But your…*rage* stopped me. You would not let me back in, or *it* would not. I thought you were lost for good, like some of the other Nulls who eventually waste away to death, never waking up again. But you…You woke on your own."

I pause with a chunk of bread at my lip, my mouth hanging open. Did she say *my rage*? I let my hand fall into my lap with the piece of bread, my mouth closing and opening a few times as my brain tries to say several things at once.

I pinch the bridge of my nose between my eyes and take a deep breath. "What do you know of my rage?"

"It attacked me. When I was in your mind trying to heal you and bring you back. You screamed at it to stop, and it did. I got out straight away. But then, whenever I tried to go back in, there was only a blackness I could not penetrate." She's looking at me with so much concern that I squirm in my seat, trying to avoid her eye. "I am so sorry, Mika."

"Sorry for *what*?" I say, lifting my arm to show the scars, then my pant leg. "You *did* heal me. I'm sorry that my…*rage* tried to hurt you."

"I can help. If you would let me. Heal the rage. Figure out why you have created a beast as a talisman in your mind to protect you."

I shake my head, not wanting to face that right now. I'm going to need my rage for a little longer. A plan is finally beginning to form.

LYSS HESITANTLY AGREES to my plan. She'd looked at me like I had lost my mind until I realized I hadn't *actually* told her that the king was an imposter. I didn't tell her it's still just a theory, that I may be wrong, and I will have killed a king. Either way, he needs to die.

I get a few more days of rest to heal, thanks to Lyss, who reports that I've still not woken up. She's made sure I'm in a position where none of the other prisoners know I am actually awake.

In my secluded cave, I stretch and move my muscles as much as I can. I'm going to need every advantage. I still don't know the Gift of the king's other man, and it's possible the Patron Gifted with fire won't come with him next time. An involuntary shiver runs down my spine and my calf stings as I remember the searing pain of the fire poker.

If only I knew where the torture trolley was located. I am already strapped to a chair when they get it, though it cannot be far, so it may as well not exist. I'm going to need to kill them *before* I'm strapped down. I'll only have mere moments before the king arrives after that.

It's a delicate balance between resting enough, exercising so I don't atrophy, and working on my weapons—one that I won't know I've gotten right until the last moment.

A large nail and a bone spoon. That is all I have to work with. Hoping it goes unnoticed, I rip off the cuff of my pant leg. Sharpening the nail on a stone until it's essentially a tiny blade, I bind it to the handle of the bone spoon. The bowl of the spoon has also been sharpened, making it a singular weapon. I would have liked two weapons, but I had nothing to reinforce the nail except the spoon handle. One missing spoon is a risk, but two would be noticed.

In between sharpening my weapon, I practice with it. I'm going to have to be precise with every move. Banking on the fact the king wants my Gift manifested, I hope the men have a standing order *not* to kill me. If they hesitate to retaliate with full force, it may give me enough of an edge.

I ask Lyss to demonstrate with me, clamping my arms together the way they do, testing the best place for my weapon. My sleeves are too short to hide it, nor do I have enough time if it's hidden in the front of my pants, under my shirt. The back of my pants is the easiest place, though risky because it can be seen.

LYSS WILL NOT BE able to hold off the king for much longer. He has expressed his desire to inspect me himself if I don't wake up soon. So tomorrow, I will miraculously wake, and the countdown will be on.

They will come for me, and I will kill them. Then I will kill the imposter king or die trying.

Reclining in my chair, I try to look as weak and exhausted as I did when they came for me last time. The more they underestimate me, the greater the likelihood I can catch them off guard. The makeshift weapon digs into my lower back. My relief at seeing the same two despicable men strengthens my resolve.

The ugly beast inside of me is prowling around my heart. Its thundering steps match my heartbeat. It takes flight, dipping down into my belly, and then tries to exit my throat. The beast is agitated by how long the walk is, incensed that it must wait longer still.

I see the cave entrance, and I take a deep breath. I have one chance. One moment. One—

"Hello dear, I thought we could do things differently this time," King Stol's slippery voice interrupts my thoughts as we round the corner into the cave. The chair is nowhere to be seen, only a set of manacles hanging from the ceiling.

Improvisation it is, then.

Fire Hands releases me to reach for the manacles while the other guard holds me. The imposter king is at the back of the cave, furthest from the entrance. It's now or never.

My heartbeat or rage thundering, I'm not sure which, I

grab my spoon blade and slice the lifeblood artery of the Patron still holding me. He lets me go to grab his throat. I swing my body and my weapon around, aiming for Fire Hands. He jumps back a step to face me, lifting his hands as a blue hue colors his palms.

Using all the force I can muster, I deliver a front kick to his groin. He flies back with a sickening crack of his head into the stone. Still, he tries to throw his fire at me, and I dodge, smelling burning hair. The nail end of my weapon slams into his eye as deep as it can go—I'm aiming for his brain. The light in his hands extinguishes.

I don't have time to see if it works, I can only hope he's incapacitated *enough*. I launch myself around and back at the other man, who tries to use his Gift to throw the manacles chained to the ceiling. They're too short to reach me, the metal clashing together echoes as I stab him in the kidney. His body facing me from the force of the blow, I stab his other lifeblood artery and shove him. He won't live long.

With both men incapacitated in less than a minute, I turn for the imposter king. He tries to flee, an opportunity arising now I am not directly in front of the cave opening. But I trip him, stabbing him once in the calf as he goes down with a pained scream.

I'm holding the slick blade at the imposter king's throat on the ground, sitting on his chest, not unlike the way I met Eryn for the first time. I press the point of the spoon blade into his throat so that a gem of his blood surfaces. He hisses and is satisfactorily terrified-looking.

I want to torture him, smash his knees, and break his fingers. But the allure of slowly watching him bleed out is winning. He's not struggling, almost as though he's frozen or hypnotized by the way I'm staring into his eyes. He doesn't speak. Neither do I.

Pressing harder still, I look deeper into the imposter

king's violet eyes. I'll watch the life drain out of him. I want to watch his life slowly fade as I press deeper and deeper.

Take. I want to *take* everything from him. I'm going to take it all.

I can't look away. I've pushed through the uncomfortable strain, and now it's taken hold of me. A scream is in my ears along with a pull.

I pull harder. My vision fills with the violet of our eyes. I cannot tell where his end and mine begin. Greed overwhelms me. I keep pulling until the greed is satiated.

My eyes snap shut as a pain explodes through my entire body. One of the men must not have been dead. I cry out as my joints flame. Every bone feels like it is only moments from breaking. My skin is stretched so thin I might pop. Then, as quickly as it started, the pain stops. I whirl around, looking for an attacker.

No one is there. Both guards are in the prone positions I left them in to die.

Underneath me is an unconscious body. Not the imposter king. Or at least, not as he was only moments before.

His clothes hang off him awkwardly as if he has shrunk inside of them. Pale skin and pointy features against a mass of wavy, light brown hair. I lift one of his eyelids. Brown eyes Oferdu, not the violet of a Patron. He's unconscious but still alive. I didn't kill him, and he's shifted into a different form. A form where I cannot see his violet eyes. My assumptions were wrong, at least in part.

Getting up causes a surge of dizziness and I pause, eyes closed, as it passes. I remove one of the dead men's belts as I keep an eye on the imposter king for any movement, then use it to restrain him. I'll think about what to do with him later. He currently doesn't *look* like the king. I should still kill him, but my bloodlust has calmed along with my rage as if both are satisfied. We could torture him for information. I need to tell the others, and they can help decide.

I stumble down the passage toward the main cave as my short sleeve gets caught, and I finger the rip at my shoulder as I continue walking awkwardly, as if my feet are too big. The rip is in a black shirt. I was wearing a filthy cream-colored shirt. This is when I notice my hands. They're large and veiny…and not my hands.

Lyss is walking toward me, her chain allowing her some distance into the entrance of the passage. "Your Majesty, is everything alright?" Lyss' voice comes, and I whip my head around to see if he's behind me.

She looks behind me and then back to me with great concern. "Sir?"

"Who do you see?" comes the deep voice of a man, causing me to stupidly slap a hand over my mouth. That's not my voice.

Fuck fuck fuck.

I walk slowly toward Lyss, and she shrinks back, my presence looming *above* her. Her panicked eyes are aimed at the ground, and I repeat myself in a whisper. I know the other prisoners cannot see us here, but they can hear us. Causing chaos is the last thing we need right now.

Refusing to look at me, and with a quiver in her voice, she whispers, "Your Majesty, I only see you."

Key. I need the key that releases the manacles. One of the dead guards will have it, so I turn and jog back down the passage, leaving Lyss with no explanation.

Running with legs that are far too long, feet far too big, and muscles much stronger than mine, I trip and crash as I go, faltering like a newly born foal. Checking the pockets of the dead men reveals the key I need. I quickly check the still unconscious *king* for anything on his person, and pocket his keys as well.

Jogging back to Lyss, who stands exactly where I left her, her eyes begin to brim with tears. "Has something happened, sir?" she asks.

"Lyss…It's me. Mika," I whisper with urgency.

She looks up at me and gasps. "Your eyes! They are violet!"

Shit. I forgot about that. Immediately, an uncomfortable pressure blooms in my eyes, and I squeeze them shut. With a slight tingle, I'm drawn to imagine myself with the same-colored eyes I saw on the unconscious imposter.

I open my eyes with a gulp of air, and Lyss' mouth drops open and snaps shut again. "Is it really you, Mika?"

"*Fuck the Divine,*" I curse. "Lyss, I think I *stole* his Gift."

CHAPTER FORTY-NINE

Lyss and I are standing at the entrance to the torture cave. Her hand is pinching her nose and covering her mouth as she stares, horrified at the sight before her. I'm not sure which is worse for her, the clear evidence of torture littered about, the two blood-covered dead bodies that soiled themselves before—or after—their death, or the unconscious pale Erduborn man in the center of the room.

"You hogtied him," she says into her hand, not a question.

"Of course. Now help me."

Lyss helps me drag the imposter king's limp form, still hogtied, to my old alcove, attaching the manacles to him.

The Divine plays a weird game when she blesses you. No Gift is the same as the next. Maybe not even when you steal it. I have the same strength—I assume—as I would as this six-foot man.

The other prisoners are stirring. I'm keeping my shifted form in case another guard comes down. I can hear their whispers, but some are not afraid to yell their queries at me or Lyss, like, "Why is she no longer manacled?" and "Who is that man?". All of which we entirely ignore for now.

Lyss grabs me and pulls me out of view of everyone else. "You need to fix your eye color," she whispers.

"What's wrong with it? I'm going to need specifics because I only ever saw his violet eyes," I say, frustrated.

"Uhh…They are just *wrong*. Can you just–" Lyss gestures vaguely in my face, "–make them…" She grimaces.

I close my eyes and think of the imposter king, and the tingle presses against my eyes, but when I open them again, Lyss scrunches her nose and tells me they're violet again. Even after she explains what they should look like, it doesn't work. That is until I remember the painting in Eryn's room, the one so scarily detailed I thought they were real. The pressure bordering on pain catches me off guard, and I scrunch them shut.

"Yes!" she hisses when I open my eyes again.

My brain gutters to a halt. I had planned to kill him, and that's it. There wasn't really an after. I thought I was likely to die trying. I certainly didn't expect to steal his Gift.

"Where's the exit?"

Lyss tips her head, and I follow her until we're at the cave opening she says will take me out.

"I have not been any further than this since I arrived. I was not sure I would ever get to see daylight again," her voice hitches, and she lets out a tiny sob.

"Do you want to come with me now? The king is secure, everyone can wait."

"No. I will not leave until we leave with all of them. They need reassurance that they are not alone or abandoned."

"I'll find Riley and the others, and we'll come and get you all out. We can figure out the next steps later. An hour. Two, tops," I say as I hand her the keys to the manacles.

Her unexpected hug makes my skin crawl. Apparently,

I'm touch-averse down to whatever is left of my blackened soul. I hug her back, my awkwardly large limbs around her softness, and then she leaves me to walk the long, dark passage alone.

The stone stairs leading up look like they're a natural occurrence. Each step is a different height and shape. When I reach the top, out of breath, I'm surprised to find no door. There is a large step down, and I am in the center of a tiny canyon. Looking left and right, sporadic patches of spidergrass sprout up from the hard-packed earth. It looks like it leads nowhere, just a hidden crack in the mountain. I follow the footprints in the sand and discover another dark cave opening on the opposite wall of the canyon, hidden behind bushes and disguised by the natural rock formation.

Fully clothed, I feel more naked like this than when I'm wearing my sneaksuit. According to the sun, it must be nearing midday, so there is no sneaking in the shadows. Keeping my shift as the imposter king, I take a tentative step into the other cave entrance.

This passage is also a long one, and I'm walking for at least five minutes before I see the end. A locked door. I fumble around with the keys. Of course, it's the second to last one I try that works. The lock clicks, and I listen and wait. But I hear nothing and no one.

Swinging the door inward, I see the back of a tapestry, and I push it out of the way to find myself in a bedroom. A grand one at that, similar to Eryn's yet much larger and significantly more gaudy. I sneak about, trying not to make a sound.

There is a washroom *fit for a king*, a short passage that ends in a door, and then another door I assume leads to the sitting room. I use a key to unlock the door at the end of the passage, confirming it's the rooms Bitty had found belonging to the late queen. They were right, it looks like it hasn't been touched in a decade.

After quietly unlocking the door to the sitting room with the third key I try, I am greeted by confusion—not mine, but the four guards who stand abruptly, scampering to attention. They all mutter apologies and bow awkwardly after I give them what I hope is a kingly glare.

"Where are Andt and Riko, Your Majesty?" one asks.

Of course. I would have been preceded by my guards, who are lying dead in a cave.

"Busy," I say with a cool indifference that I remember sent chills down my spine when I first heard the king's voice.

Eryn saved my life that day, so he needs to know what's going on, too. But Tovi first. The four men look at me like they're waiting for me to do something—say something. I'm trying to formulate my plan while pretending I know what's going on, but I need time.

"Take me to my son's doxy, the Erduborn woman," I say as I stride toward the exit. The men are scrambling behind me, one almost sprinting so that he can reach the door before me.

"Yes, Your Majesty," he all but whimpers, his violet eyes looking downward in terror.

I STRIDE through the familiar doors to the chambers I share with Tovi. She's sitting awkwardly straight in her seat, which makes me think I've interrupted something. Standing quickly, she curtsies, greeting the king in front of her. Both sets of doors finally closing, I relax so much I almost melt into the ground.

She clears her throat, schooling her facial expressions.

But not before I see everything on her face first. Tovi looks at me with barely veiled horror as I sag against the bench along the wall.

I laugh—an unhinged, breathless laugh that sounds horrifying to my ears because it's the king's voice, but somehow, it's still my laugh, which only adds fuel to my hysteria.

"I fucking missed you," I say between the hiccups of the laughter I'm trying to stem.

Tovi is slowly reaching behind her, her look turning to steel. I catch the movement in time, launching myself into a tuck and roll to avoid the blade that hits the wall behind me. My tuck and roll is more of a splat and groan as I land with a thud. This large body is useless. My mind is racing too fast to concentrate on shifting, so I resort to putting my hands up in defense as she runs for her knife.

"It's Mika! I'm Mika. Stop trying to kill your innocent friend!" I yell, with the slightest of snickers at the end. "If you give me a minute, I'll shift, but I can't do that with you throwing sharp things at me."

A thud sounds in the washroom, and the both of us whip our heads toward the noise. I get up as quickly as I can while controlling a large body that isn't my own. A gobsmacked Bitty looks between Tovi and me.

"Bitty! What the fuck?" Tovi blasts, edging toward them while still aiming the knife at me.

But Bitty ignores her and runs at me for a classic Bitty hug-slam. "It's Mika!"

For the first time since I hugged my kids in Osraed, *I'm* able to wrap someone in a hug instead of being the wrapped one. The hugged. The receiver. Unshed tears are already threatening me as I squeeze them tighter.

"How are you so sure?" I whisper, eyes squeezed shut.

"I can hear your heart."

I pull them back, holding their shoulders. "Oh, fuck off!" I laugh. "Are you serious?" A tear overflows onto the cheek that doesn't belong to me.

Bitty is nodding with their dimpled cheeks in full display as Tovi is walking toward us, knife still aimed at me. Her hand is reaching for Bitty's shoulder, still not convinced.

I need to do something before she gets stabby. Closing my eyes, I concentrate on *me*. It's not as easy as I thought, as my mind keeps wandering to all the ways I've looked over the revolutions.

The pain is easier this time, shrinking hurts much less than growing. But still, I reach for Bitty's shoulder, now above mine, to steady myself in a bout of nausea. I look down, checking to make sure I'm *me* and not a *version of me*. But it's all me, clothes, cuts, bruises, and even the stain of bile on the side of my shirt, and unfortunately, a lot more blood than I was anticipating. I stink.

The blood is still wet as if it only just happened. The blood on my hands and wrists has not even a crust of dryness. Disgusted, I wipe my hands down my shirt and look up to see Tovi still hasn't put away her knife. She pulls Bitty behind her, firmly shielding them with her imposing frame, fury in her eyes. It's not enough. Of course, it's not. The king could have just shifted into me.

We don't have time for this. "Tovi, what do you need to make you understand? Bitty knows it's me," I say with an edge of anxiety coloring my tone. We *need* to get back to Lyss.

"How?"

"I tried to kill him. He's alive. Or he was when I left him. Lyss might have killed him by now."

"*Lyss?*" they both screech.

"Buxom Nemorisborn? The *normal*-heighted twin? Definitely the flower to Riley's *overgrown red weed*."

404

Silence. I open my mouth for more rambling, but Tovi lowers her weapon. "I would hug you, but you smell *so bad*," she says, scrunching her nose and giving me a wild look. "I could have killed you. I *would* have killed you," she marvels. "That deranged laugh nearly undid me. What the fuck…"

"*'What the fuck'* yourself, Tovi! What were you thinking trying to kill the king?" My incredulous voice rises an octave with the question.

"Sorry to interrupt, but also not. *You can shift!*" Bitty exclaims.

"I can *now*. I stole his Gift…I think. He looks just like a pitiful, ordinary man now. I don't know how any of this works. But we can discuss that *later*. Right now, we need to get to Eryn, then Riley and Beans, so we can save Lyss and the others."

"Others…" they both repeat, and I sense the questions coming.

"He was torturing them," I blurt. "Us. Nulls. Trying to force Gifts to the surface."

Their eyes look me over, a closer inspection. I spot the moment they see all the new scars under the blood and death that covers me. Tovi goes to speak, concern on her face. But I shake my head, I can't talk about it yet.

"Eryn will be relieved," Bitty states, half changing the subject, and I give them an appreciative smile.

"Apparently, the king told him that we had gotten *food* poisoning—" Tovi rolls her eyes. "—and that you had taken very ill and required significant healer attention. Then refused to answer *where* you were since you weren't in the healer's wing."

I scoff. *What an asshole.*

"We all thought you were dead. Again."

I poke Bitty in the shoulder. "I promise to do my Divine hardest not to be kidnapped again, okay?"

"Sure. We'll believe that when you can go a whole moon without being kidnapped or thrown in a dungeon," Tovi tries to joke but immediately frowns at her feet and swallows hard. My heart plummets into my stomach at the same time. One day. One day, we will be able to joke about it. And I look forward to that day.

"What's the plan now?" Bitty asks before the two of us are lost in our memories.

CHAPTER FIFTY

itty reluctantly leaves via the hatch to meet us in Eryn's room. Then they'll take Tovi with them to get Riley and Beans and lead them all to the queen's old courtyard. I describe where the secret passage is behind the tapestry in the king's rooms, planning to meet in the small canyon before entering the torture caves.

The blood has begun to dry in the short time I've been myself again, so I quickly wash and change my clothes. My own stench makes me feel unwell. We gather up what little belongings we have, and I tuck my knife into my pants. Tovi puts on her cloak, hiding the fact she isn't wearing the doxy dress that she should be.

Riley. The need to see him, to apologize, to touch him, to smell him. It almost unravels me entirely. Remembering the package from Riley, I run to my bed, rage roaring louder than ever before. With a metallic taste in my mouth, I realize I'm biting the inside of my cheek. Sliding my hands along the sheets, flinging blankets and pillows, I find it exactly as I left it. I'm staring at the package in my hands when Tovi comes in looking for me.

"I didn't get to open it before he took me," I say in explanation to Tovi's baffled look.

I gently unwrap the parcel. Inside is a pile of leather, jewels, metal, and a piece of carved stone. I pick it up as a small, folded letter falls out of the package onto the ground. I'm too distracted by what's dangling in my hand to care that Tovi has picked up the folded note for me.

It's a necklace. Thin pieces of leather are woven together, with tiny blue pearls woven in. Two beautiful, handcrafted metal cuffs clasp either side of the pendant. The carved stone pendant looks to be made from white jade. My breath catches when I see it's a side view of a firecat in stunning detail. The tail is looped around and attached to the leather.

The firecat, which is already beautiful, has two gems inlaid into it: a purple amethyst in the visible eye and a forest green emerald in the shape of a tiny heart in the chest.

"What..." I rasp, throat thick with confusion, as I look up to a bright red Tovi.

Slightly frantic, she thrusts the folded letter into my hand as if it's on fire. "I shouldn't have picked this up."

"What did it... What did you... Is it bad?"

"I'll tell you if it isn't obvious when you've read it," she says over her shoulder, leaving the room as if she can't get away fast enough.

I sit down on my bed because I am having trouble multitasking simple things like standing and breathing. I gently place the necklace over my leg as I unfold the handwritten letter.

Firecat,

I wanted to give this to you in person, but I've been too much of a coward, and now I fear it might be too late. I didn't want to scare you away, and I wasn't sure how you felt. But after today, I need you to know how I feel. How my world has not been the same since you came crashing into it.

I have been asleep, choosing to waste my life in a waking nightmare. It took one fiery, pain-in-the-ass woman to punch me in the face and wake me up. And then I wanted to be awake, if I got to be in a world where she existed. Where you exist.

Mika, you've changed me, and I cannot go back. I wouldn't want to, even if I could.

You have found every crack and corner of my blackened heart, but still, I cannot get enough of you. I will never stop filling my heart with everything about you, my Firecat.

Even though I don't have your heart, you've had mine for a long time.

But it's not real love unless you feel it too. I won't force you, but I will wait for you. I have no choice, because you're it for me.

<u>I made the necklace with help from a traveling jeweler in Waadi.</u>

I still had to make the pendant, the firecat. She was hard to carve because I wanted her to be as special as you are.

The necklace is a gift and a promise. I

promise I'll keep trying to be the man deserving of your heart until the day mine stops beating. Longer, if the Divine allows it.

Yours, Riley.

I read his letter five more times. My fingers trace the words where his pen scratches the paper hard enough to make an indent. The piece of fabric it was wrapped in smells like him. I hold it against my nose and mouth, breathing in the scent of him.

Reluctantly, I wrap it back up and slip it into my pocket. It occurs to me only then that the keys are no longer there because the pocket they were in has ceased to exist. Not wanting to lose my necklace or letter, I put them on the bed and shift back into the king to test a theory. The searing pain shoots through my bones and stretches my skin. There, in the pocket of the pants I wear as the king, are the keys. *As if I'm not going to lose shit like this…*

Yet again, shifting back to myself is easier. I quickly put on the necklace and pocket the letter inside the fabric. I grit my teeth and shift into the king again, sending a silent prayer to the Divine to look after my necklace and letter.

"All good?" Tovi asks, giving me a disgusted look up and down as I walk out to meet her as the imposter king.

Unable to speak my answer, I can only nod. *I have his heart*, is on the tip of my tongue, yet I cannot say it aloud. And she doesn't push.

THE FOUR GUARDS escort Tovi and I to Eryn's rooms with no questions asked. When we arrive, I offhandedly say that Tovi can keep her cloak and usher her in.

Turning to the four men, I send the Gifted Patron and one non-Gifted, to get Lottie. I make it clear the Gifted Patron is to relieve her, and the other man can bring her here. The fewer Gifted Patrons around me right now, the better. When the two of them leave, the last two guards take up sentry by Eryn's doors. I instruct them to knock when Lottie arrives.

Finding the sitting room empty, I proceed to the closed door of Eryn's bedroom. The young prince searches my eyes as a smile tugs the corners of his lips when I enter the room.

"So that's what he looks like without his violet eyes?" Eryn says, his eyes wide.

"Can't see through *my* tricks?" I tease, flicking my hair sassily.

Eryn scrunches his face. "Oh, that's *so* disturbing."

Bitty had arrived before us and filled Eryn in. Conscious of the time this has all taken, I send them both to get Riley and Beans. Tovi borrows some of Eryn's clothes and shoes. They don't look right but are an improvement on the silky shirt and pants she was wearing. She left the cloak in the sitting room already. The two of them climb out the window as my rage bounces around my ribcage. It's broad daylight— they could be spotted at any moment.

Thankfully, they reach the bottom safely. Tovi salutes me with a rude gesture before the two of them take off running.

Silence. The chaos stops momentarily, the only sounds are Eryn and I breathing.

"This is madness," Eryn announces into our quiet contemplation.

"There's more," I say as I turn to face him. "He…he looks like you." I shake my head. "I saw the real him after I stole his power. He's got your hair, but everything is…lighter. He'd be shorter than you for sure."

I suddenly realize I can show him. I step away, bracing myself. Groaning, I double over with the uncomfortable pain and pressure of the shift.

Eryn comes to the same conclusion I did. "He's not pure Erduborn."

"Maybe half Mievaborn. Would make sense why you pass as Erduborn, since your mother was too."

"And why you pass as Mievaborn because of your mother, right?" Eryn says, studying me.

I scoff, rage rising. Eryn rolls his eyes and drags me to the mirror in his washroom.

"He's about as pale as you are. We all have the same small, sharp nose and ears," he says as he points to my features while I am in the imposter's natural form.

A flash of burning ice engulfs me. This man is my father. Eryn knows it, and somehow, I know it too with a certainty that defies all logic and sense.

"He really does look like the both of us. He's *our* father," Eryn declares, a big toothy smile breaking across his face, as he continues to look me up and down. "I knew it!"

My brother. Mine.

We return to his bedroom and Eryn slumps into the chair by his windows, leaning back with a look of self-satisfaction that changes to confusion. "How is this possible if he was sterilized?"

"*That* is something I'd like to know too, but can figure it out later. We need to decide what to do with him first."

"Our father."

I sigh, the tension coiling tighter. Until I look at him. My *brother*. "Yes. Our father."

"*You* are my sister," he says, a glisten to his eyes that sends lightning bolts that threaten to stop my heart. I can't…I don't deserve this kid.

"Unfortunately for you," I tease before changing the subject like a coward. "Hopefully, Lottie gets here soon. I'm sure Bitty and Tovi will reach Riley and Beans quickly."

"Bitty." Eryn crosses an ankle over his knee with what looks like a smirk. "They're cute."

Shaking my head. "Oh. Nope. None of that. Bitty is too old for you!"

"You're my sister for a whole minute…" Eryn grumbles. "And how much older is Riley than you, did you say?"

Five, almost six revolutions. "That's totally different!" I whisper furiously, kicking his foot with my arms crossed.

Eryn snorts and mumbles something about double standards.

I sigh. "No one can ever know that I'm your sister, Eryn. You know that, right?"

"Why not? You could be a princess!"

"No, I wouldn't be. And you wouldn't be a prince. If people know we're related, it opens up questions as to *how*. And the "how" is that there has been an imposter as the King Oferdu for a *very long time*."

"I wouldn't be the rightful heir. I'm *not* the rightful heir. *I'm not the prince*," Eryn whispers, finally understanding.

"The people would dethrone you and find some distant relative to take the crown."

Eryn's face contorts. "Riley knows…" he admits. "I told him when I threatened to kick his ass if he hurt you."

I don't know whether to laugh or…laugh harder. Riley would flatten him with a flick of his finger. Eryn knew he was my brother long before I was able to confirm it. Maybe I knew it too, with his stupid little brotherly face.

I have a brother. Eryn, this brave, endearing, funny little

creature (who towers over me), is *my* brother. I do not deserve such a Divine blessing…

CHAPTER FIFTY-ONE

A knock sounds at the sitting room door, and Eryn answers it. I concentrate on shifting into the imposter king. My bones and skin stretch, the muscles protesting as they grow and change. When I've shifted fully, I stroll out to the sitting room where Eryn stands with Lottie, the latter looking bewildered. She gives me a greeting befitting a king.

"Lottie. I really hope I judged you correctly when I met you," I say with a voice that does not belong to me. I shift back into myself, internally rolling my eyes at the theatrics of it all, but I need the shock factor.

"You!" Lottie says, looking utterly baffled. She steps in front of the prince and draws her sword, as I expected, but still to my relief.

"Good. I need you to guard him with your life, Lottie."

Eryn's looking at me over Lottie's head with one eyebrow cocked. "This is a bit dramatic, isn't it?"

"Can someone explain what the fuck is going on? Or I will run you through with my sword. Why have you impersonated the king?"

"Because there has been another man impersonating him for a decade, and I stole his power after he tortured me. Now I need to go and rescue the *rest* of the people he was torturing while I pretend to be the king, so we can do it with as little fuckery as possible. Okay?"

Lottie looks at the prince, who nods at her and swings on Tovi's cloak.

"Why me?" she asks, keeping her sword trained on me.

"Because you helped the Prince Ofnemoris give me apricots. I'm pinning everything on your moral compass to keep Eryn safe," I say this to Lottie quickly, eyeing Eryn with the cloak. "What are you doing?" I ask him.

"That was Aurelius Jasper, the second Prince Ofnemoris?" she questions with a hiss.

"Yes, he is here to save his kidnapped sister, who we *also* need to rescue. Satisfied I'm not the monster?" I ask, closing my eyes for a moment. I *am* a monster, just not *the* monster this time. Irony abounds.

"This is madness!" Lottie says, finally lowering her sword.

Eryn laughs. "That's what I said! Should we go?"

I try not to growl at the kid. "No, *we* are not going anywhere. Lottie is going to guard you here, and I'm going."

"*Technically*, you both have to do what *I* say. Prince and all," Eryn says with a cunning smile on his face, imitating the hair flick I did earlier. A challenge. He knows I can't dispute him without revealing our secret. Definitely a king in the making.

"Fine. But you're staying outside with Lottie when we get there."

Eryn gives me a smug look and flips the hood of the cloak up. Lottie looks queasy. My body begins contracting and distorting as I once again take the form of King Stol

Brud Oferdu. It's getting easier, but no less painful or uncomfortable.

"Your clothes change, too?" Lottie asks, peering at me like…well, like I've shifted into another person.

"Apparently," I mumble, shrugging away her scrutiny.

ERYN KEEPS his head down as we walk, and I hope no one takes a closer look at the *doxy* under the cloak. One Patron guard stayed behind to replace Lottie, and the other three, after some reluctance, were relieved of duty for the evening. I tell them to stay and help guard Prince Eryn's doors as there may be an intruder.

The guards are terrified of me—of King Stol. Not one of them points out what a ridiculous idea it is for us to only be escorted by one guard while there may be an intruder about. Eryn is going to need better guards.

We make it to the king's chambers without incident. Eryn throws off the cloak, and I shift back to me. I pull back the tapestry for Lottie and Eryn to enter the secret passage as an explosion rocks the castle. It came from the direction of the caves.

We run. Lottie has her sword drawn, and I am inadequately armed with only my small knife. I stumble out of the passage as another explosion rocks the canyon. Outside the cave, Beans is cradling Bitty in his lap as the Laguzborn writhes in pain and clutches their ears.

"Beans! What happened?" I scream as we run toward them. *Where is Riley and Tovi?* Dust and smoke billows from the cave entrance.

He gives me a panicked look. "Riley and Tovi ran in when Bitty said they heard Lyss scream. We waited out here.

Bitty was listening to what was going on. The explosion…"
Beans' cries. Bitty finally stops writhing in pain, falling into unconsciousness.

Riley and Tovi were *inside* during the explosion.

I'm not sure how long I stand there, frozen, my rage slicing my insides to be free. Lottie shakes me back to myself.

"Can we leave the prince with these two?" Lottie is screaming at me. I nod.

Lottie drags me with her into the cave. The dust has started to settle when we come across Lyss' and Tovi's prone forms. Both alive, but unconscious.

"Tovi?" Lottie breathes, obviously confused to see the Erduborn woman here. She picks up the women with ease, one over each shoulder as if they weigh no more than small sacks of grain. Gift of strength confirmed I observe distractedly.

I'm alert, back to myself. The sounds of moaning and crying sharpen my senses. Collapsed walls, fallen rocks, and small fires burning make the air acrid. I'm desperately looking for Riley, while also keeping an eye out for the imposter king.

A couple of conscious prisoners stumble into view, and I direct them out. I find the bodies of three dead women and a dead man still manacled, though I barely register who they are. Only that they aren't Riley.

Lottie helps me move rocks and fallen debris, carrying out casualties as we find them. Eventually, Tovi returns to help.

"Lyss is awake and is setting up a triage area. Have you found him?" she asks us, though she knows the answer. No. We have not found Riley.

Some of the royal guards have begun panicking and looking for the king. Hearing the explosions, the guards found their way *around* into the canyon via a camouflaged bend in the gorge wall. Sighing, I shift into his form. The last thing we need is everyone thinking the king has been kidnapped. The guards cry in relief when they see me. Immediately, I start barking orders.

"Guard the prince.

"Help bring the wounded and dead out of the caves.

"Cover the dead with sheets.

"Go down into the tunnels and begin clearing the collapsed one."

I get only slight pushback about not having my own personal guard, but I remind them that I have Lottie with me. When everyone we can find from the caves is outside, Lyss takes stock. The imposter king and five others are missing, as is Riley.

Lyss has healed Bitty's burst eardrums, but she cannot promise that their Gift will be the same. Bitty is still unconscious, so we won't know until they wake. Eryn holds Bitty's head in his lap, while Beans helps to clear the tunnels.

Nine are dead, three are critically wounded, and another six have superficial wounds. So much carnage. The pain of Riley missing is a knife to my organs. The two men I killed are part of the nine, having been crushed beyond recognition. Or at least beyond any recognition that they died by a handmade blade and not fallen rock.

"The main tunnel is almost clear, but we think they must have escaped further in," Tovi says with a hoarse voice.

"Do the cave systems lead to the surface somewhere?" I ask, temporarily forgetting my current appearance as the king.

Lyss leans on Tovi. "I didn't have time to investigate, but the…*assailant* must know the caves better than us."

We've made the unspoken rule not to mention the imposter king. The person responsible will be a nameless enemy. The implication that I will have to remain king for a little longer becomes more obvious as the day progresses, and my skin itches to change back to myself.

I'm getting a lot of wary—and some hostile—looks from the conscious wounded. They think I'm the king, and I don't blame them for hating this form. I instruct some of the guards to take the wounded to the healers' hall. But not Riley.

Because Riley isn't here. He isn't with the wounded.

Riley is gone.

It's been hours since the explosions. Finally, the tunnel has been cleared enough that we can follow, and I send a small army. "I want that cave system mapped," I scream. None of them bats an eye or looks at me like I'm not the king they know.

Bitty woke up with their Gift intact. They wanted to go with the army—so do I—but both Beans and I denied them. Eryn is still here, watching me as if I am on the edge of chaos and destruction. And maybe I am.

Unwillingly to leave, we have all gathered to debrief inside a tent erected just outside the entrance to the collapsed cave. This strategic placement conceals the entrance back through to the king's rooms, which have so far not been detected.

One of the other prisoners stayed with us instead of going to the healer's wing with the others—Zinniani, a Sadoriborn woman Lyss has befriended. She has the forced manifestation Gift of turning into smoke. Unfortunately, she has no concept of time when she's in smoke form and remembers nothing. Lyss assured me she would keep our secret, having already told her. She needed help after I left her, and she trusts Zinniani with her life. I tried not to let my rage slip as she told me, but she's trusted Zinniani with all of our lives now. The number of people who know about the king and my Gift *must not* increase beyond this.

Zinniani is beautiful. She must be from one of the tribes in the northern part of Sadori, as she has skin so dark it rivals the night sky. She has broad shoulders and a slim waist, holding herself with careful grace despite the atrocities inflicted upon her.

However beautiful she is, it's still startling to see a smile directed so…*lovingly* at Lyss. I'm not the only one who sees it or sees Lyss return the look in equal measure. I catch Tovi's eye, and she gives me a small, sad shrug. Lyss is leaning on Zinniani while she strokes her dark, blood-red hair, looking cozier than *friends*.

The day is already over, the sun long since set. I'll have to organize everyone's guest chambers soon, as the king. I was going to have to do *king* things. I'm going to have to *be* the king, and soon. I can't be out here overseeing everything because the king wouldn't be doing this.

I want to scream. I need my hatchets so I can annihilate *something, anything*, with my rage. I want to lead a team through the tunnels and find the imposter king. I should have ripped him apart. I need to tear him to pieces with my bare hands.

Rage slams into me harder than it ever has. As if it blames me for what's happened.

"How did he get the manacles off?" Beans breaks the deafening silence inside the tent.

"It…They were unlocked. He must have had a spare key," Lyss' small voice responds.

Of course. "Or lockpicks," I say to myself, losing the battle raging in my chest. *It's my fault he escaped.*

I should've checked him more thoroughly. Stripped him.

Instead, I left him alone with Lyss. And now he's escaped with a band of scared and dangerous people. And likely taken Riley.

I had stopped breathing normally at some point in the afternoon. I now knew Riley wasn't under the rubble, but it didn't stop my brain from imagining it. The short, sharp breaths slice my throat as if my rage is reaching up and trying to escape. Eryn puts his arm around me, and I lose control of my shape momentarily, trying to hold myself together. Trying to breathe again.

Without Riley.

Lenore and Renn, along with Sadoriborn twins Omari and Romilly and a Mievaborn named Mitta, are the missing prisoners. Except for Mitta, those missing were the imposter king's favorites.

Riley is missing.

Romilly has the forced manifestation Gift of using someone's sight and hearing or forcing them to experience hers, and Omari can induce and manipulate memories. Both are very mentally unstable, experiencing hallucinations and severe separation anxiety.

Mitta's Gift wasn't impressive, but it could be intimidating if you didn't know the truth. He could duplicate himself five times, being able to move and talk as "them" independently. But his duplicates aren't physically capable of touch or hearing anything. A gentle man, Mitta was one of the least traumatized, but he experienced a lifelong depression and sadness that was exacerbated by the torture. Lyss said he'd been making progress, but she was worried this will set him back.

Throughout the debrief, I'm only half listening. My skin prickles, and every now and then I see patches of my skin change color and texture. I'm barely holding it together. My mind is on one track. I care for Eryn, I do, and I know I'll stay and do the right thing by him and everyone else. But I want to march down those tunnels myself, not stay here, and certainly not masquerade as King Stol Brud Oferdu.

Riley is *missing*. I want to change back to myself so I can touch my necklace and run the emerald heart across my lips. Instead, I'm impersonating the impersonated inside a tent in a tiny canyon, outside the half-collapsed cave and tunnel system I was tortured in. Hysteria flushes through the blood in my veins, and I catch the laughter before it leaves my throat.

What if I can't do this? What if I can't pretend to be the king? I can kill. I can torture. I can fight. But this is beyond madness. I have no idea what I'm doing.

We will have to send word to Queen Neoniri, which will be fucking *awful* to write. Because we saved her daughter, only for her son to go missing. My heart sinks. She will also need to be told about the king and my Gift. Assurances from Lyss that she won't immediately report this to the council do nothing to alleviate my rage. Rage that is currently telling me to run, to disappear. Leave all of them and everything else behind. But I can't.

Because Riley is missing. *And it's my fault.*

One thing I know for certain is that I will find Riley. I will find him, and I will kill the imposter king—my father. Or I will die trying. And I can only think of one way I will be able to do that.

I need to be the fucking King Oferdu.

EPILOGUE
RILEY

"*L* *yss just screamed!*" *Bitty says, frantic.*

I make eye contact with Tovi, and neither of us needs to speak. We sprint for the cave entrance together. The steps lead down into near-complete darkness, but we continue running. Bursting out of the long corridor, I see my sister. My beautiful, darling sister.

A Laguzborn woman is threatening her, and Lyss looks frightened.

I do the only thing I can think of.

Without missing a step, I tackle the Laguzborn woman.

And the world goes dark.

MY EARS RING while my head pounds. The fact I'm being carried over someone's shoulder with my hands tied to my feet isn't helping matters.

"He's awake!" a small Sadoriborn woman sing-songs after sticking her face into my line of sight.

I'm flipped unceremoniously onto the ground, sending a lancing pain through my skull. When the throbbing subsides, a dozen or so people seem to be milling about in this darkened cave, though half of them look like the same person. Maybe I've taken a bigger knock to the head than I realize.

"Hello," says a man I don't recognize. *Or do I?*

His eyes are the Erduborn brown of the earth, though much about him screams Mievaborn. His big eyes and pointy features are too much like Mika's to mistake. Eryn had told me a truth I couldn't believe.

Mika. The thought of her makes me dizzy. Or maybe that's the head wound.

She stole this man's Gift.

I knew she was special the moment I laid eyes on her. Standing there, all of five foot nothing with her hands behind her back. She had commanded the room with her mere presence, especially with the black eye she was sporting. I saw the way the council president's jaw twitched when she came in late, despite her polite apologies.

"My name is Noha. I've rescued my friends here, but we're taking you with us." His smooth voice tries to placate me. "For insurance purposes."

I glare at the man, and a sharp pain bounces through my skull again.

"Would you rather be carried or walk, Riley?" he asks, his voice slippery.

"Walk. And my name is Aurelius to you."

"Fair enough. But give us any trouble, and I'll leave you for your sister—" He pauses, his smile widening to show his teeth, "—and *Mika,* to find."

Noha watches me for a moment, perhaps trying to gauge my reaction to his mention of Mika. *How does he know she would mean anything to me?* I deliberately—though with strangled effort—keep my features blank. The mention of her name cleaves a hole straight through my heart. If he knew she meant more to me than my own life, it would only endanger her further.

"There wouldn't be much left for them to find, of course," he adds.

His maniacal laugh echoes along the dark cave walls.

**If you enjoyed Null & Void,
please consider leaving a review:**

ACKNOWLEDGMENTS

I honestly have no idea where to start. I never expected that the silly little stories I've been keeping inside my head would ever make it into a real book. But when these characters refused to take no for an answer, I listened. And I'm so glad I did.

So, of course, I have to say thank you to you. Thank you to my readers. It's because of you that this book exists. If you are reading this, it likely means you read the story, and I just cannot thank you enough for taking the chance.

But this book would simply not exist without the many, many people I have had in my corner. I'm going to try and thank them all, but if I miss you, please know that it was my Swiss cheese brain and not a reflection of my care for you.

Benjamin. Thank you for letting me dive further into my chaos gremlin mode while I brought this book into the world. Your encouragement was never-ending, even when I was fully ready to pack it all in and give up. I actually cannot put into words how much your support has helped this book to exist.

To my Stinkies, who were there from the beginning. The first to read it when it was, arguably, absolute garbage. Megan, Rachael, and (my official unofficial PA) Caitlin, you have made me laugh till I cried too many times to count. You stepped up whenever I needed it, even when I didn't ask.

To the friends I have made along the way. Kimmi, CC, Braidee, where would I be without you? Probably rocking in a corner crying with a book that was never published, to be honest. You've kept me sane (or at least our insanities played together nicely…), and you helped me get this book across every single milestone all the way to the finish line. I'm so glad I bullied you into friendship with me. You're stuck with me forever now.

And finally, my editor, Shelly. Who took on my tantrums, panic attacks, and moody chaos, and still treated me with kindness and respect, which I probably didn't deserve at the end of the day. Thank you for your incredible ability to polish a turd (my unedited manuscript) into a gem.

Thank you to all of the creatives who made Null & Void the absolutely gorgeous piece of work it is. I said I wanted art, and you delivered.

Lastly, a thank you to the people who have been hyping this book up, either right from the beginning or only recently. Your excitement and enthusiasm are what will give me the momentum to write book two… so don't stop! (I joke, the characters are already yelling at me. I can't deny them—or you—the next part of their story.)

R. Moody

ABOUT THE AUTHOR

R. Moody is a dark, romantic fantasy author, with her debut novel, Null & Void, released in 2024.

As a debut indie author, R. Moody has an interest in all things fantasy and worlds that don't exist. You can expect to read about whimsical realities, political intrigue, and romance with a dash (or more) of spice.

She hopes you like kicking your feet and giggling with slow burns, fanning yourself from the spicy heat, crying—from devastation one moment to joy the next—and immersing yourself in new and exciting worlds.

R. Moody is a dreamer, one who first followed her head with numbers before her heart for stories.

An accountant for a Not-For-Profit in youth mental health, Rae spends her free time reading, writing, or researching her next fantasy romance novel to get lost in. Living in Melbourne, Australia, with her partner and angry-looking cat, Rae is the only one who uses the bookshelves; the other two don't read as voraciously.

To keep up with R. Moody or to get in touch, visit:

www.rmoodyauthor.com

or scan the QR code below:

CONTENT WARNINGS

Alcohol abuse
Colorism
Death of an animal
Death of loved ones
Explicit language
Explicit sexual content
Forced medical procedures
Forced sterilization
Graphic violence
Homophobia
Kidnapping
Non-consensual sex (references to forced sex work)
Sexual assault (not by main characters)
Suicidal ideation
Torture (on page)